WITH JUST ONE KISS

"Gray Wolf calls you Sweet Butterfly because you are beautiful and dainty, like a butterfly's wings," he said. "Gray Wolf gives you this name. It is now your given name while you are with me."

Gray Wolf quickly sealed her lips with a long, hard kiss. He could feel the pulsing in his loins and the passion flaming through him. His need for Danette was uncontrollable. With trembling fingers he caressed her silken flesh and knew the time had come to lower her to the ground, to fully possess her.

Suddenly Danette's moment of magic and sensuousness came to an abrupt halt. Why hadn't she realized where such embraces and soft-spoken words would take her and this handsome Indian? She was a woman with needs—as he was a man with just as great needs. For many reasons they could not, should not, go any further.

"No . . ." she softly argued. "I must leave, Gray Wolf. I was wrong to let you kiss me, even that first time."

"Let Gray Wolf teach you ways to love," he whispered huskily into her ear.

His warm breath teased her senses. "Gray Wolf, I've never before . . ."

"Sweet Butterfly," Gray Wolf said, reaching his hand toward her. "Don't go. Gray Wolf won't hurt you. Only love you, forever. . . ."

SAVAGE INNOCENCE

Cassie Edwards

Zebra Books
Kensington Publishing Corp.

http://www.zebrabooks.com

We have lived and loved together
Through many changing years;
We have shared each other's gladness
And wept each other's tears;
I have known ne'er a sorrow
That was long unsoothed by thee;
For thy smiles can make a summer
Where darkness else would be.

—Jefferys

Chapter One

> *I believe love, pure and true,*
> *Is to the soul a sweet, immortal dew.*
> —Townsend

1879–Duluth, Minnesota

The early afternoon of May was fast losing its appeal as low, rolling clouds quickly hid the sun behind their ominous grays. A bolt of lightning and the ensuing rumbling of thunder were just cause for eighteen-year-old Danette Thomas to decide to direct her horse and buggy in the direction of home.

Danette had spent enough hours working on her latest painting. As she glanced downward at the canvas that she had placed on the floor of her buggy, she smiled proudly. The strokes of oil paint on the canvas had dried and a scene of Lake Superior, soaring seagulls, and one lone ship with its many opened sails shone beautifully back at her. She would proudly add this painting to her collection that would, hopefully, one day be shown along with all of her other paintings on the walls of the Minnesota State Bank in downtown Duluth.

Didn't most artists have the honor of displaying their work? Surely the fact that she was a woman wouldn't be cause to set her apart from all the other artists who had proudly displayed their talents in public.

7

Danette had the need to be different. She wanted to prove her worth, to show that she wasn't like most women, who only sipped tea while working with their needlepoint. Surely her destiny wasn't to be only that of an ordinary wife with an ordinary man. Danette wanted more. Much, much more.

Having chosen to paint from the highest point of Duluth, so as to be able to see the greatest expanse of Lake Superior, Danette now found herself traveling downhill, hating these steep streets of the city. More than once a horse had lost its footing on the cobblestones and had caused a buggy to overturn, or, worse yet, a horse and buggy, suddenly out of control, had sped downward, to plunge into Saint Louis Bay.

A shudder momentarily overtook Danette. Tightening her hold on her horse's reins, she shook such thoughts from her mind. She had to be more concerned about the approaching storm. Her painting would be destroyed if the rain began. One drop of rain could ruin the many hours of her labor of love.

Peering up into the sky, Danette could feel the pressure of the wind upon her face. It was swirling dust clouds from the ground like miniature tornadoes, and the whipping of the leaves on the towering oak trees made a noise similar to that of water rushing.

The cotton bonnet that Danette had chosen to wear for the day's outing suddenly whipped from her head. It now hung down her back, blowing frantically back and forth, still tied around her neck by its pink satin ribbon.

Danette's freed coal-black hair bounced and blew in wisps around her face, into her eyes, and then back again from her shoulders. The dampness already in the air was quickly frizzing her hair even more than it already was, with its stubborn, thick and long natural curls. One hundred strokes with a brush wouldn't even be enough after this!

The buggy continued to travel downward past neat white frame houses on each side of the street. At the bottom of this steep hill, which rose gradually from Lake Superior to a height of seven hundred feet, Danette could see piers, warehouses and the row of one-story buildings that lined the lakeshore.

But before reaching this plateau she would turn off onto another street where she lived in a two-story mansion with her affluent Uncle Dwight. Though forty, her Uncle Dwight was still unwed. He had been dedicated to her since she was ten, when she had been orphaned by a raging fire that had consumed both her parents.

Yet Danette knew that she wasn't Dwight's only purpose on the earth. He was just as dedicated to making money and to politics, one as strong a drive as the other, as far as Danette could tell.

The warmth of the sun's rays gone, Danette now wished for more than her low-swept printed calico dress to protect her from the building chill of the day. The full skirt of her dress was whipping up, revealing too much of her ankles and legs.

But her concern over this was trivial in comparison to the speed with which her horse and buggy were now traveling. "Whoa! Slow down!" she shouted to her horse.

She pulled and yanked on the reins but to no avail. And when another wide zigzag of lightning forked downward from the sky followed by a fierce growl of thunder, spooking the horse even more, Danette realized that the horse was no longer in control of its wits.

Danette's clear, wide-set eyes grew wild with fear as she felt herself being carried much too quickly on downhill. The houses were now racing beside her . . . only a blur in the wind, it seemed. The sounds of the buggy wheels on the cobblestones and those of the frantic horse's hooves were surely no louder than Danette's own racing heartbeats.

"Please stop!" she once more screamed. She tried pulling the reins but only managed to get raw, sore fingers from the attempt as the leather cut into her flesh.

The long, rolling waters of the river were coming closer.

Danette looked at the frothy foam flying from her horse's mouth and listened to his heavy breathing and his wild snorting as his head jerked and shook in fear. Soon the water would be Danette's grave if she didn't jump free of the buggy.

With an erratic pulse she began inching her way across the seat, dropping the now useless reins to flip wildly in the breeze. But seeing the street rushing by below her buggy made Danette realize that to jump would most surely mean a quick death or broken, twisted bones.

She clung desperately to the seat, whispering. "I can't do it. I can't . . . jump. . . ."

Tears began to blur her vision. An empty ache was gnawing at the pit of her stomach, as she realized that death was surely near. Yet she preferred death to a future with a mangled body confined to a wheelchair, at the mercy of those who would have to care for her.

Then suddenly, above the furious noise of her rolling buggy and thundering horse the sound of another horse's hooves began drawing closer to Danette. With a quick turn of her head she caught the sight of a man riding up beside her buggy on horseback.

But, no! A closer view of his face proved to her that this wasn't just any ordinary man. It was an Indian dressed in white man's clothes . . . and he was shouting something at her. Danette leaned her head and cupped a hand over her right ear as the Indian once more yelled something at her.

"As I grab you, help me by jumping into my arms," Gray Wolf cried, taking a quick look toward the advancing, swirling water. The rivers had swollen from the spring storms and the melting of the snows from the mountains. Nothing could survive a fall into its angry, rushing nemesis. He had to work fast or his efforts would be in vain!

"How can you . . . ?" Danette cried back, doubting the sanity of the suggestion. In his attempt to rescue her, might

10

the Indian also perish along with her, possibly beneath the wheels of her buggy if his horse lost *its* footing?

"Now!" Gray Wolf yelled. "You must do it now! *Wee-wee-bee-tahn!*"

Danette felt a dizziness of sorts overcome her as she released her hold on the buggy seat and felt a strong, steellike arm move around her waist. When the Indian gave her a firm look, she suddenly remembered his orders to jump and did just that as his arm swooped her from the seat and in the blink of an eye had her securely on his lap.

Breathless, Danette quickly draped an arm about the Indian's neck and thanked God when he drew his horse to a shuddering halt with both of them safely in his saddle. In a moment of mortification she watched as her horse and buggy landed in the water, realizing that had it not been for this brave Indian, she would also be there.

Gray Wolf placed a forefinger beneath Danette's chin and urged her face around, toward his. "Are you all right?" he asked, quickly taken by her loveliness. Though her eyes were brimming with tears they didn't hide the crystal-clear blue of them. As she sniffled, her tiny, upturned nose wiggled, appearing to make the few freckles there move, as though alive. Her sensuously full lips were ruby red and her cheeks pink.

His gaze moved lower and captured her perfectly rounded breasts partially exposed by the low-swept design of her dress. Something quivered in his loins, a hunger of sorts, as his gaze traveled on downward, seeing the tininess of her waist and her utter petiteness.

Then he let his gaze move back upward to the gift of her beautiful, black, curly hair and how it framed her exquisite face. He had silently watched and studied the white women of Duluth, marveling at their differences from the Indian maidens he had known at his St. Croix village of the Chippewa Indians. But none had ever been this enchanting.

An enchantress. That was this woman ... the one with the eyes of the sky and rivers.

Ay-uh, he thought further to himself. She is *mee-kah-wah-diz-ee.*

Danette found herself staring into brilliant green eyes, surprising her to wordlessness. Most Indians' eyes were dark, as dark as the darkest nights of winter. The difference made him unique, to say the least! And with further study she found his uniqueness even more overpowering, because of the other handsome features of his beautiful, copper-colored face.

His cheekbones were high and pronounced, his nose long and straight, and his jaws powerfully set. As he studied her back with sternness, she felt the strange desire to be consumed by his wide, beautifully shaped lips, loving the feel of his tall and lean body against hers. She was finding that with his stare and his possession of her in the curve of his arms, there was not only a stirring in her heart but in her mind as well. She felt herself being drawn into the mystique of this man ... this Indian.

"I ask you again," Gray Wolf said. "Are you all right? Did I hurt you when I took you from your buggy?"

"I'm fine," she finally managed to quietly murmur, smiling softly up at him.

Her gaze traveled over his handsomely squared shoulders and then the green plaid shirt and jeans that he wore. He was a mixture of both white and red man. But she knew why. He was probably in her Uncle Dwight's employment at his lumber company. Most Indians who were seen in Duluth had traveled from their villages to work as lumberjacks for the dollars they could make to buy supplies for their people.

Danette could see pride in the Indian's eyes and concluded that there was more to this Indian than being a lumberjack. There was a quality of greatness about him ... what one might find in a powerful chief.

"Gray Wolf happy that you are all right," Gray Wolf said, feeling awkward for the first time in his twenty years of life. But he understood why. Possibly in this woman's presence he would always feel like an owl without a forest . . . lost and confused . . . and with a heart beating so wildly it might even entangle itself in his ribs and lose its sense of timing.

Danette could see his uneasiness, and she was beginning to feel it too. She moved slightly away from him. "Gray Wolf is your name?" she said in a bare whisper, slowly becoming aware of the ache in her bones from having been transferred so dramatically from her buggy to this Indian's arms.

"*Ay-uh,*" Gray Wolf said, forcing a flat tone to his voice. It wasn't good to let this white woman discover his attraction to her. In his life there could be no room for such foolish feelings. He was of the proud St. Croix band of the Chippewa. She was only white.

But then quick shame engulfed him. How could he for one minute have forgotten that his own mother was white? Lorinda . . . Red Blossom, as she had been named by her husband, the chief, had fit in well with the Indian way of life. Didn't that have to prove that another white woman might do just as well?

Danette cocked her head, frowning. "And what does *ay-uh mean?*" she asked.

"It means yes. I am Gray Wolf," Gray Wolf said, now proudly squaring his shoulders even more than they already were.

A soft pink tinge touched the soft curves of Danette's cheeks. "Oh, I see," she quietly murmured.

A flurry of feet and horse's hooves and men's loud shouts drew Danette's head quickly around. Her stomach did a strange churning when she saw her horse and buggy drifting on away from the piers that lined Front Street. No matter what the crowd of men were now doing to rescue her horse

13

and buggy, nothing was going to help. The river's current was too great.

A deep shudder consumed Danette, watching her horse's head disappear beneath the surface of the water. If not for Gray Wolf . . .

"Danette! What the hell has happened here?"

The voice of Danette's Uncle Dwight seemed to have surfaced from hell, his tone was so harsh and accusing. Danette cringed and unconsciously sank her fingers deeply into Gray Wolf's arms as Dwight came galloping down the hill behind her, to stop next to Gray Wolf's horse, glowering first at Danette, then Gray Wolf.

"Uncle Dwight," Danette said, wanting to bite her tongue for feeling the need to apologize for being with the Indian. But she knew that her uncle had only one use for an Indian. Indians worked as laborers in Dwight's lumber company, but that was as far as any Indian's personal relationship should go with any white man or woman of the community.

Danette had been warned by her Uncle Dwight to not associate with the Indians in any way . . . that most were no more than savages and should be treated accordingly.

But today . . . she had found out different.

Dwight pushed his dark frock coat back and placed a hand on one of his holstered revolvers. "Release my niece at once," he growled, scowling toward Gray Wolf.

Knowing her uncle's angry, implied affront was unwarranted, Danette's face burned hot with embarrassment for Gray Wolf. She looked toward Dwight, sometimes wondering if she knew him at all. Or maybe she knew him too well. Tall, with faded blue eyes and thinning, dark hair— she recognized the lines of his face too well, realizing they had been placed there by worry and frustration from his determination to become even richer than he already was, and by his failure to better himself politically. He even had his sights on the presidency.

His wealth showed in the way he wore the best of clothing.

He said that genteel vests and well-fitting pants had much to do with the success of mankind, and that dress was the index of man.

His trousers were tight-fitting, and a strap under each instep held the trouser leg down. He wore a fine, ruffled white linen shirt and a broad bow tie. His vest was of an elegant satin. His frockcoat was knee-length. He always had boasted of his small feet and wore shoes that were not quite large enough, and "garters" to hold up his long silk stockings.

Danette then looked slowly up onto Gray Wolf's handsome face, having felt his muscles tighten at her uncle's insulting manner. A seething rage blazed in his cold, green eyes, and his lips were set hard. But she surmised that he didn't reply to Dwight because he saw Dwight as the man who held the power in the community that an Indian chief did in the Indian community and possibly respected him for this power.

Seeing his strained silence, Danette went to Gray Wolf's defense. "Uncle Dwight, how could you act so pompous?" she said from between clenched teeth. She nodded toward the river. "Don't you see? My horse went suddenly crazed and if not for Gray Wolf I would be lost in the river. Uncle Dwight, don't you think a thank you is in order?"

Dwight looked uneasily around him, not liking the attention being drawn to him, his niece, and the Indian. It wasn't good for his image, politically, to be associated with an Indian outside his role as employer, no matter that the Indian had most surely saved Danette's life. He had to keep his constituencies happy. They not only had the power to elect him back into his senatorial seat for the state of Minnesota, but also to replace him! And he wanted to owe this Indian ... any Indian ... nothing. It wasn't healthy, any way he looked at it.

With speed, Dwight reached for Danette and drew her roughly away from Gray Wolf, onto his own lap. He glanced

15

toward the river, a bit nauseated from the realization that Danette had come so close to it.

"Uncle Dwight," Danette shrieked, feeling the awkward jerk to her body. She reached out for Gray Wolf, only succeeding at grasping onto thin air.

Placing his arm possessively about Danette's waist, Dwight wheeled his horse around and began riding away from Gray Wolf and the gaping crowd of onlookers. A light mist had just begun to fall and the smell of rain hung heavily in the air, the prelude to the usual downpour that accompanied Duluth's entry into the month of May.

"I must get you home before you catch a death of cold," Dwight said, thrusting his knees into the sides of his horse. "We'll see what became of the horse and buggy later."

Over her uncle's shoulder, Danette cast Gray Wolf a sad, defeated look. She clung to her uncle as they ascended the steep street on her uncle's strong red roan. Apologies to Gray Wolf were in order and somehow . . . somewhere . . . she would do the honors!

Another zigzag of lightning setting the darkened heavens afire with light, and the ensuing clap of thunder, crowded thoughts of Gray Wolf from Danette's mind. She welcomed the familiar comfort of her uncle's arm about her. For eight years he had been her guardian and—until only moments ago—her only protector. And this being so, it was only right that she should place her cheek against his chest and cuddle, once more feeling herself that little girl who had always looked to her uncle as a gallant knight in shining armor.

But Danette's mind wouldn't so easily let her forget those other strong arms and chest of steel, not the brilliant, penetrating green of Gray Wolf's eyes. Though her Uncle Dwight's feelings were strong against any relationship with an Indian, this Indian had awakened feelings in her that Danette had never known were possible. Just thinking of him now gave her such a sensuous thrill, her insides seemed to be taking on a pleasant, warm glow. She had to believe

16

that these were the feelings that accompanied womanhood. Smiling to herself, Danette drew her head gently away from Dwight's chest and held her face up to the wind. She said a goodbye to the little girl in her and accepted the delicious sensation of being a woman.

The rain began to fall in torrents, intermingled with round crystal pellets of hail. Danette shivered in the wet chill and tried to place her bonnet back on her head. But the wind whipped it off as quickly as she managed to get it on her wildly blowing curls.

"Your gadding about every day has got to stop, Danette," Dwight shouted, snapping the reins of his horse. "We can't have any repeat performances of today."

The ache in Danette's joints and muscles was worsening as she bounced on Dwight's lap. She squirmed when she felt his hold lessening because of the wetness of her garment. "But I must be free to go wherever and whenever I please in order to do my painting, Uncle Dwight," she shouted back. "You know how important that is to me." She blinked rain droplets from her eyelashes.

"Nothing that can get you in this much trouble is that important," he argued, giving her an angry glance. He wheeled his horse onto a side street and on past the two- and three-story imposing residences that were classified as mansions by the Sunday travelers who came to gawk after their mornings at church. Though he should be used to it, it annoyed Dwight to no end . . . this habit of the poor always wanting to get a glimpse of the rich! But then, he always had to remember . . . these people voted!

Danette's insides lost their glow, quickly replaced by a numb coldness. She looked back over her shoulder at Lake Superior. During a storm it appeared to be possessed by the devil . . . all black and menacing . . . with whitecaps lashing out at everything in their reach. And in that hellish grave were her oil paints, brushes, and canvas, and the painting that she had so proudly finished this day!

"Uncle Dwight," she cried. "It's all lost. Everything is lost."

Dwight guided his horse into a long, narrow drive and headed for his stable. "What on earth are you talking about, Danette?" he shouted, glad to finally draw rein inside the dry quarters, behind his own *manoir,* which sounded more impressive to him in French than the word "mansion."

Easing out of Dwight's arms onto a floor scattered with fresh, dry straw, Danette shook water from the skirt of her dress then raked her fingers through her dark wet hair. A look of panic was in her eyes as she looked up at Dwight.

"All of my painting oils and brushes . . . everything was in my buggy this afternoon, Uncle Dwight," she said mournfully. "Now what am I to do?"

Dwight swung himself out of the saddle and unbuckled the saddle cinch. "That's probably a blessing in disguise," he grumbled. "Now maybe you'll act as most proper ladies do."

A slow, burning anger was rising inside Danette. She found herself clenching her fists at her side. "And may I ask to what you are referring?" she asked, trying not to let Dwight sense her sarcasm. She had to remember to respect all adults . . . especially her uncle!

Swinging the saddle from his horse's back, Dwight eyed Danette speculatively. "We've spoken of this many times before," he said. "You know of what I am speaking."

Danette cupped a hand over her mouth and sneezed, then sniffled. "You would rather I sit home and do embroidery? You would rather I prick my fingers than use them to create beautifully on canvas?"

"Embroidering is creating," Dwight argued, now leading his horse to a stall.

"And would you even deprive me of eventually showing my artwork in the lobby of the Minnesota State Bank?"

"I see that type of thing as frivolity," Dwight said shallowly.

"Uncle Dwight, I thought you understood me," Danette cried. She swung around, lifted the skirt of her dress into her arms, and raced out into the rain. She hurried around toward the front door of the house. Dwight's attitude pained her so. If he didn't understand how devoted she was to her painting . . . how could she ever expect him to understand her feelings for an Indian!

Shaking her head, she had to even wonder herself about these feelings she suddenly found she had for this Indian. Why was it that it was an Indian who had set her insides aglow, when no handsome white man had ever been able to? There had been many gentlemen callers! Why hadn't she been attracted to one of them? Now life would be so complicated. . . .

The granite steps leading to the front door of the austere and beautiful Victorian house were solid and somewhat intimidating, but the granite sills of the windows were a soft, pale gray against the warm brick facade. It was one of the finest houses in Duluth, two-story, rectangular, with a wide porch and stained glass windows.

Shivering, Danette opened and closed the heavy oak door and stepped into a wide entrance hall that opened into three spacious parlors and a dining room. The portraits of the Thomas family seemed to be waiting for Danette as she walked on past them, into her favorite parlor, where a fire was raging in the fireplace.

Spreading her hands over the fire, Danette looked slowly about her, wondering how Gray Wolf would see the expensive tastes of this white family. Was he used to wigwams? Had it even been awkward for him to move into the bunkhouse-type building where all of Dwight's lumber-jacks lived?

In this parlor, dramatic red-glazed walls set off a massive mahogany Chippendale mantel and overmantel, refinished in antique Chinese red and carved with pagodas and figures of Chinese men. A bronze French Doré crystal chandelier sent a warm glow from its gaslights, settling on elegant wall and ceiling frescoes, quarter-sawn oak woodwork, and European carpeting. The Chippendale chairs and sofas were covered in the finest imported silk. Dropleaf and lamp tables were arranged generously around the room.

Dwight had purchased rare items abroad and from leading American dealers. There was the English Regency oak center table richly carved with animal, floral, and military motifs; a Chinese porcelain punch bowl with its original stand; and two magnificent twelve-foot by ten-foot Flemish tapestries, dated 1661. . . .

A rustling of feet drew Danette quickly around. She smiled warmly at Amy, who was the family cook, Danette's personal maid, and, most of all, Danette's beloved confidante, all rolled into one.

Seeing the horror in Amy's dark, wide eyes, Danette was unable to suppress a giggle. She loved her jolly, heavy-set, friend, who had taken the place of her mother, in every sense of the word. And Amy looked especially good to Danette this particular day, in her fully gathered calico dress and ruffled apron. If ever Danette needed a friend . . . it was now.

"Land sakes, Danette, what happened to you?" Amy asked. She went to Danette and began clucking and fussing over her like a mother hen. She untied the satin bow of Danette's bonnet and shook water from it over the fire.

Danette gathered the skirt of her dress up into her arms and held it out before her. "I do look a sight, don't I, Amy?" she laughed. Then she sobered. "But, Amy, I feel much worse than I look."

Amy's fingers now busied at fussing with Danette's mussed, wet hair. "You tell Amy all about it," she crooned. "But only after we get those wet clothes off and get you soakin' in a warm tub of water. Pneumonia ain't nothin' to laugh at and you're a prime candidate for such a sickness."

Danette's nose curled up into a sneeze. Feeling the wet,

clinging petticoats against her legs, she nodded. "Yes. You're right," she murmured. "Then we'll talk."

Amy placed her arm about Danette's waist and they walked together from the parlor. Murals of cherubs holding garlands of flowers and flying beneath patches of blue sky and fleecy white clouds had been painted on the walls of the staircase. A hand-blown glass chandelier that resembled large concoctions of delicately spun sugar hung from the ceiling, lighting Danette and Amy's way as they reached the second-floor landing.

"You are a sight," Amy fussed, tsk-tsking, over and over again. "I ain't nevah seen such a sight, Danette."

Danette sighed, opening the door to her bedroom. A magnificent Queen Anne pencil post bed stood in the middle of the room, a splay-leg nightstand next to it. The bed was triple-sheeted and topped with a soft, thick comforter that matched the yellow satin draperies at the two windows. Soft yellow carpeting crushed splendidly beneath Danette's feet as she stepped into her room.

Suddenly swinging around, Danette clasped onto Amy's dark, pudgy fingers. "Oh, Amy," she sighed. "Let me tell you about him. May I? Please?"

Amy's eyes bulged with shock. "Tell me about who?" she said in a near whisper. She placed a hand to Danette's cheeks, seeing the rising color of pink and the excitement dancing in her eyes. "Has a fever already set in on you? You suddenly seem to be a talkin' clean outta your head."

"No. No fever," Danette said excitedly. "It's a man, Amy. I met the most handsome man today."

Amy's thick lips lifted into a playful grin. "A man?" she said. "Yes'm. I knew it would happen. Just didn't 'spect it to happen so quickly. But my Danette is growin' up. Yes'm. It shows in your eyes." Amy circled around behind Danette and began unsnapping her dress. "Tell me about him, honey. Amy is all ears."

Danette shook herself out of her dress and let it crumple

21

into a heap at her feet. "It's not an ordinary man, Amy," she said cautiously, afraid of Amy's reaction, yet needing it. "This handsome man I met today is an Indian."

Danette flinched when she heard Amy's quick intake of breath. She stiffly watched as Amy came face to face with her. Her insides relaxed when she saw the understanding in Amy's eyes.

"This Indian you speak of," Amy said. "He has stolen your heart?"

"Entirely," Danette whispered. Then her eyes cast downward and she began wringing her hands. "Oh, Amy, what am I to do? Uncle Dwight will never allow it."

Amy took Danette's troubled hands in hers. "We'll work it out," she murmured. "If this is truly what you want, somehow we'll work it out together. Any man that can put such a sparkle in your eyes must be somethin', Danette honey. I've been waitin' to see such a sparkle and I won't do nothin' to stop it . . . be it Indian . . . or white. . . ."

Danette threw her arms about Amy's neck. "Oh, Amy, I knew I could count on you," she cried. "I love you so much. Truly I do."

"Yes'm. I know. And I loves you," Amy said, fondly patting Danette's back. "Now let's get you in that hot tub of water."

"With pleasure," Danette sighed. She was glad to have at least won Amy's approval. Now her mind was aswirl as to how she could see Gray Wolf again, for see him she must. She felt deeply that that moment when she had been in the Indian's arms had changed her life, because she ached to be with him again and knew that she must, no matter what her uncle's feelings.

Chapter Two

My kisses shall teach thy lips
The love that shall fade no more.
—Taylor

The descent of the stairs was slow and arduous for Danette. She clung to the railing, emitting a soft groan as she took another step downward, kicking the layers of petticoat and the skirt of her silk print dress away. Memories of her runaway horse and buggy flashed through her mind, causing her to shiver involuntarily. But just as quickly, another recollection as vivid but much more to her liking was there, tantalizing her to smile secretly to herself.

"Gray Wolf," she whispered, testing the Indian's name aloud on the tip of her tongue, never wanting to forget how being in his arms had made her feel.

But, oh, her uncle! Her Uncle Dwight had made his point quite clear that Gray Wolf was beneath them, and not to be made an acquaintance.

"What shall I do?" she further whispered. She took the final step from the stairs, following the aroma of the breakfast of eggs, gravy, and biscuits that would be awaiting her arrival in silver serving platters in the dining room.

"What am I to do?" Danette sighed, so wanting to see Gray Wolf again. She moved on down the hallway. Amy's chatter met Danette as she entered the dining room. This room, with its bright red fireplace and dining room furniture crafted from solid maple wood and highly figured black cherry veneers, opened onto a large garden, whose gnarled old pear trees, which had been planted when the house had first been built, were just showing a trace of blossoms.

Amy was fussing at the window, raising it, letting in the fresh smells of spring and the brilliant rays of the morning sunshine.

"Sho do hope Danette don't come down with a terrible cold after her trouble in the rain yesterday," Amy was saying, more to herself than to Dwight, pulling back the ivory-colored satin drapes as the wind began to flutter them around.

Danette smiled warmly as she moved farther into the room. "I haven't sneezed once this morning, Amy," she announced, eyeing Dwight nervously as he kept his face hidden behind the *Duluth Sentinel,* Duluth's morning newspaper.

Without even looking, Danette knew that her uncle was either studying the financial page or possibly some accounts of President Hayes and his proper wife, Lucy. Surely Danette was the farthest thing from his mind this morning. Strange that he should show the most concern when she had finally found a man who stirred her heart.

Amy swung around, clasping her hands before her when she saw Danette. "Danette, I thought you'd be sleepin' this mornin'," she exclaimed throatily. "After yesterday, you needed to stay off your feet, and above all else to stay warm, to ward off any cold that might be tryin' to creep into your delicate bones."

Danette pulled a chair from beneath the dining table and settled gracefully onto it. Spreading a lace-trimmed linen napkin across her lap, she once more smiled toward Amy. "Amy, don't you think you're trying just a bit too hard to pamper me?" she asked. "I'm a big girl now. Please don't worry so much about me."

Amy went to Danette and smoothed her pudgy fingers

over Danette's freshly brushed hair. "To me you're still that little girl, lost and bewildered over your parents' death," she crooned. "You'll always be that little girl to me, I guess even after you have a child of your own."

Danette's face showed signs of a pink blush and her eyes brightened. "Me?" she giggled. "Children? That's many years into the future, I'm sure."

Giving Danette a half smile, Amy began pouring coffee into a cup for her. "When the right man comes along, bearing children follows shortly after," she said, laughing softly.

A slow wink from Amy and a knowing nod was just cause for Danette to cast her uncle a quick glance. She knew that Amy was referring to the secret shared between them about Gray Wolf and Danette's feelings for him. This had to remain a secret! She had to caution Amy about making such careless references in the future.

Lowering the newspaper and carefully folding it in fours, Dwight eyed Danette speculatively. "And how are you feeling this morning?" he asked, laying the newspaper aside. His faded blue eyes continued to focus on Danette over his cup as he lifted it to take a long, slow sip of coffee.

"I'm just fine," Danette said, seeing that he was dressed for his usual day of work at his office. His white linen shirt was tucked and he wore a broad dark brown bow tie to match his brown frock coat.

"Why do you ask?" she quickly added. "Don't I look all right? I thought you had been too busy reading the newspaper to even notice."

"I always notice everything about you," Dwight said flatly. "I was aware of how slowly you moved into the room. I could hear. I didn't have to look your way to tell that you were possibly having a few aches and pains from yesterday's near mishap."

"Yes," Danette interjected. "A near mishap, Uncle

Dwight. You must remember that it was only a near mishap. If not for Gray Wolf . . .''

"I've a gift for you this morning," Dwight said, interrupting her. He placed his coffee cup down onto its saucer and reached beneath the table and brought out a large wrapped box. A yellow satin bow beautifully graced its exterior.

Always having loved surprises in the form of gift-wrapped boxes, Danette rose quickly from her chair. She threw her napkin on the table and rushed to Dwights side. "What is it?" she asked, waiting for Dwight to give it to her.

But just as quickly remembering his habit of bribing her, Danette once more became suspicious of his motives for choosing this moment for gift-giving, and he took a slow step backward, away from him.

"Here," Dwight said, rising, to place the box in her arms. "Open it. I think you'll approve."

Feeling a heaviness weighting her shoulders down, Danette eyed Dwight apprehensively. "Dwight, I . . .''

"Danette, open it," Dwight said, placing his hand gently on her arm. "Truly. You will think me quite a generous, thoughtful uncle this morning."

Dwight couldn't help but notice her hesitation and the look of questioning in her eyes. "What do we have here?" he said. "You've never before taken so long to unwrap any of the gifts I've given you. I must hurry on to the office. Get on with it, Danette."

Feeling her anxious heartbeat, Danette shrugged. "Oh, all right," she murmured, studying the box. Then her gaze rose upward, to meet Dwight's growing impatient stare. "If you insist, I mean," she quickly added, not wanting to show her eagerness to accept what she already knew what must surely be a bribe to keep her closer to home and away from Gray Wolf.

Dwight's eyebrows lifted. "If I insist?" he questioned. "You are behaving quite strangely this morning, Danette."

He reached for the gift. "Perhaps this isn't the proper time to give you these things, after all. Perhaps you need a few days in bed to clear your head of whatever has caused you to behave so . . . so . . . unfavorably this morning. I have to gather from such behavior that you were disturbed more by yesterday's mishap than I had originally gathered you to be."

Clinging to the gift, Danette's curiosity was too aroused to hand it over so easily to her uncle unwrapped and unseen. "No," she sighed. "I'm quite all right, Uncle Dwight. It's just that it's, well, uh, so early in the morning for gift-giving."

"I'll be gone the rest of the day, Danette," Dwight softly argued. He straightened his tie and looked nervously toward a watch he pulled from his vest pocket. "This is much better, I believe, than waiting until tomorrow."

"Tomorrow, Uncle Dwight?" Danette asked, eyes wide. "Won't you be here for dinner this evening?"

"I'm having dinner in town with a . . . a friend," he said, clearing his throat nervously. "Business, you know," he added, placing his watch back inside his pocket.

A slow blush rose to Danette's cheeks. She suspected that a woman was his business for the evening. She knew that he had several such "business acquaintances" scattered across the country, to take the place of what a wife would have offered him.

"I see," she softly said, lowering her eyes.

"Well? Then open it," Dwight said, reaching to quickly release the gift from its bow, which he let flutter to the floor.

Danette fingers worked with the sealed edges of the wrapping paper, then eagerly ripped it away, to leave her only the lid of a box to raise. With a racing pulse, she flipped the lid open, and what she saw caused a quick gasp to escape from between her lips.

"To replace what you lost," Dwight said.

Danette placed the box on the dining table and lowered

27

her fingers inside it. She savored the touch of the new canvas, the many brushes, and the tubes of fresh oil paints.

Then she spun around and threw her arms about her uncle's neck and hugged him tightly. "Uncle Dwight, you are so kind," she cried. "I love my gifts. Truly I do. I felt so badly about losing everything in the lake. Now you've replaced it all."

She kissed him on the cheek, then held back away from him, smiling. "I love you, Uncle Dwight," she murmured. "Thank you. Oh, thank you."

But though she was thanking him, she was puzzled by these particular gifts. He had always before frowned upon her hobby. Why would he so quickly replace what he had only yesterday shown his pleasure at her having lost? He was like a chameleon . . . changing moods as quickly as a chameleon changed its colors!

"I knew that you'd be pleased," Dwight said, leaning to kiss her softly on the cheek. "But you must promise me something, Danette." He stepped back and watched her features freeze but couldn't concern himself with this. He had to do what was best for her . . . and even more . . . what was best for himself.

The allure of the gifts was not so great now. Danette refused even to look their way. She had known she would have to promise him something for such generosity on his part. "What sort of promise, Uncle Dwight?" she barely whispered.

"That you will remain on the grounds of our estate while amusing yourself with your paints," he said dryly, now avoiding her look of shock and annoyance. "You have quite a view of Lake Superior and the city from our back yard. Do you need more?"

Danette stiffened. Her voice showed coolness and restraint. "One can paint the same scenery only so many times and then it becomes boring, Uncle Dwight," she said, hating the tears that were fighting to be released from the corners of her eyes. But frustrated anger always caused tears! Oh! Why was she so weak?

"Danette, I replaced your painting paraphernalia only because I thought your accident yesterday had most surely made you become aware of the dangers of being out alone on the streets of Duluth," Dwight growled, his face red with anger. "Had I known that even that hadn't changed your mind, I would have never replaced them."

Stubbornly, Danette shoved the box toward Dwight. "Take them back if you must," she snapped.

Dwight turned angrily on his heel and walked toward the door. "No. Keep them, damn it," he shouted from across his shoulder. "You are growing up into a stubborn young lady. We will talk more about that later. I must get to the office. . . ."

Danette now understood why he had given her the gifts. He was too busy to involve himself with her, and, feeling guilty for that, he had felt compelled to give her what he knew would be the best substitute for him. And wouldn't her paintings keep her busy and away from annoying him over frivolous matters that were the order of the day for most bored, restless women?

A slow smile lifted Danette's lips. She would accept his "guilt-gifts." She didn't mind his chosen substitute for himself. She loved to paint, and she loved the freedom painting afforded her.

"Danette, your uncle only means good by you," Amy said, moving to Danette to take a hand in hers. "He do love you. With all his heart, he do."

"I'm sure he does," Danette languidly sighed. "I'm sure he does." The aroma from freshly blooming lilacs blowing in from the garden reminded Danette of the day wasting away outside the walls of the house. She had new paints, canvas, and brushes . . . and she was eager to try them out.

"And you must listen to your Uncle Dwight," Amy

fussed. "You must stay closer to home. This ol' heart o' mine don't need no fright again like yesterday."

"Amy, all I can promise is to be more watchful of the steep streets," Danette said, easing her hand from Amy's steel grip. "I've lost one horse and buggy. Surely you can't think I'm anxious to lose another."

"Amy ain't worryin' none over no horse and buggy," Amy scolded, squinting her eyes, almost losing them in the deep wrinkles of her round, dark face. "It's you I fret over. From mornin' to night."

"Well, you just quit that frettin'," Danette teased, eyeing the scrambled eggs that had lost their steam. "Frettin' and stewin' won't change me one iota. You've surely better things to do with your time." She settled down onto a chair and scooted up to the table. "Like maybe bringing me warmer biscuits from the oven? I'm starved, Amy. Just absolutely starved."

"Oh, dear, Danette," Amy grumbled as she began waddling toward the door. "You are an impetuous young'un, you are."

Danette laughed softly, then ate the eggs hungrily, looking out the window at the blue sky of the day. There were no threatening clouds to ruin her outing on this day, and, if she was lucky, maybe she would even see Gray Wolf again . . . but this time . . . under much different circumstances!

Slipping her shawl from around her, Danette welcomed the sun on the bare flesh of her arms and shoulders, not having won the argument with Amy as to whether or not a shawl should be worn on her outing. She shook the shawl to the floor of her buggy, thinking the constant fussing over her to be such nonsense. She would prove that she was capable of fending for herself. She would resume her painting today and get home quite safe and sound when she was finished!

The lane Danette had chosen to direct her horse and buggy down was lined on each side by swells of blossoms on thick clusters of forsythia and lilac bushes pressed closely together. It was a painting in itself . . . all the purples and yellows, and the bees and hummingbirds actively moving from one to the other.

Inhaling, Danette savored the aroma as though it was an expensive French perfume. And it continued to follow along with her even after she guided her horse on away from the lane, onto a straight stretch of meadow that led to a secluded spot overlooking Lake Superior. She was determined to recapture the mood of the painting that had been destroyed in the river. It could never be the same . . . but surely one just as good. . . .

A seagull soaring overhead proved to Danette just how close she was to the bluff. She snapped her horse's reins and looked into the distance, then felt a trace of fear when she saw the full figure of a man standing beside a horse, looking out over Lake Superior.

Knowing the dangers of being alone, Danette drew her horse to a quick halt. She looked anxiously about her. She wished for a place to hide herself until the man went on his way. But the forest was beyond quick reach. She could either turn her horse and buggy around and go back the way she had just come or take the chance that this stranger would be an honorable man and treat her accordingly.

Determined to not be frightened away so easily, Danette lifted her chin haughtily. She flicked her reins but tensed as her horse let out a loud, irritated neigh. Though she had chosen to travel onward, there was no need to alert the man just yet to her approach. Possibly he might mount his horse and go on in a different direction without having seen her. But the turn of his head in her direction showed that the latter would not be the case. He had heard her horse. He did see her coming nearer.

Then a slow flush rose to Danette's cheeks and her heart

began to pound out of control. The man whom she had momentarily feared wasn't just any man. It was Gray Wolf! It was as though their hearts and minds had led them to one another again, for Danette had frequented this same bluff many times, and Gray Wolf had never been there before. How was it that he should know of her favorite secluded spot by the river? Fate had now led them to each other not only once . . . but twice.

Strange fluttering feelings inside her stomach overwhelmed Danette as she drew her horse and buggy to a halt next to where Gray Wolf still stood. As though in a spell, she slowly looked his way. And when their eyes met and held, they smiled unspoken words to each other.

"Hello," Danette finally managed to murmur.

"Boo-shoo," Gray Wolf replied in Indian, nodding a stiff hello back to her. His heart hammered like a drum against the wall of his chest, remembering how delicately she had lain in his arms, and how sweet she had smelled. All his senses had become strangely alive in her presence, and today, *ay-uh,* it was to be the same. The spirits had blessed him by guiding her to him again. He would have to repay them in kind by being a more humble Indian in their presence!

"Am I intruding on a private moment of yours, Gray Wolf?" Danette asked in a near whisper, knowing at least enough about Indians to know that they often communed with nature. And what better place than the loveliness of this flower-bedecked meadow overlooking the magnificence of Lake Superior?

"Gah-ween," Gray Wolf said thickly, folding his arms across his chest. "No. You are not. Gray Wolf was just thinking of home. It is the river. If I close my eyes I am beside my own people's river where the wild rice sways with the wind."

"And where might that be, Gray Wolf?" Danette asked, dropping the reins to the floor of the buggy. "Where is your Indian home?"

32

"Across the meadow and through the forest where the sacred cave stands beside our village of wigwams," Gray Wolf said, gesturing with a hand toward the green splash of forest in the distance. "It is there that my people always await and rejoice my return."

"You sound as though you so miss your people," Danette said, inching her way across the seat of her buggy. She felt awkward in his presence. She didn't know whether to stay in her buggy or climb to the ground, which would mean standing next to him.

Did she dare get so close to him? What might her heart guide her to do? She could so vividly remember the strength of his arms and her wish to be kissed by him.

But she must remember her uncle's warnings! She must! Gray Wolf was an Indian! She was white!

Her gaze traveled over him, seeing the green flannel shirt, the tight-fitting jeans on his thick-muscled legs, and the boots—all white man's attire. To only glance at him, one would believe he was white.

But then there was the copper color of his skin, and the coarse, dark hair of the Indian that hung long and straight to his shoulders. But now, as the sun danced on his hair, Danette could see faint tinges of red and had to wonder even more about this Indian with the different green eyes, and hair that seemed to change colors right before her eyes.

"Would you not miss your own home?" Gray Wolf grumbled. "Would you not miss your own people?"

A blush touched Danette's cheeks. She lowered her eyes. "Yes. I imagine I would," she said. How was he to know that she had already known such loss? Her home . . . her parents . . .

The warmth of a hand suddenly on Danette's arm drew her eyes quickly up. She swallowed hard and smiled nervously when she found Gray Wolf there, touching her, studying her with a questioning in his eyes.

33

"Your words carry a sadness in them," Gray Wolf said hoarsely. "Why is that so?"

She didn't wish to talk of sad things with this man who had strangely captured her heart. She only wished to feel happiness in his presence. For didn't he evoke such feelings inside her? She wanted to cherish this moment with him, for it might be her last!

"You are wrong," Danette said, smiling, yet feeling a weakness in her limbs that she had never felt before as his hand remained firmly in place on her arm. "I am not sad." She nodded toward the sky. "How can one be sad when the day is so lovely?" she added, letting her eyes be drawn back to his.

"Then you are all right?" he asked, concern heavy in his words. "You not suffer any from yesterday, when the weather was not so kind to you?"

"I'm fine," she said. "Perfectly fine." She turned her head from side to side and stretched her back, then laughed softly. "Except for some soreness in my back and shoulder muscles," she added. "Otherwise, I'm fine. Thanks to you, I'm even here today, Gray Wolf."

"Why you come here to river?" he asked, dropping his hand to his side.

"To paint," Danette said, nodding toward her canvas and easel on the floorboard of the buggy.

"Paint?" Gray Wolf asked, leaning over to see what she was referring to. And when he saw, he lifted his gaze and smiled at her. "Gray Wolf see. Paint. You make pictures on cloth. *O-nee-shee-shin.* That's good. May Gray Wolf watch?"

A thrill raced through Danette. Her eyes widened. "Do you really wish to?" she said excitedly. "You are interested in what I do?"

"*Ay-uh,*" Gray Wolf said, straightening his back. His gaze rose to the sky, checking the rise of the sun. "But only for a short while. Gray Wolf must go work with trees. There

34

are many trees to move to the water for travel downstream. You understand?''

''Yes,'' Danette said, feeling the need to giggle but suppressing the urge, wanting to act more a woman in this handsome man's eyes. ''I understand. I shall hurry. You will see my very first strokes of paint on my new canvas. It will always be special to me because you shared it with me.''

Gray Wolf placed his hands on Danette's waist and hesitated before lifting her from the buggy. In this moment of hesitation, their eyes once more met and held, and Danette felt herself slowly surrendering to him as his lips began to move toward hers.

It felt only right that his lips should now be slowly exploring hers in a series of sensual kisses. And when he saw that she was not going to pull away from him, Gray Wolf moved his hands upward. He twined his fingers into the thickness of her hair and tenderly held her lips in place against his, to kiss her more strongly . . . filled with passion and fire.

Danette gave herself up to the rapture. As though willed to, she laced her arms about his neck and clung to Gray Wolf, responding with a soft cry of intense pleasure under his continuing hot kisses.

The world seemed to be melting away around her as Gray Wolf's hands slowly moved from her hair and downward. A low, shaky moan escaped from between Danette's lips when she felt the sureness of his hand touch the curve of her bosom, to caress a breast through the silk of her dress. And when he set her mouth free and lowered his lips to where her breast swelled from the bodice of her dress, a giddy sort of swimming sensation began to float inside Danette's head and a sweet pain rose between her thighs.

Closing her eyes, she arched her neck backwards, lost in the newness of awakened sensations of love, and let Gray Wolf's hand search inside her dress to now cup her one breast fully.

Digging her fingernails into his shoulder, she welcomed his lips at the hollow of her throat and then lower where her heart pounded in miniature explosions. A lightheadedness overtook Danette as his lips continued to move over the exposed flesh of her bosom. Yet something deep inside began to nag away at her . . . a warning of sorts . . . telling her that this was wrong. Though she had been embraced and even kissed by other handsome men, none had been allowed these kinds of liberties with her body. . . .

Another low gasp rose shakily from her throat when Gray Wolf suddenly picked Danette up from the buggy seat and was holding her fully in his arms. Danette eyed him wonderingly, filled with passion and desire and with a need for him so great that she found herself slowly being lost to reason and time.

"You are *mee-kah-wah-diz-ee,*" Gray Wolf said huskily. "You are *wee-shko-bun.* Gray Wolf call you by name *Wee-shko-may-may-gwah.*"

Danette twined an arm about his neck and placed her cheek against the steel of his chest. "I don't understand what you're saying," she murmured, in an alarming state of heightened euphoria. And feeling the thundering of his heart against his chest made her realize that she was having the same effect on him.

"Gray Wolf says you're beautiful and sweet," he said, kissing her brow gently. "In Indian I shall call you Sweet Butterfly."

Danette sighed softly. "Sweet Butterfly?" she whispered. "How lovely. And why have you chosen that name? My name is Danette. Why not call me by my given name?"

"Gray Wolf calls you Sweet Butterfly because you are beautiful and dainty, like a butterfly's wings," he said. "Gray Wolf gives you this name. It is now your given name while you are with me."

"Sweet Butterfly," Danette whispered, testing the name. "Sweet . . ."

Gray Wolf quickly sealed her lips of further words as he kissed her hard and long. He could feel the pulsing in his loins and the passion flaming him as though a hot coal was searing his insides.

His need for her was causing his blood to spin through his veins and his heart to soar. With hunger, his fingers once more curled around the swell of her breast, and he knew the time had come to lower her to the ground, to fully possess her. He somehow feared this, having never been with a white woman before. Would it . . . could it . . . be the . . . same . . . ?

Danette's eyes widened and her pulse raced as Gray Wolf lowered her and stretched her gently on the ground. Violets and fresh green grass were her pillow and as Gray Wolf stood spread-legged over her, lowering his jeans, Danette's moments of magic and sensuousness came to an abrupt halt.

Why hadn't she realized where such embraces and soft-spoken words would take her and this handsome Indian? She was a woman, with needs . . . as he was a man with as great a need.

But Danette was now too awakened to the reality of the moment to let her own needs be fulfilled. This that they were sharing was wrong. For many reasons . . . they could not . . . should not . . . go any further with their sexual explorations of each other.

With a trembling in her limbs, Danette inched back from where Gray Wolf had placed her. Her temples pounded and blood raced to her cheeks when she saw his bared manhood and its strength jutting out before him as he stepped slowly from his jeans. It was the first time Danette had ever seen a man's private parts, and she was secretly thrilled, yet frightened.

As Gray Wolf fell to his knees beside Danette, he reached for her, his eyes searching her face imploringly. When he gently touched her face with the powerful fingers of his hand,

Danette's insides quivered and she felt her body turning to liquid as he lowered a kiss to her lips.

"No," she softly argued, yet leaning closer to him as he once more cupped her breast. "I must leave, Gray Wolf. I was wrong to let you kiss me . . . even . . . that first time."

"Let Gray Wolf teach you ways to love," he whispered huskily into her ear.

His warm breath teased her ear, drowning her in a renewed sea of sensation. "Gray Wolf, I've never before . . ." she gasped, yielding to his rain of kisses across her face.

"Gray Wolf be gentle. Gray Wolf teach. Sweet Butterfly learn. Then Sweet Butterfly teach Gray Wolf ways to paint on cloth," he said. *"Ay-uh?* Say yes to Gray Wolf, Sweet Butterfly. My heart cannot wait much longer."

His lips slipped down to her shoulder and then on to her cleavage, where he skillfully placed his tongue and set small fires where it flicked. Danette's breasts felt on fire and swollen with further want of his lips there: She wanted more but still was too afraid and finally managed to gently push his head away.

"No," she said, quietly panting. Her face was flushed crimson and her dress wrinkled and mussed as she hurriedly scrambled to her feet.

"Sweet Butterfly . . ." Gray Wolf said hoarsely, reaching a hand toward her. "Don't go. Gray Wolf won't hurt you. Only love you."

Not wanting to see the part of him that sent a strange excitement through her, Danette turned her back to him and rushed toward her buggy. "I'm sorry, Gray Wolf," she cried from across her shoulder. "I *must* go. Please understand. I've never ever let a man before."

She shuddered, now fully aware of her shameful behavior, and without a backwards glance or further words climbed aboard her buggy and set her horse to racing away from the bluff and the feelings she didn't want to have.

"Oh! How could I have?" she cried to herself. "Most

38

would now call me a . . . a . . . whore. Even Gray Wolf must think me only a guttersnipe."

Tears wetted her lashes. She didn't want to remember how delicious his hands and lips had made her feel. Never in her life had she imagined such feelings could exist!

"And never again shall they," she worried aloud. "For surely only Gray Wolf can perform such magic on my body and in my mind—and I can't allow it again. I can't."

Danette headed for home, having accomplished nothing this day except for falling more in love with an impossible dream . . . that of being able to freely love, and give of herself, to this Indian, whose passion matched her own.

Chapter Three

Let thy love in kisses rain
On my lips and eyelids pale.
—Shelley

Moody and not at all her normal self, Danette paced before the fireplace in her favorite parlor. The crinolines beneath her splendid silk dress rustled fitfully as she made first one turn before the fire and then another. Her fingers went nervously to her hair, adjusting the string of pearls she had entwined in and out of the tightly rolled bun atop her head.

Then her fingers went to the bare flesh of her throat where her dress was cut low, displaying the gentle whiteness of her bosom. All she had to do was remember Gray Wolf's lips there and she would begin a slow melting inside.

Lace draped the bodice of her dress and a faint aroma of cologne trailed after her as she finally plopped down into a chair and curled her feet in a very unladylike manner beneath her.

Heavy footsteps approaching behind the high-backed, gilt-trimmed chair in which Danette was sitting didn't even pull her away from her pensive, downcast mood. She just leaned her chin into a hand and rested her elbow on the arm of the chair, watching flames caressing logs in the grate. In her mind, the flames were fingers . . . Gray Wolf's fingers . . . and she was the log, enjoying the fire of his touch. . . .

"Danette, you missed breakfast," Dwight said, stepping

suddenly in front of her view of the fire, blocking out not only the flames but Danette's fantasy, as well.

With a jerk, she rose to her feet. Self-consciously, she straightened the lines of her dress and hoped and prayed that her uncle would attribute her red face to the fact that she had been sitting so close to the fire.

She managed a nervous laugh. "Uncle Dwight, you gave me a fright sneaking up on me so," she murmured. Her gaze took in his crisp white-ruffled shirt and the narrowness of his hips beneath the straight line of his dark, wool trousers. His vest was of an elegant satin material, fancily embroidered. Yes, he appeared successful. She only wished his concern for her were more sincere!

Dwight's dark eyebrows forked. He kneaded his chin as he silently studied her before further speaking to her. He had noticed how strangely she continued to behave since her near tragedy of over a week ago. And even more unusual for her was the fact that, according to Amy, Danette had only left the house once since that day. It wasn't at all like Danette to stay cooped inside . . . especially during the brilliant, bright days of spring!

"Sneak?" he finally said. "I'm not known for sneaking about, Danette, and I most certainly had no reason to this morning. It's you. Where does your mind stray these days? You're not at all yourself. Can you explain yourself?"

Avoiding his eyes, Danette once more toyed with the pearls in her hair. "I haven't been aware of a straying mind, as you call it," she said throatily, hardly recognizing her own voice. Had this change that had come over her . . . that of feeling like a woman . . . even changed the tone of her voice? Somehow her voice sounded sultry. . . .

"Then what would you call your continuing strange behavior?" Dwight asked, stooping to lift a log to the fire. "I've given you new paints and you ignore them?"

He straightened his back and wiped his hands on the back of his trousers. He then urged Danette's gaze to meet his by lifting her chin with his forefinger. "Want to tell Uncle Dwight all about it, honey?" he asked, winking at her. "I'm here to listen. You *are* more my daughter than my niece, you know."

Danette felt emotion grip her hard, as though being torn, and she knew that these feelings were because of her need to be with Gray Wolf, to share everything with him, and her need to be loyal to Dwight and what he expected of her, the proper, quiet, moral niece of Minnesota State Senator Dwight Thomas.

"I know," she murmured, smiling weakly. "But Uncle Dwight, I truly have nothing to confide to you. I imagine my mood is caused by the heady days of spring. They do affect a person in such a way. I'm sure even you are aware of it."

Dwight wheeled away from her and lifted his dark frock coat from the back of a chair. As he eased into it, he kept his back to her. "A man does not become affected by spring or such foolishness," he said dryly.

Swinging around, he retied his bulky bow tie and twitched his shoulders, adjusting himself to the tight confines of his coat. "A man busies his thoughts with more manly things. Business. That's what's important to a man."

"I'm sure," Danette said stiffly, not wanting to argue. She only wished to be left alone with her thoughts. Yet they always returned her to Gray Wolf, and still she could not understand this. What was this power he had over her? She had only been with him twice and she had almost let him . . .

Shaking her head to clear her thoughts, she strolled to a window and drew the drapery aside. She tensed when Dwight moved next to her.

"Amy has been instructed to pack a valise for you, Danette," he said, admiringly touching her sweep of hair. "We will be traveling by train to St. Paul early tomorrow morning."

43

A numbness overtook Danette. This was a most inopportune time for a journey to St. Paul—or *any*where. She had almost decided to go in search of Gray Wolf to see if he still considered her a friend after her last abrupt departure from him.

Twirling her skirt quickly around, Danette guardedly looked up into Dwight's faded blue eyes. "A trip to St. Paul?" she said. "Tomorrow, Uncle Dwight? Why? And why is it you spring this on me so suddenly? Why don't I ever have a say in any of our plans? What if I don't wish to go to St. Paul?"

Dwight idly scratched his brow, once more studying her, now even more confused by her behavior. She had always anxiously welcomed a journey to St. Paul, if not for the train ride alone, then for the opportunity to shop in St. Paul's elaborate, eclectic dress emporiums and even fancier millineries.

"Are you saying you do not wish to accompany me?" he questioned, furrowing his brow into a dark frown.

Showing her stubborn streak by the set of her jaw and the stiffness of her arms held tightly to her side, Danette so wanted to challenge him, but she couldn't. He was her guardian . . . a man who, in his own way, had sacrificed for her.

"I didn't say that," she said flatly. "I just asked why it is that I never have a say so in any of our plans."

"Because it is I who set the rules in this household," Dwight growled. "And by damn, you will go wherever and whenever I say."

He cleared his throat and straightened his tie. "Do I make myself clear, Danette?" he hoarsely added.

"Quite," she said, barely audible.

"Then I can expect no more question of my authority?"

"None."

Danette sighed and strolled quickly away from him and out into the hallway, headed for the staircase. But a hand on her arm made her aware of her Uncle Dwight's having followed her, and she knew that she wasn't going to escape his risen scorn so easily. She slowly turned and shrank beneath his angry stare.

"You will help Amy in choosing dresses to last for a possible two weeks' stay," he ordered.

The color quickly drained from Danette's cheeks. Two weeks! For her at this time in her life two weeks were an eternity! Gray Wolf would most surely forget that she even existed in such a lengthy absence! It had already been one full week since she had seen him!

"Two weeks?" she said weakly, voicing her dreaded worry "Uncle Dwight, why two long weeks?"

Dwight dropped his hand from her arm and looked toward the ceiling, sighing heavily. "More arguments?" he said. "Why are two weeks a thing to show such displeasure over?" His eyes were now directed toward Danette, appearing to be trying to bore holes through her, the anger was so acute in them.

Danette nervously ran her hand up and down the polished oak bannister of the staircase. "I hate the hotels we stay in when we're there," she said softly. *"You* don't have to stay in the stuffy, smelly rooms. You get to at least do your business in the beautiful State Capitol Building."

"You will spend your days shopping. . . ."

"There's just so much shopping one can do, even in St. Paul," Danette softly argued. She then straightened her back with bold determination and blurted, "Uncle Dwight, I will not go this time. I shall stay here."

Dwight's face twisted with anger as he clasped his fingers to her shoulders. "You will help Amy pack," he fumed. "And I will not hear one more disobedient word from you, will I?"

Danette swallowed back a fast-growing lump in her throat. She cringed beneath his fingers of steel, hoping not to be bruised where he so forcefully held on to her.

"No sir," she finally murmured. "You will not. And, yes, I will assist Amy in readying my valise to go to St. Paul. I'm sorry to have been so . . . so . . ."

Seeing her sweet, innocent features screwing up into near tears, Dwight drew her quickly into his arms and caressed her back. "Honey, I'm the one who's sorry," he crooned. "Don't be upset. Please try and understand my political ambitions. I *must* go to St. Paul and tend to my senatorial duties. It would be so easy to be replaced on election day."

Danette placed her arms about him, absorbing this moment of closeness with him. And, seizing the opportunity of this moment, she once more tried to argue her case. "But two weeks, Uncle Dwight?" she said. She tensed when she felt him stiffen and expected another cold, indifferent outburst from him. But instead he held her away from him and explained why, in a soft, gentle voice.

"I may also have to travel to Washington from St. Paul," he said. "This is why a longer stay may be required. President Hayes needs support on his ideas of civil service reform. I'm one who is willing to back him. It may take this trip to Washington to voice my approval in person. But first I will have to tend to some senatorial duties in St. Paul."

"I could stay here with Amy. . . ."

"I've already given Amy the time off to go visit her ailing brother, Toby."

"Oh, I see," Danette said, lowering her eyes. Then she shrugged. "All right, Uncle Dwight. If I must accompany you, I must."

Dwight urged her chin up with his forefinger and smiled warmly down at her. "I have checked around and I've found that Rettie Toliver's boardinghouse is the place to stay this time, instead of a hotel," he said, trying to reassure her. "The boardinghouse sits conveniently across from the State Capitol Building, and I've ben told it's more a home away from home than any other rental residence in St. Paul. You most surely won't mind staying there."

"Boardinghouse or hotel," Danette said sorrowfully. "There surely is no difference. A room that is mainly occupied by only a bed is not my idea of home."

"I've been told that Rettie Toliver has a niece of nearly your same age who makes her residence at this boardinghouse with her aunt," Dwight further tried to encourage her. "Perhaps you two could become friends. Possibly she will accompany you shopping. You could chat over tea and cake. If you'd let yourself, you could enjoy your stay in St. Paul with a new acquaintance to spend time with."

Once more Danette shrugged. "Perhaps," she sighed. But nothing would make her want this time away from Duluth. One step onto the train would mean leaving her heart behind.

"Her name is Amanda," Dwight said, going to the coat tree to grab his tall silk hat.

Danette took a step forward. "Whose name is Amanda?" she softly questioned.

"Rettie Toliver's niece," Dwight said, plopping his hat on his head. "You two young ladies have something in common, which could make for a faster friendship. It could cause a bond of sorts, I would think."

Lifting a silky eyebrow, Danette followed Dwight to the front door. "And what might that be?" she asked.

Dwight swung the door wide open, letting in the fresh aroma of the early May morning. Danette enjoyed the feel of the breeze, warm and enticing on her face, bare shoulders, and arms. The skirt of her dress and petticoats rustled voluptuously as they blew gently up and away from her ankles.

Dwight stepped out onto the wide porch, stretching and inhaling deeply, then turned and faced Danette. "Her parents are no longer alive either," he said matter-of-factly. "The main difference, though, is in the way her parents died."

"How *did* her parents die?" Danette asked, placing a hand to her brow as a curl escaped from the pins of her hair.

"Indians," Dwight said. "They were killed by Indians."

The pit of Danette's stomach churned menacingly. She moved a hand to her mouth to suppress a motified gasp. Indians! But, no! She didn't want to think of it. Gray Wolf wasn't that type of Indian. He was gentle. He could never kill . . .

"I shall be home early this evening, Danette," Dwight said, tipping his hat to her. "We should both retire immediately after dinner tonight because we will be boarding a train on the morrow before the sun rises."

"I understand," Danette said shallowly, following him to the granite steps. "I shall be packed, Uncle Dwight. Please don't fret anymore about it."

"No reason to fret," Dwight said, as he rushed down the steps and to the gravel walk that led around to the stables. "Your ill behavior is already forgotten."

Danette stood on the porch holding the skirt of her dress down from the whipping of the breeze. She watched as Dwight rode away on his proud mount, then turned and moved back inside the house, somehow unable to put his words about the Indians from her mind.

"How terrible," she said, shuddering. Remembering Gray Wolf made it hard for Danette to think of any Indian's being anything but warm and gentle. But historians had written of the many Indian massacres of the past years, and, yes, she knew that Indians were hated still for their heathen, savage ways.

Circling her hands to her side, she let out a soft, muffled cry. "But I love him," she whispered. "Lord, I cannot help myself. I love Gray Wolf and I must see him. Today."

His handsomeness . . . his mystique . . . her fascination for him . . . led her to her decision to, yes, defy all the propriety she had been raised with to go in search of him. She knew that no matter what anyone thought she was ready to agree to his kisses, and even more, to be with him again.

With a blush on her cheeks, Danette rushed through the house in search of Amy. "Amy! Where are you?" she yelled. "I must leave for a while. I have a sudden urge to go paint before the sun gets unbearably hot. . . ."

A slow smile lifted her lips. She would find Gray Wolf if it took her all day. Thank heavens she had her love for painting as a cover . . .

Daringly, Danette rode her buggy along Front Street, having remembered Gray Wolf's saying something about bringing the felled trees to the river for delivery to mills downstream. She drew her shawl more snugly around her shoulders and bent her head, hoping the brim of her bonnet would hide her face beneath its shadows.

Front Street was not the place for a lady of good upbringing. Besides the busy waterfront and the men scurrying to and from great ships there were the low clusters of houses known to be inhabited by rowdy Canadians and native inhabitants who worked for local traders or fisheries. The houses were no more than shanties, with makeshift tin roofs, unpainted, weather-worn outside walls, grassless lawns strewn with empty whiskey bottles and horse dung from horses that stood idly by, tied to the low limbs of trees or the posts of front porches. The aroma of filth radiated from all these things, and flies buzzed noisily from yard to yard, house to house.

A slap of the reins and Danette was carried farther down the cobblestone street, drawing nearer to the many large piers that stretched out into the Duluth Ship Canal, which had been cut through the Minnesota Point sand bar in the early 1870s.

Where there weren't piers, there were warehouses and many one-story buildings, one of which was the internationally known American Fur Company, and also a hotel, a country store, and two churches.

Danette sighed more easily, having left the questionable section of town behind her, realizing the dangers she had put herself in by being there. But searching for Gray Wolf in itself had its own element of danger. If her Uncle Dwight should happen along on horseback and discover her wanton, loose behavior, what would he do?

Loosening her shawl to let it drape down over her arms, and relaxing her shoulder muscles to lift her head to direct her vision more naturally forward, Danette could see Dwight's lumber company building towering over all else around it in the distance on the farthest stretch of Front Street where Danette did not dare travel. Her heart ached. Gray Wolf was probably there, since she hadn't succeeded in finding him anywhere else. Why hadn't she realized that would be the *only* place he would be working with lumber on the water-front? He was in her Uncle Dwight's employ.

"How much simpler it would have been if he had just been at the bluff where I last saw him," she whispered, guiding her horse left, onto the steepness of a street that would carry her upward and away from the waterfront.

She had gone first to the bluff, hoping that the river, or possibly thoughts of her, would have drawn Gray Wolf there or this beautiful early morning. The disappointment had overwhelmed her when she had found the bluff as secluded as she had before the one time she'd been there with Gray Wolf.

"I just may as well give up," Danette softly sighed. "Anyway, I was foolish for thinking I might chance seeing him again. He has his own way of life . . . I have mine."

Passing horse-drawn carriages and men on horseback traveling in the opposite direction on her steep ascent of the street, Danette nodded a friendly hello to the women and lifted her chin haughtily to the flirting eyes of the men. Most people in town knew her from their acquaintance with her senator uncle, and she hoped that none would spread gossip to him of her early morning travels on this day when she had already had too many disagreements with him.

"What I need is to go to the forest," she thought to

herself. "That way I can be alone and get a fresh painting started in peace."

She knew that if she at least got a picture sketched out on the canvas that day, her memory would help her with the details to paint later, when she was bored in her room at the boardinghouse in St. Paul. It wasn't hard to remember the bend of an aging oak tree or the twists of a grapevine with its purple clusters of grapes. Without even being there yet she could smell the pure, sweet smell of the cedar and pinewood of the forest and see the sun glowing in velvetlike strips of yellow through the ceiling of the trees.

Danette shouted to the horse, now eager to get along with her day, even if alone. Later on, she would have to supervise the packing of her valise or be sure to be severely criticized anew by her uncle.

"Hahh! Move along!"

She slapped her reins and leaned with the buggy's pull up the hill, never looking back, for fear of growing dizzy from the swirling of the waters that now stretched out many feet behind and below her.

"Oh! How I hate this city," she grumbled, urging her horse on upward. "Why would anyone place a city so sideways on a hill?"

Her thoughts were once more on Gray Wolf and how he had so bravely rescued her. She wondered if he ever would again after her uncle's rudeness to him?

"It's not the easiest thing . . ." she whispered, "to be made a fool of. Uncle Dwight should never have done that to Gray Wolf."

Her heart ached, now remembering that though she had intended to, she hadn't apologized to Gray Wolf for her uncle's nasty behavior. And now she doubted if she would ever get the chance again. Now it hadn't been only her uncle who had treated him poorly. She had also. After their intimate shared embraces she had ridden away from him without even . . . a . . . polite . . . goodbye.

Not wanting to let herself think of Gray Wolf any further, Danette headed her horse and buggy away from the city streets, onto flatter land and out across a meadow toward the fresh stretches of the forest. It would become her hideaway . . . at least for a little while, before she would have to return to the "real" world of uncles and train rides . . . and goodbyes to yesterdays. . . .

Making sure to take a turn in the road that led her away from the section of forest being worked by her uncle's men, Danette began feeling the cool shadow of the trees overhead. It had been foolish even to let herself consider looking for Gray Wolf on the acreage owned by her uncle, so close to where the lumberjacks lived in their bunkhouses on the edge of the forest. A lone woman there among the women-hungry men was a woman ready to expect anything but pleasantness.

Rape had been a word unknown to Danette before the lumberjacks. But recently rumor upon rumor of rape on the dark streets of the city had been just cause for gaslights to be doubled along the thoroughfares and for the sheriff to seek the help of more men.

The sweet fragrance of pine mingled with the damp, pungent smell of the mounds of winter-fallen leaves on the ground. Danette's nose twitched with the different fragrances, and she moved her horse and buggy on into the forest where a lane had been cut beneath the towering oak, elm, and maple trees.

Shivering with the sudden chill of the dew-laden air that had not yet escaped through the dense cover of trees, Danette drew her shawl more snugly around her shoulders. She tensed. This lane was one unfamiliar to her. She hadn't traveled this far from home since last autumn, and someone had cleared this land since that time. Danette wondered why.

Fear of the unknown caused a prickling sensation along her scalp, yet a sense of adventure lured her onward. Strange calls from birds echoed overhead and around her . . . shrieks as though from a cat, it seemed, instead of a bird! A swooping bluejay, a scampering squirrel, and Danette felt that she was the alien and the intruder in the forest's domain of little wild creatures.

The trees on both sides of her buggy had now become so dense, it was as though Danette was looking into the pitch darkness of night as she tried to see through them. Another shiver raced across her flesh. She had never felt so alone. She now wished she hadn't become so daring this morning and was out of the forest where the sun could make her feel the aliveness of the day in its warm, penetrating touch.

"I must go back," she whispered. "This is foolish. The lane goes on forever, it seems, and even when I reach the end, I may not like what I find!"

Her insides grew numb as she became aware of the narrowness of the lane and the impossibility of turning her horse and buggy around. The lane was now even barely wide enough for her buggy to pass through! Why hadn't she noticed before! It now seemed to be swallowing her up, her fear had grown to such an extreme, yet she had no other choice but to keep traveling ahead, hoping that somewhere along the way the opportunity would arise to head her horse back toward home. She had no desire to try and steer the horse and buggy backwards over the distance she had just traveled!

Suddenly Danette could see a clearing before her. She snapped her horse's reins, sending him into a faster trot, and when she reached the clearing, her pulse began to race.

She let her eyes and heart absorb the Indian wigwam that sat in the clearing, away from where the lane abruptly stopped, and her thoughts were immediately filled with Gray Wolf! Had he chosen to live away from the bunkhouse of the other lumberjacks? Did he set himself so apart from them that he felt the need to live alone?

Then, feeling foolish, remembering the many Indians in the area, she had to realize how small the chances were of this being Gray Wolf's wigwam, and a new kind of fear now caused goose pimples to rise on her flesh. If not Gray Wolf's . . . then whose? And would the owner of this wigwam be as friendly as Gray Wolf? Civilization as Danette knew it had been left behind as soon as she had first guided her horse into the newly cut lane.

Directing her horse to stop, Danette let her gaze move slowly and cautiously about her, trying to be aware of any possible quick movements that might mean a threat to her safety . . . possibly even her life.

Where trees had been cut down in the clearing, making way for the sunshine, fresh shoots of grass were trembling in the breeze. Small dogtooth violets, pale blue bird's foot, moccasin flowers and trailing arbuturs made this a place of color and peacefulness. There was a stirring inside Danette's mind . . . this could be a magnificent setting for her newest painting!

Nuthatches, sparrows and wrens were flitting about from tree to tree and a lone deer peering out from the brush made Danette smile, as she slowly lost her sense of danger, and became filled with a peacefulness that was transferring from the innocent creatures of the forest to her.

Then her gaze moved back to the wigwam. She had never seen one up close. If she left the buggy and went up to the wigwam, might an Indian step from inside it and order her away?

But once more, curiosity sent caution to the wind and Danette stepped from the buggy and began moving toward the wigwam, listening and watching, feeling like an alien, and hoping not to offend anyone if she was discovered snooping about.

Letting her shawl fall to drape loosely over the crooks of her arms, Danette observed the structure before her. The dwelling was oval with a dome-shaped top, and the sides, except the doorway, were covered with what appeared to be bulrush mats. The top was covered with rolls of birch bark.

A blanket of bright, zigzagged colors hung over the doorway, and Danette stepped up to it, feeling awkward with nothing to knock on, to announce her presence there for anyone who might be inside. She felt it only right that since she had so boldly come this far she should meet the Indian who had built this unique setting in the forest, away from the white man.

"Away from the white man," Danette slowly whispered, shrinking back from the doorway. Because the Indian chose to build away from everyone could mean a white man or woman would not be welcome. . . .

Yet, still determined to see which Indian, thinking more about Gray Wolf than about fear, she boldly stepped forward again.

"Hello, there," she said, watching the blanket at the doorway. She felt a keen weakness in her knees when the blanket rippled and shook. She then sighed deeply when she realized the movement of the blanket had been caused by a gust of wind rather than another person's presence.

"Is anybody here?" Danette once more questioned, this time more loudly.

A few heart-stopping moments passed with no reply or sound from within, and Danette came to the conclusion that she was alone. She studied the doorway. She so badly wanted to go inside, to see how an Indian lived.

But, feeling she had intruded enough, she stepped quickly back, turned, and headed back to the buggy, eager to get on with her day. Now that she knew she was alone, she would take the opportunity to quickly sketch this scene onto her canvas. Somehow by doing so she knew she would be capturing a part of Gray Wolf to always keep with her. Even if this wasn't *his* personal dwelling . . . it was his way of living . . . and her heart ached for him anew. . . .

Chapter Four

What I have lost of pleasure,
Assuage what I find of rain.
                              —Lyster

As shadows began to lengthen beside the wigwam, Danette was made suddenly aware of the passage of time. She had been caught up in the magic of her painting and had not even noticed that afternoon had come and was slipping quickly by.

Sketching on the canvas had just not been enough to satisfy her. To capture the complete esoteric quality of this setting, it had become necessary to add touches of paint to the canvas, which had inadvertently enticed Danette to work on, until only a few more strokes with the brush and she could say she had indeed had a rewarding day of painting.

But she hadn't planned to spend a full day. The dangers increased each added moment that she remained there. And now that the lowering of the sun had given her a fair warning, she would depart in haste.

Almost breathlessly, she loaded her buggy, and just as she was ready to climb aboard, she heard the distinct sound of a horse's hoofbeats drawing near, from down the lane.

A cold desperation seizing her, Danette looked wildly about her. There were no routes for escape. She had led herself into a trap . . . one she should have freed herself of long ago when she had had the chance.

But drugged from the headiness of the day and her passion for painting, her sense had been stolen from her, only to return to her now, almost paralyzing her with fear.

"What shall I do?" she whispered harshly. "Where can I go?"

Then her gaze settled on the wigwam. She could guide her horse and buggy and hide them behind the dwelling while she went inside, where she most surely could find a way to hide herself.

"But what if it's the Indian who lives there?" she worried aloud. "Surely only he uses this lane. The lane goes no farther than here."

The horse's hooves were growing even closer now. Danette saw no other choice but to hide. If not an Indian, it could be even worse . . . a lone horseman . . . a crazed, white, woman-hungry lumberjack! He could have his way with her and no one would ever hear her screams and pleas. The thickness of the forest would muffle any cries for help.

"I must try to hide in the wigwam," she said firmly, already guiding her horse toward it. "I have no choice. Possibly it's a rider, checking out the lane, and once he sees a lone Indian house he will turn and go back the way he came."

Shivering from the building chill in the late afternoon and from mounting fear, Danette secured her horse and buggy behind the wigwam. Then she crept noiselessly around to the front and slipped quietly into the wigwam, finding it dark, damp, and desolate.

With only a smoke hole in the ceiling to let in a few tinges of light, Danette groped her way around the room, feeling for furniture to either hide beneath or behind. Finding none of these things, Danette felt her entrapment worsening.

"If Gray Wolf could only be here to save me again," she whispered, still feeling around her, again reminded of him and her feelings for him by the surroundings that he was familiar with.

As she fell to her knees, her fingers came in contact with a rush mat flooring. And further exploration discovered what felt like a rolled-up blanket placed against the outer wall.

In the middle of the room, her fingers touched rocks that were warm, and closer observation showed smoldering coals beneath a thick bed of ashes inside the circle of rocks.

A faint odor of herbs tickled her nose, and in the faintness of the light Danette could see them hanging low over the firespace, possibly drying for eventual use in food, or for use as a room freshener. The aroma of the grasslike sedge plant was almost overpowering. It had probably been used in the bulrush mats.

The neighing of a horse and the answer of her own horse back to it alerted Danette that the stranger had not backtracked but had come on to the wigwam . . . and she was the same as caught . . . for now she had no choice but to sit there and wait for her eventual fate.

Swallowing hard, she watched the blanket at the doorway slowly lift and an outline of a man take its place. Though it was late afternoon there was still enough light to rush in, onto her upturned face, yet she still couldn't make out the face of the man standing there, awe-struck, she imagined, to find her huddling there.

"Wee-shko-may-may-gwah?"

Danette's senses began reeling from relief when she heard the familiar voice speaking her name in Indian. She rose quickly to her feet and went to Gray Wolf and rushed into his arms, sobbing. "Gray Wolf," she cried. "Oh, Gray Wolf, I'm so glad it's you. I was so afraid."

He held her for a moment, then urged her away from him, clasping his hands gently on her shoulders. "Why are you here?" he asked, his green eyes full of question and wonder. "How did you know of Gray Wolf's wigwam?"

"I didn't," Danette said, sniffling. She wiped her nose with the back of her hand, tremorous from his nearness and steady gaze. "I didn't know this was your wigwam. I just happened along."

"But you are here, inside," he said, gesturing with a hand. "Why are you, if you not know whose dwelling this is?"

A slow blush rose to Danette's cheeks, embarrassed now by the circumstances in which he had found her there. Quite a lengthy explanation was in order and also an apology for intruding on his privacy.

Apologies! First her Uncle Dwight had need to apologize to Gray Wolf and now herself! How could Gray Wolf even be civil to her with all this due him? He surely must think the Thomas family a rude lot and not to his liking at all!

"The lane," she said. "It attracted my attention. It wasn't here when I last was. I guess I . . . I . . . should have passed it on by but I wanted to see where it led."

"And you had to even see inside my dwelling?" Gray Wolf said hotly, walking away from her to stoop before the firespace on the floor. "What if Gray Wolf come to your dwelling and enter without asking? Your uncle would then have cause to be angry with me." He cast her an angry stare. "And you? Now that you are here, will you leave Gray Wolf again without goodbye, as you did before?"

Danette fell to her knees next to him and touched his arm. "Gray Wolf, I'm sorry," she said softly. She flinched when he jerked his arm away from her. He quickly busied himself, placing twigs and larger logs in the firespace.

Danette was not to give up so easily, not now that she had found him again. "Here. Let me help you," she said, reaching for some pieces of dry wood that lay behind Gray Wolf, next to the wall.

When he shoved her hand away and glared angrily at her, she rose slowly to her feet and inched backwards, feeling behind her for the blanket at the doorway. He didn't want her there . . . she shouldn't be there . . . so she would leave. But first she would have her say!

She watched the fire take hold amongst the stacked wood and twigs, then looked back toward Gray Wolf. With a dry, emotion-filled throat she said: "I was wrong to leave so abruptly the other day, Gray Wolf. But I was afraid of my intense feelings for you."

She watched his head move slowly around and began the usual melting inside when his eyes fell upon her, anger slowly ebbing away from them. She continued. "I've fallen in love with you, Gray Wolf. I searched and searched for you today, to tell you my feelings and to apologize for both my uncle and myself and our rude behavior. When I didn't find you, it seems fate led me to this lane which was yours and so here I am . . . baring my heart to you."

She scarcely breathed, awaiting his response, but when he did no more than continue to gaze at her, Danette couldn't help but fall once more to her knees, but this time she worked herself into his arms.

"I love you," she whispered, showering his copper face with light kisses. "Please love me back. I can't shake you from my thoughts."

His lack of response caused a coldness to cut through Danette's insides. She could feel the tightness of his muscles beneath his shirt, yet could feel also the pounding of his heart and knew that surely it was his pride causing him to not give in to her because she had already shamed him once. . . .

She drew away from him. "Don't you even care?" she asked, watching the fire cast dancing shadows on his face. She was once more made aware of his handsomeness and his mystique. He showed no emotion, as though restraint was necessary to make him a man of will.

"Did you have no feelings whatsoever for me when we came so close to making love?" she harshly spoke, searching his face for hidden answers. His eyes showed a softness but his jaw was set hard. "Was I nothing to you? You were . . . just . . . using me like you would any woman?" she added,

61

almost choking on a sob. She pushed away from him, pale and drawn. "Do you see me . . . as . . . as a whore?" she throatily gasped.

Not wanting to suffer anymore beneath his refusal to speak, even afraid of his answer should he decide to, Danette rose quickly to her feet and made her way toward the doorway.

Suddenly he was there. His hands were on her shoulders, urging her around to face him. His eyelids were heavy, his lips relaxed. "Do not go," he said hoarsely. "Stay. Gray Wolf sleep not one night since looking into your eyes of the sky and rivers. Sweet Butterfly, stay, and ease the pain in my heart."

"Gray Wolf," Danette sighed, consumed by her helpless surrender to him as he lowered his lips fiercely to hers.

Molding her closely to the contours of his body, Gray Wolf's hands swept down her back in a searching, sensuous touch. His breath became laborious when he once more became familiar with her petiteness, feeling the gentle curve of her hips.

With boldness he crept his hand between them and cupped one of her breasts. A throbbing in his groin pained him. His need for her was growing like wildfire inside him, but he couldn't help but remember their last time together, and this time he knew to practice patience.

Swallowed up in her passion for him, Danette twined her arms about his neck. She once more could tell of his intense feelings for her by the wild beating of the pulse at his throat. When his fingers found her breast, the drugged spinning of her head made a soft sort of gurgle of arousal come from her throat.

Gray Wolf's tongue quickly sought entrance to Danette's mouth and explored the hot, wet cavern there. Danette returned the assault by letting her tongue meet his in a sensuous intertwining while her fingers unlocked from about his neck, and she let her hands travel down his back to his

62

muscular male buttocks and even lower to the even more muscled strength in his thighs that were eagerly pressed against her.

Then, very brazenly, Danette's hand moved between them and stopped where the bulge beneath the tight confines of his breeches spoke to her of his readiness for her. Hearing his quick intake of breath, Danette flinched and jerked her hand quickly away.

Gray Wolf drew away from Danette, eyeing her with a heated, hungry longing, but still he would not be too hasty. He couldn't lose her again. He reached his hand to her face and ran his fingers over her gentle features, and, when her passion-heavy lashes closed and she leaned her face into his hand, Gray Wolf took her by the elbow and guided her down onto the bulrush mats beside the fire and stretched her out beneath him.

"Love is like the rivers," Gray Wolf whispered into her ear, embracing her tenderly. "It is *ah-pah-nay. Ay-uh.* It is forever. Such is my love for you, Sweet Butterfly."

His words sent Danette's senses to soaring. She lifted a finger to his chin and guided his lips to hers, first whispering, "And so is my love the same for you, Gray Wolf. Love me. Love me fully, or I shall simply die in the waiting."

Gray Wolf's green eyes met hers and held, feverish with desire, then his lips met hers in a quivering, soft kiss. A warmth coursed through Danette's veins as his hand cupped her breast and fondly kneaded it. And once more he leaned away from her, beseeching her with his eyes.

She was acutely aware of what he was silently asking of her, and, drunk now with her passion, caring about nothing but pleasing him, she rose to her feet and slowly began to undress in front of him.

Thoughts of her uncle and his warnings were tossed recklessly aside. Worries of being thought brazen were quickly forgotten. It was the power in her desire for him that led her onward. She needed to be fulfilled as much as she wanted to please the man she loved. The time to become a woman in every sense of the word had arrived, and she was ready. Oh, how she was ready!

The fire in the firespace had died to slow, flickering flames, and Gray Wolf's face showed only in soft shadows as he watched her dress slip from her shoulders. Shaking herself, Danette let the dress flutter down away from her, and she stepped out of it, leaving her with petticoats and shoes to remove.

Filled with even more of the strange, wondrous desire for this handsome Indian, Danette boldly swept the petticoats away from her, and then her shoes, until she stood trembling and quite nude before his passion-filled eyes.

Gray Wolf took in her loveliness as his gaze moved slowly over her, marveling at the soft pink color of her flesh, the sensuous curve of her hips, and the great mounds of her breasts, their even pinker tips swollen with anticipation.

Then his gaze lowered and the thundering of his heartbeat increased when he saw the dark vee of hair that covered her womanhood. When her hand instinctively suddenly covered herself there, Gray Wolf understood and went to her and knelt on his knee before her. With a trembling in his fingers he urged her hand away and lowered his lips to kiss her there, inhaling the sweet, perfumed smell of her body.

Danette clenched her hands to her side and closed her eyes to the thrill of the touch of his lips where she so throbbed with need. Her breath came in short gasps as his tongue was suddenly there, searching, hot, and caressing.

Then, feeling her senses leaving her even more, Danette became afraid and pushed at his head. "No . . ." she gasped. "Gray Wolf, what you are doing . . ."

Gray Wolf rose quickly to his feet and drew her gently into his arms. "Let love have its way this time," he said huskily, breathing warmth into her ear. "Do not let fears steal the wonders of what we have found in one another's arms. When the heart is perfectly sincere, there is no wrong in making love.''

"Gray Wolf, I . . ." she softly pleaded, becoming lethargic and limp from the ecstasy of his kisses being rained along her cheeks, lashes and throat.

Then when his lips lowered to her breast and his tongue flicked around its swollen nipple, teasing and tormenting, Danette was once more as though under a strange, magical spell as she curled her fingers through his hair and urged his face even closer.

His fingers traveled slowly down her back, then moved around and found her pulsating love mound. With the skill of a practiced lover, he began a slow caress there while tasting the sweet honey of her breast. His teeth softly nipped, his tongue swirled around the nipple's tip. And, when he felt her quivering and heard her rapturous moan, he immediately stopped his manipulations to step back away from her to quickly undress.

With a pounding heart and enflamed face, Danette watched him disrobe, loving the fine-boned frame of him, the copper color of his skin and his narrow hips. Then her gaze fell upon his swollen sex, fearful, yet she knew that this time she would welcome him inside her body. She was like liquid inside, all gushy and warm, and was ready to let her body blend with his, to become one mass of hot, melting, flesh. . . .

Stepping from the last of his clothing, Gray Wolf went to Danette and placed his hands to her hair. Slowly, but determinedly, he began to remove the pins and then the string of pearls that she had woven into her curls. Smiling, he took the string of pearls and pulled them sensuously down her body, trailing them around first one breast and then the other, and then across her navel. Watching her eyes become hazy with growing desire for him, Gray Wolf teased her further by slowly pulling the string of pearls back and forth across her swollen love mound, then dropped them to the floor when her breathing appeared to be becoming too erratic. He wanted her to reach the peak of her passion only with him inside her. He wanted to feel her rapture as he planted his seeds deeply inside her womb. She would then be his. *Ay-uh, ah-pah-nay. . . .*

His fingers worked with her hair, loosening it completely, draping it over her shoulders, and then he drew her next to him, feeling the heat of her breasts against his chest and the silk of her thighs against his legs.

Surrendering to his embrace, Danette let him once more lower her to lie on the bulrush mats. She could feel the strength in his manhood as it grazed the flesh of her thigh, causing her to flinch involuntarily. She silently feared being torn by its largeness but closed her eyes and turned her head away as he slowly began to inch it up inside her.

A sudden, sharp pain caused Danette's eyes to fly widely open and her hands to go to Gray Wolf's shoulders, to try to shove him away. "Please . . ." she softly cried. "It hurts, Gray Wolf. I mustn't go any farther with this. . . ."

Gray Wolf placed his lips to hers and kissed her gently, letting his tongue run sensuously against hers. He could feel her relaxing against him, so he once more thrust forward and then quivered as he found he had finally made a full entrance inside her moist, tight wall of love.

He drew his lips away. "Gray Wolf first with you," he mumbled huskily. "And Gray Wolf be last. You are *neen-nee-dah-ee-een.* Only mine."

Placing his face into the curve of her neck, he began his slow, sensual movements inside her. Danette's hands frantically sought out the feel of his sleek back, now working with him as she lifted her hips, welcoming the pleasure that had taken the place of the brief moment of pain.

She clung. She sighed. She tossed her head back and forth. His lips kissed her breast, his teeth chewed, and then it was as though her body had become a river of sensations, and she was all aglow with them, her mind swirling as the thrill of release tore through her in a too brief moment of overpowering ecstasy that left her limp and panting against him.

Gray Wolf smiled to himself, having achieved the proud goal of a man, that of bringing a woman into the unknown world of the agonies of sensuous ecstasies. He had succeeded well. He knew the ways of love. And now he would concentrate on his own pleasure, never being selfish in love. He was more the man by being the patient lover.

Cupping a breast with one hand and lowering his other hand to place it beneath Danette's buttocks, he began working with more eager thrusts, perspiration building on his brow. He closed his eyes, gritted his teeth, and burrowed his face into her hair, feeling the rapture mounting, like fire spreading inside him.

He groaned . . . he stiffened . . . he thrust, and suddenly the pinnacle of love was reached. He held her as though in a vise, shuddered violently against her, plunged more deeply inside her, and cried out as he felt his warm liquid being released.

Danette clung to him, totally in awe of this thing she had just shared with Gray Wolf. Nothing had ever been so beautiful, and she now knew that life would be an empty void without him. But life ahead was to be quite difficult, for her Uncle Dwight's face loomed before her, haunting her, threatening her existence as she now knew it must be.

Gray Wolf leaned up and placed a hand on her cheek, flaming her anew where he touched her. "Did Gray Wolf hurt you?" he said thickly. "This was first time for Sweet Butterfly. Gray Wolf hope you not sorry."

With a faint throbbing inside where his hugeness had so splendidly filled her, Danette felt as though she was ready to share the beauty of that moment all over again with him. But it was strange how his manhood had shrunk after his pleasure and now lay limply on her thigh! She was even in more wonder now about this man she loved and the ways his body could change right before her eyes.

"You all right . . . ?" Gray Wolf questioned, moving to lie on his side beside her. "You not speak of your feelings. You sad?"

Danette pushed herself up on an elbow and leaned her face into his and brushed a soft kiss against his lips. "Now do I look sad, Gray Wolf?" she asked, laughing softly. She knew that she should at least feel ashamed . . . or . . . guilty!

Thoughts of Dwight once more seized her. Her eyes grew wide and her face flushed as she rose quickly to her feet.

"What is it, Sweet Butterfly?" Gray Wolf questioned, following along after her as she began hurrying into her clothes.

"My uncle," she said, panting with her efforts. "He said that he would be home early this evening for dinner."

She shook herself into one petticoat after another and then into her dress, looking anxiously at Gray Wolf, who had already stepped into his jeans. "Gray Wolf, if he should ever discover where I've been . . . what I've done . . ."

Gray Wolf took a wide step and stood handsomely before her. He gently framed her face between his hands. "Sweet Butterfly do not worry so. Gray Wolf protect you even from uncle."

Danette eased away from him. "You just don't understand," she said. "My uncle is not the easiest person to talk with. He doesn't understand anything about me or why I do it. He could never understand my feelings for you."

"Because I am Indian," Gray Wolf said flatly, angrily jerking his shirt on. "I'm good enough to fell your uncle's trees to make him richer but not good enough for his niece. *Ay-uh.* He has a cold heart, angry with life."

Gray Wolf's hurtful words tore away at Danette's heart. She went to him and snuggled into his arms, clinging. "I shall always love you," she murmured. "No matter what. Please, don't even think of my uncle. Please?"

"Be my wife," Gray Wolf said, speaking softly into Danette's ear as he held her tightly against him. "That's the answer. We could go to Indian village to live. Gray Wolf one day be great chief. Gray Wolf next chief-in-line. Stay. Now. We leave when early morning sun rises. Your uncle's duties to you would be no more."

Danette's mind began swirling, and her heart was fluttering so, she felt like the butterfly that Gray Wolf had named her after, high in the sky, soaring . . . beautifully soaring. Then she had to plummet to the ground, remembering the possibility of what Gray Wolf had just asked of her.

Solemnly she withdrew from his arms and gazed longingly into his eyes. "It thrills me . . . it honors me so . . . that you have asked me to be your wife," she said, reaching to hold both his hands. She couldn't say a flat "no." There were dangers in that. He possibly would be too hurt ever to want to see her again. Yet she couldn't say yes. Not yet anyway. . . .

"But, Gray Wolf, I can't. Not now. It's too soon. We've just met. Though we can never court properly, we must at least give ourselves a bit more time."

She watched as his features became set, and she feared that he had not understood. It pained her so to think she might never see him again. Tears were in her eyes, and when one dripped onto her cheek, she turned her face away.

Strong fingers on her shoulders made her turn back to face him, and when she did she found herself once more being swallowed up in his tender embrace. She placed her cheek against the steel of his chest and sniffled.

"*Ay-uh.* We wait," Gray Wolf said. "But not long, Sweet Butterfly. Not long. My wigwam will feel your absence. My arms will reach for you and find only air. My heart will be a drum, beating for only you."

Melting against him, Danette sighed. "I promise," she said. "It won't be long." She knew not how, but she would be his wife. No love could ever be as sweet or perfect as theirs, and somehow it would be everlasting!

The face of Dwight once more swam before her eyes. She drew quickly away from Gray Wolf and finished dressing, even to twining the pearls back into her hair. And when she felt presentable enough to be scrutinized by her uncle should he arrive home before her, she gave Gray Wolf a halfhearted smile, seeing how his eyes already held a longing for her in them though she wasn't even yet gone from his sight.

Then her own smile faded away, suddenly remembering the two weeks ahead of her. She hadn't yet told Gray Wolf that they would have to be separated for this span of time. Oh! How hard it would be for both of them!

"Gray Wolf, I must travel to St. Paul with my uncle tomorrow," she said, with an air of apprehension, fearing his reaction. "I may be gone for two weeks, but when I return I shall come immediately to you. Please understand that I must go. I have no choice."

Gray Wolf clenched his fists to his side and glowered toward her. "If we were man and wife, the separation would not be necessary," he argued.

"I know," Danette sighed. She wanted to stay, to comfort him in the way she now knew how to do, but the nervous chatter of the birds in the trees outside the wigwam made her once more remember the time of day and that she had to hurry, or darkness would soon be upon her.

"I must go, Gray Wolf," she said, rushing toward the doorway to pull the blanket aside. Peering upward, she saw how the late afternoon was ribboning the sky with lines of silver, red, and rose, and she knew that somewhere the sunset was crowning the horizon in its majestic glory.

"Then Gray Wolf will go with you to protect you," Gray Wolf said, stepping on past her to his horse.

Danette went to him, pleading with her eyes as he swung

70

himself up into his saddle. "No. You'd best not," she said. "My uncle . . ."

Gray Wolf sat tall and proud in his saddle. "There are more dangers than that, should you go alone," he growled. He gestured with his hand toward the sky. "Do you not see? It soon will be dark. Dangers lurk in the shadows of the forest. I will at least see you safely away from the forest."

"All right. If you must," Danette said, still worrying about Dwight and what he might do should he see them together.

Shivering at the thought, she rushed behind the wigwam and climbed onto the seat of her buggy. She grabbed her bonnet and shawl, which she had discarded earlier in the afternoon. She tied the bonnet securely on her head and draped the shawl around her shoulders, then lifted the horse's reins and urged him around to where Gray Wolf waited.

Gray Wolf's horse fell in step next to Danette's buggy until they reached the narrow lane, then rode ahead of her, away from the clearing and the love they had shared in his wigwam. The sound of birds nestling in for the night in the trees and the rustling of leaves in the gentleness of the evening breeze were on all sides of Danette. An owl's sudden loud hoot sent her heart to racing, but she laughed nervously when Gray Wolf turned and gave her an understanding smile.

The lane didn't seem as long this time, and soon Danette and Gray Wolf were traveling along the edge of the forest, leaving its darkness behind and moving onto a meadow where prairie grass bent and blew, appearing to be a velvet bed of green. And though it was only growing dusk, the three quarter moon was already in the sky.

Danette bounced on the seat of her buggy as the wheels fell in and out of a hole in the ground. She secured herself in place again, now directing her horse and buggy onto a street where tall elm trees umbrellaed over and made a tunnel of green.

Urging her horse and buggy onward, to stop next to Gray Wolf, she gazed silently toward him, then said: "Gray Wolf, you mustn't go any farther. It's not wise."

Still able to see the moon through the trees, Gray Wolf pointed toward it. "Soon it will be Strawberry Moon," he said. "It will be time to plant the corn in my village. I must return long enough to help."

His gaze moved to her, his eyelids heavy. "Gray Wolf think Sweet Butterfly be happy there to see my people's happiness while planting alongside Gray Wolf. Come. Ride at my side."

Danette shook her head sadly. "I've already told you that I can't," she said. "But I will come to you at your wigwam when I return from St. Paul. Won't you be there? Will you be at your village? What about your job with my uncle?"

"Gray Wolf not be gone long," he growled. "There are always trees waiting to be felled. Your uncle will just have to wait until after I help my people."

"Then when I return I will come to your wigwam," she said. "And I have to ask you, Gray Wolf, why is it you live in a wigwam away from the others?"

Gray Wolf squared his shoulders proudly. "It is because I am not like the others," he boasted. "I am to one day be a great chief. I am next chief-in-line for the great . . . ."

Horse's hoofbeats drawing quickly close caused Gray Wolf's words to fade on his lips, and Danette paled as she saw her Uncle Dwight come into view. He had soon drawn rein next to her.

"My God, Danette, I've been searching and searching for you. What is going on here?" he shouted, glaring from her to Gray Wolf. He placed his hand on the revolver at his right hip and once more looked accusingly at Danette, who was sitting quite speechless with eyes wide and lips quivering. A picture of guilt, if he ever had seen one!

"What are you doing with this . . . with this savage?" he quickly blurted, with a jerk of his head. "Twice, Danette.

I've found you in his company *twice*. Can you say he's rescued you again? Ha! This time you cannot confess to such a falsehood!'' Dwight knew he would never, no, never, show the Indian that he had understood the first time he had found him with his niece . . . and that he even owed the Indian a thanks. He didn't want to encourage the Indian's friendship with Danette. He feared that it had possibly already gotten out of hand!

Danette glanced quickly toward Gray Wolf, having heard a sort of low growl from his direction. Remembering his words—that he would also protect her from her uncle—she became afraid of what he might do and even more afraid of Dwight and the gun that his hand rested threateningly upon. Gray Wolf wore no weapon! He would not be the victor here!

Quickly, she reached for her uncle and placed her hand on the hand on his revolver and held it tightly in place there. ''It's true, though,'' she lied. ''Gray Wolf did once more rescue me. I was lost in the forest. He happened along and found me and led me out.''

''How convenient,'' Dwight laughed mockingly.

''But it is true,'' Danette pleaded, seeing Gray Wolf out of the corner of her eye and how angry he was becoming. ''See, Uncle Dwight?'' she desperately continued, pointing toward her painting. ''The painting. This is why I was in the forest. I was painting.''

Dwight leaned over and saw the canvas on the floorboard of her buggy, and his face shadowed with growing anger. ''I see a painting of an Indian's wigwam,'' he growled. ''Is that supposed to lighten my anger, Danette? Was it this Indian's wigwam?''

Tears sprang forth in Danette's eyes. She was fast getting caught in her web of lies.

''You get on home,'' Dwight growled toward Danette. Then he looked at Gray Wolf. ''And as for you, Indian, if I ever see you with my niece again, I won't only see that

73

you are no longer on my payroll. I will *kill* you," he angrily hissed.

Gray Wolf glared boldly back at Dwight. "You are a man with a heart of stone," he said. "Your niece surely is no true blood relation to you. But that doesn't matter. One day she will be mine."

Wheeling his horse around, Gray Wolf thundered away from them, knowing that one day Danette . . . Sweet Butterfly . . . *would* be his, and should her uncle try to stop their marriage, Gray Wolf would be sure to be wearing a weapon then. . . .

Danette watched Gray Wolf disappear into the quickly falling shadows of night. She then looked at Dwight, hating him at this moment. "How could you have?" she cried, then jerked her reins and shouted at her horse, glad to leave Dwight behind with his questions quite unanswered, knowing that was the way it would remain! Soon she would be living in a different world . . . away . . . from him. . . .

Chapter Five

*Let none think to fly the danger
For soon or late love is his own avenger.*
—Byron

Gray Wolf had transformed himself appropriately from white man to Indian before setting out on his journey home. The white man's clothes had been left behind, and he was now attired in fringed deerskin leggings and moccasins of buckskin, thick with embroidered beads.

He wore no shirt, displaying his copper-colored thick-muscled chest, and he had worked deer tallow into his dark hair, then braided it, except for a loop of hair in which had been placed a lone eagle's feather. He had placed a band about his head and a colorful strand of beads about his neck. On the side of one of his leggings he had put a leather sheath, which enclosed a knife, and on the side of his saddle the shine of a rifle sparkled beneath the rays of the morning sun.

On his horse, a magnificent chestnut, Gray Wolf rode at a trot down a canyon, following the meanderings of a stream. Soon he would be seeing the wider expanse of the St. Croix River, and after that the many dome-shaped wigwams of his people. The separation had been too long this time. He seemed constantly to be torn between wanting to be faithful to his Indian heritage and wanting to live the life of a white man. The dollars earned by his labors as a lumberjack were few. Soon he would return to his people and never look back.

"But I first must be sure Sweet Butterfly is with me," he said aloud. "Life without her would be no life at all."

Thoughts of Danette's uncle's ridicule angered him, yet he had to remember that soon it would not matter to him at all. When Sweet Butterfly entered the Indian village with him, no white man would dare enter to try to take her back.

"Not even her uncle. . . ." he growled, doubling a fist at his side.

On one side of Gray Wolf the meadow waved with blossom, and on the other the forest was dark with foliage. The air was warm and pleasant, and Gray Wolf was enjoying this travel homeward. He felt a freedom that was a stranger to him when he lived in the white man's world. He felt as free as the *waw-be-wawa* . . . the white goose . . . flying singly in the sky, or the *omemee*, the pigeon cooing in the covert of the pine trees. Maybe the time away from these things and his people had been *o-nee-shee-shin. Ay-uh*, it had been good, because it taught him to appreciate it more upon his return.

"*En-dah-yen* . . ." he whispered. "Home. *Gee-mah-mah.*" Yes, home meant mother and father. Since he had been the only child born to his parents, Chief Yellow Feather and Red Blossom, many responsibilities had been born with him. He had often wondered if he could be as great a chief as his father. He now knew that Sweet Butterfly would be a perfect chief's wife. And wouldn't she be looked upon with favor by his mother? She too was white.

"Red Blossom still as beautiful as red poppy that grows wild in the meadow," he mumbled. "So will Sweet Butterfly be as beautiful when she reaches the age of forty! But she will bear me many sons. Our St. Croix band of the Chippewa, the Ojibway, must grow in number as well as in strength!"

His thoughts saddened. It always clouded his heart to remember the small graves beside the sacred cave. His parents had tried, and had failed at delivering healthy children besides himself into the world.

"But father has remained faithful to his one wife, and so shall I."

Then his thoughts filled with the image of an Indian maiden who would be anxiously awaiting his return to the village. Dancing Cloud! How could he have forgotten about her? She was not only his best friend Red Fox's sister, but Gray Wolf had earlier promised her his heart! How could he have forgotten?

"Sweet Butterfly has not only taken possession of my heart but also my mind," he cried aloud.

He grew silent and brooding, now remembering his times with Dancing Cloud. Until Sweet Butterfly, Dancing Cloud had performed her womanly duties quite acceptably, to his way of thinking. But now . . . since Sweet Butterfly . . . no woman could compare!

"How can I tell Dancing Cloud!" he whispered. "I do not want to hurt her! She's been devoted . . . a wife to me, though no ceremony has been performed!"

Even now he could see her waiting for him in his wigwam. The fire would be warm . . . the bulrush mats swept and smelling freshly of herbs. . . . A gnawing in his loins made him keenly aware of what they had shared together in his wigwam. It would be hard to look the other way. . . .

A noise in the brush on the left side of Gray Wolf drew his mind to the present. He tensed his shoulder muscles and grabbed his rifle from its leather pouch, peering toward the thick twists of underbrush coiling up into the lower limbs of the oak trees. The stream had led him closer to the forest's edge, where its density made it almost as dark as night.

Even so, Gray Wolf knew that an experienced horseman could always find his way through the forest, and any passerby at this point in his journey could mean a possible threat to his safety. The Chippewa village wasn't far ahead, and only the Chippewa should be traveling along this way.

A white man's presence meant not only a threat to him and his people but to the beautiful forests as well. So far, no white men like Dwight Thomas had ventured this far with their oxen and axes to clear the land of its beautiful growth. One day Gray Wolf knew that it would happen. The trees were too quickly disappearing around Duluth. A move farther north would one day begin, and then Gray Wolf would have to protect his people and their rights to stay beside the St. Croix River. *Wenebojo,* the great spirit who had made the world, had had the great owl of the forest lead Yellow Feather there many moons ago. And *Wenebojo* had so far succeeded at keeping the white man away. . . .

The neighing of a horse caused Gray Wolf to hurriedly move ahead, finding shelter behind the thickness of a huge, wide-spreading Norwegian pine tree. With his rifle poised and his finger on the trigger, he waited for the horseman to move directly in front of him. Through the limbs of the tree, Gray Wolf watched, breathless. If one shot were fired, his village would at least be alerted that trouble was near and to prepare themselves for it. They knew about warring. Though the Sioux only attacked from the north, the Chippewa were always ready for them. Through the years, the Sioux had created havoc more often than not. It was when a Chippewa maiden had been kidnapped that most blood had been shed between the two tribes.

The crackling of a twig and the scattering of winter-dried leaves and Gray Wolf knew that the intruder was near. And when he finally had full sight of the horse and its rider, Gray Wolf lowered his rifle to his side and urged his horse out, to block the way of the horse and the Indian who sat hunched in the saddle.

"You!" Gray Wolf grumbled. "Longbow, you devil-Indian. Gray Wolf had hoped to not have to see you on this return to the village."

Gray Wolf remembered Longbow's father, Flying Squirrel. Longbow had his father's identical features. As Flying

Squirrel had been, Longbow was short and small-boned, with a blemished face. The main difference between father and son was in the eyes. In Flying Squirrel's, one could read his every thought and emotion. In Longbow's eyes, a flat coldness was all that was there . . . a fathomless pit of darkness, filled with hate and mistrust.

This day he wore the typical fringed leggings and matching doeskin shirt. His sleek black hair was braided and hung to his waist, and his headband was void of a feather.

He was less than handsome . . . a crude representative for the proud tribe of the Chippewa Indians!

"You return to help your family plant corn," Longbow hissed. "So does Longbow return to help his mother, Foolish Heart. Flying Squirrel, Longbow's proud father, lies dead beneath the maples, or do you forget, Gray Wolf? Flying Squirrel died a sad, broken man, and all because of Yellow Feather and his shaming of my father those many moons ago."

"You call my father Chief Yellow Feather," Gray Wolf growled. "And you are lucky Chief Yellow Feather welcomed your mother and father back into the Chippewa village. It was both your mother and father who brought shame to the Chippewa. My father has a big heart opening his arms to their return."

"Ha! Open arms," Longbow scoffed. "Our wigwam has always had to sit away from the rest. Though now back with the Chippewa, my mother still lives the life of the outcast."

"She has wild rice and warm fires," Gray Wolf said. "She is not hungry or cold."

Longbow leaned up in his saddle and glared toward Gray Wolf. "She is all twisted and old before her time," he growled. "She deserves more than food and warmth. She needs companionship. She has been shunned long enough. Why must she always just be my responsibility? She is

79

Chippewa. She should be treated as one of the tribe . . . with respect and dignity.''

"And you, Longbow? You should be treated with such respect?'' Gray Wolf taunted, slipping his rifle back inside its leather pouch.

"*Ay-uh,*'' Longbow said stiffly. ''And why not? Longbow goes to the great city of Minneapolis and earns white man's pay while working in a flour mill. Longbow works alongside the white man . . . shows the white man the Indian is strong.''

Gray Wolf threw his head back with laughter. ''Longbow is strong because he lifts light sacks of flour?'' he said.

He rubbed laughter from his eyes, looking toward Longbow with a smile still touching his lips. ''You take a weak man's job.'' He thundered a fist against his chest, lifting his chin proudly. ''Gray Wolf takes a strong man's job. Become a lumberjack. Then you will show the white man how strong you are.''

"You always think you are better,'' Longbow growled, his face reddening with anger. ''Just because you are next chief-in-line you think you are better. Well, one day Longbow will teach you who is better. Longbow has ways.''

Gray Wolf's smile faded. He folded his arms angrily across his chest. ''What do you do besides work in mills?'' he growled. ''You wander in the forest, getting into trouble?'' He wouldn't accuse Longbow face-to-face of collaborating with the Sioux. It had always been Gray Wolf's plan to catch him in the act. Then once more a Chippewa would be shamed from the tribe. Flying Squirrel had been Chief Yellow Feather's childhood friend, yet when he reached adulthood jealously had caused him to try to deceive Yellow Feather in the worst way possible . . . by way of a woman. It had come as quite a surprise and bitter disappointment to Yellow Feather when he had discovered that his wife, Happy Flower, wasn't carrying his child, but Flying Squirrel's. Yellow Feather wouldn't have even known except that Happy Flower spoke this truth while dying. . . .

Chief Yellow Feather had told Gray Wolf that Flying Squirrel had left the village with his head hanging, still not able to confess his deceit to his best friend.

"Longbow is no dumb Indian," Longbow said sourly. "I get in no trouble. I make trouble, though, when the time is right."

Leaning over his saddle, Gray Wolf glared toward Longbow. "Is that a threat, Longbow?" he hissed. "Can I expect to keep watch over my shoulder for you? Do you hate me that much because it was I who was born to a great chief and not you?"

"It is my mother I think mostly of," Longbow snarled. "Not myself."

"Your mother was never anything but trouble," Gray Wolf said. "She always earned her name well, so I've been told. She cut other Indian maidens' hair . . . she taunted and tormented them . . . she caused trouble for my father always. Though she chose on her own to leave our village, she left in shame because of her constant foolish behavior. *Ay-uh*, she earned her name well. Your name should even be changed. Foolish Bow. *Ay-uh*. That name is best suited for you, Longbow."

Longbow lunged suddenly from his horse and toward Gray Wolf, knocking Gray Wolf from his horse. "Don't you speak of my mother so badly," Longbow yelled. "She is a good woman now. She paid for her foolish ways as a young girl. She married my father and made a good wife and mother! She's not foolish! She's not!"

Gray Wolf's back hit the ground with a bang. He groaned as his neck snapped backward with the blow. His vision momentarily blurred with the pain, but when Longbow was suddenly there, sitting astraddle him, all of his senses returned in a fierce flash of anger. Knowing his strength was twice Longbow's, all he had to do was lift his hips up from the ground and Longbow was soon the one being sat astraddle, Gray Wolf holding him by each wrist to the ground.

"You've just proven your foolishness," Gray Wolf growled, leaning down into Longbow's contorted face. "Do you forget Gray Wolf's muscles so easily? Longbow has never been victorious in battle with Gray Wolf. Never!"

Longbow pursed his lips and spat onto Gray Wolf's face. Gagging, Gray Wolf released Longbow's wrists and began wiping at his eyes. Then he felt teeth sinking into the thigh of one of his legs and rolled away from Longbow, yowling.

Longbow pounced upon him, growling like a dog. He doubled a fist and hit Gray Wolf on the chin, then found himself being once more wrestled to the ground, with Gray Wolf managing to lock him there with an arm bent behind him and Gray Wolf holding the point of a knife to his throat.

"Longbow still has much to learn about Gray Wolf," Gray Wolf hissed, edging the tip of his knife closer to Longbow's throat. Playfully, he nipped at the flesh, enjoying seeing Longbow's eyes grow wild and his color turn to that of ash in a cooled firespace. "Gray Wolf will never let Longbow win at anything. Now you best remember that, foolish son of foolish mother."

"Longbow will get you for this," Longbow said in a guttural whisper. "Some day you will pay."

Gray Wolf sank the tip of his knife barely into the flesh at Longbow's neck, causing Longbow to cry out and a slow trickle of blood to run freely from the wound.

Gray Wolf then withdrew the knife and held the bloody point before Longbow's eyes. "This is only a fraction of what Gray Wolf will do to you should you ever cross my path again," he said. "Right now you have a pinprick in your skin. The next time? Well, you will see, if there *is* ever a next time."

" 'Hate' isn't a strong enough word for how I feel about you and your family, Gray Wolf," Longbow said, rising shakily to his feet as Gray Wolf set him free, to stand and tower over him.

Gray Wolf placed his knife back into its sheath and swung himself up into his saddle. "And, Longbow, I do not wish to ride into the village in your company," he said icily. "Stay behind me."

He rode off, head held high, then turned and quickly added: "And do not try anything. Gray Wolf has eyes in the back of his head. You will be dead if you think to try and take advantage of me again."

"Once more you shame me," Longbow shouted, raising a doubled fist into the air.

"Come to the village with your tail tucked between legs," Gray Wolf taunted. "That suits you, Longbow." His hate for Longbow went back as far as when Longbow had been a teenager, sneaking around, causing all sorts of mischief in the Chippewa village. If Longbow hadn't been teasing and tormenting the girls with nasty gestures, he had picked out the weaker of the boys his age and had fought with them until bloody noses or broken teeth were the result of his game.

For a long time now, Gray Wolf had suspected that his best friend, Red Fox had come under such a sneak attack at the hands of Longbow. When, at age twelve, Red Fox had ridden back into the village with a pierced eye and had said that he had fallen from his horse onto a thorn, everyone but Gray Wolf had believed him.

Gray Wolf had suspected Longbow's being the culprit even then. But knowing Red Fox's reasons for silence . . . fear of being shamed if he revealed the truth that he had not defended himself well enough . . . Gray Wolf also waited for the truth to one day reveal itself.

But the years had passed and Red Fox had become no stronger. To most, except his true love, Amanda, he was a weak Indian who always stayed within the safe cloak of the

Indian village, fearing that to venture out would mean the possible loss of his other eye, or even worse . . . his life.

Being strong and virile himself, Gray Wolf could not understand such weakness. Yet he loved his best friend and still hoped the years adding to his age might eventually give him both strength and character. To live in the world now run by the white man . . . one had to be strong.

The sun was now directly above Gray Wolf as he rode to the edge of the gentle blue water of the St. Croix River. He cupped a hand over his eyes. On the opposite side of the river, red sandstone bluffs loomed up into the sky, while pleasant hills and stately cedars and pines cast their reflections along the shore.

Soon! Soon he would see the bold outline of the cave and then the village of wigwams clustered close by. His heart hadn't beat so since . . . since his final moments with Sweet Butterfly.

Ah! How he longed for her now. To ride into the village with her at his side could have been a proud moment.

Yet he wondered just how the Indians would have greeted her. Though his mother and her sister Amanda were a part of the Chippewa way of life, would another white woman be just as welcome?

"Gray Wolf will make it so," he promised himself.

Determined and anxious, Gray Wolf directed his horse into the water and held himself solidly in the saddle as the horse continued on its way until only its neck and head were visible. With his rifle held high over his head, Gray Wolf clucked to his horse and was relieved when the rocky bottom of the other side was reached.

Shaking itself like a dog after a bath, the horse shook and whinnied, then moved solidly onto the sandy shore.

The shadows of the sandstone bluffs followed along beside Gray Wolf until a bend in the river revealed the river's edge rich with the swaying of wild rice. Gray Wolf's heart pounded harder, knowing that around that bend his

84

people waited! What a feast there would be to welcome him home . . . the only son of the great Chief Yellow Feather!

Thrusting his knees into his horse's side, he sent him into a gallop, working his way up the steep slope of knee-high grass away from the river. Along the shore behind him, mud hens and several other types of water fowl swooped down to settle in little clusters, waiting for unwary fish.

And now, as Gray Wolf was in the middle of both meadow and forest, with each now lying on either side of him, he enjoyed hearing the scolding of the chipmunks and the squeaking of the bluejays. And then suddenly before him the great sacred cave loomed, its entrance still partially blocked by skin-tangle, ground pine, juniper and *kinnikinnick*.

Gray Wolf paused his horse before the cave, proud to know many secrets about it. His father had told him that it had been a part of his childhood dream. Yellow Feather had been guided there by his guardian spirit, the giant owl of the forest, and while looking upon the cave he had seen the face of a beautiful woman, with long, flaming red hair. He had later discovered that this vision had revealed to him Lorinda Odell . . . *ay-uh* . . . Red Blossom . . . the woman who had become Yellow Feather's wife.

"My mother," Gray Wolf said. Then a soft smile touched his lips, remembering how proudly Yellow Feather had spoken of Red Blossom's courage when she had defended herself against the evil trader Silas Konrad. She had used a gun as a man would. But she had only wounded the evil trader, and it had been Yellow Feather who had later sealed his fate on a cold, blustery winter day.

Later, Silas Konrad's and his partners' bodies had been found frozen to the trees they had been left tied to, left there as a lesson to any who might try to wrong the proud St. Croix tribe of the Chippewa.

But this cave had mainly been used to store the white man's treasures that Yellow Feather and his braves had stolen from the white man's stagecoaches and lone horsemen. It was Yellow Feather's marriage to the white woman that had abruptly brought such practices to a halt. Now the cave was used to store away rifles! Rifles stolen in the raids of the Sioux!

Not wanting to look toward the tiny mounds of earth where his dead brothers and sisters lay in their infancy, wanting to feel only happiness on his return home, Gray Wolf wheeled his horse around away from them. His heart warmed as he let his gaze settle on the village of wigwams, which had been built on a clearing close to the cave.

The dense forest of pines and hemlocks was a perfect shelter from the north and west winds and the south and east of the village had been left open to the sun. Smoke slowly spiraled up from all the smoke holes of the dwellings, and throughout the village Gray Wolf could see his father's people busy at work. Men were building canoes with peeled birch bark . . . women were stirring pots hanging low over open fires . . . older men were mending fish nets, while older women were making birch-bark trays and baskets. All of Chief Yellow Feather's people were productive, even the children, who helped pick delicious wild fruits and gathered the flowers, leaves, and roots of other plants used for food, medicines, and dyes. Many of the wild plants they collected were dried for later use. In the farther distance, where the meadow had been hoed to become the garden area of the village, many were busy hoeing, preparing the land for the corn, pumpkin, and squash to be planted.

Then Gray Wolf's gaze settled on the one log cabin in the village. His mother's. Though Chief Yellow Feather had frowned upon it, he had built this house to please his wife, and most of the Chippewa had in time grown used to this different mode of living that had invaded their lives, as they had just as quickly accepted the woman who lived there with her chief husband.

"Hahh!" Gray Wolf shouted to his horse, and he moved

on into the village, nodding and speaking to all those who gathered, chattering, about him and his horse. With a racing pulse he finally drew rein right outside the log cabin's door. He swung quickly out of his saddle just as his mother appeared at the doorway—tall, thin, and beautiful, as he always remembered her to be.

Her hair, unbound, was this day hanging like lustrous satin to her waist in its brilliant auburn colors, more red than brown, with only flecks of gray at her brow and temples. Her face was only marred by a few wrinkles at the corner of her eyes and lines around her mouth were just beginning to be visible.

She was dressed as an Indian, her deerskin dress clinging to a figure that had spread out only slightly at the waist and hips. Many strings of colorful beads cascaded about her neck, and her wristsbands and her moccasins were beautifully decorated with dyed porcupine quills.

Ay-uh, she was beautiful, and Gray Wolf now knew why it had been so easy for him to fall so deeply in love with a white woman so quickly. In Sweet Butterfly he saw so much of his mother!

"Gray Wolf! *Nin-gwis!* Son! You're home," Lorinda, known as Red Blossom to all Indians, cried. She stepped across the threshold with arms outstretched, then hugged him tightly to her as he became the boy he always was in her presence. He loved the smell of her, now realizing it was the same as Sweet Butterfly's.

Lorinda held Gray Wolf away from her and studied him. "You've been eating well," she said, nodding her head. Then the green of her eyes met and held the same color of his and she smiled slowly at him. "And do I see something different about you, my son? It is a . . . well . . . I don't know. What have you been up to?"

His hand went to his jaw and rubbed it. "Is it a bruise?" he questioned, evading the true cause of his change. "Devil Indian Longbow. He was on same trail as Gray Wolf. We

87

scuffled.'' He laughed throatily and shrugged. ''As we have for so many years, Mother.''

He wouldn't reveal the true reason he appeared to be different. It wasn't yet the time to speak of Sweet Butterfly to his mother, but he knew this difference she saw in him was from his having matured into a man, who had finally found the meaning of true love.

Lorinda's hand went to his face. ''Did he hurt you, my son?'' she asked, her face contorting with worry. ''My *mee-kah-wah-diz-ee* son with such a smooth copperface. Did he harm you?''

Embarrassed and feeling too much the man now for her fussing over him in front of the crowd of Indians gathering about the house, Gray Wolf brushed her hand away, blushing. *''Gee-mah-mah,''* he grumbled. ''Gray Wolf is fine. Do you think coward Longbow could hurt Gray Wolf? *Gah-ween-wee-kah!''*

A voice spoke suddenly from behind Gray Wolf, causing Gray Wolf's heart to skip a beat, he was so excited.

''Yellow Feather would hope not,'' Chief Yellow Feather said as he stepped through the crowd.

Gray Wolf turned on his heel and faced his father. His chest swelled with pride and a glow appeared in his eyes as he gazed almost in rapture toward him. *''Gee-bah-bah,''* he said hoarsely. ''Father, it is so good to see you.''

Chief Yellow Feather stood towering over the rest of the Indians, with perfectly squared shoulders and dark, penetrating eyes. His arms were crossed over his bare chest and his chin was held proudly high. He was attired in only a loincloth, and, of course, his headband and yellow feather placed in a coil of his coal-black braided hair. He showed signs of aging, the wrinkles on his face becoming grooves that began beneath his high cheekbones and ended at his now prominent chin.

But he was still handsome, his body still firm and his hair sleek and black . . . and his mind was keenly alert making him still the vital leader of this St. Croix band of the Chippewa Indians.

Yellow Feather took a step forward and hurriedly embraced Gray Wolf. "My son, my son," he murmured. "Welcome back into the village of our people. You have been missed. Maybe this time you stay?"

Swallowing back emotions swelling inside him, Gray Wolf embraced his father back, hating to have to disappoint him again. And seeing the watchful eyes of the people gathered about, and knowing their ears were anxious to hear everything exchanged between father and son, Gray Wolf would not say the disappointing words in front of them, to embarrass his father, as Gray Wolf knew that he would do.

"It is planting season," he instead said. "Gray Wolf has returned home to help." In a lower tone he said, "We can talk of other things later, can't we, Father?"

Frowning, Yellow Feather drew away from Gray Wolf. But seeing the intelligence in his son's hesitation to speak so openly of personal matters, he swung an arm about Gray Wolf's shoulder and began to walk with him toward the house. He gave Lorinda a lingering look, smiling warmly at her. "Our son is home, Red Blossom," he said. "A feast is in order, wouldn't you agree?"

Lorinda fell in step beside them and moved into Yellow Feather's embrace, placing an arm about his waist. *"Ayuh,"* she said proudly. "I will see that the council house is readied. We will sing and dance and eat until the sun rises again on the morrow. . . ."

Chapter Six

Love is not in our choice,
But in our fate.
—Dryden

Filled to the brim with food, dancing, and companionship, Gray Wolf lifted the blanket that led inside his wigwam and entered. The only ingredient missing that would have made this moment complete was the open arms of Sweet Butterfly awaiting him on his bed of blankets. The excitement of the full night of festivity had left him with a lusty sort of need that only a woman could fulfill ... yet he had shunned Dancing Cloud the entire night, too full of joy himself to see the hurt that he had most surely inflicted on her.

Weaving, Gray Wolf laughed aloud, having drunk too much of the concoction that had been handed him by his best friend, Red Fox. It had been white man's "tea," as Red Fox had teasingly called the whiskey that he had stolen from another more daring member of the tribe, who had himself stolen it from a white man on a raid of the Sioux.

The whiskey had burned like the fires of hell as it slid down the back of Gray Wolf's throat, but its power to lighten his mood even more had been welcomed by him and the gang of Indians his age who had also returned home for the planting season. Only Longbow had stood alone on the edge of the merry group, his eyes dark with anger and his hands continuously busy with shining the barrel of a rifle.

Though morning was lightening the horizon outside his wigwam, Gray Wolf, like all the other Chippewa, was just going to bed after the full night of celebration, with plans to begin the planting of seeds later, when the sun rose to its highest peak in the sky.

Reaching around for his bedroll, Gray Wolf stumbled over his firespace where the fire had grown cold and lifeless. Dancing Cloud had not come to the wigwam, he thought. He rolled out his blankets and then flopped down onto them, heavy, and now very aware of the tiredness of his limbs. She must have had a wounded heart from his neglect of her. But it was better now . . . than later.

Stretched out on his back, he grunted as he struggled with removing his clothes and moccasins. And once he was free of them all and quite nude, he pulled a blanket over himself and fell into a quick sleep that soon became filled with the touch and smell of his Sweet Butterfly.

A stirring inside his wigwam drew Gray Wolf semi-awake. Through a drunken haze he watched the silhouette of a woman undressing, and when she moved to his bed and stretched out beneath the blankets next to him, Gray Wolf tremored with sexual need and welcomed her there.

Strange how a dream could come to life, he thought to himself, reaching out, touching the eager, stiff point of a breast, thinking of Danette.

He then shifted his position so that he was above the silent figure of the woman, and began devouring the soft, silken flesh with passion-hungry kisses and soft probings of his tongue on the pleasure points that he had long ago memorized as being the places to touch on a woman to set her on fire, to encourage her to do likewise to him.

When a hand grazed against his swollen manhood and then returned there and began caressing him slowly, Gray Wolf closed his eyes and shook with the pleasure. Feeling the pulsating of his need building in the skilled fingers that continued to work on him, Gray Wolf lowered his lips to his bed partner's in a frenzied kiss while roughly cupping both breasts with his hands and fondly squeezing then. With his senses reeling, he brusquely brushed the hand from his sex and in one plunge drove inside the moist, tight cavern of love.

Panting, he thrust . . . he quivered . . . he moaned. And, not at all like him, he forgot to think of his partner's needs this time, so obsessed was he with his own desire, and he continued to plunge harder and harder inside her. Soon he reached the pinnacle he had been seeking, growing mindless with the intense, gratifying pleasure, and, in his momentary madness, he shouted out Sweet Butterfly's name.

Still tremoring with release, Gray Wolf was startled awake as he felt fists buffeting his chest. He now understood what he had done. The voice was not that of Sweet Butterfly. It was Dancing Cloud who had crept silently to his bed. He had still been in his dream . . . a dream inhabited only by the white woman to whom he had lost his heart.

"You speak other woman's name while still hot with passion in Dancing Cloud's arms?" Dancing Cloud cried, now pushing at Gray Wolf's chest. "Now Dancing Cloud knows why you were so aloof to her during the celebration. You *do* have another woman on your mind! Who is Sweet Butterfly, Gray Wolf? Who is she?"

Fully sober and quite angry at himself for what he had just done in his weak state of mind and even angrier at Dancing Cloud for having tricked him into these moments of lust, he growled down into her face.

"You know what you are doing here," he said. "Dancing Cloud is a tease now? Gray Wolf is ashamed of you."

"No tease," she cried, squirming beneath his hold. "Dancing Cloud always sleeps with you."

"You knew I didn't want you this night," Gray Wolf growled right back. "You come anyway like a spirit in the night."

Turning her face away, Dancing Cloud softly cried. "No

93

tease. No spirit," she whispered. "I only want you to love me again. Dancing Cloud is not dumb. I know another woman has turned your heart away. It is in Gray Wolf's eyes. It is in Gray Wolf's face. . . ."

"You knew, yet you hit me with fists when I spoke her name instead of yours?"

"Knowing hurts," she said, sniffling. "I don't want to hurt you as you hurt me. I'm sorry, Gray Wolf. Dancing Cloud shouldn't have hit you."

The morning's light was brighter now and was shining down the smoke hole in the ceiling, enough for Gray Wolf to see the innocence of the copper face so close to his. High cheekbones and wide nose and lips marked her features, and eyes as dark as the darkest night stared back up at him.

"You've been as much sister as lover," he said thickly, brushing some hair from her eyes. "You are Red Fox's sister. He is my best friend. It only seemed right I make you my wife. But now . . ."

"Now Dancing Cloud will not be your wife?" she said, choking on the words.

"Gah-ween," Gray Wolf said throatly, looking away from her, not daring to see the hurt in her eyes.

"Not even . . . second . . . wife . . ."

"Gah-ween."

Flinching, Gray Wolf watched as she scooted quickly away from him and draped her dress hurriedly over her head.

Rising on an elbow, Gray Wolf reached a hand out to her. "Dancing Cloud, wait. . . ."

But she rushed on away, through the doorway, leaving Gray Wolf lying there, miserable and suddenly low spirited.

He stretched out on his back, kneading his brow nervously. "It's all because of that firewater," he snarled. "It stole my senses and respect from me. Never will Gray Wolf drink that devil liquid again."

He felt the need to run after Dancing Cloud, to explain, yet he knew that she would have to deal with her loss in her own way. He closed his eyes and let the image of Sweet Butterfly erase all his frustrations and guilts. Soon he would reveal her to all his father's people. Soon . . . soon.

Understanding his mother's need to be kept in the shadows, ashamed of her gnarled, twisted fingers and the pain from them that she showed in her thinning face, Longbow stepped into Foolish Heart's wigwam cautiously. The bulrush mats had not been swept and rotting food lay beside a smoldering fire in the firespace. Pity . . . love . . . and disgust for his mother fused inside Longbow. And for all these mixtures of feelings, he blamed the family of Chief Yellow Feather.

But his feelings were strongest against Gray Wolf. Gray Wolf would soon have it all and Longbow nothing! Since all these feelings were festering inside Longbow like some wound left untended, he had the need to talk to someone, and his mother was the only one to whom he could confide.

"Gee-mah-mah?" he said, glancing across the wigwam, seeing her sitting so stiffly, gazing empty-eyed into the dying embers of the fire. *"Ingah-bee-dee-gay-nah?"*

In a rasp of a voice, Foolish Heart nodded her head. "Did your mother ever say you not come into her wigwam?" she scolded. With a trembling hand, she gestured toward the blankets at her side. *"Nah-mah-tah-bin.* Sit down. It's been too long, my son."

"Nee-min-weh-dum-wah-bun-min-ah," Longbow said, inching toward her, cringing when her foul smell reached his nose.

Foolish Heart laughed throatily as her eyes glistened in the shadows. *"Ay-uh.* It's good to see your mother all dried up like a prune and smelling like a fish," she tormented. "Lies come too easily for you, my son."

Longbow eased down onto the blankets beside her, seeing no signs in her features of what she had once been. Some

95

unknown crippling disease had finished what the Chippewa hadn't already done. Her exile was now even more complete than even when she had been banned from the village. She refused to let Chief Yellow Feather see her . . . even long enough to go to bathe in the river. She had only recently confided in Longbow that a part of her would always love Chief Yellow Feather, as she had done when she had been young and, yes, foolish . . . no matter what he had done to her for being foolhardy and nonthinking when she had had the honor of being his wife even before he had become the chief of their tribe of the Chippewa.

For this, Longbow hated Yellow Feather even more!

Trying to relax, Longbow crossed his legs and reached for a pipe that lay next to the firespace. Without being asked, Foolish Heart handed him a leather pouch of tobacco.

"And did you enjoy the celebration?" she asked, scorn thick in her words. "Foolish Heart heard the music and laughter. Did my son even join in the dance?"

Placing a burning twig to the tobacco set into the pipe, Longbow drew deeply from the stern, then tossed the twig back into the firespace once the tobacco's heady fragrance began erasing all other smells within the small spaces of the dwelling.

He slouched his shoulders and puffed silently for a moment. "You think Longbow would celebrate Gray Wolf's return?" he finally said. "Who celebrates Longbow's return? No one. There was no need for Longbow to dance and sing."

"You stood in the shadows and watched like a mute Indian?" Foolish Heart scolded. "My son, you are wrong. The time has come to be a man. You show Gray Wolf how much of a man by outdoing him in everything he tries."

"Mother, the time for more than that has arrived," Longbow hissed. "It is time for Longbow to seek revenge for you and Father Flying Squirrel and the way you've been shunned by the Chippewa."

He drew more angry puffs from his pipe, thinking that he would have his revenge: He would see to it that Gray Wolf's heart would first suffer many losses, and then ... and then ... he would take his life.

"Revenge?" Foolish Heart murmured, leaning forward, studying Longbow with troubled, squinted eyes. "This revenge you speak of. What do you mean to do?"

Longbow glared back at her, then smiled devilishly. "Do not worry," he said. "No harm will come to Chief Yellow Feather. Your proud chief, your first love, will not be a part of Longbow's plans."

Foolish Heart sighed shakily and let her eyes once more focus on the orange embers in the firespace. "Revenge is an ugly word, Longbow," she said solemnly. "Your father spoke the word too often. His hate ... his hurt ... killed him the same as an arrow piercing his heart."

She moved her gaze to Longbow. "Your hate will do the same for you, my son," she said. "It will swallow you in its ugliness."

"Longbow will take care of Longbow," he said, angrily rising to his feet. He knocked the ashes from his pipe into the firespace, and replaced it where he had found it.

"And what of your mother?" Foolish Heart asked, following his movements with her tear-filled eyes. "Who will take care of Foolish Heart should something happen to you?"

Longbow spun around on his heel and glared down at her. "Nothing will happen to Longbow," he growled. "And haven't I returned to plant your corn and pumpkin seeds? *Gee-mah-mah*, don't worry. Longbow will also be here for the harvest. You will not starve."

"*Gee-mah-mah* hungers for more than food."

"Longbow can only give so much of himself."

"Then you leave me now?"

"After the long day in field, Longbow will return to share the evening meal with you."

"Then it will be ready, my son."

97

Longbow rushed from the wigwam, sorrowful at heart. Life continued to be unfair to him. It seemed that all that he had in life to really call his was his mother, and she was now only a helpless lady with a whining voice.

"I must fill my days with my thoughts of vengeance," he whispered. His eye caught a movement in the forest. Taking a step forward, he peered more intensely into the shadows where the morning sunrise was coloring everything a burnt orange.

Longbow tensed. In the next moment he caught a glimpse of a woman. And to his surprise, she was moving more deeply into the forest, first walking, now breaking into a fast trot.

"Who . . . ?" Longbow murmured, idly scratching his head. He began to run toward the forest after her, now catching a glimpse of her face as she cast a quick look across her shoulder. It was Gray Wolf's woman! It was Dancing Cloud! Why was she running away into the forest? Why wasn't she sharing Gray Wolf's bed of blankets?

Stepping high over fallen, broken limbs and then tangled underbrush, Longbow continued his pursuit of Dancing Cloud. And when she collapsed, panting, beneath a low-hanging maple tree, Longbow fell to his knees beside her.

"Dancing Cloud, you run from the village? Why?"

"Leave me alone," she cried, burying her face in her hands.

Snarling, Longbow grabbed her wrists and began twisting them. "Why you run? Tell me! Now!"

Dancing Cloud's head whipped up. Her eyes were red with tears. She cried out in pain as Longbow tightened his hold on her. "You are hurting me," she then sobbed. "Why, Longbow?"

"You're not telling me what I ask," he growled.

"I'm not running away," she said, gasping for air as her pain increased. "I just wanted to be alone. That's all."

"Without Gray Wolf?"

She once more hung her head. *"Ay-uh,"* she murmured.

"But he only returned today. You should be happy. Not sad."

"I won't tell you why I'm sad," she said, suddenly stubborn. "It's not your affair. It's mine."

Having already planned for Dancing Cloud to be the first step in his vengeance, Longbow seized the opportunity at hand to achieve this goal now. "Dancing Cloud is my affair," he said. He released her wrists and whipped his knife from its sheath on his right leg.

Dancing Cloud gasped and shrank back away from Longbow, against the trunk of the tree. "What do you mean?" she asked. "What are you doing . . . with . . . that knife?"

"This," Longbow said, placing its tip next to her throat.

"Longbow, why . . . ? What are you . . . ?"

"Lift the skirt of your dress," he ordered.

"What . . . ?"

"Do as I say and don't struggle or the knife will silence you forever."

Slowly she lifted her dress, watching anxiously about her, hoping for discovery. But everyone was asleep, tired from the full night's activities. And should she scream, the knife would be even swifter!

"Lie down," Longbow said in a husky whisper.

"Please, Longbow," Dancing Cloud pleaded. The touch of the point of the knife against her neck made her aware of his crazed seriousness. She slowly stretched out on the dew-dampened grass and awaited her fate.

Longbow kept the knife at her throat as he lowered his breeches. And as he thrust his readiness inside her, he had only to take three plunges and he had had his measure of pleasure, having been without a woman for way too long now.

Dancing Cloud began to moan mournfully as she shook her head back and forth. "If Gray Wolf hadn't wronged me, I would be with him now and you couldn't have touched

99

me," she cried. "It is Gray Wolf's fault! Dancing Cloud now hates him!"

With his breeches back in place and absorbing Dancing Cloud's every word, Longbow stood threateningly over her, glaring at her. "What do you mean about Gray Wolf?" he asked, wishing his heart would quit pounding so hard. Had he raped Dancing Cloud for nothing? Didn't Gray Wolf still want her as his woman? Had Longbow's first act of vengeance been in vain? Gray Wolf would even laugh now if he knew the reason Longbow had sought pleasure with this blubbering female who was apparently no man's!

"Gray Wolf loves another!" Dancing Cloud further cried.

Longbow's eyebrows arched. He fell to his knees beside Dancing Cloud. He jerked her face around so their eyes could meet. "Gray Wolf has found himself another woman?" he asked hoarsely. "Who, Dancing Cloud? Who?"

Seeing the intense anger in Longbow's eyes, and now sorry for having revealed any truth about Gray Wolf to this crazed, jealous man, Dancing Cloud began slowly shaking her head back and forth. "I will tell you nothing else," she cried. "You are bad. I won't tell you anything you ask. Dancing Cloud hates Longbow!"

Longbow raised his hand and smacked her across the face, growling. "You tell Now," he said, hitting her over and over again.

"Sweet Butterfly is her name," Dancing Cloud finally cried, then her wails grew louder.

Longbow looked quickly about him, then he placed a hand over her mouth. "Be quiet," he hissed. "The whole tribe will be awakened and hear. Longbow has got to think. . . ."

His mind was aswirl with what he should now do. Now it wouldn't mean as much heartache to Gray Wolf that Longbow had raped Dancing Cloud. She was no longer his woman. Now Longbow would have to find this Sweet Butterfly! She was only an added ingredient in his plan. . . .

His gaze moved back to Dancing Cloud. There was still a way to cause great pain in Gray Wolf's heart as far as this woman was concerned. If she were dead . . .

It could look as though she fell upon her own knife in her sadness over losing Gray Wolf, he thought darkly to himself. Wouldn't it cause Gray Wolf much guilt for having turned her away, so that he could be free to love another woman? His guilt would be like a cloud . . . always a shroud of darkness hovering over him . . . spoiling his every movement and thought. . . .

Longbow's insides tremored and sweat beaded his brow, but it took little effort to plunge the knife into Dancing Cloud's abdomen, and he cringed only when a low sort of gurgle took the place of the scream she had tried to get out. Trembling and pale, Longbow placed the knife in Dancing Cloud's limp, lifeless hand, then slowly pulled the skirt of her dress down, not wanting the rape to be a part of the evidence when she was found.

Then he crept out of the forest and went and hung his head . . . and retched into the river.

Chapter Seven

*The winds are left behind
In the speed of my desire.*
—Taylor

The carriage moved away from the train depot. Danette sat inside this carriage, stiff-backed, next to her uncle, having felt nothing but aloofness from him since his one major stormy lecture after discovering her again with Gray Wolf. Maybe now, while they were in St. Paul, he would treat her more civilly. In the presence of others, he had no choice. He did have his reputation to protect. An uncle's being anything but kind to his niece could be labeled "cruel and heartless," to say the least!

Glancing over at Dwight, she saw how impeccably he had dressed to make his appearance before his constituents and politician cohorts. His cheeks shone from a fresh shave, his hair had been neatly trimmed, and his suit was pressed to perfection. But, oh, how Danette hated the set of his jaw! He could be such an indifferent, stubborn man.

When Dwight cast Danette a tight-lipped glance, she quickly looked away from him, not wanting to hear any more of his warnings. When it really came down to it, she much preferred his taciturn ways to his harsh words about Gray Wolf!

Seeing Danette's loveliness, Dwight once more worried about her welfare. She seemed to have grown up into a woman overnight! Even though he had insisted she wear the high-necked, ivory-colored satin dress with its abundance of embroidered lace at the throat, bodice and cuffs of the full sleeves, it didn't hide the swell of her breasts. The long strand of pearls that hung from her neck lay between her deep cleavage, emphasizing the largeness of her bosom, and her tininess everywhere else. The pearl earrings on each earlobe could be easily seen, because Danette's hair had been brought back and tied with a large satin bow. Dwight had hoped this would make her look younger, a protective shield of sorts, to cause the men's heads to turn away, instead of toward her.

But he knew he would have no control over her whatsoever while he was away from her in St. Paul. He could only hope that Rettie Toliver, the owner of the boardinghouse where she would be staying would see to it that no harm would come to Danette.

"At least while we're in St. Paul, you won't have a chance to be in the company of that Indian," he said, now speaking his worries aloud to Danette.

Danette clasped her hands tightly together on her lap. He just wouldn't give up! "Uncle Dwight, there are surely Indians in St. Paul," she taunted, casting him a sour look. "Aren't you forgetting they work in the flour mills there, as they work in the lumber camps in Duluth?"

Dwight's face reddened with anger. He crossed his legs and thumped his fingers nervously against the highly polished leather of his shoe.

"Your attempt at humor does not become you, Danette," he said dryly.

"Humor?" she argued back. "Uncle Dwight, I feel many things. But humorous? No. Not quite. Your attitude brings out anything but humor in me."

"Sarcasm then," he growled. He uncrossed his legs and reached for her hand, which she quickly drew away from him. "Danette," he said in a softer tone. "I only want what's best for you. You surely must know that."

"You have the strangest ways of showing your concern," she said icily, shaking her coiled hair to hang long and thick down her back. She had preferred a hat! But her uncle had been determined to make her look like a schoolgirl, demanding that she place her ribbon in her hair!

Well, she would show him. Once she was away from him, she would wear her hair and her clothes as she wished to do!

Danette had become anxious to meet Amanda Odell. Because of her Uncle Dwight, she had even been too protected from close female relationships! She was surprised that her uncle had even encouraged this one with Amanda, a complete stranger! But ... anything to remove her and her thoughts from Gray Wolf. Ah, yes, her Uncle Dwight did have devious ways!

"Danette, if by chance I do have to go on to Washington, I trust that you will behave accordingly," Dwight said softly, glancing around, hoping no one of the three others traveling in this carriage was a newspaper reporter. His face was always recognized. From experience he knew to be on guard at all times for anyone who might be a reporter, waiting for him to slip up by word or action, to do something that could be spread across all the major newspapers of the country. It was known that he had his eyes on the presidency.

Danette sighed heavily and leaned her head back against the cushion of the seat. "And what could I possibly do?" she said, wishing he would just let her be the woman she had recently grown into ... a woman whose heart had already been handed to a man to do with what he wished.

"Just do not make acquaintances so freely," he said, placing his hand over his mouth as he cleared his throat nervously. "Surely you know to what manner of behavior I am referring. The Indian. You were ... uh ... well ... much too ... eh ... should I say, amiable."

"Oh, Uncle Dwight, please," Danette said, then forced her eyes away from him to look out the carriage window at St. Paul's flat, straight streets, a welcome change from those of Duluth!

The houses that lined the busy thoroughfare were neat, one and two-story, some brick and some wood-framed. They all displayed trimmed yards with flowers either in windowboxes or lining the walkway that led to the front steps. The sun was bright and high in the sky, which was a velvet-blue color. As the carriage moved around a corner, the warm air rushed in through the opened window onto Danette's face, like a caress. In the distance she could see the great dome of the Minnesota State Capitol Building, where most of Minnesota's political activity took place. And across the way from the Capitol Building she knew to expect Rettie Toliver's boardinghouse. Danette couldn't help but wonder what the next two weeks held for her. Would she be bored, or might she find some excitement when she was away from her uncle?

Then she had to remember! Gray Wolf was the only excitement she now hungered for! Oh, how she already missed him!

Letting herself get lost in her fantasies of Gray Wolf, Danette was now oblivious of everything and everyone around her. And when the carriage drew to a halt and the door was thrown open, it came as such as shock that her face became aflame with embarrassment. She had at that very instant been thinking of the most sensual moment of pleasure that she had shared with Gray Wolf. . . .

"Danette, Good Lord," Dwight grumbled at her side, noticing her face and the hazy look in her eyes. "What is it now? God! Must you continue to act so . . . so strangely?"

"It is nothing, Uncle Dwight," she replied coyly, now enjoying his reaction. Then she offered her hand to him. "I do believe we've arrived at the boardinghouse. You are going to assist me from the carriage, are you not, Uncle Dwight?"

Watching her uncle's face take on a pattern of dark lines

to accompany his frown amused Danette even more. Oh, how wicked she felt enjoying his anger! But he had recently made her life almost unbearable by his strict guidelines of how he wished her to live and behave. Guardian or not, he didn't have to refuse to consider her feelings!

Dwight stepped from the carriage after the other passengers, then helped Danette down onto the gravel walk. Danette took a lingering look at the house that was to make her a possible prisoner for the amount of time she would be in St. Paul. It was a friendly-appearing sort of house, two-storey, with many windows. Its white paint glistened in the sun, and the shutters at the windows gleamed in their crimson reds. A wide porch stretched out across the front of the house, crowded with white wicker chairs and matching tables. A porch swing hung from the porch ceiling, swaying gently with the breeze, as though someone were there, swinging.

"You've enough luggage for a year, wouldn't you say?" the coachman shouted from the back of the carriage as he continued to loosen and drop Dwight's and Danette's valses and leather pieces to the ground.

"That's really no concern of yours," Dwight growled back, then coughed nervously into his cupped hand, having reminded himself to watch his manner! His anger with Danette couldn't be spread around to others! It could possibly lose him votes!

Danette swung around and gasped when she saw the coachman cart to throw her box of canvases to the ground. She rushed to him in a flurry of rustling petticoats. "Sir!" she cried. "Please, do be careful! Those are delicate canvases!"

She took the box from him and sighed heavily, then welcomed Dwight's releasing her of the burden weighting her down.

"You go on inside," Dwight said, more an order than a congenial request.

"Gladly," Danette said icily. Holding the skirt of her dress up in her arms, she moved toward the house, still studying it. There were lace curtains at the windows, and at one of the downstairs ones Danette could see the faint outline of someone sitting there, watching her.

Stepping self-consciously up the front steps and then onto the porch, Danette was suddenly welcomed by an outburst of friendship as the front door flew open, revealing a spunky, stout young lady who was offering an outstretched hand of friendship.

"You must be Danette Thomas," Amanda Odell said, stepping out to meet Danette's approach. Amanda's gaze moved on past Danette, to Dwight. "I'd know Dwight Thomas anywhere," she quickly added. "I've followed his political career in the newspapers from the very first. He's so handsome! And I'm sure quite a likeable man." She then smiled warmly toward Danette and took her hand. "And I'm sure you are just as nice, since you are his niece."

She shook Danette's hand eagerly. "I'm Amanda. Amanda Odell. Welcome to my Aunt Rettie's boardinghouse."

Amanda's enthusiasm and cheerfulness transferred itself to Danette. She laughed softly beneath Amanda's grip of steel. "It's my pleasure to meet you," she said. "And, yes, I'm Danette."

Then, observing Amanda's attire, a puzzled look passed over Danette's face. Though quite white-skinned, with crystal blue eyes and hair the color of gold, or ripe wheat, Amanda wore her hair braided, with a colorfully beaded Indian band around her head, and from beneath this band hung a straight line of bangs across her brow.

An Indian band? Danette wondered to herself. Why on earth . . .?

Then she smiled. When Dwight *sees this,* she mused to herself.

Her gaze took in the rest of Amanda. It appeared that food was her weakness, because her face was plump and round, and a dark, riding skirt hung wide and full from a thick waist.

Amanda's low-swept white blouse left nothing to the imagination. The heels of her cowboy boots now clicked noisily against the floor of the porch as she caped an arm about Danette's waist to guide her into the house.

"Come on inside," Amanda encouraged. "Meet my Aunt Rettie. She's been watching for you and your uncle's arrival. She just loves to talk to politicians. This boardinghouse has seen many coming and going for the past twenty-some-odd years."

The aroma of apple pie and chicken and dressing met Danette's approach into the house. It gave her a warm, comfortable feeling. And once she was in the house, she instantly knew that this wasn't the ordinary boardinghouse, carelessly run by stodgy people. Everything about this house spoke of warmth, character, and a sense of welcome, with its simple, framed embroidered pieces hanging along the neatly papered walls and the handmade braided rugs thrown along gleaming hardwood floors.

"In here," Amanda said, pulling Danette along beside her. "Aunt Rettie is in the parlor."

Danette smiled and glanced back across her shoulder at the hallway that led to many closed doors and then at the staircase that led up to the second floor. It wasn't a house like the one in which Danette lived. Its simpler touches were welcome to Danette. She had grown so tired of the luxuriousness of her Uncle Dwight's mansion, where one scarcely breathed for fear of knocking a crystal vase from a pedestal!

A different aroma tickled Danette's nose as she moved along with Amanda into the parlor. The arcra was so over-powering, it was as though she has stepped into a garden filled with lily of the valley blossoms. But she knew that it was only cologne and heavily used by the wearer!

The parlor in which she now stood was filled with overstuffed chairs of all designs and fabrics, and one wall was lined with books. Knickknacks crowded the tables, and a lifesized ceramic statue of a collie dog seemed to be standing guard next to a ten-foot-high-and-wide stone fireplace that showed signs of heavy use by is blackered overhead mantel. A breeze blew in from an open window, billowing the curtains out away from it.

"Amanda? Is that you, precious?" A gravelly voice suddenly spoke from somewhere in the room, startling Danette.

Amanda laughed, seeing Danette's hesitation "Yes, it is I, Aunt Rettie," she said. She then nodded toward Danette and whispered, "Go on. Go meet my aunt. She's in the rocker beside the open window. She rarely leaves it. You see, she's not at all well these days."

Danette looked toward the rocker, seeing it from behind. It stood high-backed and quite wide and moved slowly to and fro. Danette then saw pudgy fingers clasped to the arms of the rocker and realized that Rettie Toliver was there, hidden, it seemed, from all the world, except for those she viewed from her window and those who, in turn viewed her back.

Feeling strangely like an intruder, Danette tiptoed to the rocker, and before stepping around to meet Rettie, she looked toward Amanda for reassurance. When Amanda smiled and nodded, Danette moved slowly to the point of the rocker and found herself quickly under the scrutiny of an elderly lady who was so obese she completely filled out the seat of the rocker.

"Hello . . ." Danette said almost in a whisper. She reached her hand toward Rettie. 'I'm Danette Thomas. It's nice to become acquainted with you, Mrs. Toliver.'

Hoping to not appear openly rude, Danette couldn't help but intensely study Rettie. Rettie's face was very round, yet severely wrinkled, and her gray hair was thinning to the point of being almost bald and was drawn back and held by combs to her scalp. The dress Rettie wore was of a calico print with a small white collar fastened with a beautiful cameo brooch. The dress was buttoned down the front and its skirt lay long and full, yet not covering her ankles, which were so large that Danette had to wonder how Rettie managed to walk!

Rettie's hand trembled as she placed it inside Danette's. "So you are to be a guest in my boardinghouse along with your uncle?" she said in a raspy voice. "How nice. And welcome. I hope you'll enjoy your stay here."

Her bleached-out eyes looked around the corner of her chair, then back to Danette. "And where is that uncle of yours?"

"Seeing to the luggage," Danette said, hoping her canvases were being treated well enough.

"He's a great man," Rettie beamed. "Already done a lot for our great state of Minnesota."

Danette's smile faded and she eased her hand away from Rettie's. "He is quite dedicated to his senatorial duties," she said in a strained voice, hoping this elderly lady who reeked of lily of the valley cologne wouldn't detect the animosity she felt toward her uncle at the moment.

A commotion in the hallway outside the parlor drew Danette's attention quickly toward the door. Then suddenly Dwight was in the parlor, with his wide campaign smile and voice of velvet. He shook Amanda's hand, then was guided by Amanda to Rettie.

Danette stood aside and watched her uncle in action, having seen his smooth technique with new acquaintances enough times to know what to expect next. She even silently mouthed his exact next words.

"Mrs. Toliver, how nice it is to meet you," Dwight said, leaning down to shake her hand. "And, Mrs. Toliver—or may I call you Rettie—I had expected a much older lady to be the owner of such a grand establishment as Rettie Toliver's Boardinghouse."

His smile broadened and he winked. "Why, you're just

111

a young thing,'' he added, brushing a kiss against the corded knuckles of her hand.

Rettie harumphed and drew her hand quickly away, cocking a heavy gray eyebrow. ''Smooth talker,'' she said, eyeing him up and down. ''Most politicians are.'' Then a slow smile rose on her lips. ''But, son, I like ya. Can't help but like ya. Yes, do call me Rettie, and pull up a chair. Let's talk politics.''

Danette's eyes rolled to the ceiling and she groaned. Amanda moved to Danette's side and coaxed her to sit beside her on a sofa covered in a floral print.

''We must pamper my aunt,'' Amanda whispered, leaning close to Danette. ''She gets so lonely. My Uncle Matthew, Aunt Rettie's husband, died a while back. She still misses him powerfully. Just be patient, and I'll show you Flame, my horse, real soon.'' Her eyes grew wide. ''You do like horses, don't you, Danette?''

''Only for use with a buggy,'' Danette whispered back. ''I've never named one. Why did you?''

''I ride Flame,'' Amanda said, eyes even wider. ''I'd never attach him to a buggy. Never.''

Always ready to please someone who might prove to have connections to higher places, Dwight immediately drew a chair next to Rettie's rocker. ''And what do you think of our fine President Hayes?'' he asked. ''I may be traveling to Washington in the next day or so to meet with him.''

''I like the man just fine,'' Rettie said, nodding her head slowly up and down. ''He's what you might call different. Don't see too many goin' into that office of president thinkin' on only one term. His reason for that makes me admire the man.''

''His intentions to serve only one term so he could strive for civil service reform?'' Dwight said. ''Is that what you're making reference to, Rettie?''

''Exactly,'' she said raspily. ''As a one-term president he knew that he wouldn't have to give political jobs to win

112

support. Yes, sir. President Hayes based *his* appointments on merit rather than on the spoils system. He ain't only different, he's an upright, honest man.''

"Congress is refusing to act on the civil service legislation President Hayes has proposed," Dwight said, frowning.

"'Cause he's the first president to fight Congress on the civil service issue," Rettie said. "But his struggles have gained wide public support and have opened ways for later presidents to make civil service reforms."

Rettie cackled beneath her breath and gave Dwight a twisted grin. "Sure like President Hayes's wife Lucy," she said. "She don't allow no card games, smokin', dancin', or the servin' of alcoholic drinks at the White House. 'Lemonade Lucy,' some have called her, because of her set moral ways."

Dwight straightened his tie and cleared his throat nervously, never having agree with Lucy Hayes's refusal to serve drinks at formal dinners and receptions. But he couldn't voice this opinion to the already very opinionated lady taking in his every word and seeming to measure it.

"Yes," he said instead. "Rutlerford and Lucy Hayes have set a good example for every American family. And what do you think of the custom just recently introduced . . . Easter egg rolling by children on the White House lawn?"

"It'll never last," Rettie scoffed. "Maybe one more year, but not longer. When President Hayes and Lucy are gone, the next president won't think to continue the tradition and the children will be the losers."

Heavy footsteps in the hallway drew all eyes but Rettie's to the doorway. Soon a quite tall and large-boned lady came lumbering into the room. She didn't acknowledge anyone's presence in the room except for Rettie's. Going to her, she leaned over and began urging Rettie from the rocker, all the while scolding her.

"Rettie, you know it's time for your nap," Janice Belt said, placing her powerful hands to one of Rettie's elbows.

"Come on now. Give a shove. We'll get you from that chair in a jiffy and on to bed with you until supper time, and no fussing back, do you hear?"

"I've been talkin' politics," Rettie argued, puffing and growing red in the face as she struggled to rise from the rocker.

"I'm sure you have," Janice said, frowning toward Dwight. "Well, you can just talk politics later."

Dwight rose quickly from his chair and reached for Rettie's other elbow, placing his hand there to help. "Here," he said. "Let me help you. I didn't mean to tire you, Rettie."

Rettie huffed and puffed as her body came slowly from the chair. "This here's Janice Belt," she managed to say, now wheezing. "She's my nurse and companion. Couldn't do without her. I've also assigned her the duties of my boardinghouse."

Rettie's face twisted in pain as she coughed. Then, after swallowing hard, she added: "And Janice, this here's the famous Senator Dwight Thomas from Duluth."

Not even looking his way, still concentrating on her labors of the moment, Janice said, "Nice meeting you, sir. And thank you for helping, though I *am* capable of managing Rettie by myself."

"I'm sure you are," Dwight said. And as Rettie made it to her feet and was leaning heavily against Janice, he stepped aside.

Watching Rettie inch her way across the floor, Dwight went to Danette. "Hon, we'd best get settled in," he said. "I'd like to go tend to business soon."

"Amanda will show you to your rooms," Rettie said over her shoulder. "We'll talk some more before you get too involved, won't we, Dwight?" She gave him a hopeful sideways glance.

"Yes, ma'am," Dwight said. "Now you rest comfortably."

Rettie didn't reply, just cackled as she inched her way

114

out of the room. The shuffling of her feet could be heard for a few more minutes until a door banged, which meant that she had reached her room.

Danette rose from the sofa as Amanda did. Then she realized that her Uncle Dwight and Amanda had not yet been formally introduced. "Uncle Dwight," she said. "I'd like for you to meet Amanda. This is Mrs. Toliver's niece that you told me about."

Danette couldn't help but smile wickedly when she saw Dwight's eyebrows lift as his gaze settled on the colorful Indian band on Amanda's head. Though he surely must have noticed it earlier, he had been too engrossed in impressing the older member of the family to show his wonder over Amanda's choice of hair decoration.

Dwight kneaded his chin thoughtfully, leaving only one brow arched, then offered Amanda a hand. "Amanda," he said kindly. "What a pretty name for a pretty girl." He studied her face intently, then his gaze moved back to the band at her head.

Amanda's face flushed with pleasure at the handsome senator's having so politely taken her hand. She fluttered her lashes nervously and performed a half curtsy, quite an unusual thing for her to do. But he was so handsome!

"Pleased to meet you, sir," she murmured. Then she noticed how he was so strangely taken by her Indian headband, yet, thinking more about it, she understood. Didn't most people who didn't know of her ties with the Chippewa Indians wonder about the headband?

And, being reminded of the Indians by his continuing steady stare, Amanda quickly withdrew her hand, feeling disloyal to her lover, Red Fox, for even letting herself be flustered by another man, though this man was quite famous, and was one who would most surely turn any woman's eye!

"Your aunt said that you might show us to our rooms?" Dwight said, removing his watch from his vest pocket to nervously check the time.

"Yes," Amanda said, already bustling across the room. "Come with me. Your rooms are on the second floor, facin' the street. I believe you'll find them quite nice and comfortable."

Stepping out into the hallway, Dwight filled his arms with their luggage and followed along after Danette and Amanda. And once they were settled in and Amanda and Danette were alone in Danette's assigned room, the girls began getting better acquainted.

"You're an artist?" Amanda said, touching a canvas gingerly as Danette unpacked several, carefully inspecting them for damage.

Danette laughed softly. "I try to be," she said. Now that she was reassured that her canvases had taken the journey well enough, she let her gaze move slowly about the room, pleased with what she saw.

The furniture was made of solid white mahogany. The ornately carved four poster bed was beautiful with its embroidered Scalamandre silk bedspread. White lace curtains hung at the two windows where the afternoon sun shone through them in lazy streamers of gold. A comfortable chair covered in soft tones of velvet had been placed beside a table upon which sat a hurricane lamp with leaf designs painted on it to match the design in the wallpaper. An oval braided rug covered most of the floor, but where it did not, hardwood floors gleamed, freshly polished.

"Do you have any of your paintings on exhibit anywhere?" Amanda asked, plopping carelessly down on the expensive bedspread, tucking her feet beneath her, not minding that her boots were still on.

"No. Not yet," Danette sighed, opening a valise to remove some of her dresses, which she feared had already been crushed too much. "But it is my dream to be able to show my paintings one day. Perhaps I will. I'm really not sure." She wanted to say: "It's according to which direction my life takes, now that I've met Gray Wolf. . . ." But she

116

knew to not ever mention his name to anyone ... even Amanda, who wore an Indian band about her head!

Eyeing the Indian headband and settling down into a chair to rest a moment, Danette quickly blurted: "And why do you wear the band on your head, Amanda? Or do you mind telling me? Should I have asked?"

Amanda reached her hand to the band, fingering the beads sewn onto it. A slow smile lifted her lips. "Neither you nor your uncle know, do you?" she asked quietly.

"Know what?"

"I didn't think you did. I saw the questioning in your uncle's eyes."

Danette moved to the edge of her chair. "What is it you are speaking of?" she asked. "Tell me if you can. I'd like to know."

A faraway look appeared in Amanda's eyes. "It's my sister Lorinda," she murmured.

"Your sister?"

"Yes ..."

"What about her?"

"She's married to an Indian," Amanda said, watching Danette's reaction, never knowing what to expect, from person to person, when the truth was revealed. Most accepted it. But there were those who never could. And Amanda suspected Dwight Thomas to be one of the latter. Hadn't she seen it in his eyes? She hoped for better things from his niece!

A slow flush rose to Danette's face and her heart did a strange flip-flop. "Your ... sister ... ?" she said, having been rendered almost breathless by this piece of news.

"She is married to a great chief. Chief Yellow Feather," Amanda said, not quite sure how Danette was taking the news. She seemed to be *too* flustered!

"How ... interesting. ..." Danette managed in a low murmur. She wanted to ask Amanda if she might know Gray Wolf but again thought better of it. The chances were slim

117

that Amanda would know of him . . . there were many Indian tribes in the state of Minnesota.

Amanda climbed from the bed and settled on the floor at Danette's feet. "And how do you feel about this?" she asked.

"Why, I think it's a bit exciting," Danette said, laughing softly. "I think quite highly of the Indian community. Surely your sister must be proud to be married to a great chief."

Amanda grabbed Danette's hands and squeezed them. "Then you do understand? You approve?" she asked anxiously.

"Why, yes . . ."

"Then, Danette, one day soon, while you are staying here at my aunt's boardinghouse, might you like to go with me to visit my sister and her chief husband at their Indian village?"

Danette's heart began to race. How daring such a venture would be! And just maybe Gray Wolf . . . ? Then her spirits lowered.

"My uncle would never allow it," she sighed.

"Didn't he mention something about possibly traveling on to Washington from here?" Amanda asked, smiling coyly.

A slow smile caused Danette's lips to slightly tremble. "Yes," she said. "He did, at that. . . ."

"Then might we go to the Indian village while your uncle is on his own journey from St. Paul?" Amanda said, giggling.

Danette joined in and also giggled. "Yes!" she then said. "We shall!" She would not think of the dangers! She just would not. She had her own private reasons for wanting to go to an Indian village. Hadn't Gray Wolf asked for her hand in marriage? Well, it was only right that she become acquainted with another white woman who had bravely said yes to an Indian when she had been asked. . . .

Chapter Eight

I need the starshine of your
heavenly eyes,
After the day's great sun.
—Towne

Moving at a short, choppy trot on a road cut through the forest of oaks, elms and maples, the roan horse on which Danette rode still felt awkward beneath her. The saddle leather groaned . . . the bridle bit rattled . . . and the horse blew out a nervous snort as Danette tried to stay beside Amanda and her beautiful rust-colored horse, Flame.

Danette had never enjoyed riding horseback and her joints were beginning a slow ache, making her wish now she had argued more strongly for a buggy. But Amanda had argued back, saying that the trail through the forest hadn't been made for the luxuries of a buggy and that a buggy would only slow them down.

With the fear of Uncle Dwight's discovering her reckless behavior hanging threateningly over her head, Danette knew that speed was of the utmost importance here, and she had complied to Amanda's wishes and had accepted the gentlest of all the horses offered her from Rettie Toliver's stables.

"I still believe we should have told Mrs. Toliver face to face that we were leaving," Danette said, glancing over at Amanda who sat straight-backed and proud in her saddle. With her fringed buckskin dress and her hair braided,

Amanda almost could pass for an Indian. But the color of her hair and her fair skin was indeed a quick giveaway.

"You worry too much," Amanda laughed, fitting her cowboy boots more firmly into the horse's stirrups. "I told you that Aunt Rettie is quite used to my antics. The note I left for her today isn't my first. When I get the notion to go visit my sister, I go." She wasn't about to tell Danette quite yet that she had more reasons than her sister for traveling into the forest and beyond. Danette would find out soon enough about Red Fox. . . .

"But your aunt isn't well," Danette softly argued. "Won't this worry her too much?"

"No. She'll take it in stride, as she always does. You see, Aunt Rettie hasn't been the same since Uncle Matthew's death," Amanda said solemnly. "She used to be full of spunk . . . the spunkiest ol' woman you could ever meet. Most say her feistiness has rubbed off on me because she brought me up. But I'd sure like to see her the way she used to be. Just once more I'd like to see her stomp through that house, yellin' out orders to everyone."

Amanda patted the rifle slipped into a sheath close to her right leg. "She was handy with a rifle, too," she laughed. "And a shotgun. I'll never forget how she could make a man back away from her when she showed him the barrel of a shotgun."

"Why would she have a need to do that?" Danette asked, eyes wide.

"When Uncle Matthew wasn't around and a man got too ornery in our boardinghouse, Aunt Rettie had to show who was boss."

"Oh, I see," Danette said, smiling awkwardly.

Amanda whipped the rifle out and playfully twirled it around. "And I won't hesitate usin' *my* rifle if we're threatened on the trail," she said, placing the rifle back into its sheath when she saw the alarm in Danette's eyes. She let her gaze travel over Danette. "You like your new outfit?"

Danette smiled warmly toward Amanda. "It's most certainly not what my uncle had meant for me to purchase in St. Paul," she said, now glancing down at her fancily designed leather cowboy boots, her full, dark riding skirt, and the long-sleeved white blouse that had been only half-buttoned up the front. On her hands she wore soft leather gloves to protect her delicate fingers, and she had also chosen to braid her dark, thick hair. She wore a sweeping "padre" hat because of its wide, flat brim.

"Have you quit frettin' over your uncle yet?" Amanda asked, steering her horse around a muddy puddle in the center of the road. "You still afraid he might return from Washington too soon?"

"You said we'd be gone no longer than four days, didn't you, Amanda?"

Amanda shrugged. "That ought to do it," she said.

"Well, it will take Uncle Dwight much longer to go and come from Washington," Danette said, swatting at a fly that began to buzz around her face. "So if you're sure we can come and go in four days, I don't have much to worry about."

"Then will you just relax in the saddle?" Amanda laughed, reaching over to pat Danette on the leg. "You look stiffer'n a board."

"As I told you . I don't enjoy riding horseback," Danette said, placing her hand to the small of her back, stretching and groaning.

"I got you a gentle enough horse to ride," Amanda said, now giving Danette's horse a fond pat on the neck. Then she smoothed her hand over her own horse's sleek body. She laughed throatily. "You wouldn't want to ride Flame here if you're not used to horses. He's a Thoroughbred with flawless breeding, all right. But he's high-spirited and excitable."

"His mane and tail are so full and lustrous," Danette sighed. "Flame has to be the loveliest horse I've ever seen."

"Flame can be traced back directly to three Arabian stallions named Darby Arabian, Godolphin Barb, and Byerby Turk," Amanda said proudly. "Horsemen produced the Thoroughbred by crossing these fast, sturdy Arabian stallions with European horses."

"I'd like to paint him one day," Danette said, eyeing him as though she already had a paintbrush in hand, ready to make strokes on a canvas.

"You should've brought your painting equipment with you," Amanda said. "You could've somehow placed it on the side of the horse. There's much to paint out here on the trail. And especially in the Indian village. It's so beautiful there."

Danette was reminded of her painting of Gray Wolf's wigwam . . . and of Dwight's reaction to it. A shiver raced through her as she thought of his reaction should she suddenly come up with another painting with another Indian setting!

Shaking her head, she said, "No. I don't believe that would have been too wise."

"Your uncle . . . ?"

"Yes. My uncle."

Then Amanda's face drew shadows onto it when her gaze focused straight ahead. All small talk of horses, paintings, and Danette's uncle came to an abrupt halt as she rode on away from Danette, toward a fenced-off patch of ground at the side of the road.

Danette watched Amanda quickly dismount her horse and secure its reins at a low-hanging limb of a maple tree. And as Danette drew rein next to Flame, she saw what had been the sudden attraction for Amanda. Inside the white picket fence, two gravestones stood side by side, and, looking tranquil beside these gravestones, were clusters of blooming yellow jonquils.

Danette looked in silence toward the two gravestones and then back toward Amanda, wondering who could be buried there to cause Amanda to become so suddenly quiet, sad, and withdrawn.

Amanda turned her face toward Danette and motioned with a hand. "Would you like to visit my parents' graves with me?" she asked, her eyes showing tears at the corners.

Amanda's somber mood struck a chord of sadness inside Danette's heart, now remembering what her Uncle Dwight had said about Amanda's parents being dead. She was also remembering that they had been slain by Indians.

Danette's gaze moved slowly up and down Amanda and at the way she was dressed. With Amanda's parents having died in such a way, how was it that both Amanda and her sister Lorinda could associate themselves so closely with Indians?

But then . . . remembering the mystique of Gray Wolf and how he had stolen both her mind and her heart, she could understand. . . .

Dismounting and securing her horse's reins, Danette went to Amanda and slipped an arm about her waist. "Yes," she murmured. "I would like to visit your parents' graves." She swallowed hard and lowered her eyes, thinking of similar graves outside of Duluth. "You see, my parents are also dead."

"This is why you live with your uncle?"

"Yes. He became my legal guardian when I was ten."

"Aunt Rettie isn't my legal guardian," Amanda said in a near whisper as she stepped alongside Danette inside the fence. "But she's taken care of me since I was two."

"Your parents have been dead that long? Since you were two?"

"Yes . . ."

Amanda moved away from Danette and settled down on her knees next to a spot of land that had sunk a bit into the ground. She began plucking tall stems of grass away from it and tossing them over her shoulder, across the fence.

Danette stooped to one knee, across from Amanda, and

began helping her to clear the wild shoots of grass from the other grave. Her eyes went to the gravestones and she read the inscriptions. One read:

MAVIS ODELL
1814–1859
Rest In Peace

The other read:

DERRICK ODELL
1810–1859
REST IN PEACE

"I come here as often as I can," Amanda said softly. "But it's never enough. The weeds try so hard to choke the graves. I wish mother and father had been buried closer to town. Then I'd keep fresh flowers on the graves instead of these damn, ornery weeds."

"The jonquils are pretty," Danette tried to encourage her.

"Jonquils bloom for such a short time and then they look like weeds too," Amanda scoffed. She leaned back, wiping her brow with the back of her hand as the noonday sun beat down upon her. Her gaze slowly took in the land around her. "I was only a baby when it happened," she said, nodding toward a spot in the land where weeds tangled in profusion over the remains of a burned-down house.

Danette's gaze followed Amanda's and saw the bits and pieces of exposed rotting wood that lay spread across the small portion of acreage. Most of it was hid from view by tangled briars and weeds. Trailing arbutus with its shining evergreen leaves and fragrant white flowers had crept its way along the ground, choking out the wild onion and dandelion plants.

"Was this where your parents' house once stood?"

Danette asked, her voice low and filled with apprehension, not sure if Amanda wished to talk about it.

Amanda settled down onto the ground, smoothing her skirt out beneath her. She plucked a jonquil and absently twirled its long green stem around between a forefinger and thumb. "My parents were homesteading this plot of land," she finally said. "After the tragedy, Aunt Rettie and Uncle William purchased the land so my parents' graves wouldn't be disturbed."

Amanda studied the graves, sniffed the flower, then continued. "I was only a baby, so I don't remember being abducted by the Sioux. . . ."

Danette gasped. "Abducted . . . ?" she murmured.

"Yes. The Sioux killed my parents, stole me from my cradle, then set everything on fire and took me with them to their village."

"But you escaped?"

"Lorinda and Chief Yellow Feather rescued me."

"Your sister was living with the Indians even then? Even though you had been abducted by Indians and your parents had been killed by them?"

"Chief Yellow Feather is from the Chippewa. The Chippewa rarely ever warred with the white man."

"But how did your sister . . . ?"

"Lorinda had been kidnapped by a lumberjack," Amanda said, placing the jonquil on one of the graves. "Yellow Feather happened along and rescued her, but after seeing her and falling in love with her, he took her to a cave and held her hostage there. . . ."

"Good Lord," Danette said, shuddering. "A hostage!" She paused and lifted a brow inquisitively. "Yet she is now married to the Indian. Did he force her to marry him?"

"Lorinda fell in love with Yellow Feather," Amanda said, slowly rising to her feet. "She has stayed with Chief Yellow Feather because she has wanted to. And anyone who gets to know Chief Yellow Feather quickly understands why.''

Danette already understood, having herself met such an Indian. But she still didn't feel comfortable enough with her feelings to share them with Amanda. It was a secret to be held deep inside her heart, until she was in Gray Wolf's arms again. . . .

"We'd best be on our way," Amanda said, taking one last, lingering look at the graves, then the gravestones. "We should cover a lot more ground today before making camp for the night."

Danette brushed dried grass from her skirt as she rose from the ground, and walked toward the gate behind Amanda. "You really do believe we will be safe enough camping alone in the forest?" she asked, shivering involuntarily at the thought.

"I've done it many times," Amanda said. She swung her leg over her saddle and untied the reins from the tree. "If you know the land as well as I do, the perfect spot for camping can be found."

Feeling awkward with her inexperience at mounting a horse, Danette blushed as she finally got both feet in the stirrups. Then she giggled. "I'll get the hang of it soon," she said. "Lead the way, Amanda."

Moving away from the small cemetery plot, they continued along the road until the forest claimed it with its thick ground cover, and then Danette and Amanda began their journey deep into the forest. The air was strong with the scent of pine, and the trees were active with the chirping of birds. Dripping gray beards of moss trailing down from the branches of some of the trees resembled fine lace, and wild flowers showed through the bed of dead leaves in yellows, whites, and purples.

Not thinking the forest could be any darker than it already was with the sun unable to break through the thickness of the trees overhead, Danette was alarmed when things began to darken even more around her.

"We've just about traveled our limit today," Amanda soon said, glancing over her shoulder at Danette. "I know a perfect spot ahead."

The chill of impending nightfall settled on Danette's face and seemed even to be penetrating her clothes in its dampness. Dew was already settling onto the tips of the plants, resembling sparkling jewels.

"Over there," Amanda said, nodding her head.

The sound of rushing water met Danette's ears and the outline of jutting boulders could be seen in a clearing ahead. She traveled on behind Amanda until Amanda drew rein beside a creek. Peering through the semidarkness of the fast falling dusk, Danette could see a waterfall cascading over moss-covered rocks, sending a cold spray out on all sides of it. On the limbs of blue spruces and pines, drops settled like teardrops.

"I'll get us a fire going, then we can settle in for the night," Amanda said, dismounting. She looked toward Danette, reading fear in her eyes. She went to her and reached for her hand. "Come on, Danette. Truly things will be all right."

Not wanting to appear the inexperienced city girl that she in truth was, Danette refused Amanda's offer of help and swung herself out of the saddle. "I'm sure it will be," she said, unbuckling the saddle cinch as she watched Amanda working at unsaddling her own horse.

But Danette didn't feel truly safe until Amanda removed the rifle from its pouch and carried it along with her as she began gathering dry twigs for a fire.

And after a fire was burning bright and protective and their bedrolls were spread, they shared beans and hot coffee beside the warmth of the fire.

"This ain't all that bad, is it, Danette?" Amanda said,

127

leaning back on an elbow. With her plate scraped clean, she sipped leisurely from her coffee cup.

"I'm strangely relaxed," Danette laughed. She swallowed the last of her coffee and placed the empty plate and cup on the ground beside her. "In fact, I've never felt so . . . so free."

She began working her gloves from her fingers, then removed her hat and tossed it aside. "You see, my uncle has taken his duties as guardian quite seriously. He's very strict. He has even tried to keep me from painting. He would be much happier if I stayed confined in my room all day doing nothing. That way he'd know what I was doing."

"How terrible," Amanda said, visibly shuddering. "At least my aunt understands me. But I'm sure it's because she was always a free spirit herself."

A strange noise overhead, a *tseet* sort of sound, repeating over and over again, followed by soft thumping noises that sounded unlike anything Danette had ever heard before caused her to sit more upright and grow tense. "What on earth . . . ?" she whispered, looking up into the trees, but seeing nothing.

Amanda laughed and gathered the dishes and cups and began making her way toward the stream. "That's a flying squirrel," she said across her shoulder. "It's flying from tree to tree. The soft thump you heard was it landing on a tree."

Feeling foolish at her ignorance of the forest and its little creatures, Danette rose to her feet. "Let me help you with washing the dishes," she said.

Amanda shook her head. "No need," she said. "I'll only be a minute. Just stay warm by the fire. I'm sure you're not used to these nighttime temperatures. We don't want to arrive back at Aunt Rettie's with you sick with a cold."

Danette frowned, not appreciating Amanda's mothering of her. They were the same age. But she realized that because of her Uncle Dwight's constant pampering of her, Amanda probably was more practical than she.

Hugging herself, indeed feeling the cooler temperatures settling in, she settled back down on a blanket beside the fire. With another blanket wrapped around her shoulders, she watched the hypnotic flames of the fire, suddenly missing Gray Wolf. They had made love beside such a fire. . . .

The crackling of twigs close by and in the opposite direction from which Amanda had gone drew Danette quickly from her fantasies of Gray Wolf. Another snapping of twigs . . . the rustle of dried leaves . . . and an Indian stepped out from behind the tree, leading a horse behind him.

A wild shriek tore from deep inside Danette as she jumped to her feet. Then she became entangled in the blanket that she had wrapped herself in, and she fell awkwardly to the ground.

Trembling and picking herself up from where she had fallen, Danette watched the Indian wrap his reins around a limb, then stand with legs widespread, looking just as puzzled back at her. And when Danette saw that he meant her no harm, leaving his knife inside its leather sheath, she relaxed and observed him more carefully.

He was almost as handsome as Gray Wolf. But he wore a strange deerskin patch over one eye, and his shoulders weren't as broad or muscular. His sleek black hair, which was braided long down his back, was held in place by a headband with the same bead design as Amanda's, and he wore an eagle feather in the loop of his hair.

Fringed deerskin breeches, shirt, and moccasins were his attire, and his one eye was so dark it appeared black as he continued to stare back at her, now with his arms crossed over his chest.

"Red Fox!" Amanda suddenly said from behind Danette. "Why are you here?" She placed the cups and dishes on the ground, then rushed to Red Fox and eagerly embraced him.

129

Then she stepped back away from him and eyed him wonderingly as she smoothed her fingertips across his brow. "You never leave the village. Something must have happened," she said. "What is it? Nothing has happened to my sister, has it?"

Red Fox clasped his fingers onto her shoulders. "Red Fox need you," he said hoarsely, speaking English as she had. "My heart is heavy, White Blossom. My sister Dancing Cloud is dead."

Numb inside, Danette viewed the affectionate scene between Amanda and the Indian. And what had he called Amanda? White Blossom? Amanda's sister Lorinda had been given the name Red Blossom by the Indians. Was Amanda even more a part of the Indian life than she had admitted to? Were she and this Indian who called himself Red Fox . . . lovers . . . ?

Amanda paled and her heart began a slow ache. "Dancing Cloud dead?" she gasped. "How . . . ?"

Red Fox looked toward Danette, then back to Amanda. "You don't want to say in front of Danette?" Amanda whispered back to him.

Red Fox shook his head back and forth, then asked: "Who is this white woman? Were you taking her to our village?"

"Ay-uh . . ." Amanda said in a near whisper, yet not low enough to keep Danette from hearing, which caused Danette to pale and wonder even more about this new friend who even knew how to speak in Indian!

"But, why, White Blossom?" Red Fox demanded, frowning toward Danette.

"She's a *nee-gee,"* Amanda said, reassuring him. "She is a friend who not only I can trust, but also all of the Chippewa."

"But why take her to village?" Red Fox growled. "Too many strangers can bring threats to our people."

"Danette is not a threat," Amanda softly argued. "Red

130

Fox, I wanted her to meet my sister. And I grow tired of making the journey alone. Please understand?''

Red Fox cupped Amanda's chin in a hand. "White Blossom smart," he mumbled. "Red Fox not worry any longer."

"Then let me introduce you to Danette," Amanda said, taking Red Fox by the hand, guiding him closer to the fire and Danette.

Watching Danette for any signs of an unfavorable reaction, Amanda clung tightly to Red Fox's hand. "Danette, this is Red Fox," she said. "He is more than a friend. We have been close since we were babies and shared nourishment from his mother, who willingly took me into her arms when Lorinda and Chief Yellow Feather rescued me from the Sioux."

Danette no longer eyed Red Fox waringly. Instead, she offered him a hand of friendship.

"And Red Fox," Amanda continued. "This is my newfound friend—Danette."

"I'm pleased to meet you, Red Fox," Danette sincerely said, placing her hand in his. Being so close to him . . . seeing his copper-colored skin and his sculpted Indian features . . . and feeling the strong grip of his hand . . . made Danette's insides stir, so missing Gray Wolf at this moment. She had to wonder if Red Fox might know Gray Wolf, but, as before, she doubted it, realizing just how coincidental that would be. She had to keep telling herself that there were many Indians scattered about the state. Surely they knew only those of their small villages. . . .

"Nee-min-weh-dum-wah-bun-min-ah," Red Fox said, holding his shoulders straight and his head high.

Danette glanced quickly toward Amanda with a lifted eyebrow, smiling weakly.

"He says he's happy to meet you," Amanda said, smiling back an understanding toward Danette. Then she once more took Red Fox's hand and looked glumly up at him, seeing his need to talk to her, to lift some of the burden of sadness from his heart.

"We can go and talk now," she murmured. She glanced toward Danette. "Red Fox and I are going to talk beside the river. Please excuse us, Danette?"

"Yes, please do go on," Danette said, smiling nervously from Amanda to Red Fox. "I'll stay here by the fire. The air seems to be getting colder and colder."

Slowly settling back down on her blankets, Danette watched as Amanda and Red Fox walked away from her, and she saw how Amanda had worked herself close to Red Fox, into his embrace at his side. And when they exchanged a lingering kiss, Danette knew that, yes, they were, indeed, more than just friends. . . .

Chapter Nine

When sleepy birds to loving mates are calling,
I want the soothing softness of your hand.
—Gillom

Relieved to be out of the forest where the tangled barberry bushes had almost become her enemy, Danette welcomed the sight of the St. Croix River. Crossing where it was more shallow, she then found her horse slipping and sliding up a slope of shale rock, and discovered even more a challenge to staying in the saddle. Feeling the renewed aching of her joints and a dull throbbing at her temples invading her senses, she sighed with relief when they once more reached flat land.

"We should be there soon," Amanda said, riding up beside her with Red Fox trailing along behind, gloomy in his sadness over the death of his sister.

"I certainly hope so," Danette moaned. She let the reins go slack in one hand while she flexed the fingers of her other. Glancing back at Red Fox, she quietly said, "It's too bad about his sister. How did she die?"

Amanda wiped beads of perspiration from her brow. They were now beneath the steady rays of the sun, which was shining down from a brilliant blue sky. The meadow stretched out before her with its weaving grass and dots of yellow daisies. Bees buzzed from flower to flower, and a bald eagle with spread tail and wings soared through the air.

Then Amanda's thoughts were on Danette's question. The words were hard to speak, but speak them she must. It was a truth she hadn't yet accepted. She couldn't believe Dancing Cloud could ever take her own life! Even if she had lost Gray Wolf's love. Life meant too much to her to cast it aside so easily.

"She, somehow, fell upon her own knife, it seems," she finally managed to blurt. She felt no need to mention Gray Wolf. At this moment Amanda was too confused by his behavior toward Dancing Cloud to try to have to explain who he was to Danette. Who could Gray Wolf have found whom he could love more than Dancing Cloud? He had loved Dancing Cloud for forever!

Danette gasped noisily. "How horrible . . ." she said, once more glancing back at Red Fox. "Was she Red Fox's only sister?"

"Yes. And now he has no family left at all. His parents died many years ago."

Danette reached to touch one of Amanda's hands. "He has you, Amanda," she said. "He's very lucky to have you."

"Yes. And now there's even more urgency for us to be wed," Amanda said firmly.

"Wed?" Danette said, eyes wide.

"From the time we were old enough to understand a man and woman's special feelings for one another, we knew that we would one day be man and wife," Amanda said. "But I had promised Lorinda and Aunt Rettie that I first would receive schooling like all other white children."

"And you did? You went to school?"

"All twelve years."

"And now that you are finished, you still haven't married Red Fox?"

"Aunt Rettie's health became poor," Amanda sighed.

134

"I've stayed with her to return the kindness she has given me all these years." She sighed even more languidly. "But now I have another kindness to repay. If not for Red Fox's mother, Singing Cloud, I wouldn't have made it through my infant years."

"You said you shared nourishment with Red Fox?"

"We sucked from the same breast."

"Oh, I see," Danette said, blushing.

"And now that Red Fox is alone in the world, I must marry him, to fill the void in his life."

"But, love ... ?" Danette murmured. "Do you love him?"

"With all my heart," Amanda said flatly. "But I am sure you can't understand. He is an Indian. I am white."

Amanda dropped back to ride beside Red Fox. Danette smiled at them both from across her shoulder, thinking, Yes, I can understand. I *do* understand. I too love an Indian.

Then she focused her eyes straight ahead, seeing the outline of the forest ahead where a bend in the river met the protrusion of pine, cedars, towering oaks and elms. She was beginning to think they would never reach the village no matter what Amanda said. The day had become hot, the air dry, and Danette's thighs felt bruised from their constant contact with the saddle.

Removing her hat to fan herself with it, Danette reached the bend in the river. She sullenly traveled on around it, then found herself face to face with a cave, and then, close by, a village of wigwams.

St. Croix River ... a cave ... she pondered to herself, feeling a prickling of her skin. Gray Wolf had mentioned his village beside the St. Croix River ... a sacred cave. ...

But, no, she thought further, shaking her head back and forth. There were many caves, and the St. Croix River ran through the state of Minnesota for mile upon miles.

The neighing and snorting of a horse drew Danette's eyes quickly around. She found Amanda now on one side of her and Red Fox on the other. She replaced the hat on her head and traveled along beside them, silent, as they worked their way on to the outskirts of the village.

An involuntary shiver raced across Danette's flesh. She could feel the strength of the sadness of the people in the village as she looked at the few who were visible outside their wigwams. Most walked about with heads hung and paid hardly any heed to this newcomer who accompanied Amanda and Red Fox.

"We will go directly to my sister's house," Amanda said quietly. "And I must apologize for the way you've been greeted by my sister's husband's people. They mourn the loss of a loved one. You see, they are all brother and sister. If not by bloodline, then by strong bonds of the heart."

"I understand," Danette murmured.

Amanda cast her a somber glance. "I doubt if you do," she said. Then a slow smile lifted her lips. "But perhaps you can return again with me so you can share in song and dance. No one celebrates like the Indians."

"I would be honored to return again," Danette said, then grew quiet when, among the wigwams, she saw a log cabin. A warmth touched her insides when she realized that it belonged to Lorinda. Though she had married an Indian, she had somehow managed to keep something from her past. Danette wondered if Gray Wolf would be as understanding and let her live in a house instead of a wigwam. . . .

As they reached the log cabin and dismounted, Danette couldn't help but be filled with apprehension. She was a stranger in strange surroundings and had felt very much alone since Red Fox had appeared on the scene. Amanda surely hadn't meant to, but she had become distant, hard to communicate with, with Red Fox traveling at her side. Danette had even wished at times that she hadn't come.

The door of the log cabin suddenly opened, and Danette didn't have to wonder whom it was who was standing there tall and beautiful. Her red hair and fair skin gave her identity

away quite readily, and Danette knew that she was just about to meet Lorinda . . . Red Blossom.

Amanda flew immediately into Lorinda's arms. "Lorinda, I've missed you so," she murmured.

"Did Aunt Rettie give you permission this time, Amanda?" Lorinda asked, drawing away from her, studying her sister with a steady warmth in her green eyes.

Her eyes . . . Danette wondered to herself. There was something about them that was familiar. She studied them more intensely. It was only their color of green. Gray Wolf's were the same color—and of course she would notice this when Gray Wolf was so much on her mind? Oh, why did everything remind her of him?

"I left her a note," Amanda said, lowering her head as a child might do when a scolding was expected.

"Amanda!" Lorinda said, then let her gaze move to Danette, to whom she first gave a look of wonder, and then a ready smile.

Amanda turned, having noticed Lorinda's sudden silence. "I've brought a friend," she said, reaching her hand to Danette. She took Danette's hand and drew her closer. "Lorinda, this is Danette Thomas, and, Danette, this is my sister, Lorinda."

Danette smiled toward Lorinda, sweeping her eyes quickly over her and her buckskin dress and moccasins. "I'm very glad to get to meet you," she said, shaking Lorinda's hand. "I'm honored to be here in your . . . uh . . . your husband's village."

Color rose to Lorinda's face as she laughed softly, clasping onto Danette's hand, already liking her. She had so missed the companionship of white women to converse with, though the years should have made this need less in her life. Then, feeling guilty for such thoughts, as though having just been disloyal to Yellow Feather, she said, "This is not only my husband's village, but also mine."

Danette could see the pride in Lorinda's eyes when she

spoke, yet for a brief moment there, Danette had seen something else. Was this life with Lorinda's husband enough for her? Did she miss the white world?

Will I? Danette worried to herself.

"I'm sorry your people are in a state of mourning," Danette said. "Red Fox told us of . . . of . . ." She blushed. She couldn't remember Red Fox's sister's name!

"Dancing Cloud," Lorinda said, now solemn and half withdrawn. "Yes. We mourn." She took Danette by an elbow and guided her toward the doorway. "Come inside. Rest. I'm sure the journey has tired you."

"Where's Yellow Feather?" Amanda asked, clinging to Red Fox as they all moved into the house together.

"He is at the council house," Lorinda said, turning the wick higher on a kerosene lamp, sending a golden glow throughout the cabin. "Planting has been delayed because of mourning period, but it begins tomorrow and the seeds are being divided among the elders of each household."

Amanda wanted to ask how Gray Wolf was taking Dancing Cloud's death, but she decided to wait and let Lorinda bring his name into the conversation. She knew the guilt that Gray Wolf must be feeling and knew that even this was shared by his immediate family.

Danette looked around the cabin. It was simple but had all the basic needs of life. This outer room appeared to serve as both kitchen and parlor, with a woodburning cooking stove, table and chairs and storage cabinets at one end, and a sofa and chair at the other end, arranged before a massive stone fireplace.

Colorfully striped Indian blankets were used as decoration on the walls as well as throws on the sofa and chair. A crude wooden table sat against a far wall, upon which was a kerosene lamp, matching the one other lamp on the kitchen table, and a stack of books of all sizes and colors. Beside this table was an oak rocker whose arms were worn with wear. Danette imagined that Lorinda sat there for hours upon hours, reading and perhaps even fantasizing about what her other way of life could have been. . . .

A door led into another room and a faint outline of a bed could be seen. Danette sighed with relief. She had thought maybe the floor would have served as the bed, as it had in Gray Wolf's wigwam. And now, seeing that this Indian chief had let his wife live as she had most surely requested, she could hope that Gray Wolf would do the same.

"Please make yourself at home," Lorinda said, gesturing with a hand toward the sofa. "I will get us some nourishment. Would you like tea or coffee, Danette?"

"Tea would be fine," Danette murmured, settling down onto the sofa. She watched Amanda and Red Fox move to the floor, where they sat together beside the hearth of the fireplace, where no fire burned, because of the heat of the day.

But Danette wasn't seated long when a towering shadow fell across the open doorway that led to the outside. She jumped quickly to her feet, paling when an Indian who so resembled Gray Wolf, yet wasn't he, entered the room.

"Yellow Feather," Amanda said, rising to rush into his arms. She hugged him tightly and placed her cheek on his massive bare chest.

"Yellow Feather?" Danette whispered, trembling inside still, because of Yellow Feather's resemblance to Gray Wolf. It was as though she were looking at the man she loved with possibly twenty years added to his life. Yet there was the difference in Gray Wolf's eyes, and in the red cast to his hair when the sun shone directly onto it. This Indian's eyes were dark and fathomless, and his braided hair was as black and sleek as that of a raven's wing.

But his chiseled features, his nose . . . the set of his jaw . . . the cheekbones . . . and his proud, squared shoulders were, oh, so much the same. . . .

The yellow feather in his coil of hair and his loincloth

were his only attire, revealing the muscled strength of his copper-colored body.

"Who you bring to visit?" Yellow Feather asked, in English, drawing Amanda to his side, holding her affectionately there.

Amanda once more busied herself with introductions and Yellow Feather showed admiration in his eyes as he reached a hand toward Danette.

"You are welcome to my village," he said, smiling, clasping Danette's hand.

"Thank you," Danette said in a near whisper, hoping that he couldn't feel the clamminess of the palm of her hand. But he was having this effect on her. He made her miss Gray Wolf even more! She was relieved to have to her hand free of his as he stepped back away from her.

Lorinda went to Yellow Feather and stood on tiptoe to kiss him on the cheek. "Darling, did you by chance look in on Gray Wolf, to see if he needs anything?" she asked softly. "I so worry about our son."

"Gray ... Wolf ... ?" Danette whispered. Her pulse raced. Her heart pounded.

A quick dizziness overtook her. Lorinda had spoken Gray Wolf's name and had referred to him as her son! Now Danette understood so much! Gray Wolf's green eyes ... his mother's! Gray Wolf's red cast to his hair ... his mother's! And the resemblance between Gray Wolf and this powerful chief ... his father!

Fate had guided her to the man she loved yet another time, and knowing this and the shock of it was suddenly too much for Danette to grasp.

A spinning in her head caused Yellow Feather's reply to Lorinda's question to sound as though it were coming from deep inside a well, yet Danette heard his words clearly enough.

"Gray Wolf wish to be left alone," Yellow Feather said.

"He still mourns. It is hard to lose woman who was to be wife. . . ."

"Oh, no . . ." Danette whispered, feeling as though her heart were tearing into shreds. When everything turned black before her eyes, she didn't even feel the impact of her body falling onto the floor.

Seeing a face through a haze, Danette blinked her eyes nervously. She placed a hand to her forehead, feeling something damp and cold there.

"Danette, are you all right?" Amanda asked, leaning down over her, gingerly touching her cheek.

"Where am I?" Danette murmured, looking around as her vision slowly cleared. She was stretched out on a bed, in a dimly lighted room that was small and devoid of other furnishings, except for a closed trunk at the foot of the bed. She looked further around her, and when her eyes settled on Yellow Feather as he stood looking toward her from the other room, she turned her face from him. She now remembered where she was and was recalling Yellow Feather's words about Gray Wolf. Dancing Cloud had been Gray Wolf's woman . . . his future wife.

Oh, how the knowing hurt!

Amanda removed the damp cloth from Danette's brow and dropped it into a basin of water beside the bed. "You're in Lorinda's bed. And you're still not feeling well, are you, Danette?" Amanda murmured, settling down on the bed beside her. "Was it the trip? Was it too hard on you?"

"No . . ." Danette said, wishing the pain would leave her heart. "I'm fine. I don't know why I did such a foolish thing as faint." But she did know. She had lost Gray Wolf, before truly ever really having him. All along he had belonged to another. How could he have deceived her? He had asked her to be his wife.

"But you did faint, and there has to be a reason," Amanda

said. She wrung the cloth out and placed it back on Danette's brow. "Should I send for a doctor?"

Danette removed the cloth from her brow and handed it back to Amanda. She rose from the bed, trembling. "No," she said. "I don't need a doctor. I just need to return to St. Paul. Today. This minute." She choked back a sob, not wanting to reveal her inner torments to Amanda. "I've got to get out of here, Amanda. Now."

She started toward the door, but, seeing Yellow Feather's eyes still on her, she stepped back from view and leaned heavily against the wall. She hung her head, knowing that tears were near. How was she going to explain her need to escape?

She glanced toward the bed. Had Gray Wolf slept there cuddled between his parents when he was a child? Everything about this cabin . . . everyone inside it . . . was a part of Gray Wolf . . . reminding her over and over again of her deep love for him.

Amanda went to Danette and clasped onto her shoulders. "Why do you want to return to St. Paul?" she asked. "Is it something to do with Yellow Feather? It was shortly after meeting him that you fainted. And just now. When you saw him, you wouldn't go out into the room with him. Are you afraid of him?"

Danette's eyes widened. "Heavens, no," she gasped. "Please don't think that I . . ."

"Then what?" Amanda demanded. "You agreed to come. And now that you're here, you want to leave. I don't understand, Danette."

Danette shook herself free from Amanda's hold. She began a slow pacing, avoiding the doorway, not wanting to look upon Yellow Feather's handsome face again. In his features, there was so much of Gray Wolf. . . .

She wrung her hands, feeling trapped. "I really can't tell you, Amanda," she said. "It's something . . . I don't want to ever have to talk about."

Amanda went to the door and closed it, then took Danette by a hand and guided her to the bed. "Come on, Danette," she urged. "Let's sit down here and have a woman-to-woman chat. You can confide in me. I'm your friend."

"I just can't," Danette said, once more pulling away from Amanda. "You wouldn't understand." She knew that Dancing Cloud had been Amanda's true friend, and if Amanda realized that Gray Wolf had been unfaithful . . .

No. She couldn't tell!

"Well, I just can't go back to St. Paul this soon," Amanda said, plopping down on the bed. "Especially now. I am needed here. At least until I've seen and talked with Gray Wolf."

Danette paled. "Gray . . . Wolf . . . ?" she murmured, feeling almost swallowed up in her heartbeats.

"Gray Wolf is Lorinda and Yellow Feather's son," Amanda said. "I know the guilt he is feelin' at this time, and I have a duty to him, to see if I can make his burden of the heart less."

Danette inched onto the bed, next to Amanda. "Guilt?" she said, swallowing hard. "Why is it that he is feeling guilty?"

"It is rumored that Dancing Cloud fell on her knife because of her sadness over losing Gray Wolf to another woman," Amanda said solemnly.

"Another . . . woman . . . ?" Danette said, feeling a blush rise to her cheeks and her heart begin racing crazily. "What . . . other . . . woman . . . ?"

"I do not know her," Amanda said, frowning. "She must be from another tribe. But her name at least I know. Sweet Butterfly. She is to be Gray Wolf's wife, and Dancing Cloud had just been told this before she died."

Once more Danette felt a spinning in her head. But this time it was from a delirious joy that she had not been wronged by Gray Wolf! All along he had loved her when he had said that he did! She had to go to him!

But, no! How could she? How could she admit to being this Sweet Butterfly that surely most Chippewa despised because of Dancing Cloud!

Then she remembered again the words of Yellow Feather. When he had spoken of Gray Wolf's mourning, he hadn't even mentioned her name. He had only mentioned how hard it was for Gray Wolf to have lost a woman who was to be his wife.

"Doesn't Yellow Feather know the rumors of this Sweet Butterfly?" Danette suddenly blurted.

"Why, yes," Amanda said. "Chief Yellow Feather is a wise chief. He knows everything."

"But he didn't mention the name. . . ."

"And he won't. He will want most to believe that Dancing Cloud's death was accidental . . . not intentional. It will look best for Gray Wolf."

"Now that this has happened to Dancing Cloud, it will be hard for Gray Wolf to bring his other woman into this village, won't it, Amanda?" Danette asked cautiously, now full of doubts of ever being accepted by Gray Wolf's people.

"Gray Wolf is next chief-in-line," Amanda said, rising from the bed. She went to a window that had been hidden beneath a thick deerskin hide and drew the hide back and peered out. "He has the right to have more than one wife. Sweet Butterfly surely knows this. It's not her fault that Dancing Cloud is dead. It's not even Gray Wolf's fault, though guilt is heavy on his heart."

Amanda swung around, her eyes angry. "You see, I don't even believe that Dancing Cloud *did* fall purposely on her knife," she said, circling her fingers into fists at her side. "I believe someone must have killed her."

All of Amanda's words were swirling around inside Danette's head. She placed her fingers to her temples and closed her eyes, trying to sort through it all and suddenly feeling as though she had been given another chance for love. She wouldn't be blamed. She could go to Gray Wolf!

Then her insides grew cold. "Did you say that Gray Wolf could have . . . more . . . than one wife . . . at a time . . . ?" she asked, paling even more. "Chief Yellow Feather? Does he have more wives?"

Amanda laughed softly. "No. Lorinda is his only wife," she said. "It is up to the man . . . how many he wants. Gray Wolf must only want one, since he sent Dancing Cloud from his wigwam."

Danette sighed heavily. Then she wondered about something else. "Did you say that you think Dancing Cloud was murdered?" she asked, wondering if there were dangers even in such a peaceful-appearing community as this, set back, far away from the rest of the world?

"It's only because I knew Dancing Cloud so well," Amanda said, hitting her doubled fist into the palm of her hand. "She was such a happy, carefree person."

"But if she was so sad over Gray Wolf . . . ?"

"Dancing Cloud would never be that sad," Amanda hissed. "She would've given Gray Wolf up to another woman just to make Gray Wolf happy. You see, they had been friends longer than they had been lovers."

Danette flinched at the word "lover." But she had known all along that Gray Wolf's skills at making love had come . . . from . . . practice.

Feeling the need to see Gray Wolf growing stronger inside her, Danette once more paced the floor, wondering just how she was going to go about it. There was only one way. . . .

With a racing pulse, she swung around and boldly faced Amanda. "Amanda, you truly wouldn't hate Sweet Butterfly if you were to meet her?" she asked, a strain quite evident in her voice.

"I couldn't hate anyone Gray Wolf loves," Amanda said, eyeing Danette, seeing something new in her eyes, yet not understanding just what. "Why? Why do you ask?"

Danette went to Amanda and took both her hands and squeezed them affectionately. "I am your friend, aren't I,

Amanda?'' she murmured, feeling the heat rise into her cheeks from anxiety.

"You know that you are," Amanda said, searching Danette's face, seeing the sudden flush where only moments before the color had been so ashen.

"Then please understand what I am about to say," Danette said, smiling weakly.

"Danette, what on earth is it?"

"Amanda, I was once told that, in the company of Indians, I would be called Sweet Butterfly," Danette said. "Amanda —Gray Wolf . . . gave . . . me this . . . name . . . the name Sweet Butterfly. . . ."

Chapter Ten

Let the night winds touch thy brow
With the heat of my burning sigh.
—Taylor

The sun was descending behind the trees, setting the sky on fire with its fierce red color. Danette gazed intensely upon the wigwam she was approaching, wondering what Gray Wolf's reaction would be upon seeing her without first having been told that she was even in the village. Not only had Amanda encouraged Danette to go to Gray Wolf, but Lorinda had too. Chief Yellow Feather hadn't voiced his opinion. He had just stood there, silent, absorbing the sudden truth of who Danette was and what she meant to his son.

Having won approval from Amanda and then Lorinda before telling them that she was Sweet Butterfly had made her acceptance by them after they knew much easier. Lorinda had even embraced her. Danette would never forget the warmth of Lorinda's words.

"Go to my son," she had softly said. "And God bless you. I understand the mysteries of my special love for Yellow Feather. So shall you in time understand about Gray Wolf."

Danette had wanted to ask how she could be accepted so readily when Dancing Cloud had in a way died because of her. She didn't know if it was because of Lorinda's concern over her son, or because she now saw the chance of soon having another white woman in the village.

"No matter," Danette whispered. "My mind . . . my heart . . . has room for only Gray Wolf, and he is not only a heartbeat away . . . but also a footstep. . . ."

The smell of cedar and a damp pungency drifted out of the deep woods that lay beside Gray Wolf's wigwam. Shadows danced and swayed as the leaves of the trees rustled above Danette's head. But that wasn't what had given her a momentary fright. Her gaze darted around her. She sensed a presence, yet felt a stillness in the wigwams that sat scattered about on all sides of her. Smoke spiraled slowly upwards from each smoke hole, and the aroma of food cooking was heavy in the air.

Taking a deep, shaky breath, Danette once more focused on Gray Wolf's wigwam. Her face burned with its deep flush and her palms were damp with perspiration. "I must get control of myself before going in," she whispered to herself.

She wiped her hands dry on her skirt and she cleared her throat nervously. And just as she was about to reach for the colorful blanket that hung at Gray Wolf's doorway, an Indian was suddenly there and had grabbed her by the wrist.

Danette's shock and intense fear were so great that no sound would surface from her throat. It had suddenly gone dry! She couldn't even emit a whisper!

She tried to struggle free, but the Indian, attired in only a loincloth, with hate-filled dark eyes and a blemished face, was holding her with a grip of steel and now half dragging her into the dark recesses of the forest. When he had not taken her far, only to a small clearing, she finally managed to jerk herself free and regain a portion of her voice.

"Who are you?" she hissed, rubbing her raw wrists. "What do you want with me?" She could see Gray Wolf's wigwam beyond the trees . . . she could even yell and he would hear her. But this Indian, short and skinny though he was, was a threat, with his hand on the sheath that held his knife.

"Longbow listened outside Chief Yellow Feather's dwelling," he said in a growl. "You are Sweet Butterfly. You are to be Gray Wolf's wife?"

Danette blanched and her voice caught in her throat, yet she managed to say, "You were sneaking? You were listening?"

"Longbow finds out many things this way," he said. He squared his shoulders proudly. "Longbow smart."

Tossing her head haughtily, Danette stood her ground, afraid, yet even more afraid to let it show. "I wouldn't consider sneaking about your chief's house very smart," she spat. "I would even think it dangerous. Surely someone will tell him. . . ."

"Longbow kill anyone who tell," he snarled.

"Are you of this . . . this gentle tribe of the Chippewa?" Danette asked, measuring him with her eyes. "You are different from . . . from . . . Gray Wolf."

"*Ay-uh,* Longbow different," he said, laughing evilly. "And the difference makes Longbow proud."

"I would think that most would detest the likes of you," Danette said dryly.

Longbow lunged toward her and roughly grabbed both her wrists and jerked her next to his body.

"*Bee-sahn,*" he growled.

"I don't know what you just said," Danette said, flinching with pain as his hold became rougher. "But you're hurting me. Let me go!"

"Longbow first get a taste of Gray Wolf's woman," he said, laughing throatily. He hadn't expected to violate Gray Wolf's new woman so soon. His plans were working out better than he had expected!

"No!" Danette cried, now trying to kick Longbow, but he was too quick for her and jumped back, out of the way. And when she felt this brief moment of freedom, she turned and began to run toward Gray Wolf's wigwam. But, too soon, she felt hands at her waist, from behind, and she

149

couldn't stop herself from falling to the ground, with Longbow now kneeling over her.

Danette had time to shout Gray Wolf's name only once before Longbow crushed his lips down against hers.

Tasting his spittle and smelling his unbathed skin made a bitterness rise to Danette's throat. She clawed at Longbow. She tried to lift her legs to knock him from her. But his determination to rape her was giving him added strength, it seemed.

His one hand began searching up her skirt. Danette closed her eyes, groaned, and shook her head with revulsion. But when she felt Longbow suddenly being jerked from on top of her, she opened her eyes wildly and saw Gray Wolf there, holding Longbow partially in the air only briefly before he tossed him angrily against the trunk of a tree.

Danette pushed herself to her feet, trembling violently. "Gray Wolf," she said, covering her mouth with the back of her hand when Gray Wolf picked Longbow up from the ground, to hit him, which sent Longbow again sprawling against a tree.

The thud was sickening as his head hit, and Danette took a step backwards, weak-kneed, as Longbow then fell unconscious at Gray Wolf's feet.

Gray Wolf spun around on his heel, quite naked of skin except for a brief loincloth, and looked in dismay toward Danette. "Sweet Butterfly, I don't understand. . . ." he said thickly, looking from Danette to Longbow, then back again at Danette.

Having regained all her faculties, Danette burst into tears and ran into Gray Wolf's arms. "I'm so glad you came," she said. She placed a cheek to his chest and hugged him tightly. "How did you know?"

"When I heard you yell my name that one time, at first I thought I was dreaming," he said. He eased her from his arms and stepped back away from her, to frame her face between his hands. "But, being wide awake, Gray Wolf

150

know scream was real, though not understanding how it could be. How is it you are in my village, Sweet Butterfly? Why is it you are with Longbow?''

Danette shuddered violently, glancing over at Longbow. She flinched when he emitted a soft moan as he stirred on the thick cushion of fallen, dried leaves. "Can't we first get away from this horrid place?" she whispered. "Gray Wolf, please let's go to the privacy of your wigwam."

Clinging to him, Danette followed Gray Wolf into his wigwam. The dampness of the impending night had chilled her, and she welcomed the warmth of the glowing coals in Gray Wolf's firespace.

Settling down onto a spread Indian blanket beside the firespace, Danette watched as Gray Wolf added a log to the fire. He did seem withdrawn. He did appear to be deeply mourning. He did not seem at all pleased that she was there, needing the comfort of his arms and the reassurance that he still loved her.

Had Dancing Cloud's untimely death brought not only the end to Dancing Cloud's life . . . but also to the love that Gray Wolf had felt for Danette?

Oh, God, don't let that be so, Danette silently prayed to herself.

Tense, awaiting Gray Wolf's next words, she clasped her hands tightly together on her lap. Nervous trembles were plaguing her. Even her teeth were noisily chattering together, causing her lips to tremble.

Still she watched Gray Wolf. His handsomeness . . . the corded muscles of his shoulders and the beautiful color of his skin set her on fire inside, so wanting to reach out and touch him. She hungered for his lips . . . his hands. . . .

Gray Wolf finally sat down beside Danette. He crossed his arms over his chest and gave her a lingering, silent stare. Then he spoke. Deeply. Emotionally. "Gray Wolf heart heavy with sadness," he mumbled. "Gray Wolf glad you're here."

151

Suddenly he reached for her and drew her hungrily into his arms and searched her mouth with soft, wild kisses, then held her to him and burrowed his face into her hair.

"Dancing Cloud dead," he murmured. "Gray Wolf no longer hear her laugh nor see her run through the meadow like deer. Sweet Butterfly, Gray Wolf need you. How did you know to come? Did the spirits speak to you of my loss?"

Feeling many things, most of which were love and compassion for this man who wove ecstasy through her heart, Danette cradled his face in her arm and softly kissed his brow. "No," she said. "No spirits led me to you. Only my heart, dear one."

Gray Wolf looked up at her with his emerald-green eyes. No words were needed to speak of the love he had for her. If Danette had ever doubted his feelings for her before, she knew at this moment that she never would again.

"My heart begs you to stay," he said, reaching his hand to her cheek.

"Yes," she sighed, filled with rapture. "Oh, yes, yes." She leaned a kiss to his lips. "But only until tomorrow. Then I must return to St. Paul."

"St. Paul? Why St. Paul? And how did you even get here?" he asked thickly.

Danette giggled, then told him how she had met Amanda and how they had planned to come to the village and how it had come about that she discovered he was one of these particular Indians only after she had arrived there.

"Then you didn't even know I would be here?" he asked, laughing softly. "*Ay-uh,* the spirits had more to do with this than you even realize. You are here. Gray Wolf is here. Isn't that answer enough?"

"But that horrible Indian, Longbow," Danette said, visibly shuddering. "He grabbed me right outside your wigwam. Is he always so . . . so . . . foolish?"

Gray Wolf laughed throatily. "*Ay-uh,* he is," he said,

amused at the word she had chosen to describe his arch enemy. *Ay-uh,* his name should have been Foolish Bow. And wouldn't Longbow ever learn? Would it one day have to end by Longbow's death? These antics of his couldn't continue. And how dare he touch Sweet Butterfly!

Cupping his hands around Danette's chin, he drew her lips to his. He kissed her gently, then said, "If he ever gets near you again, I will have to . . ."

Danette reached a forefinger to his lips, sealing his words. "Shh," she murmured. "Let's not speak anymore of it. We're finally together, Gray Wolf. Please hold me. Please tell me you love me. Or is it too soon after Dancing Cloud's . . . ?"

"Sweet Butterfly already heal the crack in my heart with words," Gray Wolf said huskily. "No more words are needed now."

Shivers of ecstasy raced across Danette's flesh as Gray Wolf reached to unbraid her hair while his eyes spoke silently of his passion for her in their each and every blink.

Her hair now free, Danette shook it to hang long and full down her back. Her breath was coming in slow rasps as her blouse was removed, leaving her breasts free for his lips to possess. And as he lowered his head to flick his tongue around a pink-tipped nipple, Danette placed her arms about his neck and drew his head even closer. Her insides were going wild with need of him. Her hands began searching his body, feeling the sleekness of his copper-colored back and the muscles tight at his shoulders.

Lower still her hands went, touching the muscled strength of his buttocks. With his lips now searching from breast to breast, Danette daringly traced his loincloth, around to where his manhood lay only a thin layer of cloth away from her exploring fingers. With a nervous heartbeat threatening to drown her, she inched her fingers along. She felt the rippling of his flesh beneath her touch. She could hear a sensuous sigh rise from the depths of his throat as her hand finally cupped him there, feeling his hugeness and, oh, so remembering how deliciously it could fill her. . . .

Aware of his power there, Danette brazenly crept her fingers on beneath the loincloth, feeling the velvet smoothness of his shaft and its throbbing as her hand began to work slowly back and forth. Hearing his throaty moans sent a thrill through Danette, loving the knowledge that she was giving him pleasure. Filled with a blind passion, dizzy from the intensity of his effect on her, she shifted her body so she could be the aggressor, while he sighed with contentment and stretched out on his back with closed eyes and enjoyed.

In an almost-daze, Danette began trailing kisses across his body. Her tongue circled the nipples of his breasts . . . her teeth nipped at his flesh. Then she lowered kisses down across his stomach, lower even than where his hip bones jutted out, to where between these his need of her lay swollen, ready, and pulsating.

With both hands, Danette lowered his loincloth, until it was lying on the blanket at his feet. Heating up like a burning flame, Danette once more began her assault of kisses along his flesh. First at his inner thighs . . . then slowly upward until she reached his swollen need of her.

Hearing his moans and feeling his body tense up even more made Danette quite aware of the pleasure she was giving him. Placing her hands beneath his buttocks, she lifted him closer, working with him slowly, tenderly, lovingly, wanting to give her all to this man who now meant life itself to her. . . .

Gray Wolf's fingers lowered and tangled through her hair. "Sweet Butterfly . . ." he whispered huskily. He gently lifted her head away from him, smiling drunkenly down at her. *"Mee-eewh."*

"You want me to stop?" she whispered back, scooting up, then leaning over him. Her hair fell from her shoulders onto his chest, her lips grazed the flesh of his neck, and her fingers once more circled his pulsating need of her.

"Gray Wolf wants you to undress," he said huskily, cupping her breast, squeezing it. "Gray Wolf has need to see and touch you."

Seductively, Danette rose to her feet and slithered out of the rest of her clothes, until she stood boldly nude before his feasting eyes.

Gray Wolf moved to his knees, his eyes darkening with hungry intent. He framed her body between his hands as his tongue licked flames across her abdomen and lower. Like a flower, she opened herself up to him and melted inside as his lips pressed against her womanhood.

She writhed in response with soft moans repeatedly surfacing from inside her and gave herself up to the rapture. But when she could bear no more, she placed a hand to his cheek and gently urged his face away.

With passion-heavy lashes, she looked down at him. "Gray Wolf, I need you," she said. She knew that he understood when he took her hand and guided her down on the blankets, where he leaned over her with magic in his eyes as he openly appraised her naked flesh.

There was a savagery in his mouth as he suddenly bore down upon her while his palms moved seductively over her, continuing to arouse her. His fingers combed into her hair as he drew her mouth even more into his, and, when he finally entered her from below, magnificently filling her with his throbbing hardness, Danette became dizzy, her frantic passion enflaming her.

She locked her arms about his neck and her legs about his waist. She lifted her hips and her body quivered with the wild, sensuous pleasure racing through her.

"I love you," she whispered, breathless when his lips moved to the hollow of her throat, nuzzling her there. Her face was flaming . . . her throat was dry. "Gray Wolf, I'm . . ."

She could speak no more. Her body shook violently with the joy of release, filled with a blinding rage of passion.

Clinging, soaring, she returned Gray Wolf's kiss as his lips once more were there, quivering against hers. It was an exuberant, shared passion, and Danette smiled to herself when she felt his own release take hold of him, as he lunged even more feverishly inside her, until he lay next to her, limp, and breathing hard.

"It is so beautiful," Danette sighed, running her fingers through his coarse, black hair. His hair was loose, without his headband. He was only clothed in his handsomeness, and this was a threat, it seemed, to Danette's sanity, because she was feeling a renewed ache between her thighs, wanting him inside her again, to make love the whole night through, if it was humanly possible. Once she returned to the world of Uncle Dwights, who could even guess when she could be with Gray Wolf again? These moments were to be savored . . . to be used fully . . . yet wishing this to be so made her feel somewhat a wanton, loose woman. . . .

"*Ee-shqueen*," Gray Wolf said huskily, drawing her into his embrace, molding her body into his. "Do not go back to white man's world. Join with me in the planting rituals. Be as one of my people."

Her body turned to liquid as his lips lowered to her breast and tenderly kissed it. Her thirst for him was never quenched! She trembled as his hand swept down her abdomen in a sensual caress, stopping at the core of her desire, to play a symphony there as his fingers slowly moved in and out of her.

"I . . . can't . . . stay . . ." she whispered, closing her eyes as the melting sensation began in the deep recesses of her brain. "I must return. Tomorrow."

Replacing his fingers with the renewed muscled strength of his love stem, Gray Wolf began a slow laboring inside her. "How can Sweet Butterfly even think of leaving?" Gray Wolf softly argued. "Can't you see how hard it will be to ever be apart again? We are one. Can't . . . you . . . see that?"

156

Feverish with building passion, Danette cupped her breasts and offered them to him as he lowered his lips to first one and then the other. "Gray Wolf, how can you expect me to even concentrate when you're . . . you're . . . causing my mind to leave me?" she gasped. She wrapped her legs about his waist and moved with his every thrust. She twined her arms about his neck and hungrily clung to him.

"You stay," he growled. "We will soon have feast to celebrate our marriage."

"Gray Wolf . . . please . . ." Danette said, not wanting his insistence to ruin things for them. She wanted to fully enjoy the fusing of their bodies and minds. The shared flames of desire were burning quickly higher, and again resulted in an explosion that was so overpowering that they were left lying side by side, exhausted and breathless.

Rising to his feet, Gray Wolf was suddenly strangely quiet. Danette leaned up on her elbow as he scooped her clothes up into his arms and handed them toward her.

"You want me to get dressed? You want me to leave?" she asked, now worrying that she had offended him. How many times could she refuse him and still expect him to continue caring for her? In his eyes she could already see traces of wounded pride.

"Get dressed and come with me to sacred cave," Gray Wolf said thickly, shoving her clothes into her arms as she rose before him.

"Why do you want me to go with you there?" Danette asked, searching his face for answers, only seeing set features and a cool glint in his green eyes.

Then her insides took on an empty feeling, remembering Amanda's talking about the cave and how it had once been used. Yellow Feather had held Lorinda captive there! Could Gray Wolf have this in mind for *her?* Was he that determined to have his way with her when he wanted? If he could only learn patience! When the time was right, she would happily marry him! But first there were Uncle Dwight's feelings to consider.

"Gray Wolf take you to cave to share some of my past with you," he said, choosing fringed leggings to step into, instead of his loincloth.

Danette trembled, wanting to trust him but not being familiar with Indian customs, now feeling as though he was a stranger, really not sure what to expect from him next.

Slowly dressing, she said, "We've been invited to share the evening meal with your mother and father." She slipped into her boots. "And, anyway, it must be dark by now, Gray Wolf. Surely it will be too cool and dark in the cave. Maybe there are even bats inside it."

"We eat later," Gray Wolf grumbled. He placed an arm about Danette's waist. "You come with me."

Wanting only to think of their love for one another, feeling guilty for doubting him, Danette followed him out of the wigwam. Everything about them was white with moonlight. There was no one moving about, not even around the large communal fire that burned in the outdoor firespace. On one side the forest was black with shadow, conjuring up thoughts of the evil Longbow possibly there, watching and waiting for another opportunity to grab her.

"We will take a torch to the cave," Gray Wolf said, lifting one from the ground, then lighting its tip as he held it into the flames of the outdoor fire. The flames licked at the torch as Gray Wolf once more began guiding Danette on through the village.

"The *wah-wah-taysee* wave their own torches for us to follow," Gray Wolf said, laughing lightly as he squeezed Danette's waist affectionately.

Hearing his good-natured laugh lifted Danette's somewhat somber mood. She relaxed her tensed muscles and breathed a quivering sigh. "What is a *wah-wah* . . ." she murmured, softly giggling when she couldn't repeat what he had said.

"*Wah-wah-taysee*," Gray Wolf said, slowly mouthing

the Indian word. "It means fireflies. See how they are busy, rising from the grasses? It seems the moon has them by strings, pulling them upward."

Wanting to keep the mood light, Danette said, "My Uncle Dwight taught me as a little girl how to catch them and place them in jars. I would place the jar by my bed and watch the fireflies all night. Early the next morning I would set them free because I didn't want them to die on my account."

Gray Wolf's face took on a strained look. Danette wondered why and then knew it must have been her mention of Uncle Dwight. There surely could never be anything friendly between these two men, who were now the two most important people in her life.

She, too, became silent, filled with a strained, awkward sadness.

The village was now only shadows behind them as the cave came into view. The moonlight draped the cave's entrance with its shining coat of white. But to Danette the cave meant a possible threat to her freedom. But she had to dismiss such thoughts. With Gray Wolf's people near, she couldn't be held prisoner for long. And there was Amanda. Amanda would miss her and surely come to her rescue.

Casting Gray Wolf a quick glance, her insides quivered with ecstasy for him, wondering how she could even for one moment doubt his honorable intentions toward her? If he truly loved her as he professed to, he wouldn't do anything to cause her unhappiness!

Yet, there was his determination to make her his wife. . . .

Holding the undergrowth and tree limbs aside, Gray Wolf helped Danette move into the cave. A cold rush of damp air lifted her hair from her shoulders and the sound of water dripping at her side made a cold chill race up and down her spine.

Hugging herself, she peered ahead, unable to make out any shapes or forms. The cave was the blackest black that

Danette had ever seen. When Gray Wolf moved on into the cave with the torch and its dancing flames, Danette didn't even then feel any more relaxed or confident. The way was narrow where the walls were lined with a thick growth of moss and dripping moisture droplets sparkling like diamonds beneath the light's flare.

Gray Wolf once more placed his arm about Danette's waist and silently urged her onward, on past a bend in the cave, and then, surprising to Danette, a campfire could be seen burning softly at the far end.

"Gray Wolf," she gasped. "Is somebody already here before us?"

"A fire is kept burning," he said thickly. "One never knows when a rush for the guns may be required."

"Guns . . . ?" Danette said, placing a hand to her throat. Then she saw them. Hundreds of rifles standing against the side wall, their barrels shining in the firelight.

"Though we've not had a war with the Sioux for some time now, we must always be ready," he explained. "They envy us our abundance of wild rice and our land. For years they couldn't find our new home. But once they did, they sneak about like the ugly snakes they in truth are."

An involuntary shudder coursed through Danette. Duluth was at least a haven against the Sioux. They hadn't dared cause trouble for years now. The thought of living so near such savages gave her more reason to fear this place where the man she loved would one day make his home. She wondered if she could ever learn to accept his way of life, no matter the strength of her love for him!

She stepped before the fire and warmed her hands over it. "Now that we are in this cave, *why* are we?" she asked, once more looking guardedly toward the rifles.

"We will have our own private feast," Gray Wolf said hoarsely, placing his hands to her shoulders to urge her around to face him. "The moon is bright this night. I will

160

go and kill a deer to offer you as a gift, to prove my sincere love for you."

He drew her roughly into his arms and kissed her fiercely, enflaming Danette's insides anew. She laced her arms about his neck and moved her body into the curve of his, adoring the feel of him against her. She twined her fingers through his hair . . . she shot her tongue out to taste even more the sweetness of his kiss. Slowly . . . rapturously . . . all her doubts, all her fears, were dissolving into a pure delight at his nearness and the mystique of him.

Then he suddenly set her free, his eyes dark and passion-filled as he reached for a bow and arrow. "Gray Wolf won't be long," he said.

He gestured toward a blanket stretched out beside the fire. *"Ee-shqueen,"* he said forcefully. "Stay and I will soon return with a *wah-wah-skay-shee.* The strawberry moon will guide my way."

As though in a hypnotic trance, Danette lowered herself to the blanket and watched him disappear around the bend in the cave. But the ensuing silence shook Danette quickly from her enchantment with Gray Wolf, making fear slowly creep back over her. Had she ever felt so alone, so vulnerable, as now? Surely she was too far away for anyone to hear her should something or someone decide to take advantage of her.

"Longbow . . ." she whispered, trembling at the thought. "What if he saw Gray Wolf leave?"

The glare from the guns caught her eyes. She rose to her feet and moved slowly toward them. The shine of one settled in her eyes, causing her to flinch. Then she laughed nervously to herself and reached for it, grimacing when the cold of its steel barrel came in contact with her fingers.

But she felt the need for such protection and knew that she would indeed use it, if so required!

Checking to see if ammunition was in place in the gun's chamber, she sighed with relief when she found that it was, and went back and settled down on the blanket, the rifle lying protectively across her lap.

The dripping of water, the whine of the wind as it blew around the cracks and crevices of the cave's wall, and the crackling of the fire all kept Danette's senses keenly alert. She kept her eyes focused in the direction of the cave's entrance, her view impaired by the bend in the wall.

A crunching noise drew her to her feet. Someone was moving toward her on the loose rock of the cave's floor. The hair raised at the nape of Danette's neck as the footsteps drew closer and closer. Gray Wolf hadn't been gone long enough! It couldn't be he!

Raising the rifle's barrel, poising it with her finger trembling on the trigger, she breathlessly waited. Longbow would not have the opportunity to place his hand up her skirt again!

When Amanda stepped into view, Danette sighed heavily and quickly lowered the barrel of the rifle. "Good Lord," she said, shaking her head back and forth. "Amanda, I never dreamed it could be you."

"Who did you expect?" Amanda asked, going to lift the rifle from Danette's hand. She inspected it. "God. It is loaded," she gasped, then eyed Danette questioningly. "Red Fox and I saw you and Gray Wolf come to the cave. Where is he now? Why are you here alone?"

"Gray Wolf left. He said something about offering me a special gift. He's gone to shoot . . . a . . . a . . . deer."

"A gift? A deer?" Amanda said, only barely audible. A soft color of pink rose to her cheeks. She hurriedly placed the rifle with the others, then whirled around and took one of Danette's hands. "Come on, Danette," she urged. "We've got to start back for St. Paul tonight."

As Amanda began walking away from the fire, half pulling Danette along behind her, Danette softly argued . "But Gray Wolf—" she said. "When he finds me gone . . ."

"We'll leave word for Gray Wolf," Amanda argued back.

"But why must we leave now? Tonight? I thought we were returning tomorrow."

"One of my Indian friends from St. Paul just arrived here a short while ago. He brought me word that my aunt has worsened," Amanda said. "I can't wait for morning. Gray Wolf will understand. Please don't worry about him."

"I'm sorry about your aunt," Danette said, stumbling through the darkness of the cave, wishing Amanda had brought the torch. Though it was necessary to return to St. Paul earlier than planned, Danette thought Amanda had acted much too quickly after she had heard where Gray Wolf had gone.

"She takes bad spells," Amanda sighed. "One of these days, there will be one spell too many and she will be gone."

"She's such a lovely lady."

"She is quite a unique person. There could never be another Aunt Rettie," Amanda said, stopping to make her way through the profusion of growth at the cave entrance. She helped Danette out into the moonlight, then said, "You didn't tell me. Who were you expecting with the rifle ready and aimed?"

Danette's face flamed with embarrassment, not wanting to tell anyone about her unfortunate incident with Longbow. It was bad enough that Gray Wolf had to know! "No one especially," she said. "I just didn't like being left alone in the cave. That's all."

"Nothing would have happened to you in the cave," Amanda said. "If Gray Wolf left you there alone, he surely alerted some of his braves to watch the cave." She hurried Danette away from the cave, toward the village.

Danette looked about her, seeing nothing but the shine of the St. Croix River and the shadows from the trees. "I see no one," she murmured.

"You wouldn't," Amanda said, laughing throatily. "We must hurry now and say our goodbyes to Lorinda and Yellow Feather."

Danette held back from Amanda. "I must wait for Gray Wolf," she said, looking desperately about her. "I just can't disappear on him. What will he think of me?"

A movement in the darkness caused Danette's heart to lurch. Then a slow smile crept onto her face when Gray Wolf stepped boldly out of the shadows. But her smile was short-lived when he went to her and pulled her angrily away from Amanda.

"You didn't stay in cave," he growled. "Why did you leave?"

Feeling the pressure of his fingers on her wrists, hurting her, Danette tensed and desperately searched his face. Anger was written in his eyes and his jaw was firmly set. Which feeling was most prominent, hurt or anger? She could not tell. They each were fused into one.

"Amanda's aunt," she said, blinking her eyes nervously. "She has worsened. We must leave for St. Paul tonight."

"My gift of deer waits for you in the cave," Gray Wolf said hoarsely. "You cannot accept it now?"

"I'm sorry, Gray Wolf. Please understand."

"Amanda, my gift . . ." Gray Wolf said, frowning toward her. "You know of its importance."

Amanda smiled nervously. *"Ay-uh,"* she said. "But, Gray Wolf, I must return to St. Paul and Danette must return with me or my aunt and I could be in a lot of trouble. Danette's uncle is a very powerful man. Please understand. There will be another time for you and Danette. Surely you know this."

Gray Wolf drew Danette next to him, imprisoning her there. He spoke gently into her face. *"Ay-uh,"* he said. "There will be another time. You my woman." He lowered his lips to hers and kissed her sensuously and long, then released her and strolled quickly away from her.

Dazed, with a nervous heartbeat, Danette watched him until the shadows of night swallowed him up, then she looked toward Amanda. "What *is* the importance of this gift he was ready to offer me?'' she asked. ''Amanda, it was only a deer.''

''Lorinda was offered the same sort of gift and she accepted it, also not knowing its true meaning.''

''What do you mean, Amanda, by saying 'true meaning'?''

''Had you accepted the deer and shared it with Gray Wolf after cooking it, you would have been partaking in your marriage rites.''

Danette's insides took on a numbness. ''Do you mean that we . . . ?''

''Yes. Had I not intervened, by morning you would have been Gray Wolf's woman in every sense of the word. You would have been his wife. . . .''

Danette turned and looked toward the cave, speechless.

Chapter Eleven

That 'twas Heaven,
Just to be with you.
—Cory

The morning sun shone in wavy rivulets of crimsons and purples through the branches of the trees. Danette leaned up on her elbow, awakening with a start. Glancing quickly about her, she then remembered. A portion of the night had been spent in traveling and a portion in sleeping.

Her thoughts turned to Gray Wolf. Oh, how she already missed him. Yet a part of her was relieved to be away from the Indian village. She was torn with feelings about what Gray Wolf had almost succeeded at doing. Had Amanda not stopped him . . . in Gray Wolf's eyes Danette would now be his wife.

Looking over at Amanda, still asleep beneath a blanket, beside the dead ashes of their campfire, Danette hesitated to awaken her. Amanda had been so restless with worry about her aunt, she had taken forever to get to sleep. And though Danette was eager to move on out of the dark shadows of the forest, to return to civilization as she had always known it, she decided to let Amanda sleep until she woke up under her own volition.

Having seen a creek close by, Danette rose quietly from her own blanket. She shook her hair to hang long down her back and straightened the lines of her crumpled skirt and began pushing her way through the thick, tangled under-brush. Wild berries were trailing over alder branches, filling the air with a sweet, heady fragrance. Some lacy moss climbed the base of a tree. And, with the need to refresh herself, Danette lost her sense of fear. Everything was too peaceful . . . ah, so calm.

Disturbed by her presence, a deer started from the thicket and the trees came to life with birds calling out overhead, causing Danette to slow her pace and look carefully around her. For a moment there, she had felt another presence, but, seeing nothing that represented a threat to her, she moved on toward the sparkling shine of the meandering creek and fell to her knees beside it.

Through the translucent water she could see tiny minnows darting about, around and over pebbles and stones. A water spider moved along the water's surface in a jerky, skipping fashion, away from Danette's leaning shadow, leaving the water clear for her to lower her hands into it, to relish its cool, refreshing touch against her flesh.

Cupping her hands, she filled them with some water and leaned her face lower to splash the water onto it. Shivering from the icy coolness of it, she held her head back, shook her hair to hang farther down her back, and wiped her face free of most of the water with the palms of her hands.

A movement in the brush behind her made Danette's eyes widen and her heart lurch. Then she laughed awkwardly and spoke Amanda's name, thinking it surely was she. Upon awakening, seeing Danette gone, Amanda would have become momentarily frightened and would have come immediately in search of her.

"Amanda?" Danette repeated, slowly turning her head around. "Why don't you answer . . . ?" She then lost her balance and fell sideways when she saw not Amanda standing there, but the dreaded Indian, Longbow.

"Good Lord . . ." Danette gasped, growing numb with fear. She slowly pushed herself up from the ground, looking desperately around her for something to grab, to use for protecting herself. It was apparent that Longbow had followed and had been there all along, waiting and watching just for the moment that she would separate herself from Amanda and Amanda's rifle, to then finish what he had started with Danette . . . only . . . yesterday.

Longbow raced toward her and was there clasping his hands over her mouth so quickly, she didn't have time to yell for Amanda. With her wrist twisted painfully behind her back and Longbow's fingers still squeezing her lips closed, Danette wasn't in any position to struggle free.

Looking wildly up into the dark abyss of his eyes, Danette saw a cruel hatred and wondered why!

"Gee-mah-gi-ung-ah-shig-wah," he growled into her face. He jerked her close to his side and forced her to walk next to him, toward the thicker trees of the forest. *"Mah-bee-szhon,"* he said, once more in Indian, twisting her wrist even more tightly behind her.

Fear and pain fused together inside Danette's brain, making her flinch. Her heart raced . . . her legs began paining her as sharp briars began ripping at her skirt, to then enter her tender flesh.

"Gray Wolf not stop Longbow this time," Longbow laughed, bitterness ugly in its edging of his words. When he reached his horse, he removed his hands from Danette and shoved her roughly toward it.

"Why are you doing this to me?" Danette asked, rubbing her wrists. "Why me?"

"No talk. Just ride," he grumbled, gesturing toward his horse.

"I won't go with you," Danette said, boldly backing away from him, then broke into a run, panting wildly as she heard him close behind her.

Briars grabbed at her . . . low-lying limbs persisted in being in her way . . . and her side was beginning a slow, gnawing ache as she still managed to stay ahead of Longbow.

If it had been Gray Wolf in pursuit of her, she knew that she would have been overcome by him long ago. But Longbow wasn't Gray Wolf in any respect. He was a much smaller man, whose face held no emotions of love or respect for anyone. . . .

Seeing the spot where she knew she would find Amanda, hoping that she was now awake, Danette forced her feet to move onward, though she was so breathless now she was finding it hard to go on. She couldn't even yell Amanda's name, to alert her. . . .

Suddenly the birds in the trees rose with a clamor as a gunshot rang out over Danette's head. She stopped short, seeing Amanda there, with gun poised, again ready to shoot.

"Amanda, Longbow . . ." Danette panted, pointing behind her, turning her head, feeling a rush of blood to her face when she saw Longbow only a few yards behind her with a knife in his hand, raised.

Another shot rang out, and Danette saw Longbow wince as he dropped the knife to the ground, and then her stomach churned when she saw him grab at his wrist, which now had a stream of blood rolling from it, down to the ground, making a pool of red at his feet.

Covering her mouth with her hand, Danette pushed her way on through the briars and finally made it to Amanda's side, panting even more fiercely. "Thank God, Amanda," she said. She turned and looked at Longbow, who was still standing there, glaring towards them, with Amanda holding him there with her rifle still threateningly pointed toward him.

"Longbow, what in Heaven's name are you up to now?" Amanda asked incredulously. "What do you want with Danette? Is it because of Gray Wolf? Do you still want what is his? All your life you've been jealous. When will you ever learn that nothing of Gray Wolf's will ever be yours? It is meant for you to be only Longbow . . . not Chief Longbow."

Longbow squeezed his wound tightly with his other hand, finally succeeding in stopping the blood flowing from it. "White Blossom, you will pay for this," he growled. "One day, you will see."

Amanda laughed throatily. "Longbow, do you think you could ever scare me? You're no threat to anyone except yourself, especially when you play dangerous games, like trying to steal Gray Wolf's woman."

"Me go. But Longbow will one day make you pay," he growled. He turned and began running back into the forest toward his horse.

Amanda raised the barrel of her rifle toward the forest ceiling, and once more a shot rang out, causing Danette to jump with a start. She eyed Amanda speculatively, then gazed back in the direction of Longbow, who had stopped in his tracks and was now slowly turning around to face his two captors.

"Do you think I will let you go now so easily?" Amanda asked, walking slowly toward him with her rifle now pointed toward Longbow's abdomen. She nodded toward Danette. "Did you see where his horse was reined?" she said in a low voice.

"Why, yes, I did," Danette said, inching along beside Amanda.

"Go to the horse. Check it over for more weapons," Amanda said dryly. "We've got to make sure that Longbow is left with no weapons. We wouldn't be safe if he was let go with some way to make his threat good now."

"I'll go ahead and remove his rifle," Danette said. "That should do it, don't you think?"

"You'd better also check his saddlebag."

"All right."

Danette ran a wide circle around where Longbow still stood glaring. Then she once more found herself battling the sticky briars and tangled underbrush. She scanned the area with her eyes, looking for the horse. She hadn't realized just how far she had run to get away from Longbow, but finally she reached the horse and first searched in the saddlebag, surprisingly finding another sheathed knife and a derringer. On the back of his saddle he had positioned a bow and a quiver of arrows, and at the side of the saddle a rifle had been placed in its leather gunboot.

Shuddering, realizing that Longbow *was* well enough equipped to have returned to kill them, Danette quickly removed each of his weapons and began making her way back to where Amanda waited, holding Longbow still in check with the aim of her rifle. She moved on around Longbow, watching him out of the corner of her eye, then went to stand beside Amanda.

"I see he had an arsenal," Amanda said, laughing lightly. "Well, he at least won't get a chance to use them on us."

"White Blossom, Longbow always think you more man than woman, now I know it's true," Longbow grumbled. "And one day you will die like a man. Long and painful."

Fear gripped Danette's heart as she looked quickly toward Amanda. "Amanda," she whispered. "Is he . . . ?"

"He's only tryin' to scare me," Amanda said with a jerk of the head. "But he's no threat. Never."

Amanda went to Longbow and nudged him in the ribs with the barrel of her rifle. "Get along with you," she laughed. "At least wounded and without any weapons you'll be botherin' nobody else for a while."

Longbow spat at her feet, then turned and began running away, further into the forest. Danette watched until he was gone from sight, then moved to Amanda. "I'm afraid that one day he might do something terrible to you," she said, shivering. "What you have done today is something he will always remember."

Lowering her rifle, Amanda began walking toward their burned-out campfire. "Yes, he will always remember," she said. "What I have just done to him is worse than anything anyone else could have done. It is even worse than another Indian brave clipping his braids after a battle.''

Danette moved alongside Amanda, still laden down with Longbow's weapons, feeling strangely awkward with them resting in the crook of her arm and in her hands. ''What do you mean, clipping braids after a battle?'' she questioned.

''If one Indian brave clips the braids from another during or after a battle, it shames the brave whose braids have been taken,'' Amanda said, collecting the blankets from the ground, rolling them into a tight, neat roll. ''If my guess is right, Longbow won't ever ride into Chief Yellow Feather's village again. He will be too ashamed. He will be afraid that I have told what I have done to him.''

''Doesn't that make you worry even more that he will seek vengeance for what you've just done to him, Amanda?''

Amanda straightened her back and placed her hands on her hips, looking to Danette like Amanda's Aunt Rettie must have looked in her youth.

''I've always been able to take care of myself,'' Amanda said dryly. ''And Longbow knows this. He won't try anything with me.''

''But he does appear the type to sneak around to do things behind people's backs,'' Danette said, placing all the weapons on the ground beside her horse. ''I wouldn't trust him, Amanda. He could sneak up on you sometime and kill you quicker than you could blink an eye.''

''Like I said. I'm not afraid,'' Amanda said, shrugging. She began tying the blanket rolls on the backs of the saddles. ''But I do feel sorry for his mother, Foolish Heart. She's all crippled up with some sort of disease, and she depends entirely on Longbow to do the planting and harvesting for her. If he doesn't go back to the village, I don't know what will happen to her.''

''Won't the rest of the tribe help her?'' Danette asked, gathering up the rest of the camping gear, placing it all inside her saddlebag. "The Indians seem a compassionate lot. Except, of course, for Longbow."

"Foolish Heart is not like the rest of Chief Yellow Feather's people," Amanda said, picking up all of Longbow's weapons, finding space for them on her horse. "She has lived a life of isolation for many years now. It's a long story. And not a very pleasant one to tell."

"Do you mean . . . she could even die . . . alone and hungry?"

"That's quite possible," Amanda said, now standing, looking around, seeing if anything had been left behind.

"But, your sister . . . Lorinda . . ."

"Lorinda has learned the ways of the Indians," Amanda said. "As I have also done, though most of my life has been spent with my aunt. If it is meant for Foolish Heart to die alone, so be it. Lorinda would not intervene."

"But that would be cruel. . . ."

"As I'm sure some ways of the white people seem cruel to the Indians," Amanda said matter-of-factly, mounting her horse. She motioned with a hand toward Danette. "We must hurry along. We can worry about eating once we arrive in St. Paul. It is best that we put many miles between us and Longbow."

"But he has no weapons . . . and I thought you weren't afraid of him. . . ."

"It just occurred to me that he might have some friends lurking close by," Amanda said, looking cautiously about her. "It has been rumored that he has made friends with the Sioux."

"The . . . Sioux . . . ?" Danette gasped, feeling as though a cool breeze had traveled up and down her spine. "But if it is known that he has taken sides with the Sioux, how on earth has Chief Yellow Feather allowed him in the Chippewa village?"

"It is only rumored," Amanda said, smoothing some locks of golden hair beneath her headband.

Danette swung herself up into the saddle, having finally gotten used to it and the feel of it against her inner thighs. She grabbed her horse's reins and began moving along with Amanda beneath the widespread branches of the oaks, elms, and maples and onto the expanse of a wild flower-bedecked meadow. The sun felt good to Danette, who had become chilled clear through while sleeping in the dampness of the forest.

Continually glancing across her shoulder, listening for anything that might be the noise of horses following behind her, Danette was glad when they finally reached the gravesites of Amanda's parents. At least that meant they were somewhat closer to St. Paul. But then she couldn't help but remember that it was at this exact place many years ago that the Sioux had taken lives—and had taken Amanda as hostage. . . .

"Since time is of the essence, we won't stop at my parents' graves this time," Amanda said, her eyes wavering as she gazed toward the flowers that had wilted on the two spots of earth that were shadowed at this time of day by the gravestones.

"I hope your aunt is all right," Danette said.

"Like I said, she has these spells," Amanda said, wheeling her horse away from the fenced-in graves out onto the road again. "I only hope my note didn't cause this one. She's used to my doing these things. Surely my leaving had nothing to do with it."

"Maybe she was worrying about what my Uncle Dwight would do should he find out that I went along with you," Danette said, moving her horse next to Amanda's. "She was quite taken by my uncle, you know. He has the charm of a knight in shining armor. If only people knew him as I know him. He has many darker sides."

"I'm surprised at that," Amanda said, eyes wide. "He is quite a charmer and so handsome. Why hasn't he ever married? I would think the women would be flocking after him.''

Danette's features took on a pained look. "He likes for me to believe it's because of me that he's never married,'' she said. "He likes for me to believe he has given his all to the raising of me. But I know it's because of his political ambitions, and also to the making of money from his lumber business.''

"He seems to adore you, Danette," Amanda sighed. "Oh, if only I had such an uncle.''

"You do have a nephew. Gray Wolf.''

"He's too much a brother to ever be called nephew,'' Amanda said softly.

"You did have an uncle. I believe you said his name was Matthew?''

"He was elderly, like my Aunt Rettie," Amanda said. "And he wasn't my true uncle. He married my aunt quite late in life. They were only married for ten years when he died.''

"But you talk so fondly of him. . . .''

"He was a wonderful man," Amanda said. "In his youth he was a newspaperman. Even when he was older he tried his luck with a few articles for the local St. Paul newspapers. It was through him that I began reading the newspapers so avidly. It was through this foraging in the newspapers that I first read of your Uncle Dwight.''

"Amanda, you can think all the nicest things about my uncle, but I'm sure your stepuncle was just as delightful as you think my uncle is," Danette said. "It's a shame that your Uncle Matthew had to die.''

"I only hope that Aunt Rettie doesn't die just yet,'' Amanda said softly. "The world wouldn't be the same without her.''

They passed the rest of the trip in silence, and when they reached the outskirts of the city of St. Paul, Danette was made suddenly aware of how she looked. Long stares from men on horseback and women in carriages made her look down at herself to discover just how torn and mussed her skirt was. And her hair was just as unpresentable, because it hadn't had a brush taken to it since she had left St. Paul. It felt almost as tangled as the underbrush in which her skirt had become enmeshed when she was trying to escape the dreaded Longbow.

"Amanda, surely there are some backroads we can take," she said. "I do look a sight. I don't care for anyone seeing me like this. They will surely know that we've been up to something. Should any of my uncle's politician cohorts see me . . ."

Amanda reached her hand to Danette's arm and patted it fondly, as though she was once more mothering her. "I think that can be arranged," she said, laughing. "I guess it's best we don't let anyone see us like this. Aunt Rettie and my Indian friend, who delivers messages between Lorinda and Red Fox and myself, are the only ones who know I take these occasional jaunts to Chief Yellow Feather's village. Most people have grown used to my Indian headband, but I'm not sure if they would approve of anything else I might do with the Indians."

"Yet you do it frequently?" Danette asked, glad to now be on a less traveled road, lined on each side by smaller shanties, seeming to be inhabited by the poorer population of the city.

"As often as I can," Amanda said. "But now that Aunt Rettie is ailing even more than before, I'm not sure when I can return to visit my sister and Red Fox again."

"You will miss them, won't you, Amanda?"

"Without Red Fox, I only feel half alive," Amanda confessed, her eyes taking on a distant look, becoming many shades of blue.

"One day you will be able to be with him," Danette sighed. "As one day I hope to be with Gray Wolf."

Amanda cast Danette a guarded look, one that Danette

couldn't quite figure out. Then she remembered Dancing Cloud . . . and she wondered if Amanda had really forgiven her for having stood in the way of her Indian friend's happiness, and for possibly being the cause of her untimely death.

The two-story house of Rettie Toliver came into sight, directing Danette's thoughts quickly elsewhere. She grew tense, wondering what they might find there. Was Rettie dead? Had Uncle Dwight been informed of Danette's absence upon the death of Rettie Toliver? Many things scrambled together inside Danette's brain, one of them guilt for having sneaked away, instead of getting permission. It was not her custom to do anything underhanded, yet she recalled her one time with Gray Wolf at his wigwam, and she knew that that was where she had begun to change.

With the horses unsaddled and placed inside the stables, Danette and Amanda hurried side by side into the house, finding it gloomily silent and even a bit foreboding. The overpowering fragrance of lily of the valley cologne hung heavily in the air, waving them on, it seemed, down the narrow, quiet hallway, to Rettie's closed bedroom door. And just as Amanda's hand went to the doorknob, heavy footsteps and a stern voice drew her quickly around.

Janice Belt came lumbering down the hallway, her face lined with worry. "It's about time, Amanda," she scolded. "I don't understand why you do these things to your aunt. She's been worried to death about you."

Amanda and Danette sighed in unison, having promptly noticed that Rettie wasn't being referred to in the past tense.

"How is she?" Amanda asked, taking a step forward to meet Janice's approach. "I came as quickly as I could."

Janice's eyes traveled over both Amanda and Danette. She tsk-tsk'd, shaking her head forcefully back and forth. "You do not appear to be the young ladies that you were brought up to be," she further scolded, stopping with her hands on her hips. Her faded brown hair was pulled straight back from her face and held there with combs, and her face was devoid of color, as though she had never stepped out into the sun for even a brief moment.

"Janice, my aunt is your main concern. Please do not bother yourself with worrying about me or what I do," Amanda said, trying to keep her voice down, to not disturb her aunt.

"It was only this time, when your aunt became so ill, that she told me where you went," Janice said, tilting a chin haughtily. She then gave Danette a sour look. "And you? The niece of a famous senator? You also took to the wilds?" Her gaze disapproved of what she saw as she once more let her eyes travel over Danette. "Just look at you. Your clothes are even torn. What did you run into? A bear . . . ?"

Growing nervous beneath the close scrutiny and accusing words, Danette began inching away from Janice, eyeing the staircase. "Amanda, I will be up in my room," she said. "Please come and tell me soon how your aunt is."

Amanda reached for one of Danette's arms. "You can go in with me," she reassured. "Janice won't mind, will you, Janice?" She gave Janice a daring look, then turned on her heel and hurriedly opened the bedroom door.

Moving slowly into the room, Danette flinched. Mingled with the aroma of lily of the valley was a camphor-type odor, which seemed to prick the insides of Danette's nose. She felt her eyes watering and the urge to sneeze, but squeezed her nostrils together and held in her breath, until the urge quickly passed.

Then she looked through the semidarkness of the room, seeing that the dark green shade had been pulled at the one window. A kerosene lamp, barely lighted, sent a soft glow around the room, settling in deep shadows on the lifeless form on the bed. Loud snores arose from the depths of a layer of blankets where only the gray hair and wrinkled face of Rettie was visible from the chin up.

Something tugged at Danette's heart when she heard Amanda take in a deep breath and then let a sob rise from inside her throat. She watched as Amanda flew to the bed and fell to her knees, whispering Rettie's name over and over again.

Danette whirled around when Janice Belt stepped into the room and to Danette's side.

"She's pretty sick," Janice whispered, wringing her hands. "Seems this last spell has left her partially paralyzed. Now she can't even walk the least bit. I don't know what I'm going to do with her. When she's better she won't even be able to get to her rocker. The only way she's even been able to exist these past years was by watchin' the people from her parlor window."

"How terrible," Danette whispered back. "But maybe you can at least move her bed beside her bedroom window. Maybe she can be propped up on a pillow and watch from there."

A slow smile rose on Janice's face. "Land's sake," she said. "I've been so caught up in my takin' care of her and worryin', I hadn't even thought about doing that."

"If you would do it soon, maybe she would even improve more quickly now."

"Now that Amanda is back, Rettie will improve because of her," Janice said. "She always worries so about Amanda . . . especially when she's out in the forest. You know how Amanda's parents were killed."

Danette paled, yes, knowing all about the evil Sioux and what they could do to a person. Longbow wasn't even Sioux, and he had already caused her much trouble. . . .

"Yes, I know," she whispered back.

"Do you want to go over and see if Rettie wants to see that you are all right when she wakes up?" Janice asked, gesturing with a hand. "You see, this time she didn't only have Amanda to worry about, but also you."

"Yes, I know," Danette said, this time blushing instead of paling. "And, yes, I'd love to go stand beside Amanda so Mrs. Toliver can see me."

She smiled meekly at Janice as she stepped away from her, then went to stand beside Amanda as she rose from her knees. "Janice said that she's partially paralyzed," Danette whispered.

"God, no," Amanda said, placing her knuckles to her mouth, to bite down onto them.

Janice came to the bedside and stooped to straighten Rettie's blankets. "Rettie, Amanda is safely home," she said softly. "Why don't you open your eyes and see for yourself?"

The snoring became less and less and Rettie's right eye opened slowly while her left eyelid stayed closed. When she began to work her lips, only the right half of her mouth seemed to work. Her words came out all in a faint gibberish, yet one word was quite clear.

"Precious . . ."

Releasing her right hand from beneath the blankets, Rettie reached for Amanda.

"Yes, I'm here, Auntie," Amanda said, settling down on the bed beside her. "And I won't ever leave again like that. I'm sorry."

Rettie's hand went to Amanda's face and patted it fondly. "Precious," she once again managed to say. When Rettie's eyes found Danette also standing there, she managed a crooked smile, then her smile quickly faded when she saw Danette's disarray. She gave Amanda a long, questioning look.

Amanda had seen. She knew. Her aunt didn't need to speak. She placed a hand to her aunt's lined, leathery face. "It's all right," she said. "We just got tangled up in some briars in our rush to get back home to you. That's all. It's nothing to worry yourself about."

Though Danette had only met this woman, this beloved aunt, she knew that she was a wise woman, and could see that she would not believe Amanda's lies so easily.

Chapter Twelve

You kissed me! My head drooped low on your breast,
With a feeling of shelter and infinite rest.
—Hunt

Danette wiped her paintbrush dry on a cloth, admiring the completed painting of the Minnesota State Capitol Building. Surely even her uncle couldn't resist liking this painting. It reflected the pride of the Minnesota population, with its tall dome reaching up into the sky and American and state flags waving gently in the breeze. With a backdrop of blue sky and white fluffy clouds, the painting almost looked real enough for someone to walk up the Capitol's front steps.

Carefully placing her brush with her others, Danette leaned down on her knee and pulled another painting from beneath her bed. She removed the painting of the Capitol from her easel and stood it up against a wall to finish drying. Then she placed the other one on the easel and felt the soaring of her heart as she traced the classic Indian nose, then the high cheekbones so skillfully etched and then painted. But it was the eyes that were so beautifully real. They seemed to touch her soul as she stood there beneath their hypnotic gaze of emerald green.

Though Gray Wolf hadn't been there to pose for the painting in person, it had been from the heart that Danette had taken each stroke of the paintbrush, turning him into life for her to be near, if only on canvas. Two full weeks had now passed since they had been together.

Studying how she had succeeded at blending red tones into his hair, she tried to envision what it would be like to, indeed, marry him and live with the Indians. Had she seen loneliness in Lorinda's eyes? Would it be hard to learn the ways of the Indians? Wouldn't it in a sense be the same as being a newborn baby, being taught how to speak all over again? Though many Indians talked in the English language, there were so many who didn't!

Flipping her hair back from her eyes, Danette began slowly pacing the floor. There were so many things to consider when thinking of marrying Gray Wolf, one of which was the dreaded Longbow. He seemed to have made it his goal in life to make her miserable! Was it something truly to do with Gray Wolf? What had Amanda said . . . something about Longbow's being jealous of Gray Wolf?

A light tapping on the bedroom door drew Danette quickly around. Straightening the lines of her low-necked, blue-flowered dress, she went to the door and found Amanda there, dressed in her usual dark skirt and white blouse. But there was something else about Amanda this day . . . A paleness of sorts.

"Amanda, are you all right?" Danette asked, ushering her into the bedroom. "Is it your aunt? Has she worsened?"

Amanda sighed heavily and plopped down into a chair, placing a foot beneath her. She thumped her fingers on the arm of the chair, appearing to be deep in thought.

Danette settled down onto the edge of the bed and folded her hands on her lap. "Amanda, what is it?" she asked quietly. "Can I help in some way? You look so distraught."

"I haven't told anyone," Amanda said sullenly. She looked toward the open door, then rose from the chair and quietly closed it.

"You haven't told anyone what?" Danette persisted, lifting an eyebrow quizzically.

Arranging herself in the chair again, Amanda gave Danette a wavering stare. "Danette, I truly don't know what to do," she said in a near whisper. "Now that my aunt is worse, my dilemma worsens."

"Whatever are you talking about, Amanda?" Danette said, leaning forward.

"Red Fox and I have been waitin' for the right time, but now it's gotten way out of hand," she said, blushing. "Now we can't be together like I had thought. I must stay and see to Aunt Rettie. She has become pitifully helpless."

Amanda hung her head into a hand, shaking it slowly back and forth. "And there will be no disguising it from anyone any longer."

Danette rose slowly from the bed, eyeing Amanda even more closely. "Disguise?" she murmured. "What are you talking about, Amanda?"

"It's so hard to say," Amanda said, color rising to her cheeks in profuse pinks. "I haven't told a soul, except for Red Fox. Not even my sister knows."

Danette went to Amanda and placed her hand affectionately on her shoulder. "Amanda, whatever it is, you can tell me," she said. "Though we've only known each other for such a short time, I feel as though I could confide anything in you. You've been so understanding about Gray Wolf's and my relationship. If it would make things easier for you, tell me what's bothering you and I promise to not breathe a word of it to anyone."

Amanda looked imploringly up into Danette's eyes. "Danette, I'm five months pregnant," she said, letting her voice drop off to a mere whisper when the word "pregnant" was reached.

Danette was taken aback by the news. She dropped her hand to her side and couldn't help but let her eyes move to Amanda's stomach. There was no obvious swell there, yet Amanda had just said that she was five months pregnant!

"Red Fox and I shouldn't have waited so long. Now our

child will be born . . . in . . . shame," Amanda said, her head hung.

"Shame?" Danette thought to herself, which had to mean that Amanda and Red Fox hadn't married.

Not having expected this type of news, Danette was wordless. She swung around, hiding the blush of her cheeks from Amanda. What could she say? Amanda was pregnant with Red Fox's child and they had not exchanged vows. No. No one would understand. She could see just why Amanda had kept this a secret. Wouldn't she do the same herself . . . if she was pregnant with Gray Wolf's child out of wedlock?

Unconsciously Danette's hands went to her own abdomen and touched herself softly there. It could happen! She and Gray Wolf had been together in such an intimate way!

But, no. It was nothing to worry herself about. At this moment in time, all thoughts . . . all concern . . . had to be directed toward Amanda. What could she now do? Marry Red Fox! Yes! Immediately!

Turning slowly, feeling guilty for having reacted so to the announcement, Danette reached for Amanda and urged her up from the chair. It was time for Danette to do some mothering. Up to this point, it had been Amanda who had done this for Danette!

Drawing her into her arms, Danette hugged Amanda and tried to comfort her. "Amanda, what can I do?" she whispered. "I want to help you. If you want me to, somehow, return with you to the St. Croix village so you can exchange vows with Red Fox, I shall."

Tears formed at Amanda's eyes, something quite out of character for her! She blinked them back and swallowed hard. Then she stepped away from Danette, chin held haughtily up, showing that she was still the strong person she had always been, though feeling quite confused at what she should do now that things had suddenly changed in her life where her aunt was concerned.

"I will go to Red Fox alone," she said, touching her

abdomen, patting it, as though by doing so she could calm the tiny baby coiled inside her. "We will have the marital rites in privacy, and then I will return and have my child here at my aunt's house and raise it without Red Fox until . . . until my aunt needs me no longer. I cannot leave my aunt. Being partially paralyzed is even worse for her than death. So my abandonment of her at this time would only cause her mental anguish . . . something she does not need more of at this time."

A low sort of a growl surfaced from between Amanda's lips. She hit her fist into the palm of her hand. "I don't know why we waited so long," she said. "Time has a way of slipping on by, though. And Red Fox had said that he would come to St. Paul to live, to work in the flour mills. I had waited, hoping, but he never did, and now I know he never will. So my waiting for him has been in vain. It is now the time to make all these wrongs right. I will go to him this one more time. But it seems wrong that I have to do all the giving in to him. Yet I do know that he is not the strongest of the braves of the St. Croix of the Chippewa, and he needs my understanding, which I am willing to give, because I love him so much."

Danette studied Amanda's full figure, still confused at how well Amanda had disguised her pregnancy. "But, Amanda, you don't look at all pregnant," she suddenly blurted. "Five months? Usually at five months one's stomach is *quite* swollen with child. How have you managed so well to hide it from everyone?"

"Since I'm already quite fleshy, it helps to hide my pregnancy," Amanda sighed. "And I have taken it upon myself to bind my stomach with cloths. But it is gettin' much too miserable to bind myself in such a way for much longer. The truth will have to be told, even more than just my pregnancy."

"What do you mean, Amanda?"

"It will become known that my child might possibly be Indian, and that my sister Lorinda is married to an Indian."

"No one knows about Lorinda?" Danette gasped.

"Not too many," Amanda sighed. "People can be so cold and cruel."

"Yes, I'm sure," Danette said, thinking of her Uncle Dwight and his reaction to Gray Wolf. She had to know that in her future lay such complications, for she would marry Gray Wolf eventually.

Amanda went to the painting of Gray Wolf. With her fingers, she traced his chiseled features, her eyes once more misting with tears. "You captured him wholly on canvas, Danette," she said. "Just as you have captured his heart."

"My nights . . . my days . . . all of my thoughts are filled with Gray Wolf," Danette said, moving to Amanda's side, to also admire the painting. "I love him with all of my heart. And one day I hope to make him proud as I stand at his side as his wife."

"Don't wait too long," Amanda sighed. "If he chooses to make you his soon, agree. Life passes by much too quickly. Go with him. Share life with him. As you see, I am floundering in my way of life. And each day without Red Fox is a day lost to me, and now I have not even the hope to be with him soon. I do owe my aunt. . . ."

Heavy footsteps outside in the hallway and then a loud knock on the door made Danette swirl around to stare toward the door, though knowing who it was. No one but Janice Belt made such sounds when walking. It seemed that the floor might cave in beneath her, her steps were so pronounced and heavy.

"Danette, your uncle has just suddenly arrived," Janice spoke through the closed door. "He is downstairs, waiting to see you. He says he is anxious to return to Duluth, so put speed in your steps, child."

Paling, Danette placed her hands to her cheeks. She turned to face Amanda, then looked quickly at the painting of Gray

188

Wolf so boldly perched on the easel. "Uncle Dwight," she gasped. "He mustn't see this painting of Gray Wolf. He mustn't."

"I can keep it for you," Amanda said, showing a keen understanding in her eyes. "No one will ever see it."

"No," Danette said, shaking her head back and forth. "I must take it with me. It's as close as I can get to having *him* with me."

She scurried around the room, looking for a way in which to disguise it, to be able to take it to Duluth with her. Then she stopped and laughed softly. "I don't know why I'm fretting so," she said. "Uncle Dwight never shows interest in my work. Why would he now?"

She eyed the painting of the Capitol. "I can't even show him that," she said. "He might be so pleased, it just might make him ask to see more of my work, though it is wishful thinking on my part, I am sure."

She removed the painting from the easel and placed it on the bed, then gathered all of her other canvases from where they had been stored beneath the bed and made sure that the painting of Gray Wolf was well hidden between them. "There. That ought to do it," she said, just as Janice Belt opened the door with a jerk.

"Danette ... Amanda ..." she said sourly, glancing tight-lipped from one to the other. "Didn't you hear me speaking to you from outside the door? What are you two up to? Some sort of meanness?"

Amanda and Danette exchanged troubled glances, then both hurried to Janice and each took one of her arms and ushered her back out of the room. "No," Amanda said. "Nothing like that. We were just discussing the weather, weren't we, Danette?" She leaned forward, giving Danette a soft smile of forced innocence.

"Yes, the weather," Danette said, clearing her throat nervously. "It is such a beautiful day for a train trip to

189

Duluth. My uncle knows how to pick his days for traveling, wouldn't you say, Janice?''

Janice harumphed loudly and moved away from Amanda and Danette, hurrying down the staircase before them.

"Whew!" Danette said, brushing a row of beaded perspiration from her brow. "That was too close. Is she always so ready to barge into a room unannounced?''

"She has strange ways," Amanda laughed. "But she is quite good for my aunt. I don't know what we would've done without Janice. She's been quite a devoted nurse and companion. And she even knows her figures quite well, and keeps good ledgers for the boardinghouse.''

"Well, I'm glad I have only Amy around *my* house.''

"Amy?''

"She's my personal maid and my confidante.''

"Does she know about Gray Wolf?''

"Yes. She guessed right away when I became infatuated with a man," Danette said, still feeling the relief that had rushed over her when Amy had been so understanding when she found out that Gray Wolf was the man . . . and that Gray Wolf was an Indian.

No more words were exchanged. Uncle Dwight claimed their full attention as he nervously paced back and forth at the foot of the staircase. When he heard the footsteps approaching, he looked up into Danette's eyes, then met her approach, taking the steps quickly upward, to hug her into his embrace.

"So, I see the stay here has been rewarding for you," he chuckled, now studying her face. "You've even more color in your cheeks than before. And your eyes show a pleasantness.''

"I'm quite all right," Danette said, letting him take her elbow to guide her on down the stairs.

"So it was a wise decision, was it not, that I leave you at Rettie Toliver's boardinghouse while I tended to important business in Washington?''

190

"Quite a wise decision," Danette said, giving Amanda a quick glance.

"And how *is* your aunt?" Dwight asked, giving Amanda a lingering look, frowning when his eyes once more settled on her Indian headband.

Taking the last step, Amanda turned and eyed Dwight sadly. "Didn't Janice tell you?" she murmured.

Dwight reached a hand to his brightly printed bow tie, absently fussing with it. "Tell me what?" he asked, looking from Amanda to Danette.

"My aunt has worsened these past two weeks," Amanda said, nodding toward her aunt's closed door. "She had a spell, which has left her partially paralyzed."

"God. How terrible," Dwight groaned.

"But seeing you would perk her up somewhat," Amanda said, smiling softly up at him, once more taken in by his sleek handsomeness, and, yes, once more feeling guilty, especially with her pregnancy soon to be spoken aloud.

Dwight turned to Danette. "Perhaps you could pack your belongings while I visit with Rettie for a short while," he said. "But we must hurry. I've already gotten tickets for the next train to Duluth."

"I shan't be long, Uncle Dwight," Danette said, half curtsying. Then she was compelled to hug him, now realizing just how much she had missed him. Oh, she was always so confused by her feelings for him. First she loved him . . . then she detested him.

Again she hugged him, loving his aftershave and the crisp smell of cigars on his dark tailored suit. Then she gave Amanda a lingering look and rushed on up the stairs, breathless at the thought of returning to Duluth, and possibly to the arms of Gray Wolf.

Surely Gray Wolf would be through with the planting of the crops at his village and would have returned to Duluth. Surely he missed her just as much and would be watching for her return to her home! Oh, how she ached for him. She only had to close her eyes to feel his lips against hers, and his hands arousing in her such a feeling of delight that it seemed almost too sweet to be true.

Slipping the hatpin from her hat, then the gloves from her hands, Danette looked around her room, oddly feeling like a stranger there, though it had been her private room since she had first arrived to live with her uncle. But it seemed to her now that the past several weeks had changed so much in her life that what she had once thought to be the norm for her was forever transformed.

She now knew other ways of life. She could never return to the old ways, even if her uncle was there, a constant reminder of what life was supposed to be for her. She had to keep telling herself over and over again that she was a famous senator's niece. She was of the affluent class. She was . . . oh, sweet Lord . . . she was in love with Gray Wolf and couldn't refuse herself the lingering thoughts of him, or fail to realize how much she missed him.

Tossing her hat on her bed, Danette went to her bedroom window and stared dreamily from it. Not far from where she now stood was Gray Wolf's wigwam. Only a short ride in her carriage and she could be there . . . possibly in his arms.

"Danette," Amy spoke suddenly from behind her. "I hope it won't be too hard on you while I'm away tendin' to my brother."

Danette swung around and smiled toward Amy, feeling a tug at her heart, already missing her personal maid. It had come as quite a surprise when Amy had broken the news to her and Uncle Dwight upon their arrival back home from St. Paul that she would be leaving them permanently to go take care of her ailing brother, who was too ill to take care of himself any longer. And since he had no wife or children, Amy had been the only one he could ask for, though it would take her away from her weekly salary and the family she had adopted as her own. But Amy, with her big heart, had said yes, and was going to be gone by sunup the next morning.

"I'm sure Uncle Dwight will find someone to take your place quite soon," Danette said, hugging Amy affectionately. "And whenever you can return, you know your position will always be given back to you."

"Yes'm," Amy said, hugging Danette back. "That's what I was told before your Uncle Dwight rode off."

Danette's heart raced and her eyes grew anxious as she pulled free of Amy's arms. "Uncle Dwight is gone?" she said in a near whisper, looking toward the open door. "Did he say when he would return, Amy?"

"He said he would take dinner with you," Amy said, now fussing around the room, already organizing Danette's clothes in drawers and placing cologne and face creams on Danette's dressing table.

Danette rushed to Amy and clasped her fingers onto her shoulders, to draw her around to meet her beseeching eyes. "Amy, would you understand if I said that I had to also leave for a spell?" she said, waiting anxiously for an answer.

"Amy understands," Amy chuckled, raising a hand to pat one of Danette's. "You've been away from your man for too long. You want to go to him, don't you?"

"I don't want to hurt your feelings by leaving, since this will be your last evening with us for a time," Danette said, once more in Amy's arms, hugging her tightly. "I'm going to miss you so. I truly am."

"Amy'll be near for you when you need to talk, darlin'," Amy said, caressing Danette's back. "Only across town. You can come and talk anytime. You knows that."

Danette drew away from her and searched Amy's face for signs of hurt. "You really don't mind if I leave? Tell me the truth, Amy," she said. "I wouldn't hurt your feelings for the world."

Amy whirled around and began unpacking a valise, then motioned with her hand. "Shoo," she said. "Scat. Get on outta here. We can say our goodbyes tonight after dinner. Go to your man. That's more important than anything else. Your eyes are just a-sparklin', talkin' 'bout him."

Danette rushed to a mirror that was inset onto the back side of her bedroom door and posed, brushing her hair back from her rosy cheeks. She inspected her dress, seeing that its lines were straight and that the fully gathered skirt was lying perfectly away from the many layers of petticoats beneath it.

Then her fingers went to her throat. She ran her fingers across the smooth velvet of her exposed flesh there, dropping her gaze lower, seeing the swell of her breasts, wondering why they appeared to be larger. They even seemed at times to be hot and swollen. Yet this wasn't the time to wonder about such foolish things. Not with the chance to go to Gray Wolf. Time was short. The afternoon sun was already dipping too low in the sky. She had to time this right to return before her Uncle Dwight did.

"I will need my shawl and a bonnet, Amy," she said. She looked toward the boxed canvases on her bed, having to be sure her canvas displaying Gray Wolf was first hidden from view before she left. She wouldn't even chance showing it to Amy. This was hers . . . alone . . . to share only with her dreams of the future.

"And should you not make it home before . . ."

"I shall," Danette said determinedly, slipping the canvas from the box to place it behind the headboard of her bed while Amy was looking in the opposite direction. Then, breathing with relief, she gladly accepted the shawl and bonnet and quickly readied herself for her outing.

With a quick kiss on Amy's cheek, Danette flew down the stairs and out to the stables. Scoffing at the use of a carriage, needing the time that would be spent securing her horse to hurry up her escape, she, for the first time ever, placed a saddle her uncle had bought for only himself on the back of her tawny, sleek horse and swung herself up into it.

"If Uncle Dwight should see me now, oh, what would he do?" Danette giggled, clucking to the horse, leading him on out onto the angling streets of Duluth.

With the ribbon of her bonnet and the skirt of her dress whipping in the wind, Danette made her way up the steep streets until finally the straight stretch of meadow lay ahead of her, and beyond it the black depths of the forest.

A shiver raced up and down Danette's spine, as she realized the daring nature of this second visit alone to the forest, knowing that at any time she could be accosted by one or even more undesirables.

But her need to see if Gray Wolf had returned from his time at his village was stronger than her fear. She rode like the wind until she found herself again in the narrow lane, where shadows of the trees danced on all sides of her and the profusion of birds clamored overhead. When the clearing appeared before her, Danette's insides took on a strange queasiness. But she now understood this feeling ... this feeling of desire and endless love for Gray Wolf.

With a quickening pulse, she urged her horse even more quickly onward, glad now that she had learned how to ride horseback. It seemed that Amanda had taught her many things. . . .

A flush rose to her cheeks when she was finally able to see the wigwam. Though it was quite a warm day, there was a trace of smoke spiraling upward from the smoke hole, which had to mean that ... Gray Wolf ... was ... there!

Trembling, Danette rode up to the wigwam and dismounted, and, just as she turned around to walk toward Gray Wolf's dwelling, he was there, tall in his handsomeness, yet with a sour, brooding look, his arms stubbornly folded across his chest.

Attired in boots, jeans, and a cotton, plaid shirt, he was

apparently trying to return to the ways of dress that matched his white man's occupation.

Either way, Danette loved him with all of her heart. But she didn't like his continuing pouting manner as she slowly began walking toward him. She wanted him to rush toward her, to take her up into his arms, to carry her to his bed of blankets.

"So you have returned to your uncle's city?" Gray Wolf grumbled, his features still stern and lacking any signs of feelings for her.

Only his eyes could possibly give him away. Danette moved to stand in front of him and gazed into the emerald greens, and, yes, could see his passion for her lying in their depths. Perhaps only a kiss and then his stubborn Indian pride would melt away, and he would accept her now, while she could be with him, if for only the moment.

"Yes," Danette said, untying the bow of her bonnet. "We only just returned. And you? When did you? And did you get your crops planted in time?"

"Gray Wolf only just arrive," he said, without expression. "And, *ay-uh,* the St. Croix band of the Chippewa have planted their seeds."

Danette whipped the bonnet from her head and shook her hair to hang long and loose down her back. Then she slowly slipped the shawl from around her shoulders, revealing the nervous heartbeat in the hollow of her throat, and revealing even more than that to Gray Wolf as his gaze lowered and his arms came down to his side.

"Why have you come, Sweet Butterfly?" he growled, forcing his eyes upward. "You were anxious to leave my village. You did not share my feast I offered you."

Danette blushed, remembering the meaning of the gift of venison. "You know why, Gray Wolf," she said, hoping her eyes would not waver as he continued to hold her in place with the force of *his* eyes. "Amanda had to return to her aunt. She was ailing. You know that was the reason for

196

my goodbye to you. Otherwise, I would have stayed. Even if you had meant to trick me, I would have innocently stayed, and I would now possibly be . . . your . . ."

"Neen-gee-wee-oo," he said, interrupting her. *"Ay-uh,* I would have made you my wife by trickery, since you avoid becoming my wife in any other way. Your love not strong enough, it seems, Sweet Butterfly."

Danette reached out her hand and touched the smoothness of his arm, thrilling with the contact of her flesh against his. "My love is forever, Gray Wolf," she said softly. "I have come to you now, to prove my love for you. Please hold me. We are wasting precious time. My uncle will expect me back for the evening meal. Please understand that the time will come for us to never say goodbye again."

Unable to hold back any longer, Gray Wolf embraced her long and sweet, and, with a quivering to his lips, searched her face with sensual kisses, then found her lips and bore down upon them. A shiver of desire coursed through Danette as she fit herself into his lean, sinewy body. Wildly flinging her bonnet away, she let him sweep her fully up into his arms and carry her into the wigwam, where a lazy fire danced in the firespace and blankets were spread neatly over the bulrush mat flooring.

"You turn Gray Wolf's heart to liquid," Gray Wolf said huskily as he lowered Danette to the blankets. "No woman ever do this before."

His fingers were busy unsnapping her dress, and as he lowered it and her petticoats away from her his eyes feasted on the heaving of her breasts. As though magically drawn to it, he lowered his mouth to the ripe swell of a nipple and flicked a tongue around its hardness.

An euphoric state swept over Danette as the mushiness of her insides grew fiercely warm with building passion. She welcomed his lips on her other breast and then trembled as his lips lowered and his tongue circled her navel.

Aware of the many ways he could make love to her, this

afternoon Danette hungered for only one. "Gray Wolf," she murmured, breathing erratically as his head moved lower, "not in that way. Fill me, my love, with your manly strength . . . with your hardness . . . until I cry out your name in rapture." She reached her slender fingers to his face. "I want to feel it, my love," she murmured. "I want to drown in ecstasy. . . ."

Moving to his feet, Gray Wolf began to undress, too slowly, it seemed, as though making her wait would make her pleasure even more.

"Gray Wolf return to village for wild rice harvest," he said, tossing his shirt aside. "I will return no more to this place called Duluth. If you do not follow me then, you do not follow me at all."

A numbness caused a weakness to circle Danette's heart. "And when is . . . is . . . the wild rice harvest?" she asked, keeping her eyes from watching his jeans drop to the floor, exposing the part of him that caused such a drugged rapture to capture her soul.

"In the autumn, when leaves turn the color of gold and others turn so crimson they appear to be on fire," he said, tossing his jeans aside. "At that time, I will stay with my father's people. I will be there to help see to it that our band of Indians survives the long, cold days and nights of winter."

He pulled his boots off and dropped them to the floor, then knelt down over her. "But, Sweet Butterfly, I need you there to warm my bed," he said hoarsely, trailing his fingers across the gentle curve of her hips. "If not you, then perhaps someone else. With Dancing Cloud's death, I was crudely reminded how quickly life passes. And Gray Wolf will not live life alone. A woman will be at my side. Always."

The thought of Gray Wolf's embracing another woman made Danette turn cold, as though someone had splashed water on her from a mountain-fed stream. She leaned up on one elbow and stared into his blazing eyes. "You wouldn't . . ." she gasped. "You couldn't . . ."

"Sweet Butterfly says no too many times," Gray Wolf growled. "Wounded pride not become next-chief-in-line. Gray Wolf need woman to show father's people he is virile. A true man . . ."

He brushed his lips against her ear, whispering, "And Gray Wolf all man, as Sweet Butterfly all woman . . ."

"But, Gray Wolf . . ." Danette softly argued, trying to fight the sexual excitement building inside her.

"You have summer to make up mind," he said huskily, as he drove himself inside her, swiftly, surely. "Gray Wolf make love to you often. Sweet Butterfly won't be able say no."

"I must convince my uncle. . . ."

"Uncle cannot make your body tremble with passion," Gray Wolf said, kissing the hollow of her throat. "Forget uncle. Think only of Gray Wolf."

With a sob of pure joy, Danette twined her arms about his neck and clung to him, arching her hips to meet his every thrust. "Yes, yes," she whispered with a sigh. "There is only you, Gray Wolf. And when you are ready to leave for your village in the autumn, I will be at your side."

Gray Wolf kissed her with savagery, and together they climbed the stairsteps to ecstasy. For the moment, all seemed perfect in their love for each other. . . .

im like the pendulum of a clock. ''Raoul can
nt me to prove it, brown skin?''

's eyes narrowed and his jaw tightened. He
long enough to wipe perspiration from his
the sweat from running into his eyes to half
s coarse black hair lay hot and heavy against
s neck, and he felt quite confined in the white
jeans, and shirt. If he were back at his village,
he would be in only his loincloth!

no English?'' Raoul teased. ''Raoul learned
well.'' He gestured with a hand, smiling
? I use no French words when I communicate.

rned that the best way to deal with Raoul was
, Gray Wolf gave him a sour glance, smelling
's offensive odor, which emanated from his
t and the knit cap perched atop his head.

placed his back to Raoul, once more absorbed
He was making sure to cut close to the ground,
ting wood by leaving a high stump.

blow with the axe, and the wedge flew from
he tree. And since no other lumberjack was
Volf had to share the two-man crosscut saw
nd together they began laboring, working the
p'' back and forth against the white pine's

had purposely chosen this white pine. It was
rable tree for lumber because it was tall, soft,
d longlasting. Though having yet to win favor
Thomas, Gray Wolf still worked hard, mainly
an Indian's ways of working were anything

e began to groan and creak, Gray Wolf and
d back away from it with their saw, and both
ng out in unison, shouting, ''Tim . . . berrrr . . .''
ent crashing to the ground.

Chapter Thirteen

Oh! Love is like a rose,
And a month it may not see,
Ere it withers where it grows.
—Bailey

August. A hot month, though usually in Duluth one could
at least expect a breeze from Lake Superior.

With the parlor windows open wide, Danette tried to busy
her fingers with embroidery, to make at least an honest effort
to please her Uncle Dwight before springing the news of
her upcoming departure from Duluth and her eventual marriage to Gray Wolf.

Oh, how often she had tried to have the courage to tell
him! But the words had always seemed to freeze on the tip
of her tongue. And as each day passed, the task had grown
no easier. She just knew that he would never understand,
and she now even thought that she might have to leave
without telling him!

''But that would be so unfair to him,'' she whispered,
quietly ouching as she pricked her finger with the clumsiness
of her needle.

Throwing her head back against the high-backed soft
velveteen chair, she closed her eyes and sighed. She began
fanning herself with her embroidery piece, counting the
minutes until she could once more sneak away and meet
with Gray Wolf. The summer had been filled with many such

rendezvous ... and, luckily ... without further interference from her uncle.

"Uncle Dwight just continues to involve himself in things other than myself," she further whispered aloud to herself. "Perhaps my absence will mean nothing at all to him. At this stage in his political career, I am probably even in his way."

The clock on the fireplace mantel began striking, and when it sounded out the lazy, long hour of noon, Danette's eyes sprung wide open. She had promised to meet Gray Wolf at his wigwam shortly after noon. Working in the forest so close to his wigwam had made it easy for him to break away to meet with her, for it was never possible for her to leave home during the evening hours. Her Uncle Dwight's questions would be many ... and his suspicions would once more be aroused.

Dropping her needlework on the chair, Danette rushed to a mirror out in the foyer. Yes. She was presentable enough with her cotton dress without petticoats beneath it and her hair combed back and held in place by combs behind her ears.

Seductively low, and much cooler that way, Danette's bodice revealed her even fuller breasts, puzzling her more and more each day. Did gratification in love cause one's breasts to mature so? Or was it something else that she was yet to understand? Her awareness of her own feelings had greatly increased since she had met Gray Wolf, most of the time leaving her with a dreamy sort of lightheadedness that kept her head in the clouds at all hours of the day and night.

Leaning closer to the mirror, Danette let a soft giggle emerge from her throat. "There's no need to pinch my cheeks for added color," she whispered. "The thought of being with Gray Wolf does this readily enough for me."

Not having Amy or Dwight to account to, with only a substitute personal maid who had not yet learned ways to fuss over her, Danette was free to leave without notice. And,

this being the case, she hurrie
soon was on her way to wha
rendezvous with Gray Wolf.
month of September would show
leaves, and it would be then that
to her old way of life and say h

The men called foresters, who
the woods before the loggers to
be cut, had come and gone. Gray
fellers were now hard at work cutt

Gray Wolf had become an exper
knowing how to drop a tree exactly
could avoid striking other trees or hit
break or damage the trunk of the fall

Standing back to study a tree, Gray
which way he wanted it to fall. After ey
began swinging his axe, striking heavy b
make an undercut, to cut a wedge-shaped
tree trunk.

Continuing to chop away at the tree trun
undercut on the side of the tree that he wante
the ground, he tried to ignore the sudo
side. Raoul. A hefty French lumberjack
to arouse a hate so deep inside Gray
almost understand the animal instinc
to listen to this man's abusive words

It seemed to Gray Wolf that the F
ment and tease—and not only Gray
brute with foul breath and a full
leave no one alone, boasting that h
thing better than anyone else.

"So the tree will come tumbli
eh?" Raoul laughed idly, swin

The sound of the thud echoed throughout the forest, causing deer to run from their cover and birds to rise from their nests. "We do good together," Raoul said, patting Gray Wolf on the back. "You not so bad after all."

Chuckling, Raoul pulled a watch from his front pocket. "I leave you now, Indian," he said, giving Gray Wolf a guarded glance. "I have duty elsewhere."

Glad to be rid of him, and having his own appointment to keep, warming inside at the thought of Danette waiting for him at his dwelling, Gray Wolf began clearing his prize of its limbs. He then let the "buckers" take over, to saw the trunk of the tree into logs twelve to forty feet long, before being skidded on drags to the central place in the woods, to be stored there until transported by oxen to the sawmill.

As Gray Wolf headed for his horse, he saw that many lumberjacks were busy branding the logs. This was necessary because of the countless individuals and companies cutting lumber. Each company had its own mark, so when the logs reached the mill they could be separated and credited to the proper owner.

"Soon I will leave all this behind me," Gray Wolf mumbled to himself. "The time to return to my people is near, to never leave them again."

He swung himself up into his saddle, wheeled his horse around, and directed it away from the confusion of the lumber camp. His heart beat like a drum, remembering Sweet Butterfly's promise to him. She was to return with him to his village, to one day share his glory as wife of the chief of the St. Croix band of the Chippewa! No words had yet been spoken of children, but Gray Wolf wanted many sons! He had felt such a loneliness as a child with no brothers to share in the hunt.

Ay-uh, there would be many sons born to him and his Sweet Butterfly, and what a feast there would be when news reached him of his first to be born. . . .

Danette was enjoying the breeze caressing her face, neck, and arms as her horse trotted toward the narrow lane that led to Gray Wolf's dwelling. Even the whipping of her skirt against her legs was giving her a relief of sorts. Yet she knew that one day soon she might be wishing for the warm days of August. When the winter winds howled and the snow covered everything with its blanket of white, would she be warm enough in her husband's wigwam?

Surely he would build her a house, as Chief Yellow Feather had done for his wife, she worried to herself. She needed the space not only for comfort, but for her paintings. This was the one thing in her life she would not leave behind. And she knew that Gray Wolf understood. Even more than that. He admired her skills and praised her for them ... something her uncle had never done.

Feeling, ah, deliciously free, Danette bounced leisurely in the saddle, anticipating the pleasurable moments ahead. In Gray Wolf's arms, she became a wild and wanton thing, experiencing with him a kind of savage innocence. . . .

Danette's horse whinnied loudly and threw its head to the side when suddenly a horseman moved out of the shadows of the forest, and toward Danette.

Having become reckless in her hunger to be with Gray Wolf, Danette had once again lost all sense of fear. But now . . . at this moment . . . fear came back to her, as she saw the burliness of this man, whose face was mostly hidden behind a beard and whose eyes were raking over her, quite visibly reflecting lustful thoughts.

Frantic, Danette eyed the narrow lane only a few feet ahead, wondering if Gray Wolf was yet at his dwelling, ready to defend her should she scream out his name.

But time was not on her side. She could move no farther. The man was already there, grabbing her horse's reins from her, and emitting a sort of growl mixed with an ugly laugh.

"Raoul finally get you for himself," he said, dismounting from his horse, and holding tightly to Danette's horse's reins.

"Please return my reins, sir," Danette said, trying to sound strong and courageous, though her stomach felt as though its bottom had dropped from it.

Raoul forked his heavy eyebrows and licked his lips hungrily. "Only after I get a taste of you will I let you go on to your love nest," he said. With force he jerked her from her saddle and pinioned her against him. "If you're good enough for an Indian then you're good enough for a Frenchman, wouldn't you say, pretty thing?"

His fingers were coarse and leathery as he placed them at her throat and let them then travel lower until they were inside her dress, cupping her breasts.

Danette was reminded of Longbow and how he had attempted to take advantage of her. And now another man? What did she do to invite such things to happen to her? And how did this man know of Gray Wolf, unless he had watched and had seen them together.

The thought of his watching her and Gray Wolf together sent sparks of anger into her eyes. "You unhand me," she screamed, flailing her arms and trying to kick him. Her skirt continued to get in the way.

"Kick all you want, but you won't get away from Raoul," he laughed, roughly leading her away from the road, on into the forest.

"Why me?" Danette cried, wincing as Raoul tightened his hold on her wrist, to urge her downward onto a thick bed of dried leaves.

"Why not you?" he said huskily, leaning down over her. He held her with one hand and worked with the buttons of his breeches with the other. "I see no other woman. You are here. Raoul is here. I need what you give Indian. Why be stingy?"

Danette raised a hand and struck him on the face, but his

207

thick whiskers had cushioned her blow. "You beast," she hissed. "If Gray Wolf doesn't find you to kill you then my uncle will. After I tell my Uncle Dwight . . ."

"You wouldn't dare," he chuckled. "Then I'd have to tell him you'd been meeting an Indian and letting him fondle your lovely little body."

Seeing the part of him now exposed that could give her anything but pleasure, Danette shuddered violently at the thought of what was just about to happen. A bitterness of sorts rose up into her throat when his free hand quickly whisked the skirt of her dress up. His large, rough hand began a slow exploration.

"You are so soft," he said, breathing hard. "Your skin is like the petal of a rose." He lowered his lips to her chest and kissed her wetly there, then tore her dress away from her breast with the sharpness of his teeth.

"Please . . . don't . . ." Danette pleaded, trying to push his head away with her free hand. But he just continued his assault, now sucking hard on her nipple, hurting Danette as his teeth then suddenly ground into it.

"And, now, my sweet," Raoul said in a growl. "Raoul can wait no longer. . . ."

Danette could feel the largeness of his manhood throbbing against her inner thigh and knew that soon he would be invading her, where only Gray Wolf had been.

"You just can't," Danette said, squirming and fighting again. But he was too strong. His body held her in place as his hand began guiding his sex closer and closer. . . .

Danette closed her eyes and tried to scream, but Raoul's lips were suddenly there, kissing her wetly. The vile smell of him was so strong, Danette's eyes opened wildly, still trying to push him away from her but not succeeding.

A stirring in the brush at her side and a flash of movement caught Danette's eye, and the next thing she saw was the shine of a knife as its blade moved downward and into the flesh of Raoul's left shoulder.

Raoul jerked clumsily away from Danette, yowling, clutching onto his bleeding shoulder, giving Danette room now to see Gray Wolf standing there with blood dripping from his knife.

"Gray Wolf . . ." she sighed shakily in a low whisper, quickly lowering the skirt of her dress. She began inching slowly up from the ground, watching Gray Wolf as he posed himself, ready to pounce on Raoul, if the need arose.

Raoul moved to his feet, glowering toward Gray Wolf. His shirt was streaked with blood, his breeches still unbuttoned. Fumbling, he replaced his shrunken sex inside his breeches and finally managed to get the buttons back in place. "You die for this, Indian," he growled. "No one gets away with making a fool out of Raoul."

"No one touches my woman," Gray Wolf growled back. "Frenchman, you're lucky I didn't plunge knife into your heart."

"You'd be much better off if you had," Raoul laughed. He began inching away from the forest, not even giving Danette a backwards glance. "I'll get you, Indian," he once more warned, then hurried on to his horse and rode away.

Gray Wolf bent and wiped the blood from his knife on some dried leaves, then replaced it inside his sheath. Then, heavy-lidded, full of a mixture of many feelings, he went to Danette and slowly drew her into his arms. "My Sweet Butterfly," he crooned. "You're too beautiful and innocent. All men want you."

Danette clung to him, trembling. "You always are there, to protect me," she murmured.

"You soon will be with me all the time," he grumbled. "All dangers will be no more. No man try to touch my wife. Then it would mean instant death . . . not just a minor wound in shoulder."

Drawing gently away from him, Danette looked down at her torn dress. "Look at what he did," she said. "How am I to even go back home? Everyone will see. . . ."

209

"I should have killed him," Gray Wolf growled.

Danette placed a finger to his lips. "Shhh," she said. "Let's talk no more of it. Let's go to your wigwam."

"But your dress . . . ?" Gray Wolf asked, lifting the torn flap and placing it over her exposed breast. Hate caused his eyes to narrow. "I shall kill him for this. One day soon . . ."

"And if you did, *you* would then be killed," Danette softly argued. "Do you really want to be lynched? Then how could I become the wife of the next chief-in-line?"

"Ay-uh," he said thickly, tracing her features with the tip of his forefinger. "You are right. Why make trouble in white community now? Soon you and I will both no longer be a part of it."

"Ay-uh," Danette said, giggling softly.

Gray Wolf let out a hearty laugh. "Indian word sounds good on your lips," he said, placing an arm about her waist. "One day you will know ways to say more than yes in Indian."

Danette welcomed his strong hands at her waist as he lifted her up into her saddle. "I will learn all your ways, Gray Wolf," she said, smiling down at him.

"Ay-uh. It will be so," he said hoarsely, mounting his own horse.

Gray Wolf rode on ahead of Danette, straight and tall in the saddle, watching cautiously on all sides, until they were finally safely inside his wigwam.

"No fire today," Gray Wolf said. "This day of August like fire itself. The rains have forgotten where to fall this summer."

He knelt over a basin of water and splashed some onto his face. Danette moved behind him and reached around him to unbutton his shirt, splaying her fingers across his flesh. She felt the usual sweet pain between her thighs, already needing him there.

With slow movements she removed his shirt, then urged

210

him around to face her. "I love you," she whispered, working herself into his arms, snuggling against his bare chest. She tremored sensuously as his fingers began working on the buttons at the back of her dress. And when his hand made contact with her flesh, caressing her back, she emitted a soft moan of rapture.

"You are more beautiful each day," Gray Wolf said, now smoothing her dress down, over her shoulders, and then her hips. His lips moved to her breast and kissed a nipple to tautness while his hands completed the task of disrobing her.

With soft, fluttering kisses, he moved his lips across her abdomen, then back upward to her lips, where she eagerly awaited him.

Locking her arms about his neck, Danette pressed her breasts against his chest, grinding herself more into him as her fingers worked with his jeans, to lower them. And when he was nude and she could feel the whole of him against her, she once more became euphoric in her love for him.

Wrapping a leg about him, she managed to draw him down over her as she stretched out on her back on the bulrush mats.

"Make me forget everything but you, Gray Wolf," Danette whispered, raking her fingernails over his buttocks as he positioned his manhood inside her. "Make my mind become a melting liquid. . . ."

"Your desire blends with my own," Gray Wolf said huskily. He flicked his tongue inside her ear and smiled when he felt her tremble and heard her sigh. "The spirits bless our union. They smile upon my choice of woman, or else they would not have brought me to your rescue, not once, but twice in the forest. The next time you are alone there, give thanks to them, my Sweet Butterfly."

"Yes," she murmured. "Yes, yes. I will."

His lips fell upon hers with savagery, and his tongue probed and found hers waiting. As their tongues played, so

211

did their bodies. Danette arched her hips, moving with his each and every thrust. Her fingers could not stay still on his body. While his buttocks lifted and fell, she placed her hands there and marveled at his muscled strength.

Daring, wanting to experience it all, now that she knew that his love for her was forever, she let her fingers search even more over the curve of his buttocks and around to the front of him, and once she found the vee of curly hair there, she cupped the part of him that lay like a sack and wondered even more about the softness of him.

Gray Wolf placed his lips against her cheek and emitted a throaty moan as Danette's fingers gently squeezed and explored this part of him that she had never touched before. There was such a mystery about a man and his body. But it was this mystery that seemed to heighten the pleasure that Gray Wolf was so skilled in giving.

Relaxing her hold on him, Danette leaned her mouth to the softness of his neck. The magical glow was burning higher inside her as his thrusts became harder and more frequent.

"Gray Wolf, it is so sweet," she sighed, trembling as her mind became giddy with the ecstasy of the moment as they once more succeeded in sharing the ultimate joy of release at the same time.

Perspiration glistened on both their bodies, their hair wet with their efforts. Gray Wolf eased away from Danette, laughing throatily. "We make heat as well as love," he said, wiping beads of perspiration from his brow.

"But soon we will wish for warmer days," Danette said, leaning up on her elbow to admire the man she loved. His copper-colored skin shone in its wetness and his hair was even darker, it seemed, than before. In the shadows of the wigwam, the red streaks were not visible. But the green of his eyes was quite prominent as he teasingly placed his face into hers, laughing softly.

"I will bathe you now, my Sweet Butterfly," he said. "I

have no perfumed oils, but I do have water.'' He kissed her gently on the lips. ''I will make you as fresh as a lily in a pond.''

''What . . . ?'' Danette giggled. ''You will what?''

''Just relax. Gray Wolf show you.''

Danette stretched out on the coolness of the bulrush mats and sighed leisurely as Gray Wolf squeezed cool water from a cloth onto the tips of her toes, then slowly on up her legs, to her inner thighs. She watched breathlessly as Gray Wolf placed the cloth back into its basin and began to massage her feet and legs sensuously with his hands, until all the water had been absorbed into her flesh.

Again he removed the cloth from the basin and smiled devilishly as he squeezed cool droplets from it onto her love mound. He spread her legs and squeezed even more water there, sending a shiver of delight up and down Danette's spine.

When he once more dropped the cloth and began to massage her where he had left the sparkle of water, Danette's insides grew deliciously weak with the feelings engulfing her, and she wondered how such a small spot on her body could cause such waves of sensation to splash through her.

Quivering, she welcomed his lips there, and in a flash she had once more been sent into another world of bright colors.

Opening her eyes, she smiled lazily down at him as he looked up at her still with deviltry in his expression. ''And this is the bath you mentioned?'' she giggled. ''Good Lord, Gray Wolf, if you don't stop, I'll be too weak to mount my horse to return home.''

''We could then leave tonight for my village,'' he said, rising to a sitting position. ''You ride on my horse with me.''

Danette's face took on a paleness. She rose from the mats and reached for her dress. ''No,'' she said, shaking her head. ''Tonight I have something else to do.''

''And what is that?''

"Tonight I tell Uncle Dwight about us," she said, buttoning her dress. "This must be the night. I know that I can wait no longer."

Gray Wolf stood and slipped into his jeans. "Sweet Butterfly shouldn't have waited so long," he grumbled. "Gray Wolf will leave. Soon."

"I know," Danette said, working with the rip of her dress, worrying about it. Then she went to Gray Wolf and twined her arms about his neck. "And, darling, thank you so much for understanding why I first have to tell my uncle about us. I am all he has."

"That not true," Gray Wolf argued. "He has himself. He is a man in love with self."

Danette laughed softly, kissing him affectionately on a cheek. "Yes, he is," she said. "But I don't think he's even aware of that."

"Gray Wolf follow you to town," he said, breaking away from her to slip into the rest of his clothes. "Men like Raoul are many in your uncle's lumber camp. I should have known you were not safe."

"Who is this Raoul?" Danette asked, stepping into her shoes. "He is such an ugly, horrible man."

"He is one nobody likes," Gray Wolf growled. "Forget him. He not bother you again."

"But, you?" Danette said, going to Gray Wolf, framing his face between her hands. "He threatened you. Will you be safe?"

"Did you not hear Gray Wolf also threaten him?"

"*Ay-uh . . .*"

"He is the one who should worry. Not Gray Wolf."

"But . . ."

"No buts," Gray Wolf said, lowering her hands from his face, gently kissing the palms of each. "Now you go. Tell uncle. We leave together soon for my village."

"Should he try and stop me . . . ?"

"Then I will just take you," Gray Wolf said flatly. "I

214

have waited long enough. No uncle stand in my way any longer.''

He stepped back and studied her torn dress. Then he picked up one of his other shirts and began to rip it apart until he had a long, narrow strip to hand her. ''Here. Drape this on your shoulders,'' he said. ''No one will even notice. It look like a cotton shawl. Anything to keep eyes from your body.''

Danette blushed and accepted the length of cloth. She did as he said and felt relieved that her breast was finally hidden from view. She leaned up on tiptoe and kissed him softly on the lips. ''Thank you,'' she murmured. ''You do seem to think of everything.''

''We will go now,'' he said. ''I will follow.''

''If you must . . .''

''I must.''

Danette went to her horse and swung herself up into her saddle, looking back toward the wigwam. The next time she would be there would be when she and Gray Wolf were readying themselves for their journey to his village.

With a blush of happiness rising to her cheeks, Danette gave Gray Wolf a smile over her shoulder, then rode on away, glad when his horse overtook hers and moved on ahead of her.

Soon they would be together for the rest of their lives! Danette now felt assured that nothing could stand in the way of their happiness. Even the thought of her Uncle Dwight no longer frightened her.

Chapter Fourteen

Out of a world of laughter,
Suddenly I am sad.
— Russell

Dwight leaned heavily over his ledgers, studying the figures. So far, this was the best year yet for his lumber business. If the figures kept in the black the rest of the year he could hire an assistant, then have more time to devote to his political aspirations. All of his responsibilities were taking a toll on his health. He knew this. But there was so much to do in this world of opportunities, and he wanted to do it all.

Slamming the ledger closed, Dwight rose from his chair and moved from behind his stately oak desk. He wore no tie or jacket today and even his shirt had been unbuttoned halfway to his waist. He lifted a half-smoked cigar from an ashtray, thrust it between his lips, and strolled to his office window. Being six floors up, he could see for miles and miles. In one direction he saw the shimmering waters of Lake Superior and in the other his beloved trees.

Raking a hand through his hair, he studied the leaves of the trees. Most were wilted. "Damn," he uttered to himself, pulling his cigar from his mouth. "How long has it been now since we've had rain? This has to be the dryest summer in the history of Minnesota."

He shook his head wearily. "One bolt of lightning could

erase my profits I might have even in the future," he continued to agonize. "If lightning strikes just one tree . . . as dry as it is . . . it would all go up in flames. Even Lake Superior's being so close wouldn't be of any help. The forest is too dry. It's as though it's already been baked!"

Dwight swung around and went back to his desk and plopped into his chair. He crushed his cigar out. "I won't think about it," he said. "I just won't let myself think about it. It can't happen. It can't."

A loud knock on his closed office door drew his attention away from his worries about forest fires and his ruined lumber business. "Yes? Who is it?" he said in almost a growl.

The door opened in a jerk, revealing an angry Raoul, his shoulder still oozing blood onto his shirt. "I must talk with you," Raoul said, rushing on into the room, clutching onto his wounded shoulder.

Dwight paled and rose hurriedly from his chair and went to Raoul. "My God, Raoul, what happened to you?" he gasped, stepping closer to get a better look. "How did this happen? It looks as though you've been stabbed."

"A damn Indian," Raoul growled. "There's got to be something done about those damn Indians you've got working side by side with us normal folk."

"How did it happen? Why did an Indian attack you? Did you provoke him in any way?"

"Raoul did nothing," Raoul spat angrily. "I was riding along and he pulled me from my horse and stabbed me."

"But why on earth would an Indian do that to you?"

Raoul slumped down into a chair, avoiding Dwight's eyes. He knew how smart this man was. He was a United States senator, wasn't he? Surely he could see a lie, if met head on. So Raoul had to be sure to be convincing! "It's the heat," he said. "It's got tempers up in the camp. And anything provokes a damn Indian."

Raoul glanced at Dwight, smiling when he saw a mask

218

of hate shadow his face. Yes, he had taken the bait, and there would be a lynching for sure. But he had to be careful. He couldn't let Dwight find out the true reason the Indian had attacked him. *Then* there would be a hanging all right. His. There was a strong penalty for rape now in Duluth. But only if one got caught. . . .

Dwight kneaded his chin. He walked back to the window and looked down onto the streets of Duluth. Suddenly he was reminded of Gray Wolf. It had been some time now since he had worried about Danette and the Indian. She had appeared content enough painting this past summer. "One battle won with an Indian, and now another?" he thought to himself. "But at least this one will not harm my reputation, with my niece no part of the quarrel."

Swinging around, he faced Raoul. "Do you know the Indian's name?" he blurted.

Raoul's eyes wavered. Though he knew the name, he was afraid to mention it. Somehow it could connect him with Danette and what he had tried with her.

No. No names. But faces! Ah, he would know the face!

"No," he lied. "But Raoul can point him out to you. Isn't that enough when a lynching is in the makin'?"

Disappointed that the name Gray Wolf hadn't been spoken, still feeling that to have that Indian dead would give him even more reason to breathe easily where Danette was concerned, Dwight frowned toward Raoul. "You work with the Indians and you don't know their names?" he persisted.

Raoul shrugged. "An Indian is an Indian," he said. "Most don't talk. Just grunt. How's one to know names when the savages don't communicate? Raoul know English well. The savages? Ha! All they know is mumbo jumbo!"

Dwight began fastening the buttons of his shirt. "All right," he said. "Just as long as you can point him out to me. I guess that's all that matters."

"Raoul can," Raoul said anxiously, rising to his feet,

letting out a loud groan when a sharp pain shot through his shoulder.

Dwight jerked a bow tie from his desktop and began placing it about his neck. He nodded toward Raoul's shoulder. "First you go and get that looked into," he said. "Then gather some men together and I'll meet you at the courthouse steps in a little while."

Raoul's eyes narrowed. "What you going to do before you go to courthouse?" he asked cautiously, worrying about Danette and what she might say to Dwight, should Dwight see her first. But surely Danette wouldn't tell him about what had happened. She then would have to tell him where she had been, and why. No decent woman traveled so far from the city alone.

"I must go home and warn my niece," Dwight said, fitting into his jacket. "She has a tendency to travel too far from home these days, to paint. You see, she's an artist."

Raoul paled. So she *did* have a reason to be so far from home other than to meet with the Indian! Damn! Would she tell? But it was a chance he had to take. He had to think that she would be too embarrassed by the incident. Then he had to smile broadly. If she told her uncle that Raoul had tried to rape her she in turn would have to reveal to him how it had then not come about! She would have to mention Gray Wolf's name, and then Dwight would ask how the Indian had just happened along!

Smiling, Raoul walked toward the door. "I will go to get my shoulder patched up, then gather together men," he said. "We'll wait for you at the courthouse just as you say."

Dwight nodded as Raoul walked from the room. He then hurried from his office himself and down the six flights of stairs and on outdoors. Swinging his leg over his horse, he suddenly thought of Danette and how she would take such a lynching.

"She has to realize that this attack by an Indian cannot go unnoticed by the community," he argued to himself. "If one Indian gets away with attacking a white man, then others could follow. It could cause unrest all over again in Duluth. No. I must see to it that no Indian gets away with anything like this, now . . . or ever.''

Danette sneaked into the house, relieved that no one was around to see her disarray. It was good to know that these days of sneaking about were drawing to a close. And she would not wait another moment once Dwight was home from his office. She would immediately tell him of her plans.

"But, oh, he will be so angry,'' she sighed, hurrying up the stairs. "He will never approve. What shall I even do?''

The afternoon had slipped by much too quickly, and Danette knew that she didn't have much time to make herself presentable.

"A bath isn't required,'' she laughed to herself, remembering the cool water that Gray Wolf had playfully splashed over her body.

"Ah, what a master at making love he is,'' she said, tossing aside the makeshift cotton shawl that he had presented her with to hide her torn dress.

As she undressed, she watched herself in her mirror, seeing how he had seen her, again marveling at the size of her breasts. Cupping them, she studied them even more closely, seeing their healthy, pink tinge. "My love for Gray Wolf has budded my breasts,'' she giggled.

Then she swirled around and gathered up her soiled clothes, discarded them, then chose another such cool dress, but this time one of a soft silk with braided tufts of satin at the bodice and the tightly drawn waist.

"My waist too?'' Danette whispered, standing sideways, seeing how the waist puckered at its seams. "I am also larger there?''

Shrugging, she hurriedly brushed her hair, fussing at its thick, natural curls. Then she tensed, hearing a horse drawing close by outside. "Uncle Dwight," she whispered, moving to the window, looking down from it to the gravel drive. "Good Lord, I just barely beat him home. Why is he always so punctual? One would think that his business affairs would at least delay him a bit."

But, breathing a sigh of relief that she was presentable enough to meet him at the door, she forgot how close she had come to not being home before him and rushed out of the room and down the staircase. She was standing there, hands clasped tightly together before her, when he stepped through the front door.

"Well. What have we here?" Dwight asked, going to Danette, kissing her softly on her cheek. "Standing waiting for your uncle?"

Danette placed her hand to his cheek as he kissed her, and kissed him back from the corner of her mouth, trembling inside, knowing the ordeal she had before her. But she had to do it now. She couldn't delay any longer. And what if that lumberjack went to Dwight and told him that he had seen her with Gray Wolf?

But, no, he wouldn't! she thought further to herself. He was raping me!

Swallowing hard, she stepped back from her uncle and began to speak but stopped abruptly when she saw a moodiness in his eyes that she hadn't seen before. And when he gave her a lingering, questioning look, she had to wonder what he had to tell her. She could see it coming in the way he raked his fingers through his hair. He always did this when he was disturbed about something. And she knew that it had nothing to do with her having been with Gray Wolf that afternoon, because he would already be outraged! He didn't spare words when speaking of Gray Wolf and her relationship!

So . . . what . . . was . . . it . . . ?

"Would you like a glass of wine, Danette?" Dwight asked, moving on into the parlor, to a wine decanter. He gave her a backwards glance as she followed him into the room. Then he poured a glass of wine and offered it to her, lifting an eyebrow in her direction.

"No. I don't care for wine," Danette said, settling down into a chair. "You know that, Uncle Dwight." She straightened her skirt and eyed him speculatively. "And, get on with whatever you have to say, Uncle Dwight," she quickly added. "I can always tell when you have something on your mind. What is it now?"

Dwight took the glass of wine and went and sat down opposite Danette. He crossed his legs and twirled the long-stemmed wine glass slowly around between his fingers.

"One of my men came to me with a wounded shoulder," Dwight began. If he had been looking toward Danette, he would have seen her grow quite pale, but, he, instead, was watching the sparkling of the red wine in his glass. "Raoul. He said an Indian jumped him and stabbed him with a knife," he continued.

Danette's heart fluttered wildly. She closed her eyes, sighing to herself. At first, she had thought he was going to say that Raoul . . .

She cleared her throat nervously and focused back on her uncle, relieved at least that her name was surely not going to be brought into the conversation or it would have already been!

But what was this mood he was in? Had Raoul said which Indian? And what was Raoul's purpose in going to her uncle? A numbness was slowly taking hold of her insides, and she dreaded to hear the answer.

"An Indian?" she murmured, trying to calm her hands on her lap by clasping them tightly together.

"Yes," Dwight said. "An Indian." He took a long, slow sip of wine, now looking at her over the tip of the glass. Why did the mention of an Indian cause such an ashen color to appear on her cheeks? Was Danette still friendly with that Indian?

223

"And why did an Indian ... uh ... stab this man, did you say his name was ... uh ... Raoul?"

"It was an unprovoked attack," Dwight said, slamming his empty glass down on a table, rising from his chair. He went to his desk and pulled a pistol from a drawer. He determinedly began fitting bullets into its chambers.

Danette slowly rose from her chair as she watched him loading his pistol. "What are you doing, Uncle Dwight?" she asked, inching toward him.

"We cannot let these things happen in our community," Dwight said, giving her a brooding glance. "No Indian can be made to think he can get away with such a thing or we can have more and more attacks and that could lead to much unrest and bloodshed."

He pulled a gunbelt from his desk drawer and began fitting it around his waist. "No. We will nip this in the bud. Right now. Then the Indians will know their place. We don't give them jobs for them to go around wounding the white men who work by their side."

"You ... mean ... to kill ... the Indian?" Danette said, wishing her heart would quit racing so. It threatened to drown her, it was thundering so against her chest! But what if Gray Wolf ...?

"Yes. Exactly," Dwight said flatly.

Danette shook her head, to clear her thoughts of how this could turn out.

"Which ... Indian ... Uncle Dwight?" she managed to say in a strained whisper, hoping that this evil man named Raoul would have forgotten Gray Wolf's name.

Dwight slipped the pistol into its holster, dropped a few more bullets into his front, right trouser's pocket, then turned and clasped onto Danette's shoulders. "No name was given," he said thickly. "And, Danette, I don't like what I see in your reaction to this thing I am about to do. You haven't been talking with Gray Wolf again, have you? I've

224

given you privileges to travel wherever you like, hoping that I could trust you. Have I been wrong?''

Danette knew that her time to tell him about Gray Wolf had to be delayed again! And, though this Raoul hadn't mentioned a name, he knew Gray Wolf well enough to identify him. Raoul even knew where Gray Wolf lived!

She had to go to Gray Wolf! She had to warn him! Everything had suddenly changed, and all because of this ugly man Raoul who in truth had been committing the wrong. Oh, if she could only tell Dwight that he had been raping her when Gray Wolf . . .

But she couldn't say the word "rape" to her uncle. She had somehow been guilty for causing this man Raoul to even want to rape her! She had disobeyed her Uncle Dwight by being that far from home! She had disobeyed him by going to Gray Wolf!

But that doesn't matter now, she thought to herself. I am going to leave with him anyway. I must do what I must. . . .

"Uncle Dwight," she said, following him as he moved out into the foyer, toward the front door. "I have something to tell . . ."

Dwight swung around and faced her. "Later, Danette," he said. "I have to hurry. I don't care to get caught out in the forest after dark hunting for a crazed Indian. And you stay put. Do you hear? You wouldn't be safe out on the streets now for sure!"

"But, Uncle Dwight," she said, rushing after him as he stepped on out onto the porch. "Please listen . . ."

Dwight turned on his heel and glowered toward her. "I said later," he growled. "Please do not pester me so, Danette. Not at a time like this. I've things to do besides listen to your babble—and what would it be about? Painting?''

He laughed sarcastically and took off in a run toward the stables, leaving Danette standing there, aghast at how crude her uncle could be at times. If she had even had the chance to tell him of the attempted rape, would he have listened? It was going to make him even more important in the community to lynch an Indian . . . a threat to the peace-loving people of Duluth.

"All he truly does care about is himself," she fumed, slamming the front door shut with a bang. Seething, she watched him ride away, then didn't stop to get a wrap, but went on outside and saddled and mounted her own horse and headed toward the forest.

The lane seemed longer and darker than ever before as Danette rode down it. She kept remembering Raoul and how he had suddenly been there. And it was because of Raoul that Gray Wolf's life was in sudden danger!

"I must get to Gray Wolf first," Danette worried aloud. "I must."

Her main concern was that he might not be at his wigwam, but in the forest, still laboring. How could she go to the forest to warn him? How would she even know where to look?

Looking toward the sky, Danette spoke a soft prayer. "Please, Lord," she whispered. "Let him be home."

A delicate breeze fell across her face, calming her, as though, somehow, she knew that her prayer would be answered. Gray Wolf didn't deserve harsh treatment. And God as she knew him just wouldn't let Gray Wolf suffer for something that he had done only in bravery while protecting *her*.

Shaking her hair down her back, she clucked to her horse and snapped her reins and felt a quiet joy as she discovered smoke spiraling upward from the smoke hole of Gray Wolf's wigwam. She could even smell the aroma of rabbit cooking and knew that Gray Wolf was there, preparing his evening meal.

With tears of relief sparkling at the corners of her eyes,

Danette quickly dismounted and ran to the doorspace of the wigwam and hurried inside. When Gray Wolf turned with a start, discovering her there, she could see that her alarm had transferred to him.

"What is it?" he asked, rushing to her. He looked down into her eyes, seeing the tears. "Is it your uncle? Did he say no? You will go away with me anyway, won't you?"

Shaking her head slowly back and forth, Danette sniffled. "It's my uncle all right," she said solemnly. "But it has nothing to do with my telling him about us."

Gray Wolf's face clouded with disappointment. "You didn't tell him?" he growled. "You said that you would. Do you come to tell me that you have changed your mind? That you want to live the rest of your life with your uncle instead of the man you love?"

Danette raised a hand to his cheek. "No," she murmured. "That isn't it at all, Gray Wolf." She swallowed hard. "Oh, how do I tell you?"

"Tell me what?"

"I must tell you and quickly," she said, lowering her eyes. "This Raoul, the one you stabbed, well, he went to my uncle and lied about why he was stabbed." Her eyes moved slowly upward. "He said that you attacked him for no reason. And there are men gathering to come in search of you. There will be a lynching, Gray Wolf, if they find you. You must leave. Now. You can't let them find you."

Gray Wolf walked angrily away from her and began pacing. "Gray Wolf should've killed Frenchman," he grumbled. "Gray Wolf will kill Frenchman. Let them come. If I have to, I will kill them all."

Danette paled. She rushed to Gray Wolf and took both his hands in hers. "Gray Wolf, no," she cried. "There will be many of them. There is no way you can fight them. Please! Go now. Go to your village where you will be safe."

"Gray Wolf no run like scared rabbit," he said firmly. "Gray Wolf stay. Fight." He squared his shoulders and

227

tilted his chin proudly. "Gray Wolf next chief-in-line. Gray Wolf brave."

Feeling desperation seizing her, Danette began shaking her head hurriedly back and forth. "No," she cried. "Please listen to reason, Gray Wolf. These men have had a long, boring summer. They're probably hungering for such excitement as a hanging. And you will be the one filling a moment of idleness these men have found while working so far from their homelands, for my uncle."

"Gray Wolf not run," Gray Wolf growled, picking up his rifle, holding it defiantly up into the air. "Gray Wolf fight!"

"Then we will have no future together," Danette said, sobbing. "There is no way you can fight off the throng of men that will come hunting for you. There will be no wedding, Gray Wolf. You will be dead. I know it."

Gray Wolf went to Danette and looked solemnly down into her face. *"Ay-uh,* what you say makes sense. I do have my future to consider. I must not be vain in my actions. But if I leave now, Sweet Butterfly, you can't ride alongside," he said. "It can be too dangerous. You would have to come later."

"Yes," she said eagerly. "Yes. I will follow later. Amanda can accompany me to your village."

"And you will come soon?" he asked, lifting her hair from her neck, admiring her loveliness as though it might be his last chance to do so.

"Yes," she murmured. "I promise. I will come. Soon."

"Then Gray Wolf will go," he said angrily. "But I will remember, always, how the white man still hunt Indian like animal."

"Not all who are white do these things," Danette whispered, leaning into his embrace, hugging him tightly to her. "I'm white and I love you more than life itself. Please love me back, Gray Wolf. I am going to miss you so."

Gray Wolf leaned his rifle against the wall of the wigwam

and drew her so close to him their hearts seemed to be beating as one. Their breaths intermingled as lips sought lips in a gentle kiss.

Twining her fingers through his hair, Danette sighed. "I will come soon," she whispered. "Then we can be wed. Until then, Gray Wolf, I will only be half alive."

"You will bear me many sons?" he said huskily, then kissed the hollow of her throat.

Danette's eyes flew wide open. He hadn't mentioned children before. She hadn't even considered them! The thought of mothering his children was a thrill quite unique to her, and it made a rapturous glow spread throughout her insides.

She threw her head back in sheer ecstasy as his lips moved lower and kissed the upper swell of her breasts. "Yes," she whispered. "I will bear you many sons. And, God grant, they will all be as handsome as you."

"Together we will reign over the St. Croix band of the Chippewa," he said, now framing her face between his hands. "You will be at my side as Red Blossom has so faithfully stood at Chief Yellow Feather's side."

"*Ay-uh* ..." Danette said, giggling when she saw his pride in her in his eyes when she once more proved her skill at saying yes in Indian.

Then she sobered, remembering the threat of the arrival of the posse. "But, Gray Wolf, please leave now. Hurry. The men could be here at any time now. They were to meet at the courthouse. My uncle is to lead them. Seems he never gets enough attention. This way he will be whispered about for weeks ... maybe months to come. The senator who defended the whole city of Duluth from Indians."

"This man ... your uncle ... he is a man who will one day find his end in an ugly way," Gray Wolf growled, gathering together his Indian attire.

Danette shivered at his cold words. But surely Gray Wolf didn't mean anything by them. He was just angry and hurt.

Anyone would hate the man responsible for threatening his life. . . .

Danette watched, trembling, as Gray Wolf changed himself into an Indian by removing all of his white man's clothes. In their place he put on only a loincloth, moccasins, and a headband with an eagle feather secured into a coil of his hair at the back of his head.

And after he had speedily braided his hair and stood boldly over her with sternness in his features, Danette saw only the Indian in him and felt her heart soaring in her love for him, never having quite loved him as much as she did at this moment.

Blinded with tears, she flew into his arms and sobbed against his chest of steel. "I'm so frightened for you," she cried, looking up into his green eyes. "What if they do catch you? Oh, Gray Wolf, I just couldn't live without you."

"They won't catch me," he said dryly. "Gray Wolf know the forest better than any white man. My horse move like a deer. You go home. Don't worry another moment about it. Just believe me when I say that I will be safe. Tonight when the moon is full, look onto it and know that I am safe in my village. And I will be looking at the moon at the same time as you, and in its reflection, I will be there with you."

Arm in arm they left the wigwam, and Danette walked with him to his horse. As he mounted it, she tried to keep the tears from once more rushing from her eyes. Instead, she looked adoringly up at him and blew him a kiss, and, after a long, studious look back at her, he was gone.

"God be with you," she whispered, watching him disappear into the shadows.

Chapter Fifteen

The happy sweet laughter of love without pain,
Young love, the strong love, burning in the rain.
—Eastman

Heat lightning flashed in the sky in faint pale orange, not enough to make the darkness of night any lighter, only more ominous. Not a whisper of a breeze could be heard blowing through the leaves of the trees as Danette stood at her open bedroom window watching for Dwight. Upon her return from having warned Gray Wolf, the house had seemed like a tomb. If Dwight succeeded at his task. . . .

Danette shook her head furiously. "No," she said. "I won't let myself even think on the possibilities of that happening. Gray Wolf had a head start. He knows the secrets of the forest as no white man does."

Wringing her hands, Danette moved from the window and began an anxious pacing. She glanced toward the clock on the fireplace mantel, thinking the hands must be frozen, they had moved so slowly these past few minutes.

"How much longer?" she murmured, throwing her head back, closing her eyes. "I can't bear much more of this wondering and waiting. Gray Wolf, oh, Gray Wolf, this is my fault. If I hadn't become so careless . . ."

The sound of a horse's hoofbeats in the distance made Danette's heart become the thunder the heat lightning did not project from the heavens. Trembling, she raced down the stairs and to the open front door and awaited her uncle's arrival inside the house. Possibly he had given up and had ordered all the men back to their houses. This was something quite new to her uncle . . . tracking an Indian. Surely he had not been successful.

Feeling the heat rise to her cheeks from her anxious state, Danette placed the palms of her hands to her face, to try and cool it. She just couldn't let her Uncle Dwight see her so concerned. Yet, wouldn't he understand? Even though he had never wanted to admit it, he most surely had to know her feelings for Gray Wolf!

Heavy footsteps on the porch made Danette take a step backwards, almost stumbling on the last step of the staircase. She grabbed at the bannister to steady herself and smiled awkwardly when her Uncle Dwight stepped into the foyer. Then her smile faded when she saw something new in her uncle's eyes. It was not a look of someone who had been unsuccessful. Good Lord! Had he actually found Gray Wolf and . . . ?

"So I see you've waited up for me," Dwight said, untying his bow tie, jerking it from around his neck. "You didn't have to do that, Danette." He pulled his jacket off and hung it on a coat tree, glancing across his shoulder as he continued to watch the anxious tremble of her lips and the clasping and unclasping of her hands.

"Uncle, did you find . . . ?" she asked with a break in her voice.

"Yes," he said blandly. "The deed is done. The Indian Gray Wolf is dead. The hanging is over."

Danette placed a hand to her heart, feeling as though a thousand arrows had pierced her there. Her head began a crazy spinning and she couldn't stop seeing many faces of Dwight in her dizziness as she crumpled to the floor in an unconscious heap.

Danette awakened in a haze. Through her wet, tear-soaked lashes, she saw an unfamiliar face leaning down over her. Blinking her eyes nervously and kneading her brow, she very slowly regained the focus of her eyes and realized that she was in her bedroom, in her bed. But who was this stranger standing over her?

Then, as though a bolt of lightning had struck her, she remembered. Gray Wolf! He had been hung. . . .

Again bitter tears tore from the corners of her eyes. She bit her lower lip to keep the sobs from surfacing and she clutched desperately onto the blanket that had been placed over her after someone had taken the liberty of removing her street clothes and dressed her in one of her cotton gowns.

"There, there," the man beside her bed spoke in a soothing tone as he took one of her hands in his. "You mustn't cry. It isn't good for you."

Danette tried to jerk her hand away, not wanting anyone near her at this time. She wanted to mourn alone for her lost loved one. No one could ever take his place. It was as though her heart had been torn from inside her. She felt nothing but an emptiness and even wished she were dead.

Dwight's voice spoke up from across the room, where he was standing out of Danette's view, beside the bedroom window. "Danette, quit that crying," he said dryly. "Dr. Ross is here to help. How can he if you continue to be hysterical?"

Danette placed a hand to her mouth and let her eyes move slowly to where her uncle stood. She couldn't hate anyone as much as she hated him at this moment. He had taken the most important thing in life away from her. He had murdered the man she loved!

When her eyes met her Uncle Dwight's and held, she could see in them that he understood her plight and she knew that he could care less that she was in such a state. The reason he wished that she would behave more rationally was only because she was embarrassing him!

Shaking her head back and forth, she turned her eyes away from him, never wanting to even see him again. What love she had had for him was like a puff of smoke in the wind, blown away. . . .

Yet whether or not she wanted to accept it, he was all that she had left in the world. She had to act civil toward him until she could gather together in her mind what her next move must be.

She watched as Dr. Ross went to Dwight and had a quiet council. When Dwight moved from the room, frowning over his shoulder toward Danette, a slow chill raced across her flesh. Nothing could ever be the same again! Nothing!

Dr. Ross, with his snow-white hair and round face, and his black suit and matching tie, moved back beside her bed. He scooted a chair beside it and settled his short, squat body down into it, all the while watching Danette through pale gray, squinted eyes. His nose was bulbous and his lips narrow, and he smelled of camphor.

"We must have us a little talk, young lady," he said in a deep, gruff voice. "We need to talk in privacy. That's why I asked your uncle to leave the room. No need in embarrassin' you. You seem distraught enough as it is. Is it because you know that you're with child? Can't you handle the knowin', young lady? Is it because you're afraid the young man will refuse to marry you?"

The doctor's words sounded as though he was speaking them from deep inside a well, as Danette grew more and more numb inside. What was he saying? How could he say that she was with child? Why would he say such a thing? She wasn't with child! She was crying because she had just lost Gray Wolf!

But Danette couldn't tell the doctor that. She couldn't

pour out her feelings to anyone. She was alone. Oh, so utterly alone!

Dr. Ross leaned closer to Danette. "Young lady, don't you hear what I'm sayin' to you? You are in a dilemma, to say the least," he said in a near whisper. "It is quite obvious that your uncle knows nothing of your pregnancy. Why haven't you confided in him? He must know. It is of the utmost importance that he find a way to keep his constituency from finding out or it will ruin his career as senator in this fine state of Minnesota. Who is the responsible man? Tell me. I shall go to him and, by God, he will marry you!"

Danette's eyes widened in horror. The doctor was adamant in saying that she was with child! He would only be so, if . . .

Covering her eyes with her hands, Danette began frantically shaking her head back and forth. "No," she cried. "No. It can't be. I can't be . . . pregnant. . . ."

Dr. Ross removed her hands from her face and spoke more firmly to her. "Yes, you are, young lady," he said flatly. "Upon my first arrival here I examined you thoroughly. There is no doubt in my mind that you are carrying a child, though you are only a few weeks into your pregnancy. Didn't you even suspect? The tears. Your state . . ."

Danette's eyes cleared. Her heart ached. Her face paled. She was remembering how she had just recently been so confused by how much larger her breasts were becoming. She now also remembered that her "monthly weeps" had not occurred this past month, although this had not been alarming to her, since she had been irregular since this unpleasant phenomenon had begun when she was twelve. All the signs of pregnancy had been there and she hadn't even thought to suspect!

Trying to not envision Gray Wolf hanging from the end of a rope, feeling violently ill when such a thought crept over her, she once again began to cry. The father of her unborn child was dead . . . and at the hands of her uncle.

"Danette, please get control of yourself or I shall have to give you quite a large dose of laudanum," Dr. Ross scolded. "And I do not like to see my patients numbed by the drug . . . especially my pregnant patients."

"Just leave me alone," Danette whispered. "I don't want to hear anything else you have to say. Leave me alone. Do you hear?"

Dr. Ross rose from his chair and stood gloomily over her. "That is not the way I do things," he growled. "I am being paid quite well to tend to you and, by God, I will give your Uncle Dwight his money's worth. Now, young lady, you must do as I say if you don't want your uncle disgraced in this city. First, we must include him in our confidences. He must know. He has to find a way to handle the situation."

Danette's head shot quickly around, her eyes wide with pleading. She grabbed for Dr. Ross's hand. "No," she said. "He mustn't know."

She swallowed back a growing lump in her throat, seeing shadows cross the elderly doctor's face, knowing that he was not going to agree with her. "Please give me time to adjust to the fact that I am pregnant before telling my uncle," she quickly added. "Please, Dr. Ross. I need time. If you are truly concerned for my welfare as a patient, you want to do what's best for me, don't you?"

"But he should know. . . ."

"It won't hurt to wait just maybe one more week, will it?" she continued to plead. She knew not why but she *did* have to have time to straighten this all out in her head, though in the end, it would be her uncle who would surely be carrying the burden of her and of her and Gray Wolf's child!

Oh, the thought of her Uncle Dwight with the baby instead of Gray Wolf made a renewed hurt and anger splash throughout her! What in life was ever fair?

"All right," Dr. Ross said, furrowing his brow. "But for only one week. Then we shall tell him. Together."

Danette sighed heavily. "Thank you at least for this," she said.

"Now then, we must discuss the father of your unborn child," Dr. Ross said, settling down into the chair again, leaning over her. "He must be forced to marry you. I shall go to him. Tell me his name, Danette. Do not be ashamed to speak his name aloud. I do know how to handle these things. And, darlin', you are not the only young lady to become with child before havin' legal papers attachin' you to a young man. It happens more than not. The only reason people don't know about it is because the two in question rush to the preacher and tie the knot."

Gray Wolf's face flashed before Danette's eyes. She could see a pleading in them, remembering the many times he had asked her to leave for his village with him, with her only putting him off until "later." If it had not been for her fear of telling her Uncle Dwight, she would have a husband . . . and her husband would be . . . alive.

Tears blurred her vision once again. "No," she said. "There is no name that I can hand you, sir."

"Time is of the essence," he growled. "You cannot wait long. Everyone will know."

Not knowing what she could do, she reached for his hand and squeezed it. "I am pleading with you, sir, to give me time even for this," she said. "I will take care of this in my own way. I do not need you to clear up the problems I have created for myself. I will talk to the man . . . in . . . question. I promise."

Lies did not become her. She wondered if he could read it in her eyes that she had just told him a falsehood.

But it did not matter to her at all what he thought about her or her condition. All that mattered to her was now gone from her life.

Yet a slow glow was rising inside her. If she was with child . . . Gray Wolf's child . . . she would always have with her a part of him—and what a blessing the pregnancy suddenly was!

"A man sometimes needs the barrel of a shotgun to convince him what is best for him," Dr. Ross grumbled, lifting a black bag to his chair, snapping it closed. He turned and faced Danette. "I can point that barrel for you, if it comes to that. I am quite devoted to your uncle, you see."

"Most are," Danette said in a whisper, turning her face from him. Then she met his steady stare and shook her head back and forth. "No. That will not be necessary in my case. I will take care of this. Do not worry one minute about it."

Lifting the bag from the chair, Dr. Ross let it hang at his side. "We shall see," he said dryly. "In one week, we shall see."

Danette watched him leave the room, then slowly rose from the bed, trembling in the knees as she began to move about the room, gathering up her clothes. She had things to do. It seemed that in Gray Wolf's death she had suddenly become stronger, for she did have things to do, and they were things for him.

Though it would break her heart over and over again, she did have Gray Wolf to place before her own feelings. There would be no one else to do this dreaded task. It was up to her to claim Gray Wolf's body and return it to his people. Suddenly what people might think made no difference to her whatsoever. Let her Uncle Dwight squirm himself out of it once it became knowledge who it was who had come asking for Gray Wolf's body!

"In death Gray Wolf will be even more a threat to you, Uncle Dwight," Danette said, feeling a need for vengeance and knowing this was the only way.

"But what about my child?" she whispered, flipping her dress over her head. "What am I to do?"

Completely dressed now, and having adequately brushed her hair, Danette forced her shoulders back and her head high and moved out of the room. She stood at the head of the staircase until she heard the doctor's departure, then walked weak-limbed on down the stairs, to boldly confront her uncle with her decision.

And after she did, he was taken aback, even to the extent that he dropped a glass of wine on the carpet, the wine spreading at his feet like ink on a blotter.

"You want to what . . . ?" he shouted, his face flaming with rage.

"I want to take Gray Wolf's body back to his people for proper burial rites," she said, feeling sick with the thought of seeing him dead, but knowing that this was what he would want. To be . . . with his people. Oh, what a mourning there would be for the next chief-in-line. Danette could almost hear the wails of grief for their fallen chief's son!

She closed her eyes and turned her head away from her uncle's accusing stare and sealed her lips tightly, afraid of what she might say next to this man who had stolen her love from her.

Dwight went to Danette and grabbed her wrist and forced her around, to face him. "You can't do that," he said. "Why would you even want to? He proved his savage ways when he stabbed Raoul unprovoked."

"You are wrong," Danette cried, trying to suppress a sob. "It was Gray Wolf who was wronged. He was rescuing me from that beast Raoul when Raoul was attempting to rape me. This was the reason Raoul was stabbed. Good Lord, Uncle Dwight, don't you see the mistake you have made? You killed Gray Wolf for naught. It was Raoul who should have been hung from the end of a rope. Not Gray . . . Wolf."

Dwight stepped back away from her, paling. "Raoul was . . . raping . . . you . . . ?" he said in a strained voice. "My God, Danette, why didn't you tell me?"

"I tried," she screamed. "You left me standing there with the words unspoken. As you always do, Uncle Dwight. You never listen when you need to be listening."

She swung away from him and moved to the fireplace mantel and rested her arm against it, staring blankly into the cold, gray ashes beneath the grate. She felt a part of the ashes. Dead. "It is my duty to take Gray Wolf back to his people," she said quietly. "This was the man I was going to marry."

She swung around, fury in her eyes. "Yes," she screamed. "I was about to tell you when . . . when . . ."

Dwight went to her and slapped her across the face, snapping her head recklessly back. "Shut up, Danette," he shouted. "Don't say anything else. I've heard enough."

Stunned, never having been struck by her uncle before, Danette reached a hand to her cheek where it flamed with his fingerprints. "Uncle, you . . . you struck me," she murmured. "Did you hate Gray Wolf . . . so . . . much . . . ?"

"It is only right that he is dead," Dwight growled. "If not for wronging a white man, for wronging my niece."

"He never wronged me," she cried. "I loved him. We were in love. Uncle Dwight, didn't you ever fall in love? Have you always been so hard? Hasn't your heart ever ached to hold the one you love in your arms? Are you truly so coldhearted as you appear at this moment?"

Dwight turned and glared toward Danette. She could see his pulse throbbing in his temple and felt as though she had never known him.

"I will hear no more from you," he said, pointing toward the staircase. "You return to your room. Possibly there is more wrong with you than just having lost an Indian from your life. Perhaps you have become deranged."

Danette stood her ground, stiffening her arms to her side. "I shall not return to my room," she said. "I shall go and claim Gray Wolf's body. You cannot stop me. From here on out, I will be my own person, no matter what you say or do."

Yet she was still worrying about her child. Alone? Could she survive, raising the child alone? No. It seemed not at all possible. Yet how could she stand another moment with this ... this ... man, who by bloodline was her uncle, her only living relative?

"That is quite impossible," Dwight growled, placing a cigar between his lips, lighting it. "Yes, claiming the Indian's body is quite impossible." He looked toward Danette with forked eyebrows, watching her, wishing none of this had come about. He had lost so much ground with her now, would he ever be able to reclaim it? He needed her in his campaign for the presidency! Not only did she look good at his side, he had been admired by so many for having raised her!

"And why is that?" she fumed. "All I have to do is go by buggy. I shall recover his body and leave for his village tonight."

Dwight puffed eagerly on his cigar, then said, "Like I said. That is not possible."

"We shall see what is and what is not possible," Danette said, rushing toward the staircase to go to her room to pack her things, for forever, she had to think at this moment.

"No need to bother," Dwight said, moving to the foot of the staircase, peering up at her swooshing skirt as she reached the second-floor landing.

"Oh, Uncle Dwight, give up," she shouted, moving on toward her bedroom, ignoring that he was close behind her now, rushing toward her.

Dwight moved to her and grabbed her roughly by an arm and turned her to face him. "Listen to me," he said, his cigar hanging from the corner of his mouth. "You can't do this, because there is no body to recover."

Danette felt the usual spinning of her head that she experienced whenever she didn't grasp what was being revealed to her. "What did you say?" she asked, teetering.

"We dumped the body into the lake," Dwight said, absently shrugging. "We felt it the easiest way out of this ugly situation. No body. No trouble."

Danette's eyes lowered. "Good Lord," she said, shaking her head. "Uncle Dwight . . . you aren't . . . even human."

Then she squirmed away from him. "How could you?" she screamed, doubling her fists to her side. "How could you do such a terrible thing? Gray Wolf? You threw Gray Wolf's body into the lake?"

A bitterness rose into her throat. She rushed over to a basin on her nightstand and hung her head over it, retching. Her stomach felt as though it was going to tear from inside her the more that she retched. Her head became light and tears burned at her eyes. She couldn't let herself think of Gray Wolf at the bottom of the dark abyss of the lake. She couldn't! If she did, she would forever be ill!

The thought of Chief Yellow Feather and Lorinda caused her quickly to recover. When they heard what had happened to their son . . .

Raising her head, wiping her face with a towel, she turned and stared angrily at her uncle. "You do not know what you have done here," she said. "You don't even know who it was you have murdered."

"It was a damn Indian," Dwight said, once more shrugging. "It was an Indian who was causing trouble. That's all anyone needs to know."

"He was to be the next chief of the St. Croix band of the Chippewa," she hissed. "Chief Yellow Feather will avenge his death. Then what will you tell your constituency? What then, Uncle?"

She laughed as she saw her uncle's mouth drop open and his cigar hang limply from one corner, threatening to fall to the floor.

"Yes, Uncle Dwight, you did yourself good when you killed the man who was to be the next chief of the kind, peaceful Chippewa, who might now decide to not be so congenial."

She began gathering clothes from her wardrobe. She

pulled a valise from beneath her bed and began packing her clothes into it.

"What do you think you're doing, Danette?"

"I need to get away," she said. "I'd like to go visit Amanda for a while. Maybe in time I can forget all that has happened here. But, Uncle Dwight, I do doubt that."

She wasn't about to tell him that she wasn't going to Amanda's . . . only to Amanda's. Once she got there, she and Amanda would travel to Gray Wolf's village and tell them the sad news of their fallen brave.

Danette looked down at her abdomen, knowing that one day it would be quite swollen, with all her secrets revealed to the naked eye. This, also, was her reason for wanting to go to St. Paul. She had the need to talk with Amanda about her pregnancy. If anyone would understand her feelings, Amanda would.

Dwight removed his cigar from between his lips and circled it around, between his thumb and forefinger. "Yes," he said. "Maybe that's what you need. Rettie Toliver's boardinghouse could serve as your place of seclusion until all talk of this Indian thing is a thing of the past."

He went to Danette and lifted her chin with his other forefinger. "And, Danette, while you're there, try to get some sun," he added. "You look quite pale."

Danette flinched beneath his touch and recoiled back, away from him. An involuntary shudder raced through her, and she wondered if this would be her reaction to him from now on, whenever he drew near to her.

"Also, you may take in some last minute horseback riding and swimming with Amanda before the temperatures turn too cool to do so," he also added. "Amanda has a way about her. She can help you to forget this . . . this infatuation you had for that Indian."

Danette wanted to lash out at him . . . tell him the truth about Amanda . . . laugh about it to his face . . . tell him that he wasn't so smart after all. But too many truths had

243

already been revealed this night, and most of them cut through her heart until she knew that it most surely must be bleeding inside her.

"Yes," she said, nodding. "You're right. Amanda is a unique person. She does have quite a way about her. I'm sure she will help me with any problem I may have."

She smiled to herself as she folded a skirt and placed it inside her valise, thinking it amusing that he didn't realize the double meaning to her statement.

"You must not leave until morning, though," Dwight said, going to the valise, placing his hand in the way as Danette started to place a nightgown inside it. "What you should do is go to bed, get some rest, then finish packing in the morning and I'll drive you to the depot, for you to catch the first train to St. Paul."

Sighing, Danette slouched down onto the edge of the bed, yes, feeling too heavy to make any more attempts at moving this evening. She had the weight of the world on her shoulders this night, it seemed. "Yes," she said. "You're right. I am almost too exhausted to move. I will retire for the night, Uncle Dwight. And I will be ready when the sun rises in the morning."

She wanted to thank him for being so understanding but then realized the mockery of any words of thanks she might now hand his way. She had to remember Gray Wolf! How he had died! She must never let her uncle's suave manner make her forget!

"I'm glad to see that you've settled down," Dwight said, leaning a kiss to her brow. "You had me worried there for a while. Things will be all right, Danette. You'll see. This time in your life will be like a flicker from a candle. Life is fleeting. Only an image it seems, sometimes."

"Yes," Danette said sullenly. "An image." The image of Gray Wolf and his handsomeness flashed across her eyes. Strange how she thought this image could never fade. It was as though he were still alive ... there with her ... offering her a hand to guide her on her way.

Shaking her head to clear her thoughts, she rose to her feet. "Yes, Uncle Dwight, I will be all right," she said flatly. "Now, please. I do want to retire."

Dwight walked toward the door, giving her occasional backward glances, then disappeared out into the hallway, leaving Danette woefully alone with her aching heart, her memories, and her scalding eyes, which once more flowed freely with tears.

Going to the window, she drew back a drape and looked toward the shimmering waters of Lake Superior. "Oh, Lord, at one time I thought nothing could be as beautiful as that water," she whispered. "Now it is as it has been sometimes at night ... like the devil ... and this time, it holds the body of my loved one as his grave forever. . . .

"I shall always love you, Gray Wolf," she said. "Always. In death as in life. Forever."

Something drew her eyes upward to where the circle of the moon was shining brightly and fully. It was then that she remembered Gray Wolf's parting words. "Tonight when the moon is full, look into it. In its reflection I will be there with you."

Lifting her hand toward the moon, Danette whispered, "Gray Wolf, in its reflection, you will always be with me. . . ."

Chapter Sixteen

Eyes full of starlight,
moist over fire,
Full of young wonder,
touch my desire!
—Anonymous

The journey was a solemn one. Danette and Amanda had spent only a few moments of silent vigil beside Amanda's parents' graves, then one night in the forest, and now they were traveling toward the shine of the St. Croix River. Low-hanging thunderheads were hiding the bright, scorching rays of the sun beneath them, and the air had a heaviness to it, as though it was wrapping a cloak of humidity about Danette's shoulders, threatening to completely engulf her.

Pulling her heavy riding skirt up from her knees, she relished the touch of what breeze the trees were able to blow around her. Perspiration laced her brow and her upper lip, and all these things didn't help to lift the oppressive sadness that continued to linger about her heart.

It had helped her to share with Amanda the sad news they were taking to Chief Yellow Feather and Lorinda. Rettie Toliver hadn't been told because of her forever weakening condition. One bad piece of news looked as though it might be the end of her, so, at all costs, she was being spared.

"And how are you feeling now?" Amanda asked, moving her horse next to Danette's. "I must tell you, you don't look so good. Maybe you shouldn't be riding in your condition. Did the doctor give you any suggestions as to what you could or could not do? With me, I'm used to ridin' horseback. It won't hurt me or my baby.''

Danette looked down at Amanda's abdomen, seeing how it was so obvious that she was with child. Amanda had accepted her pregnancy and was no longer afraid of what the townspeople might say about it.

Danette had a different sort of problem. She hadn't decided yet when, or if, she would ever tell Chief Yellow Feather and Lorinda about *her* pregnancy. Should she, they might make claim to the child, and she wanted Gray Wolf's child all to herself!

"I'm fine," she finally answered. "And, no. The doctor didn't give me any specific instructions except . . . except that I should wed quite hurriedly." She swallowed hard. "But you and I know that this is not possible."

"I can't believe that such a man as your uncle would be responsible for an innocent Indian's hanging," Amanda said, smoothing a gloved hand over her horse's mane.

"At the time, he didn't know that Gray Wolf was innocent," Danette said. "Only later, Amanda. Only later. He wouldn't listen when I tried to tell him."

"And to discard the body as he did?" Amanda said, shivering. "How inhumane."

Danette felt her insides rippling, as though waves on an ocean. "Please, Amanda," she said. "Let's not talk any more about it. I grow so ill when I think of Gray Wolf. . . .''

"I understand," Amanda said, reaching a hand to Danette's arm. "Please forgive me. I know how hard this must be for you. It's hard for me, too, you know. Gray Wolf was my blood relative, and I loved him dearly. He was special. Quite special. He would have made a great chief."

"Amanda, there is a special favor I must ask of you."

"Anything," Amanda said. "You know that I want to help you in your sorrow."

"You mustn't tell your sister or Chief Yellow Feather about my pregnancy."

"Why would you want to keep it from them?"

"With Gray Wolf gone, they might want to make claim to his child because Gray Wolf was the next chief-in-line. They may want to keep our child, especially if it is a son, to raise as a chief. This just can't happen. I will want to raise my child. I could never give up my child to anyone for any reason."

Amanda's face screwed up into a frown. She looked over at Danette, silent at first, then said, "But knowing the Chippewa as I do, I know they will want the child if it is a son. And, Danette, that would only be their right. It is because of the white man that they have lost their son. They wouldn't want to also lose a grandson."

"Good Lord, Amanda," Danette gasped. "I can't believe you would actually say that." She glanced down at Amanda's swollen abdomen. "And what about yourself? Would you give up your child so easily?"

"My child can never be a great chief," Amanda said. "You must remember. Gray Wolf would eventually have been his people's leader. His son would also."

Danette drew her horse to an abrupt halt, causing it to shudder and whinny. "Then perhaps I should turn back," she said, feeling threatened. "My duty to the Chippewa stops right here. You can go and tell them about Gray Wolf. I fear the outcome for both me and my child, should I go with you."

Amanda wheeled her horse around and moved it next to Danette's. "Danette, please don't take that attitude," she murmured. "And why not consider living with the Chippewa? You know that you are unhappy with your uncle. God! He's a villain, to say the least. Lorinda and Chief Yellow Feather would see to it that you would have anything you wanted. It wouldn't be a terrible existence. I, too, will eventually live with the Chippewa. I look forward to it."

Danette slowly shook her head. "Without Gray Wolf? No. I could not," she said. "Living with the Chippewa would be a constant reminder of what I have lost."

"You have to learn to live with your losses," Amanda said, leaning, softly stroking Danette's cheek. "Think about it, Danette. Your son, if you have a son, will one day be a great chief! Would you deprive him such an honor?"

Tears stung at the corners of Danette's eyes. The pain was still there, stabbing her heart. This was too soon to be thinking so hard on anything. "Amanda, I will continue on to the village with you only if you promise to not say anything to Lorinda or Chief Yellow Feather," she said, wiping a tear from her cheek. "I need time. For all of this. Surely you can understand. You also hurt because of the loss of Gray Wolf. Think of how I hurt. If you had just lost Red Fox . . ."

Amanda interrupted. "I don't even want to think of such a thing happening," she said. "And, yes, I promise not to say anything. You are a dear friend . . . one I wouldn't want to lose."

Danette's shoulders slumped with intense relief. "Thank you," she said. "I appreciate your kindness."

"Then shall we proceed?" Amanda said, peering upward into the sky, seeing the gray swirls of clouds, yet doubting if any rain would fall from them. It had been so long since rain had blessed the state of Minnesota that one had to wonder if it ever would again.

"Yes. Let's get this dreaded thing over with," Danette sighed. "How hard it will be to reveal the truth of Gray Wolf's death! And my own uncle is responsible. Possibly Lorinda and Chief Yellow Feather will even hate me because of my relation with the man who took their son's life."

"They know as well as you and I that there are evil men in the world," Amanda said sourly, sending her horse into a slow trot. "They will never associate him with you. They know you are filled with compassion for their people. They know your love for Gray Wolf.''

"He is dead," Danette said, lowering her eyes. "Whenever will I be able to accept such a truth? My arms are still warm from our last embrace. My lips still tingle from his kisses."

"Danette, don't," Amanda urged, giving Danette a wistful look. "You are only going to make things worse for yourself. It's good to remember, but don't dwell on it. For your child's sake, please do not torture yourself so."

"Yes, I know," Danette said, swallowing hard. "I will have to practice a stronger will and think only on the future. When our child runs in the meadow . . . when our child looks upon my face . . ."

She looked woefully toward the sky, groaning. "But when our child looks upon my face I will always see Gray Wolf," she cried. "Oh, God, I just want to die, my grief is so strong!"

A muffled sound of a horse's hooves became evident through the forest. Amanda drew her horse up next to Danette's. "Listen," she said. "Someone is approaching."

A cold chill engulfed Danette, remembering Longbow. "Should we seek cover, Amanda?" she whispered. "What if it's . . ."

Then her words froze on her lips when she saw the perfect image of Gray Wolf materializing, approaching her and Amanda. A lightheadedness swept over Danette and she began weaving in the saddle, stopped only by the quick rescue of Amanda's outstretched arm.

"Gray Wolf . . ." Amanda gasped, squinting her eyes, trying to look with greater scrutiny at the approaching figure on horseback. "How . . . ?"

Danette's heart fluttered wildly . . . her face became colored with a vivid rose splash . . . and her eyes moved over Gray Wolf in a wild fashion . . . now knowing that what she was seeing was not a figment of her imagination . . . but the real thing!

"Gray Wolf," she cried, urging her horse onward, quickly meeting him halfway. She jumped from her horse and went to him and let him lift her from the ground, onto his lap. She smothered his face in kisses, crying and laughing at the same time.

Gray Wolf chuckled amusedly. "You kiss me as though you haven't seen me in many moons," he said, embracing her, marveling at the greeting she continued to bestow upon him.

Danette clung to him, reveling in the touch of his strong body of steel, not understanding why, but joyous at the discovery! "I thought you were dead," she finally murmured, kissing him once again lightly on his lips. "Gray Wolf, oh, Gray Wolf, you are not. You are here, with me, holding me! I won't have to deliver such terrible news to your village after all!"

Gray Wolf's brow furrowed as he looked down at her with wonder. "You thought Gray Wolf dead?" he said. "Why did you?"

"If not you, then who?" Amanda said, riding up next to Gray Wolf.

Settling down, breathing much more easily now, Danette's face clouded, yes, wondering whom had been tossed into Lake Superior instead of Gray Wolf, though she had to admit to the honest feeling of thankfulness that it had been someone else!

"What are you talking about?" Gray Wolf exclaimed, looking from Danette to Amanda.

"My uncle," Danette said, lowering her eyes. "When he went looking for an Indian to hang, he found one." Then her eyes flew wide open, searching Gray Wolf's face: Never, no never, would she get enough of him now that she had him with her again.

"Your uncle . . . hung . . . an Indian?" Gray Wolf growled, his green eyes now ablaze with anger.

"Yes," Danette said. "And he led me to believe that . . . it . . . was you, Gray Wolf."

"That evil liar," Gray Wolf snarled.

"When he came back to the house after having searched for you, Uncle Dwight said that there had been a hanging and that they had thrown the Indian . . . they had thrown you . . . into Lake Superior."

Once more she clung to him, placing her cheek to his bare chest. "Oh, Gray Wolf, I have died inside, over and over again, believing it was you," she cried.

"So Raoul didn't care which Indian he pointed out to your uncle when I couldn't be found," he growled. "They had to hang someone so they hung the first Indian that crossed their path."

"But Uncle Dwight had to know that it wasn't you," Danette said, once more searching Gray Wolf's face. "Why did he tell me that it was you? Why did they hang an innocent Indian?"

"They needed to see an Indian suffer one more time," Gray Wolf grumbled. "And your uncle thought by telling you it was me he would never have to worry about you coming to me again. He lied. On purpose, he lied, Sweet Butterfly."

"I never did know him, did I?" Danette said solemnly. "He only uses people for his own purposes in life. And to think that once I actually worshipped the man."

"That's only natural," Amanda tried to console her. "He took you in when you had nowhere else to go."

"Yes," Danette sighed. "He did."

"I wonder which Indian," Amanda worried aloud.

"Maybe there wasn't even a hanging," Danette said, pulling away from Gray Wolf. "If my uncle lies so easily, maybe he even lied about that. If he only wanted to keep me from you, wasn't this lie the easiest way to do so? Perhaps no Indian was hanged after all."

She again snuggled up next to him, sinfully happy.

"One day he will pay for all his actions," Gray Wolf said. "If not for hanging an Indian, then for lying."

Amanda silently studied Danette, seeing how limply she lay against Gray Wolf's chest and suddenly remembering the child. Now, if not more than before they had discovered Gray Wolf alive, the unborn child had to be protected from all harm. Danette had to get somewhere quickly, to rest.

Looking through the trees, seeing the shine from the St. Croix River, she knew the village was not far ahead. "Gray Wolf, perhaps we should go on into the village," she said, not knowing how she could show her concern for Danette without having to tell him of the child—and that should be Danette's honor!

"Ay-uh," he said. "Your journey has been long and filled with emotion. You both need rest." His gaze fell upon Amanda's swollen abdomen. A slow smile rose to his lips. "We must take care of Red Fox's son, mustn't we, White Blossom?"

Amanda patted her abdomen and nodded a yes, then gave Danette a knowing glance but said nothing.

"Sweet Butterfly take the rest of the journey to village with me on my horse," Gray Wolf said, lowering a sweet kiss to the tip of Danette's nose. "You take her horse, White Blossom. We will meet you there."

"Ay-uh," Amanda said, reaching for Danette's horse's reins, glowing with happiness inside at seeing Gray Wolf and Danette so happily content in one another's arms. "You go on ahead. I will soon follow."

"I plan to take Sweet Butterfly immediately to my wigwam," Gray Wolf said thickly. "You tell Mother and Father we will meet with them later."

"Ay-uh," Amanda once more said, smiling back an understanding in their direction. There would be love made in

Gray Wolf's wigwam as never before. Two hearts reunited
. . . two souls . . . and a child on the way . . . !

Danette was glad that the evening was fast approaching,
not wanting to be openly stared at by all the village people
as she rode into camp on Gray Wolf's lap. Her love for him
was a personal, private one . . . one that she didn't wish to
share with anyone. Now that she had him with her again,
she would savor each and every moment with him, but she
wanted these moments alone . . . not with a whole village
of Indians.

Had they thought their brave dead, how they would now
have reason to celebrate his life! Well, Danette wanted to
celebrate all right! But in her own way . . . in privacy!

The large communal fire burned brightly in the distance,
reflecting orange onto the low-hanging clouds of the continuing impending storm. Seeing this in the sky, Danette knew
that the village was close by and tried to prepare herself for
whatever sort of welcome Gray Wolf had had many years
to grow accustomed to. But then she still had to remind
herself that they had no reason to celebrate! They hadn't
known what her fears had been! It would surely be just a
usual entry into the village, without much notice!

"You cling as though no tomorrow, Sweet Butterfly,"
Gray Wolf whispered into her ear, silently amazed at her
sudden presence this day, a prayer to the spirits fulfilled, it
seemed, for he had only moments before having seen her
been thinking of her, wishing to be with her.

"Only moments ago, I had thought there was not,"
Danette sighed. "Tomorrows without you would be no
tomorrows at all, Gray Wolf."

"Sweet Butterfly love Gray Wolf so much?"

"Ay-uh . . ."

He chuckled, burrowing his nose into the depths of her
hair, then directed his full attention to crossing the St. Croix
River, searching its bottom for the shallow spot through
which to take his beloved across. And when that was found

and conquered and the other side reached, they rode on past the sacred cave, and into the waving shadows of the communal fire's glow, where several elderly squaws knelt, stirring food in a large, blackened pot.

"They prepare venison," Gray Wolf said, nodding toward them. "There is never enough food, it seems. It is a task that has to be fought day in and day out."

Danette was reminded of Longbow's mother, Foolish Heart, and had to wonder about her. Had Longbow left her to die alone? Had she even already died?

But Danette couldn't ask Gray Wolf any of these questions, for she had decided long ago not to reveal to him what had happened with her and Amanda and Longbow. Longbow was surely gone, to never bother any of them again. He had been shamed by Amanda's gunshot wound. He wouldn't dare show his face again to the Chippewa, for fear of their laughing and ridiculing him. The thought made Danette's insides relax even more, knowing that the one Indian that she truly feared was no longer a threat.

Danette clung to Gray Wolf as he spoke to each Indian he passed until they were finally in seclusion inside his wigwam and desperately rushing into one another's arms.

"Gray Wolf miss you," he said, raining kisses along her face, kissing her lashes shut, then her lips, while his hands were quickly disrobing her.

"No more than I missed you, Gray Wolf," Danette whispered, having only his loincloth to drop from around his hips to the floor.

Eager hands explored eager bodies ... mouth sought mouth in a frenzied passion ... until Danette and Gray Wolf slithered together down onto the bulrush mat and let their bodies fuse into one.

Danette searched Gray Wolf's body with her hands as he plunged his hardness inside her. She let out a soft murmur of passion as his lips found her breast, stiffening her nipple into a sharp peak as his teeth played and his tongue flicked.

"Gray Wolf, oh, how I do love you," she cried, lifting her hips, eagerly meeting his thrusts, feeling the heat rising, hotter, threatening to scorch her insides with fiery flames. "When I thought you were . . ."

Gray Wolf placed a hand gently over her lips. *"Gah-ween,"* he said huskily. "Do not speak anymore about it. Gray Wolf not so easily done away with. I told you that."

He soothed the palms of his hands across her cheeks, devouring her with his eyes. The fire from his firespace shone like gems back at him in the depths of her blue pools of eyes, and her lips were partially open, inviting, beautifully red. He crushed his mouth down to hers, dizzying in the pure sweet taste of her, and his body trembled in the ecstasy of the moment.

The melting glow inside Danette's head became heightened when Gray Wolf touched her love mound and began slowly stroking her there, in unison with his steady thrusts inside her. Squirming, making herself more accessible, she sighed hungrily as his tongue once more found her breast and caressed it with his lips.

Danette cupped the breast and guided its nipple inside Gray Wolf's mouth, and when he began suckling from it a strange wondrous sensation at the pit of her stomach made Danette arch her back even more and cry out her rapture as he also shuddered desperately inside her, filling her once again with his love.

Still weak from passion, Danette smiled drunkenly up at Gray Wolf as he leaned away from her, still caressing her abdomen, as though he suspected the change in her there, where a baby lay, curled, waiting for its day of birth.

Danette touched the back of his hand and caused it to press even harder against her. "Gray Wolf, do you feel anything different?" she whispered, marveling at the peacefulness that she had once again found with him.

Being with him . . . touching him . . . kissing him . . . made such a joy inside her, she now knew that she couldn't

257

have made it without him, had he in truth been dead. She had only fooled herself, thinking to be able to awaken each day knowing she would never see him again. How could she have ever thought for one minute that life would go on without him? He *was* life! He was her soul!

Gray Wolf leaned up on his elbow and studied her abdomen, forking an eyebrow. "Different?" he mumbled. "What should Gray Wolf see? Touching you disturbs my mind so, how can Gray Wolf be expected to see a difference?"

He bent his back and let his lips kiss where his hand had just been. *"Gah-ween,"* he said. "You no look different. You no taste different. You still sweet like pollen removed from the loveliest flower."

Danette giggled. "Gray Wolf, kiss me there again," she urged.

Gray Wolf gazed up at her with amusement. "You not get enough of Gray Wolf?" he laughed, then kept his eyes on her as he again planted a kiss on the tender flesh of her abdomen.

Danette reached up and entangled her fingers through his hair. "You have just given your child one of his first kisses of life," she said, smiling.

Gray Wolf's head jerked quickly up, his eyes wide. He looked toward Danette with his mouth open, having become wordless, something quite out of the ordinary for him. But had he heard her right?

He once more placed his hand to her abdomen and ran it across the small swell of it, then again questioned her with his eyes.

"Ah-bee-no-gee?" he said in a near whisper. "Sweet Butterfly, you carry baby inside you? You carry our child? Perhaps . . . a . . . a . . . son . . . ?"

Danette giggled and reached a hand to his cheek and softly touched him. *"Ay-uh,"* she said. "Our child. And, yes, perhaps a son. One of many, my love."

Gray Wolf doubled his fists and raised his arms as he

258

shouted in jubilation. "A feast!" he cried. "We must have a feast to celebrate!"

Then his face shadowed. "But first we must marry, Sweet Butterfly," he said, framing her face between his hands.

"*Ay-uh,* we must," she said, near to tears, so engulfed was she by happiness.

"But I must first do something else," he said thickly. "Will Sweet Butterfly understand if Gray Wolf puts marriage rites off until later? I was out in forest for a reason. I must finish what I started before anything else."

The thought of delaying the marriage now placed fear inside her heart, realizing how much she had feared and dreaded carrying his child, unwed, before she had known that he was alive. What if something now happened to him before they married?

But she scoffed at the thought. Hadn't he just moments ago said that nothing could harm him? Yet, what was this thing pulling him away from her so soon after she had found him?

"I've delayed our marriage, myself, for my own reasons many times," she said, rising to a sitting position, accepting a kiss as he leaned it to the tip of her nose. "So whatever your reasons are, I shall agree to them."

She hesitated and scooted over, to fit into his embrace by the fire. "What is the reason, Gray Wolf?"

"Red Fox," Gray Wolf said quietly. "He has not been seen for two days and two nights. I was in search of him when I came across you and White Blossom in the forest."

Danette leaned out away from him, feeling cold inside, knowing how Amanda must be feeling at this moment, having surely been told. "What do you think may have happened to him?" she asked, yet not wanting to hear the answer, fearing for Red Fox and Amanda. And there was their unborn child!

"No one knows," Gray Wolf said. "It is not like Red Fox to go far. It has been since he was a child that he feared going far from the village. He is not one of the stronger braves of our people.''

He once again was filled with doubts. But he could never prove Longbow's meanness in these incidents that kept happening to the Chippewa. Without proof . . . there could be no vengeance.

A shiver raced across Danette's flesh. ''You don't think . . . he's . . . ?''

''He should be back in village,'' Gray Wolf answered. ''That's all I can say.''

He let his hand cup one of Danette's breasts as his lips bent to kiss its pink tip. ''You wait for Gray Wolf's return?''

''Gray Wolf, while there has to be a delay anyway, let me return to my home and get my things,'' she said, gasping as the pleasure once more began to take hold of her the more his hands and lips moved across her body.

''You no need white man things to live in Indian village,'' he grumbled.

''Gray Wolf, had I known you were alive and I was coming to be with you, I would have brought my paintings, canvases, brushes, and paints,'' she said, trembling as he continued to try to make her mindless. ''I had only come without them because I had no idea . . . you . . . you were here. Please? Understand. I want my personal things with me. Somehow I feel it necessary. You see, I will be leaving behind the ways I have always known. It will be hard for me to make an adjustment as it is. Why must I completely? I will be happier with some of my things with me from the very first.''

''But your uncle?''

''It will just be a temporary game I will play with him,'' Danette said, laughing at the thought of when her Uncle Dwight would discover her and her things gone. ''I must do it in this way. Don't you see, Gray Wolf? I would be happier.''

''Then you must know the other task I have planned after

I find Red Fox," he said, pulling her back down on top of him, fitting her body into his.

"And what is that?" she asked in her heady, weakened condition, as he once more entered her from below, already working inside her.

"I ... must ... go see which Indian—if it was an Indian—was hung by the white man," he said, perspiration lacing his brow as his pleasure mounted.

Danette wanted to remain sober, to argue with him, but the lethargy was quickly taking over inside her brain as he cupped her breasts and fondled them as his hardness filled her, over and over again. "It could be dangerous," she managed to utter, closing her eyes, licking her lips as the ecstasy swam through her in torrents of a delicious warmth.

"Gray Wolf can take care of Gray Wolf," he said hoarsely, drawing her lips to his, kissing her long and hard as their bodies convulsed into the other and they once more found the secrets of life in their moment of rapture.

Slipping away from him, Danette lay breathless on the bulrush mats, eyes closed. "Amanda?" she said in a bare whisper. "What ... about ... Amanda ... ?"

"Now that you feel you have to return to Duluth, I suggest you encourage Amanda to return with you to St. Paul," Gray Wolf said, pulling on his loincloth. "It's best she busies herself at this time. Then I will send word when Red Fox is found, or I will tell her myself on my way to Duluth."

"I hope you or your braves will carry good news to Amanda."

"And when will you return to my village?" he asked, reaching to draw her up into his arms.

"As soon as it's humanly possible," she murmured, gazing upon his handsomeness, so serenely happy that her worries about him had all been for naught! She feared letting him out of her sight again, but knew that life had to be lived and that she had to continue trusting that nothing would take him away from her.

"We will have a combined feast upon your return," he said. "For a marriage and a child. It will be a celebration of all celebrations."

"If only Red Fox . . ."

"We will pray to the spirits to lead him safely home," he said.

A low rumble of thunder sounded in the distance. Danette threw herself into Gray Wolf's arms, thinking of the fullness of the moon that she had looked upon the night that she thought she had lost him forever. In its reflection she *had* seen him. Surely she had.

Chapter Seventeen

I will not let thee go,
I hold thee by too many bonds.
—Bridges

The train rolled along the tracks, jostling Danette as she sat stiff-backed next to her uncle. She gave him a slow glance, having been surprised to the point of becoming wordless when she had found him waiting for her at Rettie Toliver's boardinghouse upon her return from Gray Wolf's village. His ensuing coolness to Amanda had been unforgivable and embarrassing. But somehow he had discovered the Toliver family's secret and now knew their deep involvement with Gray Wolf and his family.

The air inside the train was so close it was stifling. It reminded Danette of a stove, all stoked up and burning hot. Had any late August ever been as hot? Not only were the trees of the forest scorched, but also the streams had gone dry. If not for the great rivers of the state, all would be lost for the people of Minnesota.

Yet there had continued to be a dull grayness to the sky these past several days, with still only a threat of rain. A great flash of lightning zigzagged across the sky, momentarily lighting up the train's interior, followed by a loud, clear crack of thunder, a sure sign that this bolt of lightning had struck something close by in the forest.

Dwight leaned closer to the window, peering into the

forest. "I don't like it," he worried, kneading his chin. "A fire is imminent. Surely that bolt of lighting struck one of those damn lifeless tress. The forest could go up like a match . . . in one angry puff."

The wind whined around the St. Paul and Duluth Railway train as it proceeded on its way, chug-chugging leisurely along. Soot from the train's engine blew into the open window at Dwight's side, settling on his face and in his eyes. Cursing, he removed a handkerchief from his inner jacket pocket and busied himself at removing the black streaks from his nose and beneath his eyes.

A faint odor of smoke drifted in through the window, alerting Danette to look past Dwight and out the window. But seeing nothing, she dismissed the smell as coming from the train's "tender," where a fire was kept roaring during the entire trip.

"Such an inconvenience, Danette," Dwight grumbled, replacing his handkerchief inside his pocket, giving her a sour look.

Danette emitted a bothered sigh. "To what are you referring?" she said, fanning herself with her embroidered velvet purse. Her hair had been styled atop her head in a fancy swirl to get it off her neck in an effort to make her comfortably cool. And though her silk dress was tighter than usual at her waist, it reflected her loveliness with its silk-threaded, embroidered, low-swept bodice and its yards and yards of gathered skirt.

"The fact that I had to go to St. Paul to return you, bodily, to Duluth, where I can keep my eye on you."

Danette shook her head sadly. But she knew that this one more time with her uncle would be her last and she would play out the charade to the end, for soon she would be with Gray Wolf for the rest of their lives, and she would never let her Uncle Dwight cause her any more confused heartache.

"And, Uncle Dwight, now that you have done this, what are your plans for me?" she tested, giving him a shadowed look. In his proper attire, looking so impeccable, and yes, handsome, Danette was reminded of her old admiration for him and even now felt the urge to touch him, to feel as she used to feel, as though he alone could make her feel secure in her life, knowing that he was always there, looking after her. But he had overstepped his bounds as guardian.

"We'll see," he said dryly. "But one thing I will forbid is your continued acquaintance with Gray Wolf." He fussed with his bow tie, placing a forefinger between it and his neck, making space there, as though trying to make it easier for him to breathe.

"You see," he murmured, leaning closer to Danette. "I found your portrait of Gray Wolf in your bedroom. How many times have you seen him behind my back? And even to go to his village? Disgraceful, Danette. Your mother and father would turn over in their graves if they knew."

Tears glistened at the corners of Danette's eyes. She circled her fingers into tight fists on her lap. "How could you even question me so after what you did?" she whispered back. "Uncle Dwight, you told me that you had killed Gray Wolf. Don't you know how cruel that was? A part of me was dead until I found him alive! You are the disgrace in the Thomas family. Not *I!*"

"It seemed an easy out," he grumbled. "Gray Wolf was a threat to our relationship. I couldn't let that continue, Danette."

"And was there even an Indian hanging?" she asked, covering her mouth with her hand, shuddering at the thought of the time that she had thought it had been Gray Wolf!

"Is it important to know?" he returned, crossing his legs. "You will have no more contact with the Indian community."

"I need to know if you are, indeed, that heartless!"

"Then set your mind at ease. No one died that night. No one."

Danette's eyes and face grew hot with anger. "You even

265

went so far as to tell that type of lie to me?" she gasped. "Uncle Dwight, how could you?"

"I do what is necessary."

"You have succeeded only in alienating me, your only living relative."

Dwight took one of her hands and squeezed it hard as she tried to wriggle it away from him. "Danette, you owe me," he said thickly. "From here on out, remember this. There will always be only the two of us. You are mine. Nobody else's."

Danette's eyes widened and her pulse raced. She looked toward her uncle and saw something new in his eyes. It was more than possessiveness. It was a look of desire—what a man feels for a woman when he wants her sexually!

"Uncle Dwight, you . . ." she whispered, numb, now realizing why he had never wed. In his twisted mind, he had thought that once she grew into womanhood, she would forever be his, in every sense of the word!

The thought not only surprised but repelled her!

Another bolt of lightning and a crack of thunder rumbled and smoke became quite evident outside the train window, drawing Danette's thoughts away from her Uncle Dwight and her newest discovery about him. When the smoke swirled around, leaving a space to look through, Danette saw that the forest was speckled with small fires.

Then her attention was quickly drawn elsewhere, to a man running down the aisle of the train, shouting something almost incomprehensible, his words garbled.

Dwight stepped over Danette and grabbed the man by his wrist and stopped him, swinging him around to face him. "What are you shouting?" he said. "Did you say something about Duluth?"

"A man just rode up on horseback and shouted to the engineer that Duluth is on fire," he said, recoiling as Dwight strengthened his hold.

"Duluth . . . is on fire?" Dwight gasped loudly.

"The whole damn countryside is burnin'," the man cried. "Let me go. I need to alert everyone on this train. We could be doomed unless we reach a body of water. Everybody needs to be told!"

Wisps of smoke drifted in through the train windows. Dwight released his hold on the man and fell sideways as the train suddenly jerked to a shuddering halt. "What the . . . ?" he said, steadying himself against a seat, wiping smoke from his face as it thickened around him.

There was suddenly a panic in the air as women, children, and men alike rose from their seats, shoving and pushing, trampling on each other. Dwight moved toward Danette with an outstretched hand. "We'll die in this trap," he shouted. "We've got to get out of here! Seems the train is on fire!"

Once more he fell across the seat, knocking the wind momentarily from him as the train took on a backwards plunge. The wheels screeched . . . the people screamed . . . but it was only Dwight who had become aware of what the train engineer was attempting to do. Only a couple of miles back the train had crossed over the bridge that had been built over Chain Lake, one of the many smaller lakes that stretched out like a chain from the wider expanses of Lake Superior. The engineer was trying to get the train to this lake so that his passengers could try to find safety in the water.

Then it came to Dwight like a flash. This fire was more than a threat to people. It was a threat to his entire future! Without the trees . . . and with Duluth burning . . . he *had* no future. All would be gone that he had worked so hard for all these years. And hadn't he in a sense already lost even Danette?

"Danette!" he said, shaking his head, suddenly once more aware of now . . . the present . . . and what was happening all around him. The fire had overtaken the train while it kept racing backwards. Everywhere Dwight looked, he saw flames. The seats were burning. The ceiling was ablaze. The walls were smoldering and smoking and spitting out balls of flame. Screams tore through the air.

Dwight placed a hand over his mouth and nostrils, fighting to see through the dense smoke where Danette had been sitting. But she wasn't there. She was gone! But where . . . ?

Stumbling, fighting off the flames that threatened to engulf him, Dwight began searching frantically for Danette, and when he found her huddled behind a seat farther up in the coach where the flames weren't as bad, he grabbed her hand and pulled her up next to him.

"We must hurry!" he shouted. "The heat has caused the air to rise, which in turn has made the flames even hotter. It's caused a chain reaction of sorts in the forest . . . producing a wind that is roaring, carrying the flames with it. Everything and everybody in its path is in danger!"

The glass windows of the train snapped and cracked in the fierce heat, beginning to toss splinters of glass in all directions, like weapons. Danette covered her face with her hands and let Dwight continue guiding her to the back of the coach, feeling as though the end of the world had come and nothing they attempted would help. Gray Wolf flashed before her eyes, and she thought she would never see him again, and even wondered if his village was being burned as everything else in the world seemed to be in the process of doing.

When a piece of flying glass pierced Danette's upper left arm, she cried out in pain and winced as Dwight quickly freed her of the glass and guided her by his arm about her waist on out, onto the burning caboose.

"We're there!" Dwight shouted. "I see the river." He also saw bodies tumbling from the train, down the steep banks of the river, some burning, some with their clothes smoldering and gray spirals of smoke rising from them.

The screams multiplied, and the heavens raged with an inferno of flames as the fire spread through the forest ceiling, setting off fresh fires as each treetop was reached. Then, as the train drew to a grinding halt, a loud rumble followed when the burning bridge that the train had just crossed fell tumbling into the muddy waters below it, burying some people beneath its debris and setting off even more fires with its timbers of red flames.

"Come on," Dwight said, urging Danette onto the ground. He half dragged and half carried her to their goal— a small portion of the water that wasn't already inhabited. Danette swung at the flames that had caught onto the skirt of her dress, and when she looked toward Dwight she screamed, seeing his jacket in full flames that threatened to scorch his face as they rose quickly upward.

Dwight fought with the jacket, trying to remove it, then began swatting at his hair as the pomade he had applied to it seemed to grab out at the flames, inviting them to dance and sway through his hair, like miniature orange elves.

Danette desperately began swinging her hands at the flames, crying, sobbing his name over and over again. But he just continued to drag her toward the water, and when they reached it, he gave her a great shove and fell to the ground and rolled on it, trying then to protect himself from the flames that had quickly engulfed him.

Danette stumbled around on the muddy bottom of the river, trying to stand, watching in desperation as her uncle was perishing right before her eyes. "Uncle Dwight!" she screamed. "Oh, God, Uncle Dwight . . ."

She felt a bitterness rising in her throat. She suddenly wasn't only seeing her uncle burning before her eyes, but also her parents.

"Why? Oh, why . . . ?" she cried, turning her eyes to the fiery heavens.

She then turned her eyes away and held her face in her hands, but only momentarily, for she became aware of the heat on the flesh of her legs where she stood in the shallow water. She looked quickly down at the skirt of her dress and saw that some burning debris had fallen around her in the water and had once more set her clothes on fire.

"No," she cried. "Oh, God, no."

She threw herself down into the water, oblivious now of all the cries for help around her, knowing that she was in just as much danger as everyone else was. All above her the trees were crimson with fire. Limbs were breaking off, unmercifully falling on and around the people who sought refuge in the water, which, because of the lack of rain, was too shallow to give much protection.

Danette could only stay beneath the water for short intervals, and each time she rose to the surface her arms would once more become an attraction to the flames, and before long many welts had risen on her flesh.

Sorrowfully heavy at heart over the death of her uncle, whose body she couldn't even see now in the raging fire, Danette couldn't control her sobs. She trembled with weakening knees and tried to close her ears to the torturous screams and the howling of the wind on all sides of her.

She splashed water on herself continuously and dipped her head into the lake over and over again, keeping her hair wet. But nothing could stop the smell of her scorched flesh from rising into her nose nor the lightheadedness that was now engulfing her.

Clutching at her abdomen, she remembered her child and cried out Gray Wolf's name as she crumpled slowly down into the water. But before her head lowered beneath the water's surface, Danette suddenly felt strong arms about her waist.

Laboring to keep her eyes open, to hold on to consciousness, Danette looked through a haze of smoke and tears and made out a figure of a man who was covering her with a large strip of wetted deerskin. With the man partially hidden beneath his own strip of wet deerskin, Danette was only able to catch a glimpse of his eyes, and somehow she thought she had seen something familiar about them. But the smoke

... the ache in her head ... the burning of her eyes kept her from focusing enough to make out who it was.

"Sweet Butterfly, Gray Wolf will get you to safety," she heard, then went delirious with joy when she knew who her rescuer was. Once again Gray Wolf was saving her from imminent death. She wanted to hug him, tell him how happy she was to see him, but it was all she could do to keep herself from falling into a state of shock from all that she had experienced and was still experiencing. In Gray Wolf's arms, she went limp and closed her eyes, knowing no more than his strength ... his nearness ... and thanking God for them both.

Breathing hard, wracked with fiery pains on her arms, legs, and face, Danette awakened. With her each and every movement she had added pain. She looked slowly around her, then erupted into a quivering smile when she saw Gray Wolf close by, erecting what appeared to be a wigwam.

Licking her parched, cracked lips, Danette tried to speak his name, but only a shallow whisper surfaced. She blinked her eyes slowly, hurting even there, and tried to reach her hand into the air to draw his attention to her, but her arm seemed heavy, like a dead weight, making her give up, to wait until he came to her under his own volition.

Recalling the horror of what had happened, Danette shuddered violently, then looked desperately up at the trees, watching for flames to lap away at the leaves overhead. But there were no flames ... no smoke....

There was only the chatter of the birds, and the soft whisper of a breeze as it blew through the wilted leaves of the gigantic oak that towered over Danette, as she lay stretched out on a blanket, naked.

Gray Wolf worked in haste, knowing that he had to get Sweet Butterfly into a soft bed of blankets, out of the approaching damp hours of the night. She was in no condition to travel to his village. Her burns had first to be treated, given a chance to heal, and then, only then would he return her to his people, where he would never let her wander from them again unless he was with her to watch over her and their unborn child.

"My son," he grumbled, feeling his gut do a slow twisting. "What if all of this has caused her to lose our child?"

Gray Wolf stopped long enough to gaze toward Danette, knowing that he had come close to losing her forever. One moment longer and she would have perished, not by fire, but by water. When he had caught her, she had been half-conscious and would have drowned for sure had she fallen all the way into the water.

Gray Wolf took a sudden step forward, dropping his arm-load of birchbark to the ground. "Sweet Butterfly?" he whispered. Had she moved? Had she awakened?

Danette slowly turned her head toward the shine of the water, wondering which river Gray Wolf had found refuge beside. Would the fires follow them? Would they perish together in the end? Had it been foolish to stop, even for a moment?

"No . . ." she finally managed to scream, shaking her head fitfully back and forth, though every movement was a torment to her.

Gray Wolf ran to Danette and fell to his knees beside her. "Sweet Butterfly . . ." he said thickly. "You cry out?"

Danette slowly turned her head his way and painfully moved her hand, to touch him. "Gray . . . Wolf . . ." she whispered raspily. "My . . . love . . ."

Gray Wolf sat down on the ground and slowly lifted her head onto his lap. "Gray Wolf heal your burns with herbs," he said. "This why you no wear clothes. You will heal more quickly. Sweet Butterfly will be all right. We will stay beside the river in wigwam until you are well enough to travel again."

He brushed her hair softly back from her eyes and saw

the mask of pain her face made, crushing his heart, feeling helpless though he was doing everything humanly possible to make her comfortable and well.

"It's all so horrible," Danette said, becoming teary-eyed. She licked her lips. "My uncle . . ."

Gray Wolf lifted a tin cup of water to her lips and gave her a small, slow drink. *"Ay-uh,* Gray Wolf knows," he said thickly.

"How . . . ?"

"While delirious in sleep, you tell of his fate," Gray Wolf said, lowering the cup from her lips. "While delirious you say many things. But you need fear no more. Gray Wolf protect you. Always."

"How did you know to . . . to find me . . . ?"

Gray Wolf placed the cup on the ground and his face drew shadows onto it as he avoided Danette's eyes. "News of Red Fox had to be taken to White Blossom," he said hoarsely. "White Blossom said you'd just left by train with your uncle, so I follow."

"News? What news? Did . . . you . . . find Red Fox . . . ?"

"Ay-uh . . ."

"And . . . ?"

"The news was not good," Gray Wolf said, moving his gaze to meet hers.

Danette's heart ached anew. "No," she whispered. "Not him also. This is a time of many deaths. What can it . . . all . . . mean . . . ?"

"Red Fox look like he fell from his horse," Gray Wolf said painfully. "His neck was broken. It was like in his youth, when he said he injure himself when he fell upon a thorn and hurt his eye. Gray Wolf not believe it then . . . and not believe it now."

"You think . . . ?"

"Me know," Gray Wolf announced loudly. "One day I find that Longbow and kill him slowly, with no mercy."

"Is Longbow . . . no . . . longer of the Chippewa?"

273

"He will always be Chippewa by birth but not by action or deed," Gray Wolf growled. "He most surely is now a part of the snakelike Sioux. Even his mother Foolish Heart is gone. He must have sneaked into camp and steal her away like a ghost in the night."

"Amanda . . . ?"

"Heartbroken," Gray Wolf said sadly. "She leave for the burial rites. They should already be over by now. Everyone understand my absence. It was my deed to also find out who the Indian was who your uncle murdered. If it was Chippewa . . ."

Danette shook her head slowly back and forth. "It was . . . not . . . Chippewa. . . ." she said, each breath now an effort on her part, as though her lungs were scorched, possibly fused to her chest.

"How does Sweet Butterfly know this?"

She hated saying his name, feeling guilty for having been unpleasant to her Uncle Dwight only moments before his death. Would she ever forgive herself? He had only meant the best for her. He had even saved her . . . losing his own life in the process!

But then she remembered his future, unnatural intentions for her, and was sickened anew.

"My Uncle Dwight," she whispered. "He . . . confessed to me . . . that there was no death that night."

"Then it was a trick?"

"Yes. A terrible trick," Danette said, closing her eyes wistfully, feeling, oh, so badly, the need to let sleep overcome her. But she was afraid to sleep. She was afraid that possibly she might not awaken again. . . .

A slight whiff of smoke spiraling through the air through the treetops caused her eyes to open. She clasped onto Gray Wolf's hand. "The . . . fire . . ." she softly cried. "It will overtake us. We . . . shall . . . die. . . ."

"There are many bodies of water between us and the raging fingers of the fire," Gray Wolf said, moistening her lips with water from the cup. "We are safe. We traveled far. The St. Croix River is running freely and calmly at our side. We only have it to follow when we head on to the village. You must remember. Smoke like we left behind travels much distance. Do not let it frighten you."

"Duluth . . . ?"

"While searching for you in the fire, I heard shouts from some that Duluth was gone," he said. "Others said that only a small part was burned."

"My uncle's house, my beloved paintings," she murmured. Then her eyes grew wild. "And Amy," she cried.

"Amy?"

"My personal maid," she said. "Deer, sweet Amy . . ." She once more found herself fighting sleep.

"One day you will forget all sadness," Gray Wolf crooned, cradling her head, slowly rocking her back and forth.

"Never . . ." she whispered, closing her eyes.

Gray Wolf stared numbly at the very slight swell of her abdomen, hypnotically watching her heartbeat there, wondering if there still was another heartbeat, in the cocoon of her womb.

As though she had read his thoughts, Danette's hand went to her stomach. It was still smooth, free of burns, and she had to wonder about her child. Could all the trauma she had experienced cause the loss of her and Gray Wolf's child? Would such a tragedy give way to future tragedies, causing her to never be able to bear children for the man she loved?

Gray Wolf eased her head from his lap. "Gray Wolf must finish dwelling before nightfall," he said, lowering a kiss to her parched lips. "Tonight you will lie beside me, safe, and soon your burns will heal, to be no more."

"I . . . love . . . you. . . ." she whispered, painfully smiling at him as he rose from his haunches and proceeded with his labors. Occasionally he would glance her way with a worried

275

look, which then would seem to give cause for him to rush on, even more quickly.

Still wary should the fire spread even this far, no matter what Gray Wolf said, Danette turned her head toward the river, and gradually she let its presence become like a tonic to her. The sky was only barely overcast and the stream was still and tranquil. It had overflowed its margins because of a dam that had been made by beavers. Trees stood knee-deep in the water and water-lilies floated, dainty in their faint pinks and yellows. The rushes waved and whispered and the sunshine fell in specks around Danette.

Softly dozing, she dreamed of her Uncle Dwight and the flames he could no longer fight. Screams . . . shouts . . . the snapping of the fire . . . the howl of the wind. . . .

"Gray Wolf!" Danette screamed, unable to bear any more of the thoughts that continued to haunt her.

Gray Wolf was there in a rush and very carefully lifted her up into his arms, trying his best to not touch the rawness of any of her burns. "The wigwam is ready," he said quietly, taking the softest of steps, as though his feet weren't even touching the ground. She knew that he could be gentle, but never before had he been this gentle.

Stooping, Gray Wolf carried her inside the dwelling and placed her on blankets beside a softly burning fire in a firespace.

Danette flinched when she looked wildly into the flames, wondering if flames of a fire would forever haunt and torment her.

Shivering, she groaned as Gray Wolf moved his arms from beneath her, stirring her body too much with his movements.

"Is a fire needed?" she finally managed to question, looking painfully away from it.

"To keep off chill," he said, settling down beside her, now slowly bathing her burns with a clear, fresh-smelling substance that he had stirred together in a cup. "And, Sweet Butterfly, these medicinal herbs are required. They should be applied often to heal the flesh. Tomorrow I will boil cedar boughs in water over fire to purify air.''

Danette winced beneath the painful touch. She felt beads of perspiration rise on her brow and she had the urge to cry out. But she had more the need to show her bravery and instead bit her lower lip and bore the pain in silence.

A flash of lightning and the ensuing rumble of thunder caused Danette to quickly lose her bravery and desperately grab Gray Wolf's arm, causing him to spill the medicine at his feet.

"Sweet Butterfly . . . ?" he said, questioning her with his eyes.

"Didn't you hear . . . ?"

"Ay-uh," he said. "Thunder."

"Gray Wolf, what if . . . ?"

Gray Wolf cupped a hand to his right ear. "Do *you* not hear?" he said, leaning toward the doorspace.

Danette's breath slowed and a slow smile drew her lips upward. "Is it . . . is it . . . really raining?" she asked, flooded with a joyous relief, knowing that nothing could sound so sweet or be so welcome.

"Rain," Gray Wolf said, jumping to his feet and rushing outside. He raised his face to the gentle grays of the sky and spread his arms above his head, tasting the freshness of the rain on his lips and feeling its coolness on his face.

"Thank you, *Wenebojo,* spirit who made the world," he chanted. He cupped his hands and patiently let the rain splash into them, then went to Danette and knelt beside her.

"Ay-uh," he said. "Rain. I've brought some to you." He placed his hands beneath her nose and let her inhale the fresh outdoor fragrance of it, then placed some on her lips to taste.

"The drought is now over," he said. "Now is time for rejoicing. With rain, comes life."

"If it . . . could have . . . been sooner. . . ."

Gray Wolf leaned a kiss to the tip of her nose. "Sweet

Butterfly, be happy for now, not sad for what could have been."

"It is not an . . . easy . . . task."

"Life is no easy task, but the living live it."

Danette lifted a hand shakily to his face. "Are you always so . . . so wise . . . ?"

Gray Wolf chuckled. "Gray Wolf certainly hope so," he said. "As you are always beautiful."

Though ravaged with pain, Danette managed a blush. "I know what . . . a . . . sight I must . . . be," she whispered. "Gray Wolf, your love for me must truly be . . . be . . . strong."

"*Ay-uh,* it is," he said, stretching out beside her, so wanting to embrace her, but knowing that would come later, after she had healed.

"*Ay-uh,* it is," he repeated, at least taking her hand, bringing it to his lips, kissing it.

Chapter Eighteen

Come live with me and be my love,
And we will all the pleasures prove. . . .
— Marlowe

Raindrops sparkled on the tips of the leaves in the shining mist of early morning. Danette drew the Indian blanket aside at the doorspace and inhaled the fragrance of damp pine needles and earth. At this moment, in the peacefulness that surrounded her, it was almost impossible for her to believe all the tragedy that had befallen her and her friend Amanda.

"Uncle Dwight and Red Fox," she sighed. "How quickly and unexpected death comes. . . ."

Feeling the warmth of an arm circling her waist and the male strength of Gray Wolf moving against her body from behind, Danette's eyes closed in ecstasy. If she would just let it happen, it could be easy to forget, with Gray Wolf there to help her.

With Gray Wolf's herbs, it had taken, almost miraculously, only a few days for her burns to begin healing. Now they were only slight blemishes, no longer painful to the touch, and Danette knew that the time had come to make a decision about what she must do about her Uncle Dwight's estate, which would now be hers. It was probably believed that she had perished in the fire along with State Senator Dwight Thomas.

"Sweet Butterfly beautiful with child," Gray Wolf said

279

huskily, drawing her even closer against him, with his chest against her back. His fingers circled her breasts and gently squeezed them.

"And milk is readying for our tiny *ah-bee-no-gee*," he added. "*Ay-uh*, we will have a healthy son who will carry our name on, even after our death."

Shivering more from delight than the morning chill, Danette turned and faced Gray Wolf. Placing her hands to his cheeks, she gazed rapturously into his green eyes, feeling guilty for her happiness, when she should be mourning her Uncle Dwight's death.

But, somehow, the tears had been spent for a man who had thought enough of himself during life to leave almost no room for anyone else's grieving for him.

"Gray Wolf, I am now well enough to travel," she said. "You do know what has to be done, don't you?"

"Even in death your uncle still stands in the way of our happiness," Gray Wolf said, frowning.

"For only a little longer, Gray Wolf," Danette murmured. "Only for a little while longer. Please understand?"

"Gray Wolf accompany you to Duluth," he said. "On same horse, we will ride into the city of Duluth together."

"I will not argue against that," she said, knowing not what to expect when she arrived there. Should the city be gone, it might even be easier for her, for then it would be easier to walk away, to think of it no more.

But she did have to go to Duluth, to see for herself, and then to place all of the legal aspects of the estate in the hands of her uncle's lawyer. If things were still intact and salvageable, she would have everything placed in trust for her and Gray Wolf's children, to assure them of a trouble-free future.

It would be the only thing left them by her Uncle Dwight. Her children would never discover the evil side of his character . . . the side that had wanted Gray Wolf, their father, dead.

"Your eyes take on a look of sadness," Gray Wolf said, reading in her expression that she would not forget her recent trauma so easily. Seeing her uncle burn to death would haunt her, possibly forever. And, hadn't her parents died in the same, agonizing way . . . ?

"Gray Wolf, I was once more spared," she said. "Please help me to understand and be happy for it."

"You were born for a purpose," he said, drawing her into his arms, holding her tightly. "As I was also. It was meant for Gray Wolf to be chief and Sweet Butterfly chief's wife. The spirits are wise. Do not doubt reason for being. As great spirit Manido control weather, great spirit Wenebojo control our fate."

"Hold me," Danette whispered. "Just please hold me." She lifted her face to his, clinging, and watched as his lips lowered sensuously to hers.

Effervescent bubbles of desire bounced and burst inside her as his tongue slowly probed inside her mouth.

With the need to feel the whole of him, Danette's hands began moving over his bare flesh, having long ago lost all modesty in his presence. For the past several days they had shared the wigwam without a trace of clothes on. But only now had he tried to approach her sexually because of his earlier fears of hurting her where her burns lay, red and raw.

But now, with healed wounds and hearts on fire with building passion for one another, his need for her showed in the swollen strength of his manhood pressed hungrily against her thigh.

Gray Wolf's hands teased and tormented Danette as he moved them across her back and down her spine. They cupped the cheeks of her buttocks and playfully squeezed her there.

"Sweet Butterfly, my mind is spinning with want of you," he said huskily. He placed his sex against her furry mound and slowly moved it up and down, tantalizing her almost into mindlessness.

281

"It's been so long," Danette whispered, taking in a shuddering breath as one of his fingers entered her from below and began a slow, circular movement inside her. She opened herself up to him and let the sweet pain/pleasure take hold, as never before.

"*Ay-uh*," Gray Wolf said. "Too long."

With the guidance of spirals of sunshine glistening through the branches of the trees, Gray Wolf lifted Danette up into his arms and carried her toward the shine of the St. Croix River. On a bluff, only barely shadowed by tall oak trees, Gray Wolf spread Danette out onto a thick bed of springy, green moss. She looked like an offering to the great Indian spirits, but to Gray Wolf she was only his, and he lowered himself down over her.

"You healed enough, Sweet Butterfly?" he asked, shakily running a forefinger over her delicate facial features. "Gray Wolf can be patient longer, if you say so."

Danette twined her arms about his neck and smiled peacefully up at him. "Your herbs were like magic to my flesh," she said. "As your hands and lips are magic to my soul."

With an intense throbbing in his loins and his heart full of love, Gray Wolf crushed his lips against hers while skillfully placing his swollen strength inside her.

Feeling the passion rising, having the need of this sort of escape to help mend her inner wounds, Danette raised her hips to join in their bodies' dance of ecstasy.

Becoming breathless now, Danette's eyes closed, her fingers locked together behind his neck. She writhed beneath him as his tongue flicked back and forth between her breasts.

The swimming feeling inside her head began unwarned, and together she and Gray Wolf shook and trembled, then lay, clinging, laughing softly into one another's hair at the wetness of their perspiration-beaded bodies.

"*Ay-uh*, you are well enough," Gray Wolf softly laughed, kissing her neck, below her left ear. Then he drew away from her and pushed her hair back from her eyes. "Did it

282

feel as though you were a bird, soaring, when the pleasure was at its greatest?"

"No," she said, smiling softly up at him.

"*Gah-ween?*" he exclaimed, eyeing her with an arched eyebrow.

"No," she teased.

"You no enjoy?"

"*Ay-uh*, I did," she said, giggling.

"Then how it make you feel, if not like a bird?"

"Gray Wolf, I felt like a beautiful butterfly," she said, watching a slow laugh lift his lips and the color of his eyes take on many shades of green, as he understood her meaning.

"A butterfly with lacy wings," he said, running a hand down her stomach, causing her flesh to ripple with the pleasure of his added touch.

"Well, not so lacy that everyone could see and know me so intimately," she said. "Only you, my love. Only you."

"As it shall always be," Gray Wolf said.

Danette rose slowly from the ground, stretching her arms above her head, yawning. "This is a lazy, peaceful place, Gray Wolf," she sighed. "One I hate to leave. It's a world without people, except for only us."

She welcomed him at her side and leaned into his embrace as his arm linked about her waist. "Don't you feel it, Gray Wolf?" she whispered. "The sense of forever? The feeling that no matter what happens anywhere else, this particular place will go on forever, as it has since the beginning of time?"

She gestured with her hand. "When we are dead even. The river will run, the sun will shine, the birds will sing. . . ."

Gray Wolf urged her around to face him. His features were stern, his eyes unwavering. "These feelings you have are good," he said. "It means you are understanding life as an Indian sees it. So much of our thoughts are guided by nature. We live by nature's rules. You will make Gray Wolf good wife."

Danette settled into his arms, hugging him as she placed her cheek against his chest. "But I must prepare myself for my journey to Duluth," she said, shuddering at the thought. "I must go today. There are things that must be done."

"We will have one last swim in river," Gray Wolf said. "It, as well as my herbs, has helped to make you well. The St. Croix River holds many spirits. They bless your body when they touch you."

"All right," Danette said, turning to look from the steep bluff. Several mornings she had watched Gray Wolf dive gracefully from the bluff. Until this day she had only gone to where the grassy slope led her slowly into the water. But today she felt well enough to dive alongside him. Her unborn child had proven its strength to her by staying peacefully alive inside her, though she had suffered much from the damnable, raging fire. So, Danette knew that her child would also not suffer from the physical activity of a dive and a swim!

Gray Wolf began leading her by the hand toward the grassy slope, but Danette held back. "Let's dive together," she said, watching his jaw tighten and his brow furrow. "I am well enough, Gray Wolf. And I have dived quite often from the bluffs over Lake Superior. This is one thing my uncle taught me quite well. He always preached the importance of swimming, when you live so close to a large body of water."

Gray Wolf placed his hand gently to the slight swell of her abdomen. *"Ah-bee-no-gee?"* he mumbled.

Danette laughed softly. She covered his hand with hers. "You said 'baby' in Indian?" she asked.

"Ay-uh."

"Do you see, Gray Wolf, I'm learning your way of speaking quite well."

"This make Gray Wolf proud," he said. "But once more I question you. Will dive into water harm baby? So many

284

Indian women lose babies while in womb. Sweet Butterfly must do everything to keep this from happening.''

"Gray Wolf, I am not Indian,'' she said. "I will probably bear you many sons without one ounce of trouble. And if I'm strong, so is our unborn child. One day he will show you his strength in the way he will kick inside me.''

"Gray Wolf will be touching you a lot, to experience it also,'' he said, laughing lightly.

He bent and kissed her abdomen. "There, my son,'' he said throatily. "You have had your morning kiss from your *gee-bah-bah*.''

Danette giggled, then broke free and ran to the edge of the bluff and posed for her dive. "Come on, Gray Wolf, dive beside me,'' she said, taking in his virile form as he moved toward her.

She loved the powerful cords of his leg muscles and the way his hips narrowed. Her heart pounded as she let her gaze settle on the part of him that sent her senses to reeling with only one plunge inside her. Before Gray Wolf, passion . . . rapture . . . ecstasy . . . had been words foreign to her. She had been so innocent!

He posed next to her, and together they began their plummet downward. Danette relished the feel of the air rushing against her face and the feel of weightlessness as she waited for her first contact with the water. She closed her eyes and let her body move gracefully into the water and on to the bottom of the river where Gray Wolf eased himself next to her and together, arm in arm, they floated back to the surface and broke through, laughing.

"My Sweet Butterfly now become as fish,'' Gray Wolf said, nuzzling her neck. "Is there anything my woman cannot do? You swim as easily as you walk.''

Treading water, Danette turned to face him, shaking her hair from her eyes. "I want to prove to you that I am worthy to one day become the chief's wife,'' she said softly. "Until only recently, I was not as strong as I'm sure you wished me to be. I depended too much on others. Even Amanda, White Blossom, felt the need to mother me."

"Gray Wolf never see this weakness you speak of," he said hoarsely. "You strong in my eyes."

Pulling her into his arms, he placed his renewed swollen desire for her against her leg. Clinging, she draped an arm about his shoulder and welcomed his lips claiming hers in a fiery kiss.

"Gray Wolf, not again . . . so soon . . ." she teased as he set her momentarily free from his lips, to ease a hand down to where she ached with need for him. The water made his gentle caresses even more sensual. She arched her head back and let out a soft moan. Then he once more was there, embracing her, fighting to keep afloat as their bodies began tangling until he was inside her, working frantically in and out of her.

Danette laughed huskily. "Gray Wolf, what we are trying to do is surely impossible in the water," she said, trying to stay locked to him as she held tightly around his neck.

The water splashed into her eyes, momentarily blinding her, causing her to giggle even more throatily. She knew that the euphoric feeling was slowly engulfing her, no matter that her head was fighting to remain at the surface of the water and that Gray Wolf had to do all that was in his power to keep them both from plunging to the bottom of the river because of their added weight and desperate manipulations of each other's body.

"Everything in love is possible," Gray Wolf said, holding her even more tightly, shuddering with the thrill of having her breasts next to his chest, warm and wet, and, oh, so beautifully huge with their unborn child's milk.

"I'm beginning to believe that is so," Danette said, closing her eyes, now depending solely on him to keep her from drowning as she felt her mind slowly drifting from her, as though she was a part of the water now, floating, forever floating.

Suddenly a violent shudder erupted throughout her, causing her to cry out with pleasure, her cry echoing back at her over and over again, through the hills and the meadows, added to them by Gray Wolf's loud chant as his body also quaked and stiffened.

Softly laughing, Danette felt him loose his grip on her body. She swam away from him, still trembling from the intense pleasure he had once more given her. She looked back over her shoulder, teasing him, and began taking swifter strokes as she saw him plunge deep down into the water so she lost sight of him.

Suddenly his hands were there, beneath the water, encircling both her ankles and pulling her downward. And as she moved gracefully into his waiting arms, she twined her arms about his neck and welcomed his lips soft and sweet against hers, until together they once again had to rush to the surface, coughing and laughing for the breaths of air they so desperately needed.

"Gray Wolf, this has to stop," Danette said, running her fingers through her hair. "We cannot spend the rest of eternity just making love. Remember? I do have my duties awaiting me."

"*Ay-uh*," Gray Wolf grumbled, tossing his head, now swimming toward shore, moody in his unhappiness at what she had to do. He had hoped that she would just place all of her past completely behind her now, but he had to remember that she had her ways . . . as he had his. He had to give in to her . . . as she would give in to him when the need arose. That was what the word "sharing" meant. An understanding of the other's needs. But it was hard! He didn't understand much of the white man's world, though he had tried . . . by working in it.

Moving on to the blowing grass of the shore, Gray Wolf turned and offered Danette his hand, to help her out beside him.

Danette took his hand, looking into his eyes, seeing their

troubled look. But she had no choice but to return to Duluth. Possibly it would be her last time.

Now securely on the ground, she raked her fingers through her hair and tossed it back from her shoulders, already feeling the warm rays of the sun drying it. She thought wearily about the dress that she would be wearing to Duluth. It was filled with many burn holes, a sad reminder of that fateful day in her life.

But she had no other to wear. At least she had been able to wash it in the river, to cleanse it of its ugly smell of smoke.

But nothing would ever remove the remembrance of that day . . . especially while she had to wear the dress that she had worn while watching her Uncle Dwight . . . perish . . . right before her eyes.

Closing her eyes, gritting her teeth, she tried to not let the memory take hold of her again. If it did, she might scream. Not only was she haunted by her uncle's eyes filled with horrible pain, but also by the memory of her parents and her new knowledge of exactly how they must have suffered, since they also had died in such a fire.

Gray Wolf moved to Danette and clasped his fingers gently to her shoulders and gently shook her. "You are once more lost in thought," he growled. "You must fight these times when the remembering wants to take hold of you. You must put it all behind you. All the pain . . . the fire . . ."

Danette sobbed throatily, then let her eyes turn to him, seeing his concern for her in the lines of his face. "Yes," she murmured. "I must. I will. But only after I go to Duluth and as quickly leave it and my uncle's house behind me."

"Then Sweet Butterfly, let's do it," Gray Wolf said. "Now."

Dreading the task even more than she had realized, Danette eased from Gray Wolf's hold and moved to the ground, where she settled onto a thick bed of grass. She couldn't stop the tremors from taking charge of her as she again fought memories of that day.

Gray Wolf sat down next to her and wrapped his arms about his knees. "It is so hard?" he murmured.

"*Ay-uh,*" she said, plucking grass, tossing it into the river. "It is."

"Then why do it?"

"I told you. I must."

"Then go," he growled.

"In a little while," Danette murmured. Her eyes moved away from the river and captured a gleaming against the brown mat of fallen leaves beneath the oak tree. She leaned closer and saw flowers so white and fragile they were almost unreal. The stems and bracts as well as the flowers were without a vestige of color. They were completely translucent white.

Gray Wolf saw where she looked and placed a hand to hers as she started to pluck a slender stem. "Do not pluck ghost flower," he told her. "You violate tribal taboo."

"What ... ?" Danette asked, studying the flower, not understanding.

"They are ghost flowers," Gray Wolf said. "Notice how they are shaped like peace pipe?"

"Why, yes," she said. "I can see it now."

"Spirits smoke these ghost peace pipes in Happy Hunting Ground."

"What do you mean, Gray Wolf?"

"They smoke Little Spirit peace pipes. Smoke peace pipe and forget," he said. "Ghosts of the peace pipes the spirits smoke when they first come to the Happy Hunting Grounds. When they smoke their pipes of peace, they forget quarrels and can live happy and at peace always."

"It's a beautiful myth."

Gray Wolf's face took on angry shadows. "No myth," he growled. "Truth."

Danette reached a hand to his face. "I'm sorry, Gray Wolf," she said. "I didn't mean to upset you."

He shook his head and forced a smile. "You will learn my ways in time," he said. "This word 'lawyer' you speak of is as foreign to me as ghost flower is to you. You use that word a lot lately."

"Yes. I will be letting a lawyer settle all of my uncle's affairs," Danette said, rising slowly to her feet. "And I've procrastinated long enough. I guess I'd best do it today, Gray Wolf."

"Best done and over with, then we begin our life without any more interruptions," he said, walking alongside her to the wigwam.

Silently Danette dressed, watching Gray Wolf as he gathered together everything they had used there. Once she was ready, she left the wigwam and went to his horse and waited for him. As he dismantled the wigwam, it seemed to Danette that parts of her were being removed. The days and nights in the wigwam with Gray Wolf had become such a special time, something never to be recaptured. From here on out, she would forever be sharing him with his people. He was a chosen one, a leader.

"It is done," Gray Wolf said without a backwards glance as he helped Danette onto the horse.

"But why did you have to destroy it?" Danette asked, now only seeing the wigwam's frame left standing, like a skeleton, devoid of flesh.

"When Chippewa move on, the dwelling is never left for another to use," he grumbled. "Our moments together there will not be allowed to be shared by another."

"I see," Danette murmured, now sitting in his shadows as he sat tall in his saddle behind her.

Gray Wolf held her against him with one hand and his reins with the other and guided his horse into the forest. There was a difference today. The rain had fed the maple's roots, making the sugar rise upward, causing some of the leaves to take on a slight crimson cast. The yellow leaves of the elms and poison ivy vines twining about an old oak seemed to have magically changed overnight to bright red.

"Windigo haunt winter woods soon," Gray Wolf said, looking sourly about him at the change in the trees.

"This Windigo you speak of," Danette said. "Is this another of your Indian spirits?"

"Yes," he said. "He is a giant who slay the deer and rabbit by blowing icy breath on faces and limbs. He cause much heartache for Indians. If animals freeze, they no good to Indian."

A tinge of scorched trees was suddenly there, in the air. In the distance, remains of burned trees rose from the earth in ghostly caricatures of what once was, sending an involuntary shiver to race across Danette's face.

"Seems Windigo will be deprived of many things this winter," she said sullenly. "I'm sure the fire not only ravaged the trees, but surely also many innocent wild things in its path."

"*Ay-uh,*" Gray Wolf said, leading his horse on toward and into the gray ashes damp with after-rain. The forest was eerily quiet, with only an occasional sharp, momentary cry from a confused bird in flight.

The farther they traveled, the worse the desolation and ruin. And then the railroad track was before them. The steel was strangely curled away from the ground, twisted from the intense heat of the fire.

Danette turned her head away to where only the engine of a train still stood intact, fallen to its side deep into a ravine, where the bridge had burned and had fallen into the river, where Danette had found refuge . . . and where she had seen not only her uncle, but many people die. . . .

"Please, Gray Wolf," she said. "Hurry and take me on by this place."

Danette closed her eyes and placed her cheek against Gray Wolf's chest. "Tell me when it's safe to look again,

Gray Wolf,'' she murmured, wondering if it would ever be safe again. She felt as though she was in hell and silently thanked God that she wasn't alone.

She clung to Gray Wolf's chest, and when a voice broke through the silence, she opened her eyes wildly and found herself staring into a face quite familiar to her.

"Frenchman . . ." Gray Wolf growled.

"Raoul . . ." Danette gasped.

Chapter Nineteen

The kind, the brave, the sweet
Walk with us no more.
—Chadwick

In a flash of movement, Gray Wolf removed his rifle from its sheath and was pointing it toward Raoul, who didn't react except to laugh cynically as he remained untouched, it seemed, by the threat of Gray Wolf's renewed anger against him.

"Indian, Raoul wants no trouble," Raoul said. He ran a hand across his singed whiskers. "These past several days have been trouble enough for me. Let me pass on by you. Duluth holds my interest no more. Raoul is in search of new adventure, but not the kind you are threatening me with."

"It was a mistake to not kill you before. The same mistake must not be made again," Gray Wolf growled. "Frenchman, you are trouble no matter where adventure take you. No one safe when you're around."

Danette placed her hand on the rifle and lowered its barrel. "Gray Wolf, let him go," she encouraged. "There have been enough deaths. And what harm can he be to us now? He says he is leaving Duluth, which means he must be leaving this entire area. The fire has destroyed so much, he will surely travel far away to seek his new life."

"It will never be far enough," Gray Wolf said. "He not to be trusted. Ever."

"Gray Wolf, perhaps this is the time to place all bitterness behind you," Danette further encouraged. "Our future together is almost a reality. Please do nothing now to threaten this happiness we have been searching for since our first meeting. Gray Wolf, our child . . ."

Gray Wolf gave Danette a scowl, then looked back toward Raoul as he nodded. *"Ay-uh,"* he grumbled. "You are right. As always, you prove to me that you are wise choice for chief's wife."

"Then you will let him pass?"

"This time," Gray Wolf growled. "But if he cross my path again . . ."

"He says he is leaving," Danette said. "We will never see him again."

Gray Wolf clucked to his horse and guided it to stand next to Raoul's. With his rifle once more aimed at Raoul, Gray Wolf said, "Be on your way, Frenchman. But if you ever return to cause me or my woman trouble, a bullet won't even be enough for you to put you out of your misery once I finish with you."

Raoul spat over his shoulder, laughed, and snapped his horse's reins. "Raoul is scared," he laughed, even more cynically. "Indian, you put the fear of God in Raoul." He gave Danette a silent, appraising look, then moved away, trailing laughter along behind him.

Gray Wolf's face reddened with anger. "He shouldn't be allowed to live," he said, dropping his rifle back inside its sheath. "Gray Wolf see trouble ahead. This Frenchman have evil in his eye and heart. *Ay-uh,* a bullet should be used this day to stop him from all his tomorrows of trouble he spreads."

Danette hugged Gray Wolf. "Do not worry so, Gray Wolf," she said. "It makes one become old before one's time."

"Better to worry and live to old age than to not and be slain from carelessness."

"Let's just be on our way and get this dreaded chore over with," Danette said, sighing, looking into the distance, still seeing nothing but a scorched landscape of fallen trees and burned underbrush.

"You prepared for the worst?" Gray Wolf asked, seeing the continued desolation and hearing the silence of the forest.

"The worst has already been left behind," she murmured. "The day of the fire was the worst, Gray Wolf."

"Ay-uh," he mumbled.

They rode in a strained silence until they reached the outskirts of Duluth. To Danette's amazement, the destruction wasn't half what she had expected. Most of the taller buildings on the lakefront were still intact, apparently only the shanties on Front Street having been destroyed. On the skyline, Danette could see her uncle's taller lumber company building, and she felt a relief of sorts, though she had never felt much interest in what he did in his lumber business. Now she wondered about their house. Had it been also spared? So much of her life had been spent inside that mansion on the hill. And her paintings! How she hoped to find them intact. Especially the one she had painted of Gray Wolf! Yet hadn't her Uncle Dwight said that he had found that painting? In his anger, he had probably destroyed it.

"Shall we continue on our way?" Gray Wolf asked, watching carriages, men on horseback, and buggies moving about the streets. Most were ignoring them, even though it was unusual to see an Indian and a white woman together. But the anxiety and preoccupation of all those who passed them was evident in their eyes and the frowns of their faces . . . they had either lost their futures because of the fire or had been spared, but only barely.

Gray Wolf's main interest was in the horses. Hopefully, he would be able to secure Danette a horse before they were ready to make the long journey back to his village. He was again worrying about his child's welfare. It was of the utmost importance to make Danette as comfortable as possible, to ensure their unborn child's comfort as well.

"Yes, Gray Wolf," Danette said, shaking her hair, causing it to ripple down her back, thick and full in its dark, lustrous black. "Avoid the busier thoroughfares. Let's go immediately to my house. I'm anxious to see how it fared through the fire."

With a nod, Gray Wolf directed his horse on around the outskirts of town, then on up the steep street that led to another flatter street, which was Danette's. As they began to travel down this street, Danette was all eyes. Some houses had burned and some had not. It was as though the winds had whipped the fire around as a tornado might travel, leaving a twisted path of destruction, where some property owners had been lucky and others had not.

Danette tensed the closer they drew to her house, and then her heart pounded furiously as Gray Wolf guided his horse down the gravel drive toward all that remained of what once had been one of the most magnificent mansions of Duluth.

"Good Lord," Danette gasped, grabbing for Gray Wolf's arm to steady her against the shock, as she saw that part of the house was a mere shell while the other half still stood proud and hardly touched at all. Only its paint had begun to peel close to the half that had burned.

"At least some of it was saved," Gray Wolf said, drawing rein beside a hitching rail.

Danette, numb from the discovery, let her eyes scale the wall of the house, to the window of her room, breathing more easily when she saw that it at least had been spared. "I must go inside," she said, anxious.

"It could be dangerous," Gray Wolf warned. "The floor most surely is made weak by the heat of the fire."

"I must see," Danette said firmly, jumping from the horse. "If I can at least save my paintings, I must."

Gray Wolf dismounted and placed an arm about her waist, walking alongside her toward the house, and then carefully on up the steps to the wide porch, which dropped suddenly off where the fire had burned and stopped.

With trembling fingers Danette opened the great oak door and pushed it back, flinching at its loud and ominous creak. A strong aroma of smoke met her as she stepped into the foyer. She placed her hand to her throat as she stood and observed it all. On the left side of her sunlight shone through the shell of remains . . . and on the right, she saw the furniture and walls of the room that hadn't burned all covered with a blanket of black dust and blown ashes.

"It's horrible," she cried. "Everything is ruined. If not by the fire, by the smoke."

Rain droplets, left from the rains of the past few days, dripped eerily from the roof that was exposed to the left of them. And a crazed sparrow, having gotten lost in the debris, began flapping wildly from wall to wall in the room to her right.

Then Danette's eyes moved to the staircase. Dare she? Half of it seemed scorched, while the other half appeared quite strong enough to step upon.

"I must go to my room," she said, giving Gray Wolf a guarded glance, seeing his disapproval in the shadows of his eyes.

"If you must, you must," he grumbled. "I will go with you. But we must be careful where we step. One wrong move and we could go right through the ceiling."

"I will gather together a few of my belongings, my paintings, and then we shall leave," Danette said, taking the first careful step upward. "And then I must go and talk with Uncle Dwight's lawyer. I will let him take care of the rest of the problems that have to do with this house and Dwight's business."

"We will then leave for village," Gray Wolf said, determination strong in his voice. "Duluth will finally be a thing of your past, Sweet Butterfly."

Danette thought long and hard about that. A part of her dream hadn't come true, and now she doubted it ever would. Oh, how she had wanted to have a formal showing of her paintings! Her uncle had frowned upon this—but now that he was gone . . . !

But, no. Such a thought was foolish. Gray Wolf wouldn't ever understand this side of her. Vain! He would think she was vain to want to draw attention to herself in such a manner. But she could argue this point! It was not to herself she would be drawing this attention . . . but to her paintings! Her talent!

Thinking about this at this time is utter foolishness, she argued to herself. With so much else to worry about and settle, a display of her artwork was the last thing she should have on her mind!

But, what a dream it had been during her long, lonely nights before she had met Gray Wolf!

Reaching the second-floor landing, Danette took in a deep, quivering breath, seeing again how the fire had seemed purposely to divide the house in two. On the side where she had her room, it had been spared. On the other, where her uncle had slept, it had been burned.

Shivering from a damp breeze blowing through the burned, black remains of the house on the one side of her, Danette moved away from it, toward her own room, whose door was ajar.

"In here," Danette urged, taking Gray Wolf by his hand, pushing her bedroom door more widely open. But when she stepped inside, she gasped.

"Amy?" she said, quickly dropping Gray Wolf's hand, taken aback when she saw Amy standing there, removing Danette's clothes from her wardrobe, folding them and placing them in boxes.

Amy dropped a dress to the floor and placed her hands

to her mouth as her eyes grew wider than almost humanly possible. "Lordie be," Amy cried. "It is my Danette come back from the dead!"

Danette didn't quite grasp what Amy had said, being so filled with joy herself that Amy hadn't perished in the fire, and she rushed to her and grabbed her into her arms and hugged her fiercely.

"Amy," she sighed. "I was so worried about you. The fire. You made it through the fire all right."

Amy was shivering so, her voice rattled as she spoke, pulling free of Danette's hold. "Is it truly you, Danette?" she asked, placing a hand to Danette's face, tracing her features. "Lordy, Danette, you ain't a ghost, come to haunt me for takin' liberty with your clothes?"

Danette laughed awkwardly, taking Amy's hand away from her face, to fondly hold it. "Amy, what on earth are you talking about?" she said. "Why would you think I was a ghost, of all things? And what do you mean by saying you are taking liberty with my clothes?"

A slow smile rose on Amy's face, and then one of jubilation. "Land sakes, Danette," she cried, now hugging her tightly. "It *is* you. It ain't no ghost. You didn't burn, after all. The memorial for you was in haste, to be sure now!"

"Memorial?" Danette gasped, stepping back, aghast at what she was now beginning to understand. She looked toward Gray Wolf, then back to Amy. "You thought I was dead?" she said. "Amy, a memorial has already been held in my honor?"

Amy plopped down into a chair, hanging her head into her hand. "For you and Mr. Dwight," she mumbled. "I was here sortin' through your things, to give them to the needy who came out of the fire with only their lives."

Danette fell to her knees before Amy and urged Amy to look at her. "Amy, don't fret so about it," she said. "It's understandable. I guess everyone would think I was dead. I was with Uncle Dwight on that train. And thank you for

299

remembering me in such a way. But I am alive, Amy. Alive and well, and I have come to see to it that things are taken care of before I leave again with Gray Wolf.''

Amy looked shyly toward Gray Wolf ... Gray Wolf looked firmly back at her.

"This is the man in your painting,'' Amy said, now smiling. "This is the man who stole your heart?''

"Yes,'' Danette said, going to link her arm through Gray Wolf's. "And soon we will be man and wife. As soon as we arrive back at his village.''

"Mr. Dwight ... ?''

"Uncle Dwight didn't make it through the fire,'' Danette said somberly. "He perished in ... the ... flames.''

Amy turned her eyes away and let out a sorrowful groan. Danette rushed to her and embraced her. "It's all right, Amy,'' she crooned. "Please don't become upset all over again.''

Amy wiped tears from her eyes with her short, pudgy fingers and then patted Danette affectionately on the back. "At least you are alive,'' she said. "And I will replace your dresses real quick, Danette. You are here to wear them. Thank goodness, you are here to wear them.''

Danette stopped Amy as she began replacing the dresses on hangers. "No,'' she said. "Go ahead. Keep the ones you have already packed and even more than those. You know that Uncle Dwight let me spend quite freely for clothes. And, Amy, I will only need a few dresses for my journey into the forest to live with Gray Wolf and his people.''

"It ain't right, somehow,'' Amy fussed, still replacing Danette's dresses in her wardrobe. "These be your clothes, Danette. It ain't right to hand them out to others.''

Danette laughed lightly, removing the dresses from the hangers as quickly as Amy was replacing them. "Amy,'' she said. "Will you listen? I won't need these.''

She was remembering how Lorinda had been dressed. She had worn beautifully beaded buckskin dresses, and Danette

300

thought this more appropriate than her frilly silk and satin garments. She didn't want to stick out like a sore thumb when she lived with Gray Wolf's people. She would learn all his ways, even the way to dress.

"You choose the ones you do want," Amy said, stepping back, folding her hands before her.

Danette smiled warmly back at her and began sorting through her things until she had a small pile of her favorites, in case she should need to travel to St. Paul or Duluth, should the need arise to argue over her uncle's business affairs!

Then her heart seemed to stand still as she looked desperately around the room, suddenly remembering her sole purpose for being here. "My paintings?" she gasped, seeing none in sight. "Where are they?"

Amy went to Danette and placed a hand to her face, gently touching her cheek. "Shh," she said, smiling. "Don't fret none. Your paintings are quite safe."

Danette breathed a shuddering sigh of relief. "But, where, Amy?" she anxiously said. "They were here. In my room."

"Mr. Dwight's lawyer, Charles Klein, took them," Amy said. "He said somethin' 'bout them being so good he was going to see to it that they were showed off somehow."

Danette's pulse raced. Her cheeks flamed with excitement. "What did you say . . . ?" she murmured.

"Charles Klein said that he's going to place your paintings in the bank, on the walls, for everybody to see," Amy said matter-of-factly. She eyed Danette more intently. "Danette, did I say somethin' wrong? Your face is flushed somethin' terrible."

With her eyes wide and her heart thundering inside her, Danette shook her head back and forth. "No," she said. "You didn't say anything wrong. You said something quite good." She flew to Gray Wolf and grabbed his hands into hers. "Gray Wolf, did you hear? My paintings! They are to be on display at the bank. I've always wanted this."

Gray Wolf didn't share her enthusiasm. Instead, he moved away from her, his eyes cold as steel.

Danette went to him and faced him. "Gray Wolf, what is it?" she murmured. "You should be happy for me."

"Sweet Butterfly once more caught up in white man's world," he growled. "This will delay our journey back to village. It will cause our marriage celebration to not be so soon."

Danette felt suddenly torn between Gray Wolf and her desire to see her paintings on display. She wanted to be a part of both worlds now that the opportunity had arisen. Yet, she couldn't do anything to make Gray Wolf think less of her, possibly cause him to even love her less!

With a proud tilt of her chin, she chose her love for Gray Wolf over her need to become famous for her talents. Maybe one day she could return . . . see how her other dream had come true.

But now . . . so much had stood in the way of her and Gray Wolf's complete happiness. Nothing else could . . . no matter what it was.

"All right, Gray Wolf," she said, gathering up more clothes out of her drawers to place inside a valise. "Whatever you want. I do understand."

Though a part of her heart was aching, she wouldn't . . . no . . . she wouldn't give in to her other need now.

After two valises were packed, Danette leaned down and searched with her hands beneath her bed. Smiling, she felt the box of blank canvases, then found the rest of her painting equipment there, stored, unharmed. She had been wise to do this before she had last left, or they, too, would possibly have been taken by anyone who had assumed she was dead.

Directing Gray Wolf's attention to all of these, she watched him take them from the room, and then the packed valises. "And now I must take one final look at what is left of my uncle's private sitting room," she said, ignoring the frown being directed at her by Amy.

With a weakness in her knees, Danette moved slowly down the hallway and stepped cautiously over the charred remains of floor that stretched out only partially intact across the room, where the furniture was half burned and half standing.

"Danette, you musn't . . ." Amy warned, reaching out for Danette. "The floor . . ."

"Amy, please," Danette argued softly back at her. "I feel I must." Something tore at her heart, remembering the good years, when she had loved her Uncle Dwight with all of her heart. She wanted to remember these times with him, not the last weeks and months, when she had discovered the ugly and selfish side of him. Loving was much easier than hating, especially when it was only a memory that she had to deal with.

Inching her way across the floor, something caught her eye, causing her insides to feel as though splashed with cold, icy water. "No," she gasped, placing her hand to her throat, feeling a spasm of distaste erupting there. "He couldn't have done that. . . ."

Only barely scorched by the hands of the fire, the painting of Gray Wolf sat on the floor in the far corner away from the worst-ravaged part of the room. Feeling a dizziness overcoming her, Danette saw how her Uncle Dwight had taken a knife to the painting and had carved it up, slice by slice, until Gray Wolf's face had been made to take on a grotesqueness unlike anything Danette had ever seen in her entire life.

Unthinking, no longer worrying about the condition of the floor of the room, Danette raced to the painting of Gray Wolf. She began to reach for it, sobbing, when suddenly a crackling and popping at her feet and the ensuing feeling of falling downward through space caused a scream to emerge from the depths of her throat. She felt only a twinge of pain when she crumpled, twisted, on the floor of what had once been her Uncle Dwight's private library, located on the first floor directly beneath his private sitting room, where she mercifully was thrown into a quick unconsciousness.

An agonizing ache in her lower abdomen drew Danette from a fitful sleep. Groaning, she placed her hand where she hurt, then awakened fully with a start, looking in fright around her. In this gloomy room where she lay she could smell the distinct aroma of stale cigar smoke. The walls were covered with a dusty gray wallpaper and framed diplomas, yellow with age.

The bed on which she lay was spread with clean, white sheets smelling of bleach, and the blanket covering her nude body was of a scratchy wool fabric, making her flesh itch.

Grabbing at her abdomen when another pain shot through her, Danette began to sob. "Where am I?" she cried. "Whose room is this?"

A door burst open and Gray Wolf rushed into the room and fell to his knees beside the bed. He cupped her face into his hands, tears sparkling in his eyes. "Sweet Butterfly," he whispered hoarsely. "You cried out. You are finally awake. It took so long for you to wake up."

Danette licked her parched lips and searched Gray Wolf's face for answers. "Gray Wolf, what has happened . . . to me . . . ?" she asked. "Why am I here? Where am I?"

"You are in Dr. Ross's house," he said thickly. "You fell. You fell . . . through . . . the floor of your uncle's room."

Frowning, thinking hard, Danette was finally able to remember. She closed her eyes and bit her lower lip, now remembering falling and the moment of instant pain when her body had made contact with the floor.

"No," she said, desperately shaking her head back and forth. The pain wracked her body once again. "Not that," she cried, realizing what the pain in that particular area of her body had to mean.

She reached a hand to Gray Wolf's face. "Please tell me that our child . . . is . . . all right. . . ." she said, breathless with fright.

Gray Wolf's eyes lowered. He took her hand and held it to his lips as he emitted a soft sob. He began shaking his head slowly back and forth. *"Gah-ween,"* he murmured. "We will have to wait another time for a celebration of news of Sweet Butterfly being with child. This child of ours . . . is . . . no more."

Not wanting to believe this, Danette placed her hands over her ears and closed her eyes. "No," she cried. "It isn't true. You are mistaken. I'm strong. I couldn't have lost the child. I couldn't have."

Gray Wolf moved to sit beside Danette on the edge of the bed. He eased her head up, to rest on his lap. He cradled her there, rocking her slowly back and forth. "Do not cry," he crooned. "There will be others. You'll see. We shall have many, many sons."

Danette wrapped an arm about him, clinging. Her tears wet his flesh where her cheek lay against his chest. "But what if I can't have any more children?" she cried. "That happens so often after miscarrying. Gray Wolf, you know the importance of you having a son."

"Ay-uh . . ."

Danette grew numb inside. She raised her face away from him and looked into his eyes. "And if I can't?" she whispered. "Does this mean you will take another . . . another . . . wife . . . ?"

His refusal to answer and the set of his jaw was answer enough to Danette. She knew that a chief *must* have a son, no matter how many wives it took to bear him one.

Turning her face from his, she grew first hurt, then angry. She pulled free from his embrace and moved painfully across the bed. "By damn, Gray Wolf, I will be the *only* wife, if it's the last thing I do," she said, swinging her legs around, letting her feet touch the floor.

"And what do you think you're doing?" he growled, rising, going around to the other side of the bed. He stood over her with his hands on his hips.

"We have a celebration awaiting us in your village," she said thickly, moving, wobbling to her feet, grabbing for the edge of the bed when a moment of lightheadedness swept over her. "And we will have that celebration. I will become your wife. Real soon. This is one celebration that won't be stopped!"

"Sweet Butterfly have to wait until strong enough to travel," Gray Wolf said, forcefully grasping onto her arms, to lower her once more to the bed.

Holding back tears, Danette tried to struggle free of his grip of steel, but she only grew breathless and had to give in to him and stretch back down onto the mattress, panting.

"Why?" she cried. "Why must life continue to be filled with so many miseries? Is God punishing me for something I do not know about? What have I done to deserve all these misfortunes? What did our child do to warrant not being born?"

Gray Wolf wet a cloth and placed it across her brow. "Hush, my woman," he said. "Words only upset you now. Rest is what you need. We have plenty of time for talk, and the celebration will wait for you. Without you there will *be* no celebration of marriage. Hush. Rest. Gray Wolf's love for you is strong. Remember this and let your limbs grow stronger each day, to ready you for our journey back to our home."

Danette blinked her eyes, shaking drops of tears to her cheeks. Then she said, "Our home? You already call your home our home, and we are not yet wed?"

"My sweet one, we are the same as wed," he said thickly. "Our hearts are one, as are our souls. And we will have another child. The spirits will bless us. Just have patience. Just have faith."

"My faith runs thin," Danette said, once more licking

her parched lips. A pain shot like a lightning bolt down through her, causing her to moan and flinch. "How can I practice faith when I am still in such pain from having lost our child?"

"It will pass," Gray Wolf whispered. "As all these bad memories will pass."

"None of my memories of this will pass," Danette said, placing her hand where her baby had once lain inside her, curled peacefully, trustingly. . . .

"It was just a bad thing . . . you went into your uncle's room when it was not safe," Gray Wolf said, wringing out the cloth, again placing it on her brow.

Danette's eyes squinted, slowly remembering just why she had gone all the way into her uncle's scorched sitting room. It had been something drawing her there. What . . . had . . . it . . . been . . . ?

Then her eyes flew wide open. "It was my portrait of *you,*" she cried, grabbing Gray Wolf's hand. "Gray Wolf, the only painting of mine that won't be on display on the walls of the bank is my portrait of . . . *you.* . . ."

"What about the painting?" he said, eyebrows arched. "What it have to do with any of this?"

"I saw it in my uncle's private sitting room," she said, paling even more than she already had. She was vividly remembering how Gray Wolf's portrait had been slashed, as though her Uncle Dwight had been some sort of maniac to have done something so incredibly insane.

"This was why you went in there?"

"Yes," she murmured. "And when I saw it, wholly saw it . . ."

She turned her eyes away from Gray Wolf and swallowed hard. "Oh, Gray Wolf," she sobbed. "It was so horrible. What he did to your portrait was oh, so horrible. He must have hated you so much."

Then she sobered, much too quickly, it seemed to Gray Wolf.

307

"It is as though my uncle planned all of this," she whispered. "He has somehow reached out from death and is still ruling my life. He made me lose the child."

She clasped onto Gray Wolf's hands, desperation seizing her. "Don't you see, Gray Wolf?" she cried. "He will always be here to ruin everything for me. In death as . . . in . . . life . . . somehow he will always manage to do this. Somehow I have to find a way to show him that he . . . that he cannot do this to me . . . to us."

Chapter Twenty

Her fairness, wedded to a star,
Is whiter than all lilies are.
                                        —O'Brien

Several weeks had passed, the wild rice had been gathered and stored for winter, and Gray Wolf and Danette had made their promises of everlasting love and devotion to each other in the privacy of their wigwam at Gray Wolf's village. The loss of their child had delayed the celebration of marriage, but the day had finally arrived when Danette felt she could once more look to the future, and the village people were buzzing with excitement, preparing for feasting and dancing.

"My wife, the day has come to formally introduce you to my father's and my people," Gray Wolf said huskily from his bed of blankets, reaching to pull Danette closer to him, exploring the satin of her flesh with his hand.

Gray Wolf circled his fingers around one of her breasts. "And the time is right, Sweet Butterfly, to make another child begin to grow inside you," he murmured. "The winter will be long and lazy. It's a perfect time for baby to lie safely inside you. Do not fear losing it also."

Danette sighed shakily. "I fear more than that," she said. "What if I do not become with child again? Would your people then have cause for another such celebration as they plan today . . . but for you taking a second wife . . . ?"

Gray Wolf rose over her, his green eyes hazy with desire.

"We will not doubt our love," he said. "Not today, not ever, Sweet Butterfly. It is our day. Do you not hear the drums? Do you not hear the flute being played by the river? It is a day of hope . . . not doubt."

He lowered himself over her and gathered her into his arms. His lips sought hers in a hot, demanding kiss, while his fingers lowered to the soft flesh between her thighs and probed deeply inside her, stirring up flames of passion that she hadn't felt since the loss of their child.

"My love . . ." she whispered as his lips lowered to the ripe bud of her breast, and his tongue sensuously circled it.

Becoming dizzy with the intense feelings of desire shooting through her, Danette arched her hips, inviting him to fully possess her, as never before. Trembling, she moved her hand to his magnificent hardness and guided him inside her. She became almost mindless when she felt how he so completely filled her, and, as he began moving inside her, she locked her legs about him and closed her eyes and enjoyed the ecstasy of the moment.

Gray Wolf leaned over her, gazing down at her with burning eyes. The muscles at his shoulders corded as he held himself there, motionless, while his lower torso kept up a steady, almost magical movement.

With a moan of ecstasy, Danette's heartbeats keeping rhythm with his each and every thrust, she twined her fingers through his unbraided hair and forced his mouth to hers, kissing him fiercely and long. Spirals of colors seemed to be floating through her brain as the fire of his kiss grew more intense. The touch of his fingers on her breasts caused a melody inside her, rising to a crescendo, it seemed, and, as the sweet pain of release began to take hold, her body shook violently against Gray Wolf's as his own stiffened and then released his liquid warmth inside her.

Clinging, still soaring, Danette showed kisses across Gray Wolf's face. She felt the wetness of tears on his cheek and knew that they were her own. "I cry tears of joy, my love," she whispered.

"And why this feeling of joy?" he asked, his eyelids still heavy in his spent passion for her.

"Because I'm with you," she said, smiling sweetly up at him. "I should never forget how lucky I am to have found you. All else is unimportant to me now."

Gray Wolf lowered a kiss to her lips, then murmured, "Do not forget child. We must concentrate on child."

His words . . . the importance of having a child . . . his sudden obsession with having a child . . . sent a cold chill around Danette's heart. She had to get pregnant again. And soon. All she had to do was look around her in the Indian village to see the many young, ripe squaws who would be willing. . . .

Rising to her feet, forcing a soft laugh, Danette reached for Gray Wolf. "Do you not hear the drums? Do you not hear the flute being played by the river?" she teased. "The celebration won't truly start without us, will it? Let's dress. Let's celebrate all our tomorrows, Gray Wolf."

"Our vows should have been exchanged long ago," he said, rising from their bed of love. He began working the deer tallow into his hair that was used to keep it smooth and in place. "Things not in our control kept getting in the way. But today it is done and it is *ah-pay-nay*. Forever."

"I hope your people will accept me as they have your mother," Danette said, now pulling a brush through her wild tangle of hair.

"The woman Gray Wolf choose for wife will be accepted," he said, now braiding his hair. "Have no fear, my love."

With her hair now untangled and glistening, Danette eyed the dress that she would be wearing this day . . . her wedding day. As a child, she had dreamed of something quite different for her special day. Lace . . . satin . . . frills . . . a veil partially hiding her half-downcast, shy blue eyes. . . .

"This dress is lovely," she blurted, placing all thoughts of fancy weddings behind her. She had to remember that the wedding vows had already been exchanged in private, and that the dress was for the celebration, not a wedding ceremony.

She had much to learn of her husband's Indian ways. And she had the rest of her life in which to do this. It was like a dream . . . her being with Gray Wolf here in his village. Many months had passed since their first embrace. It was now October, and some snowflakes had even been seen spitting from the sky.

"White Blossom make it especially for you. She send it to you to wear this day."

"I wonder if Amanda . . . I mean White Blossom . . . has arrived yet," she said, slipping the deerskin dress over her head. She was finding it hard to remember to call Amanda White Blossom. Her mind was crowded with remembering, it seemed.

"White Blossom be here. No fret," Gray Wolf said. "She just move slower these days. Her and Red Fox's child slow her down. Most say she heavy with son. Red Fox would be proud."

A twinge of guilt touched Danette's heart, feeling, oh, so empty where her own child had lain. If she hadn't been so foolish! She shouldn't have entered her uncle's private sitting room, knowing the condition of the floor. But the portrait of Gray Wolf! How grotesque her uncle had made it!

Busying herself, to erase all guilt and sorrow from her mind, Danette began placing colorful beads around her neck. They matched the colors of the beadwork design on the front of her Indian dress, which included flower petals and leaves, the favorite embroidery subjects of the Chippewa woodland.

"Should Amanda even be traveling in her condition?" Danette worried aloud, now understanding the fragilities of pregnancies.

"She strong," Gray Wolf said, slipping his fringe-trimmed leggings on, followed by a beaded vest with bear and flower designs.

"I still worry about her," Danette said, frowning when she eyed her own set of leggings that she had been instructed to wear because of the cooler temperatures. She had never worn breeches, and with a dress wouldn't they look comical?

Yet seeing Gray Wolf's displeasure at her hesitation in the narrowing of his eyes, she shrugged slightly and stepped into them, relieved that her dress hid them mostly from view as she pulled its skirt down over them.

Gray Wolf, now with his headband and eagle feather adorning his head, and Danette with her own matching headband holding her hair in place, embraced quickly. Gray Wolf's lips searched her face with kisses. "Gray Wolf proud of new wife," he whispered huskily.

He tilted her chin with his forefinger and looked upon her delicate features as though seeing her for the first time. With an excited blush having risen to her cheeks, and her wide, innocent blue eyes heavy with thick, lustrous lashes, she was achingly beautiful.

The small dots of freckles on her nose made her look like a child bride, yet her sensuously full lips the color of the wild poppy reminded him of what she could do to his mind when she used the skills of her lips on him, and he knew that she was all woman.

Danette splayed her fingers against his bare chest, beneath his vest. "And, you, my husband, are so handsome," she said, feeling the hypnotic effect his green eyes had on her as he held her there, gazing down at her.

She giggled and shook her head slowly back and forth. "And, my husband, if you don't quit looking at me in such a way, we shall never make it to the celebration," she whispered. "You are causing my insides to melt with desire."

"Sweet Butterfly so lovely," he said huskily. He lowered his lips to hers, softly quivering with feeling.

Clinging, Danette felt a peaceful happiness engulf her. At this moment, life was sweet again. Surely nothing could ever again spoil the relationship she and Gray Wolf had found together.

"I love you so," she whispered as he drew away from her, still holding her in bondage by the dark passion in his eyes. "I shall always love you, Gray Wolf."

The beating of the drums, the lone flute, and the songs of the Indians continued outside the wigwam, even seeming to have grown louder. The aroma of venison and fish cooking over the large outdoor firespace filled the air with a delightful fragrance.

"The time has come to make appearance," Gray Wolf said, smiling as he broke his eyes away from her to look toward the blanket that hung over the doorspace.

"My only goal in life is to make you happy, Gray Wolf," Danette murmured. She stood on tiptoes and kissed him softly on the cheek. "And to make you proud."

"Then your goals have been reached," he chuckled. "Because Gray Wolf is both happy and proud."

He offered her his arm and nodded toward the doorspace. "My wife, let us celebrate," he said.

"Ay-uh . . ." Danette said, laughing softly as she saw Gray Wolf smile.

The soles of her moccasins radiated a cool dampness through to her feet as Danette stepped out onto the dew-dampened grass outside the wigwam, still clinging to Gray Wolf. The bite of the air nipped at her face, and she was now grateful for the leggings and the long arms of her buckskin dress. Her eyes moved to Gray Wolf, seeing his bare arms and the way the breeze blew his vest out and away from his bare chest, and she worried about his welfare. Yet she knew how foolish it was to worry about him. The many years of braving the moods of winter and summers

314

had conditioned his skin to any and all radical changes in temperatures. Danette knew that it would take much time for her own tender flesh to become as conditioned, if it ever did. . . .

Danette walked alongside Gray Wolf, aware of the hush brought on by her presence and feeling many eyes on her, openly scrutinizing her. Swallowing hard, she smiled to all those who smiled at her. She held her chin proudly high as she watched the Indians forming a wide circle around a huge fire, in front of what she had been told was the council house, where all important business of the St. Croix band of the Chippewa was decided upon. Today the business was to accept another white woman into the village . . . the wife of the next-chief-in-line.

Danette drew in a quick breath when she caught sight of Chief Yellow Feather and Lorinda already settled comfortably on blankets, in the quickly forming circle of Indians. Chief Yellow Feather was the epitome of handsomeness, sitting tall and proud, adorned by his Chippewa tribal headdress of brightly colored feathers stitched onto leather. The headdress was five feet long, covered with beads of every size, color, and description. His clothes were white doeskin, fringed, and worked with beads matching those of his headdress. His face showed strength and a sternness, and his dark eyes a sort of restraint when he looked in Danette's direction. Yet she could see a quivering of his lips, as though he was suppressing a smile.

Danette smiled warmly toward him, momentarily lowering her eyes bashfully, then let her gaze move to Lorinda, seeing her extreme loveliness. Lorinda's red flame of hair hung long and satiny down her back, only showing flecks of gray at the temples. In her exquisite face there was a serene contentment, and her emerald-colored eyes beamed understanding back at Danette . . . an understanding of the meaning of this special day, which would begin a lifetime of special days for this woman who was in love with her one and only son.

In a fringed and beaded white doeskin dress, Lorinda fit in with the Indians settling down around her, despite the differences in the color of her skin, eyes, and hair. But she so obviously belonged there, that Danette suddenly envied her, wondering if she would ever fit in as well.

Gray Wolf directed Danette to stand before Chief Yellow Feather and Lorinda. "Father . . . Mother . . . my wife, Sweet Butterfly," he said hoarsely, bowing his head, but keeping his eyes on his father, seeing acceptance in the way his father nodded a silent hello to Danette and then himself.

"Come and sit beside me, Danette," Lorinda said, patting the blanket beside her. "Gray Wolf must sit at his father's right side during the celebration."

"Must he?" Danette whispered, leaning down to Lorinda. She didn't want to be separated from Gray Wolf. She wanted him near, to take his hand if the urge so arose inside her.

Lorinda took one of Danette's hands and urged her downward, beside her. "It is the custom," she murmured. "From this day forth, Gray Wolf will be instructed in the ways of the chief."

Danette's face grew somber. "But we have only just spoken our vows," she whispered back, crossing her legs beneath her. "The celebration is for us. We should at least sit together."

Lorinda fondly patted Danette's hand. "The celebration is for many things," she said. "Today my son is a man. Many sons can come from his union to you. It is important that he learn from his father, so he in turn can teach his own sons."

Looking around the circle of Indians, Danette could see many petite, beautiful squaws, and on most of their faces she could see a mask of jealousy. Again Danette was reminded of her lost child and the importance of quickly becoming with child again.

316

"I see," she finally murmured. "I will not interfere in my husband's duties."

"Enjoy yourself," Lorinda said. "Don't worry so much about things. You will discover, as I did many years ago, that life among the Chippewa has many rewards."

"Life with Gray Wolf is my reward," Danette said, leaning forward giving him a loving glance, which he silently returned to her.

"The celebration truly begins now," Lorinda said, nodding toward several Indians who were now circling the fire, chanting and dancing to the boom boom of the drums' steady beats."

Chanting "Hi-ya-ya," the Indians' feet picked up the rhythm of the drums, their bodies swaying and their arms tossing, first right and then left, as they shuffled around the roaring fire.

All those who were still seated, men, women, and children alike, joined in with an incessant clapping of their hands and nodding of their heads. The excitement grew. The drums filled the forests and meadow with their echo, and the blue sky reflected the orange of the great fire, as though there was another sun in the heaven.

Suddenly a band of small children wormed their way through their elders and began their own dance. They were naked except for moccasins and brief embroidered loincloths. Painted in exotic patterns, their skin shone with grease covering them from head to toe.

Dashing around the fire, their heads bobbing, and looking as though they were in a trance, the children moved rapidly to the beat of the drums. Pausing in unison, they looked as though they were aiming an imaginary arrow.

"They are performing the 'Hunting of the Deer' dance," Lorinda said, leaning closer to Danette. "See how the elders step aside, proud to let their children and grandchildren show they have learned this dance so well?"

"It is a beautiful dance," Danette whispered back, seeing

317

how the pantomine continued. The children appeared to be pretending to be finishing off a stricken deer with imaginary hunting knives as they raised their hands, then plunged them just as quickly to the ground.

Cheers broke loose through the crowd as the children fell back away from the fire. They soon lost themselves in the frenzied excitement of other children playing what appeared to be a game of hide and seek, shrieking, running about from tree to tree, wigwam to wigwam.

"They are content with life," Danette said, once more longing for her own child.

"Satisfaction begets contentment," Lorinda said.

"Ay-uh . . ." Danette replied, then felt a blush rise to her cheeks when she saw Lorinda glancing quickly at her, having heard Danette's first Indian word spoken so easily. They exchanged warm smiles and then helped to pass along the wooden dishes laden with food.

Among the offerings were smoked fish rolled neatly in birchbark, cakes of maple sugar, strips of dried pumpkin, fried wild rice, and grease-soaked slices of cooked venison.

Afterwards, cone-shaped bark cups filled with spring water were passed around. The water was quite welcome to Danette after she had sampled each of all these foods, not wanting to offend by refusing.

And then another different sort of drink was offered to her. It was a concoction of wild cherry twigs and wintergreen added to water. Slowly sipping this delicious liquid that had been warmed over the fire, Danette tried to get Gray Wolf's attention. To her chagrin, he continued to be kept in a steady conference with his chief father, and jealousy began slowly to weave itself around her heart.

The drums suddenly ceased and a great hush fell over the crowd as an Indian brave rode into the village, leading a horse behind him upon which had been tied a bundle wrapped in an Indian blanket.

A stirring of feet and shallow whispers broke the silence

318

as the brave grew closer, revealing an even smaller wrapped bundle in the crook of his left arm.

"What . . . ?" Danette began, noticing how the one horse looked so much like Amanda's prized horse Flame, but Lorinda softly placed her hand to Danette's lips, silencing her further words.

A weak baby's cry from the direction of the lone rider caused a flow of gasps to vibrate around and through the circle of Indians. Danette watched in the strained silence as Chief Yellow Feather and Gray Wolf rose to their feet and met the brave's approach halfway.

Soft mumblings were exchanged from Chief Yellow Feather to the lone rider. And when Chief Yellow Feather's head dropped and he moved his mournful eyes to Lorinda, Lorinda rose quickly to her feet and rushed to her husband's side.

Gray Wolf looked toward Danette and motioned for her to come to him. Fear-laden, Danette rose, trembling, to her feet, and made her way through the Indians. When she was beside Gray Wolf and could see into his face more clearly, she knew the celebration would be no more today.

"What *is* it?" Danette whispered, flinching when a baby's cry once more came from the bundle in the Indian brave's arm. Danette eyed Gray Wolf questioningly. "Who?" she whispered. But he did not hear her. His eyes were glued elsewhere and his face was ashen pale.

Danette followed his gaze, which had stopped at the large, wrapped bundle on the other horse's back. It was in the shape . . . of . . . a body. But . . . whose . . . ?

Hearing a painful cry arise from Lorinda after Chief Yellow Feather had spoken softly to her, Danette reached for Gray Wolf, now afraid to know the answers to her silent questions.

"Not my sister," Lorinda whimpered, crying softly now as she moved toward the wrapped body. "Not Amanda. It just can't be Amanda."

Yellow Feather grabbed her arm and stopped her and looked sternly down at her, shaking his head. *"Gah-ween,"* he mumbled. "Do not look."

Lorinda shook herself free and walked stiffly to the blanket and slowly pulled back one end. Her whole body shook as she let out a loud gasp. Then she replaced the corner of the blanket and walked with her head hung toward her house.

"Give me the child," Gray Wolf ordered, stretching his arms out to the Indian brave.

Danette's insides were cold with shock and grief. She watched, wide-eyed, as the small bundle was placed in her husband's arms. And when he turned and offered her the baby, she swallowed back tears and shakily accepted it, not yet understanding whose it was, nor how any of this had happened. One thing she did now know was that somehow it was Amanda wrapped in that blanket, and knowing this ate away at her heart. . . .

Feeling the soft weight of the bundled baby in her arms and hearing its even softer whimpers, Danette eyed Gray Wolf wonderingly.

"White Blossom's," Gray Wolf said thickly, nodding toward the baby.

Danette's mouth dropped open and her heart skipped a beat. "Amanda's?" she whispered, paling. "Is this child truly . . . Amanda's . . . ?"

"Ay-uh," Gray Wolf said solemnly. "Take the child to our dwelling. Gray Wolf will follow soon. Then I will tell you about it."

"All right," Danette said, drawing the small bundle to her bosom, marveling at how tiny it must be. Stepping lightly, she left the stunned crowd of Indians behind her and went on to her and Gray Wolf's wigwam, trying to understand how these tragedies could continue to happen.

The baby wriggled an arm free of the blanket and Danette's breath caught in her throat as she saw the tiniest of fingers, then fingernails, and then realized the color of the

320

skin. "Indian," she whispered. "Amanda, your child has the beautiful, copper coloring of the Indian."

Feeling that this child was a blessing at such a time of sadness, Danette rushed into her and Gray Wolf's wigwam, now anxious to see all of the baby. Almost breathless, she gently placed the small bundle on an Indian blanket, next to the soft glow of the fire in the fire space. And as she slowly drew the blanket aside, her heart grew warm with a sudden love and compassion for the tiny, delicate baby girl looking up at her with crystal-clear blue eyes and blonde fuzz where hair would one day grow.

Danette's eyes filled with tears as she lifted the baby into her arms and drew her closely to her bosom, to cradle her there. "You are orphaned so young in life," she whispered, still unable to grasp onto the reality of Amanda's being dead. The question of how and why kept racing through her mind. Amanda had always been quite capable of taking care of herself. Nothing had been a threat to her. Not even Longbow!

"Longbow!" she said, stiffening. "Did . . . he . . . ?"

Gray Wolf entered the wigwam, his eyes cold with hate and his face tightly drawn, dulling his handsomeness. He fell to one knee beside Danette and gently touched the baby's arm.

"She is brought into this world only to be first acquainted with violence," he said. "For this we should make it up to her by giving her a special name."

His brow creased with a frown as he became deep in thought. Then he spoke again. "She shall be called Kee-way-din-ah-nung. North Star. Its beauty in the evening sky outshines all others. It is a star of strength, yet gentle beauty."

"That's lovely," Danette said, then noticed North Star hungrily sucking on a fist. It only now occurred to her that the child had not only lost her mother, but her source of nourishment as well.

Danette eyed Gray Wolf wildly. "She will starve!" she whispered harshly.

"Give North Star to me," Gray Wolf said, outstretching his arms for the light burden of the child to be placed there. "She will be fed. She will share breasts with another newly born member of our tribe. She will survive as her own mother did those many moons ago when she shared nourishment with her love, Red Fox."

Danette gently placed North Star in Gray Wolf's arms. "Gray Wolf, I must know how this all happened," she murmured. "Amanda was always capable of taking care of herself. Did she die while giving birth, or what?"

Her heart melted, seeing how gently Gray Wolf held the child, knowing that he would one day make such a loving father for his own children. . . .

"North Star must have decided to enter the world while White Blossom on journey here, to share in our wedding celebration," Gray Wolf said, rocking North Star back and forth in his arms.

"Then I am right? She died while giving birth?"

"Gah-ween," Gray Wolf growled. "She did not."

Danette's eyes widened. "Then how, Gray Wolf?" she asked, fearing the answer.

"Only in White Blossom's weakened condition after just giving birth to a child could anyone take advantage of her, and kill her."

"Killed?" Danette said, placing a hand to her throat.

"By knife," Gray Wolf said, in a low, angry growl.

"Good Lord," Danette said, turning her head away from Gray Wolf. She closed her eyes, trying not to envision how it could have happened. But, somehow, Longbow was there, poised with a bloody knife in his hand, and laughing. . . .

Gray Wolf rose to his feet. "North Star must be placed with proper squaw who has good supply of milk in breasts, then all St. Croix band of Chippewa braves go on war party, to kill one responsible for White Blossom's death."

"Who . . . ?" Danette asked, pushing herself up from the floor.

"White Blossom whisper name before dying," he grumbled. "She said the name Longbow quite clearly."

"Longbow . . ." Danette whispered, so vividly remembering his threats to Amanda. At the time, Amanda had laughed at him. But never had she imagined him to be so evil as to kill her after she had just given birth to a child.

"*Ay-uh*," Gray Wolf said. "At least he did spare the child."

"Who found Amanda?"

"The scout who brought her and North Star to the village," Gray Wolf said. "Father had sent him to look for White Blossom when she didn't arrive as expected."

Danette lowered her eyes. "If only he could have been sooner."

"He wasn't," Gray Wolf said. "And now we Chippewa do what must be done to avenge death of loved one."

"You will leave soon?"

"*Ay-uh* . . ." Gray Wolf said. He nodded toward the shine of a rifle barrel standing against the wall in the corner of the wigwam. "Place the rifle next to your bed and keep one eye open all night. Longbow surely not foolish enough to come to village now, but since he *is* so foolish, one never knows what to expect of his ugly, cold heart."

Danette stood beside him and placed her arm about his waist and leaned against his chest, watching the baby and aching anew inside. "I will be all right," she said. "But will the child? Who will raise her, Gray Wolf?"

"Gray Wolf's *gee-mah-mah* and *gee-bah-bah*," he said hoarsely. "North Star will fill the void in my mother and father's lives, since *gee-mah-mah* only successfully gave birth to one child. North Star will be as baby sister to both Sweet Butterfly and Gray Wolf."

"But Lorinda . . . your mother . . . didn't even stop to

look at North Star. She . . . she walked away from her as though she didn't even exist.''

''Her grief over loss of sister was as heavy as ice frozen over St. Croix River in winter,'' Gray Wolf said. ''It will be as river in spring. Her grief will soon melt away, leaving room for budding of love for sister's child. North Star will be special child . . . loved and cherished by all.''

Standing on tiptoe, Danette swiftly kissed Gray Wolf, swelling inside with respect for him. ''You are the special one,'' she murmured. ''I'm so glad you're mine.''

''Must go now,'' he said, looking heavy-lidded down at her. ''I will return soon. Please keep bed warm for me?''

''Not only our bed, but my arms,'' Danette said, already missing him. She touched his cheek gently. ''And please do return to me, my love. My heart will beat out the minutes until you are back with me, unharmed.''

''I am good at hunt,'' he said, setting his jaw firmly. ''Gray Wolf always return victorious.'' He turned and with only a quick, backwards glance, left Danette standing there shivering from remorse over Amanda and fear for her husband.

She settled down beside the fire and added more wood to it. ''Life is such a mockery at times,'' she whispered. ''Just when one thinks to relax and be content, misfortunes once more are there, to remind you to never take even a moment of shared happiness for granted.''

Tensing, she heard the loud war chants and the thundering of horses and then the silence that ensued, and knew that she, until this moment, had never known what the word ''alone'' truly meant. . . .

Chapter Twenty-One

> Alas, how easily things go wrong!
> A sigh too much, or a kiss too long. . . .
> —MacDonald

Unable to close her eyes without seeing Amanda, as though she was there in the room with her, Danette had left her bed, to busy herself with painting. With a canvas on her easel, facing the light from the fire, a new portrait of Gray Wolf was taking shape. This one would be hers forever. She wouldn't let anything happen to it.

Sadness seemed to be hanging over her like a shroud. These past several months had taught her what life was outside the once protective walls of her uncle's house, and she was learning from it all to be a little on the hard side. Bitterness for all that had happened was causing this change in her.

"Destroying Gray Wolf's portrait was the last straw," Danette whispered. "I shall show Uncle Dwight. I shall."

Determined to prove to herself and her dead uncle that she was capable of more than her uncle had given her credit for, Danette had decided to not sell her Uncle Dwight's business. It was now hers, and, somehow, by making it an even more successful venture than even her uncle had managed to do, she felt as though she would finally get even with her uncle, because it *was* hers . . . and no longer his.

She had given Charles Klein, now her lawyer, the power

of attorney for her lumber business, and she was going to run it by proxy. And since most of the forests north of Duluth had been spared by the ravaging fire, ah, how profitable a venture this would be!

Gray Wolf hadn't liked her decision to do this, having wanted her to leave all her white ways behind her. But, somehow, having another man again wanting to completely run her life didn't sit well with her. It had taken the death of her child to awaken her to this decision. If she couldn't bear Gray Wolf a son, might he not take another wife, and might Danette someday find herself superfluous?

Knowing this, Danette had wanted something to fall back onto, something to give some semblance of stability to her life. If Gray Wolf turned his back on her, she could always return to Duluth and lose herself in her business.

Danette had even given orders to rebuild the Thomas mansion, leaving Amy in charge in her absence. In this way, Danette would always have a house awaiting her if she needed to return to take care of any problems with her business.

"And I want my children to have an education," she whispered. "Gray Wolf will surely want this for our children. There is no schooling here at the Indian village."

She knew that acquiring such an education would possibly mean months away from Gray Wolf while their children attended school. But an education would be required for an heir to the Thomas wealth. . . .

"I had too many days to think while lying in that drab doctor's house," she sighed. She had had many hours to think about the past and the future. She had decided much during those days, while her heart had been healing over the loss of her child.

A baby's cry in the distance tore through Danette. She was quickly reminded of Amanda's child. North Star had at least been given a chance. But . . . Amanda . . . ? No. It still didn't seem real that this could have happened. Yet it had happened, and pity Longbow when Gray Wolf and Chief Yellow Feather caught up with him!

Shuddering at the thought, Danette took another stroke with her brush, placing color to Gray Wolf's eyes, enchanted always by the green. . . .

A hush-hush of moccasin-covered feet outside her doorspace caused Danette to tense and look toward it. A slight movement of the blanket hanging there made her take a step backwards, remembering Gray Wolf's warnings about Longbow and how Longbow's foolishness might lead him back to the village.

The flash of the rifle barrel that Gray Wolf had left for her caught Danette's eyes. She began to move toward it but was stopped when Longbow was suddenly in the wigwam, standing threateningly between her and the rifle, holding his own rifle pointed toward her.

Danette's breath caught in her throat. Then she managed to gasp. "You, Longbow! Good Lord, it *is* you," she said, looking him up and down.

Her heartbeat was going wild with fear and she wondered how he had slipped past the guards that she had seen after having heard Gray Wolf and his braves ride from the village. Enough braves had been left behind, she had thought, to truly feel protected. But Longbow had somehow eluded them all!

"You do as told or one bullet will silence you forever," Longbow growled. He nodded toward the doorspace. "Come. You go with me to Sioux village. Death too good for Gray Wolf's woman. Longbow has other plans for you."

"You . . . you . . . murdering, evil Indian," Danette hissed, regaining some of her bravery. "I won't go with you. And if you fire one bullet from that rifle, you will be the same as dead. Everyone will hear you. Your death will be slow and painful."

Anger flared in her eyes. "How could you have killed Amanda? She was such a good, decent person. And she had just given birth to a child. And was it you who killed Red Fox? Do you hate Gray Wolf so much that you must keep on with this vengeance?"

"Gray Wolf have too much," Longbow growled. "Longbow have nothing." His pitted face twisted into a scheming smile. "But now, Longbow has you. You will go to Sioux village with me."

"You have turned traitor to the Chippewa so easily?" Danette asked, stepping up next to the portrait of Gray Wolf, placing her back to it. Slowly she placed her brush to the wet paints of the freshly painted portrait and began smearing them into words, though it cut away at her heart for having to destroy another painting of Gray Wolf.

But she had to leave a message for Gray Wolf. She needed to lead him to her, for she saw that she wouldn't be able to get out of going with Longbow. She knew that his hate was so strong for Gray Wolf that he would kill her even if it did mean losing his own life in the process . . . all because he would want to be victorious in one more act of vengeance against the man he hated.

Hoping enough paint had been left on the brush to mingle with the wet strokes already on the canvas, Danette worked until the word "Sioux" and then "Longbow" had been hopefully written for Gray Wolf to see when he returned and found her gone.

Longbow kept an eye on her as he leaned down and jerked a blanket from the floor. "Put this around you," he ordered. "Winds are cold. Ride is long."

"As if you care if I get cold or not," Danette said, once more eyeing the rifle standing in the corner. She dropped her paintbrush to the floor and began inching toward it. She had to at least try to defend herself. But Longbow was there in a flash, twisting her arm painfully behind her.

Danette flinched and felt tears move to her eyes as the pain became severe. "Do you enjoy hurting . . . killing women . . . ?" she managed to say in a strain. "Longbow, you are not ... even ... a man. I imagine you've accomplished everything in life by hurting ones who are smaller than you."

Then she had to laugh. "Yet, who could be smaller? You are nothing but a tiny, warped Indian. You could never stand up to Gray Wolf. And when he finds you, he will readily prove this to you."

"Go, white woman," Longbow snarled, giving her a shove toward the doorspace. "And you be quiet. We must walk into the forest without being noticed."

Then the portrait of Gray Wolf caught his eye. Danette's insides froze as she watched him study the portrait with an arched eyebrow. Now he would see that she had left instructions for Gray Wolf! All would be hopeless. Surely Longbow would pitch the portrait into the fire, to destroy all the evidence!

"So white woman paints?" Longbow said, giving her an appraising glance, then once more studied the portrait. *"Ay-uh.* Good. Longbow compliment you, white woman."

Danette sighed and relaxed her shoulders. She had forgotten that most of the Indians hadn't been taught to read or write. Most hadn't been as fortunate in this as Gray Wolf, having a white woman for a mother.

"And what do you plan to do with it?" she dared. "Destroy it as you do everything else you get near?"

"Gah-ween," Longbow said, shrugging. "Gray Wolf can have this. Doesn't matter to Longbow if painting is left to haunt Gray Wolf. This reminder slowly kill him. At least until Longbow has the chance."

Danette paled. So in time he did also plan to kill Gray Wolf. She glanced toward the portrait, relieved that she could make out the words that she had smeared there. Gray Wolf would know where to find her and Longbow and do what was necessary, to end Longbow's days of vengeful killings. She only prayed that Gray Wolf would do so quickly enough.

Longbow stepped toward Danette and nudged her roughly in the abdomen with the barrel of his rifle, then forced the Indian blanket into her arms. "Go. I will be right behind you. You let out one sound from your mouth and you will be dead."

Trembling, Danette placed the blanket about her shoulders, then stepped outside into the total darkness of night. The air was damp and the wind cutting as it blew around the corner of the wigwam. A strong aroma of wood burning lay heavy in the air as all the wigwams emitted spirals of smoke upward from their smoke holes.

The one larger, communal fire had died down to only embers, and the Indians of the village were all out of sight, except for the braves who stood, rifles ready, too far from Danette for her to expect them to see and rescue her. It was too dark. Longbow was too swift. He gave Danette a hateful shove, causing her to stumble on into the black of the forest, where she was made to hurry onward, getting tangled in underbrush and scratching her legs with briars as they pierced her buckskin leggings.

"Keep moving," Longbow ordered, continuously shoving her.

"Gray Wolf will find you," Danette said, panting. Sweat beads sparkled on her brow, though the wind whipped in icy shreds against her face. "Longbow, you won't get away with this. Gray Wolf is determined. His hate for you already is great."

"Let him come to Sioux village," Longbow laughed.

"*Ay-uh,*" Danette said, laughing also. "Let yourself be a part of the snakelike Sioux so they will hide you behind their backs, being the coward you are, Longbow."

Longbow grabbed her by her wrist and jerked her to him, glowering down into her face. "Watch your words, white woman," he snarled. "Or you no make it to Sioux village before I have my way with you. You beg for mercy before

I get finished. I just stand and laugh at you and then throw your remains back into Gray Wolf's face.''

Danette's insides seemed to crawl, knowing that his hate for her was sincere, yet not understanding such a hate, since he didn't even know her. But knowing Gray Wolf was enough for Longbow . . . and she was now a part of Gray Wolf . . . his wife.

Longbow threw Danette to the ground and stood threateningly over her with the barrel of his rifle staring down into her face. He laughed mockingly, aiming. ''It is so simple,'' he said. ''One pull from my trigger and you be no more, white woman.''

Danette ached from the rough treatment and her lower abdomen throbbed, having still occasional faint reminders that she had not so long ago gone through the trauma of having lost a child. Her hair swept over her eyes as she lowered her head in pain. She clutched at her stomach, groaning. Then, having the need to show strength to get her through this new dilemma, she shook her hair back and looked up at him, daring him with the set of her jaw and the flashing of her eyes.

''Shoot me,'' she said. ''Go ahead. But then your fun would be over much too quickly, wouldn't it, ugly, foolish Indian?''

She knew that he could do so much to her without first killing her. There was a strong possibility of rape. Yet she had to show that she was not afraid. He wouldn't be able to see the nervous chattering of her teeth in the darkness of night, would he? She just had to be sure to not let her voice quiver.

Strength. She had to keep thinking about showing strength! Maybe that was what was needed to defeat this Chippewa-turned-Sioux!

Longbow lowered the barrel of his rifle, then stopped and slapped her across the face. Her neck snapped as her head moved with the blow, and she could feel a trickle of blood running from the corner of her mouth.

She angrily wiped the salty blood away and still defied him with a stubborn set to her jaw. "Hit me again, Longbow," she dared, drawing the blanket around her as she rose to her feet. "I am on my feet now. Hit me again. There's no one here to see how you shame yourself by beating up a defenseless woman."

Danette didn't know where her words might lead her. Possibly even to death's door. But she had to torment him at every opportunity. Only by doing this could she keep from falling apart from fear!

"White woman talk too much," Longbow grumbled. He sank his fingers into her arm and began forcing her to walk alongside him. "Longbow have fun with you later. It's best to first get as far from village as possible. When Gray Wolf can't find me one place, he will search another. Longbow will be long gone with you by the time Gray Wolf arrive here."

"How do you know?" Danette said, momentarily slipping on some dew-laden leaves.

"Longbow observe much," he laughed. "Gray Wolf and Chief Yellow Feather ride in other direction. They leave village handy for me to come and take white woman. The braves they leave behind are lazy braves. They see only what they want to see. No like fight. *Ay-uh.* They are like dogs with tails tucked between hind legs. The worst of cowards."

Panting for breath, Danette's chest began to pain her. Coughing, feeling her lungs aching for want of air, she half collapsed. But Longbow jerked her back to her feet.

"Did you walk from the Sioux village?" Danette asked, licking her parched lips. "Will we have . . . to . . . continue walking much . . . longer . . . ?"

"Horse close by now," Longbow grumbled. "Longbow

had to come to Chief Yellow Feather's village without noise. Horse make noise.''

"Thank the Lord there is a horse," Danette sighed. "How . . . much . . . farther?''

Longbow laughed sarcastically. "Your words of bravery have lessened?'' he said.

"I'm tired," Danette whispered. "That doesn't make me less brave.''

"Before the night is over, you will have many reasons to be tired," Longbow said, stopping, jerking her around to face him. "You pretty woman. Longbow have much fun with you when we arrive safely to Sioux village.'' He placed his hand roughly behind her head and drew her lips to his.

Squirming, moaning, flailing her arms, Danette tried to work herself free. His kiss was repugnant to her. He smelled of sweat and the aged deer tallow that he had worked heavily into his hair. And his kiss was wet, causing his spittle to dribble down her chin.

Pulling her next to him so that her breasts were crushing against his chest, Longbow let out a guttural sigh as his tongue sought entrance through her teeth. Danette cringed and went cold inside when she felt his male hardness growing against her thigh, and, knowing the true threat of that, she raised a knee upward and slammed it into his groin.

Yowling, Longbow lunged away from her. He dropped his rifle to the ground, clutching at himself where he throbbed achingly.

Danette eyed the rifle. It was too close to his feet. She didn't dare reach for it. Then she eyed the direction from which they had just traveled. Yes, the village was far behind them, but she had no choice but to try to reach it again. If not the village, perhaps a place to hide until Gray Wolf came in search of her and Longbow.

Not looking back, Danette began to run, blind. She had never known the forest to be as dark or as threatening. With every lift of the foot she expected either Longbow to grab her or an animal to jump out at her.

Sobbing lightly, hurting even more now, she continued to run. Briars scratched her ankles and legs, low-hanging limbs scraped against her face. She stumbled and fell across a fallen log in her path, then picked herself up again and once more began her flight of fear. But suddenly there was a heavy panting close behind her and an arm around her waist.

"No," she screamed, struggling. "Let me go!"

But she was once more pinioned against Longbow, his face so near hers that she could smell the thickened spittle of his breath.

"White woman, Longbow should kill you now," he growled. "The next time you do anything like that, Longbow *will* kill you. Death doesn't keep a man from enjoying a woman's body. You still be warm inside many hours. Pleasure even more, knowing you dead."

A bitterness rose in Danette's throat. She placed her hand over her mouth and gulped hard, knowing that she might retch at any moment. Longbow was deranged! Shouldn't she have known, though, that he was? One doesn't go around killing innocent people unless one is deranged. But to rape a woman after ... she ... was dead? That was something unthinkable, and surely he was only trying to put more fear into her by saying such a vile thing! Surely he wouldn't ... !

Danette didn't say a word back to him. She just accepted his arm about her waist, urging her father into the forest, and when they finally reached the horse, she was glad. If she had had to walk much farther, she most surely would have had to have been dragged! Her knees were weak, her feet swollen and sore. Each step had become a torture. And now? What could she expect at the end of the journey? Death? Slow, true torture? Rape? Possibly rape by many Indians? She knew to expect many things from the Sioux!

Settling on an Indian blanket behind Longbow, Danette clung around his waist. She tried to hold her head up but gave in to her lethargy, and, though she hated doing it, she couldn't help but place a cheek against his back and fall into a fitful sleep while he held onto her arms in front of him.

Head bobbing, her eyes fluttering wildly open, Danette awakened, seeing that the morning was showing its pale oranges from a sunrise that was visible on the horizon across a wide stretch of meadow.

Straightening her back, blinking her eyes, Danette focused on a river in the distance. "Where are we?" she asked, wriggling on the horse, her thighs numb from having been in one position for so long. "How far have we ridden, Longbow?"

"We ride all night," he said thickly. "We soon will be at the Sioux village."

Danette's stomach growled from hunger. Her mouth was dry with need of water. But she wouldn't admit any of these things to her captor. She would die first!

Holding her shoulders back, she flung her hair from her eyes and rode the rest of the way in silence, tensing when she caught sight of what had to be the Sioux Indian village nestled beneath trees and on the shore of a river that was unknown to her.

Looking more closely, the nearer they came to the village, Danette noticed that the Sioux dwellings were different from those of the Chippewa. They were in a tipi style, with many colorful paintings on their outer birchbark shells. And, though it was early in the morning, the village was buzzing with activity, the Indians looking no different from the Chippewa in their attire and the way in which they wore their hair and colorful beads.

"We are here," Longbow said forcefully. "You keep quiet. You will be taken immediately to Longbow's tipi."

"Ha!" Danette scoffed. "You act as though I am a threat

to you. What's the matter? Are the Sioux kinder than you? Would they disapprove of you stealing the wife of the St. Croix band of the Chippewa's next chief-in-line?''

"You speak vows with Gray Wolf already?" Longbow said. "Good. That makes your capture even better. You draw much attention to Longbow by the Chippewa. This will show them that Longbow strong. Not weak!"

Knowing that it was useless to argue with Longbow, Danette grew silent and observed all that was going on around her. The ground had been trampled down to form a hard, smooth surface throughout the Sioux camp. Around and around the tipis dozens of children were chasing each other. Screaming and laughing, they played, attired in a full outfit of fringed buckskin, their coarse black hair braided to their waists. Danette was unable to distinguish the boys from the girls.

In the center of the circle of tipis, there were fires in long trenches filled with coals, over which the carcasses of animals were roasting. Women crouched, turning spits. Danette's nose caught the odor of burned flesh, hair, and grease. And then her eyes widened, as she got a closer look at the carcasses being cooked as she and Longbow rode up next to the outdoor cooking space. She recognized a young bear and a beaver, as well as other smaller animals, all being roasted whole, with claws, eyes, and everything still intact, and seeing this made Danette gag and quickly lose her appetite. It was like a cannibal orgy, seeing animals cooked in such a way!

Turning her eyes away from the horrid sight, she watched as Longbow kicked at several village dogs as they circled around the horse, sniffling and growling. "Pester someone else," he shouted. "Longbow has business this morning, you lazy, no-good beasts!"

His shouting drew quick attention to him and his riding companion. The women stopped turning the spits . . . the children stopped their playing . . . and the Sioux Indian

336

braves who had been walking about performing their usual morning duties stopped to stare and silently watch Longbow and Danette pass by.

In the many eyes focused on her, Danette saw hate and coldness, and now she knew the true meaning of fear . . . !

Putting his horse into a lope, Longbow hurried to the outer edge of the circle of tipis and finally drew rein before one. "You now at Longbow's dwelling," he growled. He dismounted and lifted Danette down to the ground. "Go inside. I follow shortly."

Hesitating, Danette looked from Longbow to the tipi entrance, wondering if she was going to seal her fate by entering his dwelling.

"Mah-szhon," Longbow growled, giving Danette a rough shove.

Hungry, thirsty, and aching from the long, endless ride on horseback, Danette turned and slowly pulled the deerskin entrance flap aside and stepped inside. Her nose cringed at the sudden aroma of herbs. It was a smell similar to the medication Gray Wolf had used on her burns. She looked slowly around her. The conical-shaped room was dreary, the only light being that cast downward from the smoke hole at the top of the tipi and a soft glow from a fire in the center of the room.

Danette stopped and rubbed her eyes, and when they finally adjusted to the semidarkness, she was able to make out the figure of a woman sitting slouched beside the slow-burning fire.

"Who are you?" the woman asked in a husky, shaky voice, in English. "What do you want in my son's tipi?"

Danette took a step closer. When she got a better look at the woman, she flinched, seeing how crippled and old she looked, and then she remembered Gray Wolf and Amanda's speaking of Foolish Heart . . . Longbow's mother!

"My name is Danette," she finally said in a near whisper. Foolish Heart squinted her eyes. "Step closer," she said.

337

"My eyes are failing me. You are only a shadow to me."
She placed more wood on the fire, and, when it blazed
upward, casting more light on Danette, Foolish Heart saw
clearly enough who it was that her son had brought to the
village of the Sioux.

"You are Gray Wolf's woman!" she gasped. "Why has
my son brought you here?"

Danette didn't know the relationship between mother and
son, whether it was friendly, or one of noncommunication.
She didn't know if pleading with this crippled woman would
be useless or if possibly she might have an ally here. Surely
no mother could approve of her son's behaving so improp-
erly! Yet Danette knew that Foolish Heart had been forced
to live the life of the shamed for all those years by the
Chippewa, and possibly had the need for vengeance herself!

"Don't you know, truly know, why I am here?" Danette
asked, taking another step forward, seeking the warmth from
the fire. A sort of pain shot through her heart when she got
an even better look at Foolish Heart. She was gaunt, as
though her skin had been stretched tightly across her bones,
with twisted and grotesque fingers. She only looked half
alive. Yet there was still spirit and strength in her dark,
fathomless eyes, and Danette suspected that this woman had
been quite a personable figure when she had been young
and trying to win Yellow Feather's favor.

"*Gah-ween,*" Foolish Heart said sourly. "If Foolish
Heart know, Foolish Heart wouldn't ask. Words are never
wasted with me. Now give me direct answer. Why you here
in village of the Sioux?"

"Not by choice," Danette snapped. She settled to her
knees beside the fire and held her hands near the flames,
rubbing them briskly together, absorbing the warmth into
her flesh.

Foolish Heart lowered her eyes. "My son is up to foolishness again," she mumbled. "His heart is full of hate. Will
. . . it . . . ever . . . end?"

338

"Then you don't . . . approve?" Danette asked, eyes wide with hope.

Foolish Heart's eyes flashed. *"Nee-mee-nwa-bah-dahn?"* she said scornfully. "Foolish Heart approve of nothing son does anymore. Does white woman believe Foolish Heart, a Chippewa, want to be in Sioux camp? Foolish Heart the same as dead here. Longbow wrong to bring *gee-mah-mah* to such a place. My shame has never been greater."

"Why *did* he bring you here?" Danette asked softly.

"One day he come to wigwam with wound in wrist," Foolish Heart said. "He let *gee-mah-mah* doctor it, then say that we must go to Sioux camp. He shamed himself by letting another Chippewa shoot him, so felt the need to live away from the Chippewa village."

"But to live with . . . the . . . Sioux?"

"Foolish Heart's heart has never understood."

Danette's shoulders relaxed, realizing she was with a friend, not an enemy. Perhaps . . . just perhaps . . .

She scooted closer to Foolish Heart, smelling the stronger aroma of herbs. Her throat burned and her eyes stung and she knew that Foolish Heart must be using the medication for her hands and bent, crippled back.

"Foolish Heart . . ." she said, but was interrupted.

"Where is son now?" Foolish Heart said, watching the doorspace.

"He will be here. Soon," Danette said. "And before he comes, I want to talk to you, Foolish Heart. There is much that you need to know. And possibly you can help me." She lowered her eyes. "You see, I fear for my life in the company of your son, Longbow."

Foolish Heart's wrinkled face took on shadows. "Longbow not that hungry for revenge," she said. "You safe. He just torment Gray Wolf by bringing you here. Vengeance does ugly things to my son's mind. One day he will be swallowed up by it all."

Fearing Longbow's entrance at any moment, Danette

began speaking almost desperately. "Foolish Heart, please listen," she said. She wanted to take one of the crippled woman's hands in hers, a sort of better communication between two wronged women, yet hated touching a hand that looked as dried up as a dead leaf in winter. Instead, Danette placed her hands in her lap, wishing her heart would quit beating so quickly from fear and apprehension.

First, Danette explained how Longbow had really received the wound in his wrist, then quickly blurted, "Your son has killed. Once, possibly two or three times. We only have proof of the one time."

Foolish Heart leaned forward, rasping as her breathing became shallow. "What . . . are . . . you saying . . . ?" she murmured.

"Amanda . . . White Blossom," Danette said sadly, swallowing back the lump that rose in her throat whenever she remembered her dear friend's fate.

"What about . . . White . . . Blossom . . . ?" Foolish Heart asked, her lips nervously quivering.

Danette looked forcefully toward Foolish Heart. "Longbow stabbed her to death," she said. "He had threatened her the day she shot him, and he carried out his threat."

She shook her head sadly, then continued, "And Foolish Heart, he committed such a murder right after White Blossom . . . had . . . given birth to . . . a child."

Foolish Heart gasped and turned her head away from Danette. *"Gah-ween . . ."* she whispered. "Not Longbow. He couldn't. . . ."

Danette reached for Foolish Heart's hand, once more reconsidering, placing her hands back on her own lap. She clasped and unclasped them anxiously. *"Ay-uh,* he did," she said.

Foolish Heart's head swung around. Her eyes were red-streaked with the blossoming of tears. "You . . . speak . . . in Indian?" she murmured.

"Ay-uh," Danette said proudly. "I know some words

340

and will one day know them all. You see, it is my duty to learn your language. I am now Gray Wolf's wife."

"And Longbow has taken Gray Wolf's wife . . . captive. . . ." Foolish Heart mumbled. She lowered her face into her hands and softly wept. "Foolish Heart do not know son. He is not his father's son. Flying Squirrel's heart pined for his people. He did not kill nor steal other Indian's woman for vengeance."

Seeing this mother's torment, Danette scooted next to Foolish Heart and forgot her earlier apprehension, slowly placing an arm about the bony shoulders. "I'm sorry," she murmured. "But you must hear the rest."

"Ah-nway-bin?"

"There have been two other deaths, and everyone believes Longbow is responsible."

"Who . . . ?"

"First there was Dancing Cloud," Danette said, watching Foolish Heart's face take on a twisted expression. "And also . . . Red . . . Fox."

"Gah-ween . . ." Foolish Heart said throatily.

"Everyone does suspect Longbow is responsible. But without proof, nothing could be done about it."

"Proof of White Blossom's death? You have that?"

"Ay-uh. She was not yet dead when one of Chief Yellow Feather's braves found her. She spoke Longbow's name quite clearly. There is no doubt that he is the one responsible."

Foolish Heart's eyes took on a distant look as she stared into the flames of the fire. "Yellow Feather . . ." she whispered. "My husband . . . Yellow Feather."

Knowing the whole story of Foolish Heart and Yellow Feather's earlier relationship, Danette knew what Foolish Heart must be thinking, and her own heart ached for the woman who was remembering a love that had been refused her.

Foolish Heart's whole body trembled as she began push-

341

ing herself slowly up from the floor. *"Gah-ween,"* she said. "Longbow will not be allowed to harm you. Enough shame has been brought to me by the hands of my son."

Foolish Heart's eyes showed twinklings of tears in their corners. "Oh, how Yellow Feather must hate me now," she whispered. "To bear such a son as Longbow . . . ?" She shook her head sadly and walked, bent, toward a rifle that stood against the wall of the tipi.

Danette rose slowly to her feet, watching, barely breathing, as Foolish Heart then settled herself on the floor at the doorspace, blocking the way. "What . . . are . . . you . . . doing . . . ?" she asked, edging toward her.

"My son will not be allowed to enter," Foolish Heart said stubbornly, feeling remorse, and something else inside her that she had lost long ago in her sadness over how her life had turned out. It was good to feel the old, fiery spirit that had so long ago gotten her into so much trouble! These past years, she had just given in to being an ugly, aging woman, waiting for the day when the spirits would take her to the Happy Hunting Ground.

But now . . . she once more had a purpose in life . . . and she only hoped that she would be given this opportunity to show Yellow Feather that she could still be something besides . . . foolish.

"You will do this . . . for . . . me . . . ?" Danette asked, looking down upon Foolish Heart, who now looked anything but ready for the burial rites! In Foolish Heart's eyes, Danette could see life . . . hope.

"Foolish Heart do this for you, but mostly for Chief Yellow Feather," Foolish Heart said flatly, tilting her chin haughtily. "My son has brought too much grief into my chief's heart already. He will not be allowed to do so again."

Danette looked at the rifle and the way Foolish Heart's crooked finger was poised on its trigger. "You . . . would . . . kill . . . your own . . . son . . . ?" she whispered.

"Ay-uh," Foolish Heart said thickly. "If Longbow

342

doesn't obey, I will kill him. It will only get him out of his misery. He wallows in his own pity like a wounded pup. A bullet would stop it all.''

"But . . . your own son . . . ?"

"Longbow stopped being Foolish Heart's son when he began his killing of the Chippewa," Foolish Heart said. "No matter what has happened to me in the past, the Chippewa are my people. They are Longbow's people! He has disgraced his father Flying Squirrel's memory, as he is disgracing me while I am still alive!"

The deerskin flap at the doorspace suddenly flipped open and in its shadow Longbow stood, gaping wonderingly down at his mother. *"Gee-mah-mah?"* he said thickly, taking a step backwards. "What you do? You sit like crazy woman with gun on your lap."

"Go away," Foolish Heart said, staring with anger up into her son's eyes. "You not needed here."

"This Longbow's tipi," he said, taking a step, but stopping when the barrel of the rifle was raised and pointed in his direction. He gasped. *"Gee-mah-mah,* why you do this? Let me enter."

"You bring Gray Wolf's woman to visit?" Foolish Heart said sarcastically, laughing.

"Gah-ween," Longbow said, placing a hand on the knife at his waist. "You know that I do not. She is a part of my vengeance against the Chippewa, *gee-mah-mah*. But surely you know this. She must already have told you. You know. Now let me enter my tipi. Longbow has much to do."

"And what is it you have to do?" Foolish Heart hissed. "Do you expect Foolish Heart to turn her eyes away while you rape white woman? Isn't that your purpose for bringing her here? Or do you plan to kill her also?"

"None of this is any of your business," Longbow snarled back at his mother, then gave Danette an ugly, cold stare.

"Foolish Heart make it her business," Foolish Heart said, motioning with the gun. "You go away. I won't allow you

343

to hurt Gray Wolf's wife. She stay here with me until Gray Wolf and Chief Yellow Feather come for her."

"You can't do this," Longbow growled. He began to step around his mother but was stopped when she took the butt of the rifle and hit it against one of his knees, causing him to recoil and let out a loud yelp of pain.

"A bullet will be next," Foolish Heart said flatly.

Longbow rubbed his sore knee, red-faced with hurt pride and anger. "This how you repay me for all the years of devotion to you, *gee-mah-mah?*" he snarled. "After Father's death, you were taken care of by only one person. And by who? By son."

"Foolish Heart rather be dead," she said in a near whisper.

"Longbow even kill for you," he shouted, flailing his hands into the air. "More than once. My vengeance is also for you to celebrate. Longbow did it for you."

Danette gasped, paling. Foolish Heart's hands began to quiver, her head slightly and nervously to bob.

"What did ... Longbow ... say ... ?" Foolish Heart said in a rasp.

"Our vengeance is almost complete, *gee-mah-mah,*" he said proudly, smiling toward her.

"Who ... did ... you ... kill ... ?" Foolish Heart prodded.

Longbow glanced quickly at Danette, then back at his mother. "Names?" he whispered. *"Gee-mah-mah* needs names? Isn't it enough to know that son performed the deeds in the name of vengeance?"

"Names, Longbow ..." Foolish Heart hissed, narrowing her eyes.

"Dancing Cloud ... Red Fox ... White Blossom ..."

Foolish Heart let out a throaty sob, then looked coldly into her son's eyes. "Longbow, either you leave or Foolish Heart be forced to do what heart aches to never have to do," she said, her voice cracking with emotion.

"You wouldn't shoot son!" Longbow said, folding his arms defiantly across his chest.

"Longbow no son of Foolish Heart any longer," Foolish Heart said, her voice once more cracking. "Son die long ago."

Longbow's head lowered and he turned his back to her. "Son is alive," he said, emitting a throaty sob. "Son is alive!"

Longbow walked away, leaving a heavy silence behind him. Danette stood, breathless, watching Foolish Heart's shoulders quaking with sobs. Swallowing hard, Danette went and settled down on the floor beside the fire, knowing it was best to let this mother lose herself privately in her grief.

Danette picked up a stick and began stirring the fire wondering what the next day would bring.

Chapter Twenty-Two

*I arise from dreams of thee
In the first sweet sleep of night. . . .*
—Shelley

Two full days had come and gone and Danette still didn't know her fate. Longbow hadn't shown his face again to his mother, and Danette had just begun to wonder what meanness he now might be up to.

"The pain has lessened since you've been kind enough to apply the herbal medication generously to my feeble back," Foolish Heart said, closing her eyes, relaxing beneath the manipulations of Danette's deft fingers.

"This is the least I can do to repay you for your kindness to me," Danette said, running her fingers across Foolish Heart's shoulders, feeling the knots there, each almost the size of walnuts. "If not for you, I don't know what Longbow would have managed to do to me."

"Please do not speak of him to me," Foolish Heart said softly. "The pain around my heart is worse than in the crippled bones of my body."

"I'm sorry," Danette said. She lifted one of Foolish Heart's hands and began massaging the herbal medication into her fingers, rubbing the liquid into the coarse skin, working with each until the full liquid had been absorbed. "I shall not mention him again."

"Tell me of Yellow Feather," Foolish Heart said, her eyes shining.

"What do you want to hear?"

"That he asked about me when he discovered me gone from Chippewa village."

Danette blushed. "But, Foolish Heart, I do not know," she murmured. "I have rarely even spoken with Chief Yellow Feather. He shows . . . such . . . restraint when in my presence. I sometimes even think he doesn't like me."

Foolish Heart cackled throatily and bobbed her head up and down. *"Ay-uh,"* she said. "Yellow Feather would be this way. He always practiced such restraint when he was a young boy. When looking into his eyes, no one could tell any of his feelings. He was the proud son of Chief Wind Whisper, and he had to show that he was as strong and had the will of an ox."

"Gray Wolf isn't as restrained in his actions," Danette said, lowering her hands into a basin of water, cleansing them of the herbal medication. "Perhaps it is because it is not so required now to look cold and withdrawn as it was in the past. No wars are being fought between white man and Indian. Gray Wolf accepted me right away, though I was white."

"You beautiful," Foolish Heart laughed. "This is why. Just as Red Blossom was as beautiful and turned Yellow Feather's head those many years ago."

Massaging her own fingers now, Foolish Heart's eyes took on another distant stare. "If not for Red Blossom, things might have been different for Foolish Heart and Yellow Feather. . . ."

"But you married a man who loved you," Danette said, wanting to make Foolish Heart understand that she had been lucky to have found a man who had loved her.

"Ay-uh, Flying Squirrel loved me," Foolish Heart sighed. "I'll never forget how Flying Squirrel found me half frozen and dead and made me well again. It was during those days

of happiness with him that our son . . . Longbow . . . was . . . conceived. . . ."

Her eyes lowered. *"Gah-ween,"* she murmured. "Longbow is not forgotten so easily by his mother. He was my son for so long. He did care for me after Flying Squirrel died. Now I regret saying to him that he no longer my son." She looked toward the doorspace, a worry frown creasing her brow. "Where is he? It's been two days. . . ."

Danette didn't want to say that possibly Longbow had been captured by Gray Wolf and put to death. But deep in her heart, she hoped this would be true. She had begun to hope that each movement outside the tipi was Gray Wolf, come to rescue her. How many days would it take? Would the first true snowfall of the winter stop him from traveling so far from the Chippewa village?

The aroma of snow was in the air as the wind blew through the thin strip of deerskin at the doorspace. This morning, upon first awakening, Danette's heart had lurched at seeing the blanket of white that was spread out, across the land. The hundreds of pine trees surrounding the village looked like many more tipis in their shrouds of white. Yes, it was beautiful. But it served no useful purpose for Danette, for it was now muffling each and every movement that was made outside the tipi walls.

"Do Indians travel as easily in snow?" Danette suddenly blurted, rising. She held the entrance flap back, looking out onto the beautiful setting of white. The branches of the trees above her creaked and groaned as the wind blew in fiery, ugly gusts. Everywhere she looked it was a crystal fairyland. Trees, bushes, and even the grass blades and weed stalks along the edge of the forest were encrusted with frosty snow. Snow was piled upon snow, and as the wind blew it whirled and drifted.

Yet, the snowstorm hadn't kept the Indians from their daily chores. The women of the village were taking turns at the communal fire, preparing the meat for the day's meal,

349

and Danette had been told by Foolish Heart that the others worked even harder, inside their private dwellings, pounding maize or dressing the deerskin. The braves, dressed in furs and snowshoes, hunted even more fiercely for the deer that hadn't fled into the deeper recesses of the forest.

In the distance, Danette could make out several boys playing together near the river, throwing snowballs and laughing. And Danette wondered if anyone understood that she was being held prisoner, as well as why no one had come to see to her release now that Longbow had chosen to make himself scarce!

"Winter travel is made with sledge and snowshoes," Foolish Heart said, now preparing their noonday meal over the fire in the firespace. A strong aroma of fish was floating through the air, the last of what Longbow had supplied his mother with the day before his arrival at the Sioux camp with Danette as his hostage.

"Then if Gray Wolf and Chief Yellow Feather are still searching for me, they will find me?" Danette asked, dropping the entrance flap closed, shivering in the chill that had wrapped itself around her.

"They will find you," Foolish Heart said. *"Ay-uh,* they will find you. But will they find Longbow? I now fear for my son's safety. He is my only son. Without him, I will become as forever barren."

"Let's just try to force ourselves to think on the joyous side of life today," Danette said, settling down on a bulrush mat across from Foolish Heart. "Let's just be thankful that we are alive and able to enjoy one another's company."

"It has been good," Foolish Heart said, offering Danette a plate of fish. "The years have been lonely ones. Most Chippewa women ignored my presence, because I was the one to be left alone, out of my circle of people."

"If you had a chance to return to Chief Yellow Feather's village, would you go?" Danette asked, cringing when she took her first taste of the fish. It was more grease than meat,

350

and it stuck to the roof of her mouth , and made her teeth feel as though they had a thick coating of slime on them.

"*Ay-uh,*" Foolish Heart said. "The only reason I left was because Longbow said that he could never return. Foolish Heart's first thoughts were that without son's planted corn and gathered wild rice to give to me to cook, I would surely starve."

"But now? Would it be any different?" Danette asked, forking an eyebrow. "If Longbow is gone . . . you would be in the same position, would you not?"

"This getting to know you and the chance to defend you against the wrong my son has wrought upon you proved to me that I once again can do for myself as well as anyone else. Though this body is crooked and wracked with pain, it will no longer keep me to myself, waiting for death."

Danette leaned forward, her eyes bright. "Foolish Heart, if you return with me to the Chippewa village, I, for sure, will see to it that nothing bad ever comes your way," she said firmly. "Just you wait and see. I will make all wrongs right for you."

Tears sparkled at the corners of Foolish Heart's eyes. "These things we are speaking of are what dreams are made of," she said, laughing softly. "Foolish Heart knows this can never be. Now that Longbow has left a trail of blood, his *gee-mah-mah* could never be made welcome again in the Chippewa village. It's even worse than when I was made to feel like an outcast before. Then there had been no deaths. Only foolish deeds."

"Just don't you worry," Danette promised. "I will be there. Do you forget? I am the wife of the next chief-in-line."

"*Ay-uh,*" Foolish Heart said, lowering her eyes. "And Foolish Heart feel humble in your presence, beautiful, sweet one."

"Sweet Butterfly," Danette giggled. "Gray Wolf calls me Sweet Butterfly."

A look of admiration came into Foolish Heart's eyes. *"Ay-uh,"* she sighed. "Gray Wolf gave you rightful name. If only my son could have met someone like you and forgot his vengeful ways . . ."

"Even with my being white, you can feel this way?"

"Even though you are white," Foolish Heart said. "You more friend than any other in my life." She blinked her eyes, then added: "Except for Flying Squirrel. He was best friend. And, *ay-uh,* life has been empty without him."

A sound of barking dogs and men talking right outside the tipi drew Danette quickly to her feet. Her heart thundered wildly inside her, hoping that Gray Wolf had finally come for her. She rushed to the entrance flap and pulled it aside, her smile fading when she saw two frowning Sioux braves looking back at her, dullness in their dark, fathomless eyes.

Stepping back, afraid, Danette began to tremble. Then her eyes went to the sledge behind the six snarling, wolfish dogs, and she saw a bundle, then recognized the shape of a body.

Fear struck at Danette's heart. Had Gray Wolf been found . . . and murdered . . . by the snakelike Sioux? Was this the Sioux's cruel way of bringing him to her? Dead? Being pulled by a pack of dogs?

But then she had to remember that, no, it surely couldn't be Gray Wolf. Gray Wolf wasn't alone in his hunt. Chief Yellow Feather and many braves would have surely accompanied him! She looked wildly about, seeing no one else, then took a step outside the tipi into the ankle-deep snow and bravely faced the Sioux braves.

"Yes? What do you want?" she asked, seeing that they didn't continue on their way and had definitely stopped at this tipi for a purpose.

Seeing a blank expression mask their faces, Danette suddenly realized that they surely didn't understand English. Feeling frustrated, she stepped aside as Foolish Heart came

352

to stand beside her, completely wrapped in an Indian blanket thrown about her shoulders.

Danette listened as they exchanged words in Indian, then watched as Foolish Heart came toward the bundle on the sledge, to slowly lift a corner back to stare at the victim.

Danette flinched when she heard a slow chanting sound rise from deep inside Foolish Heart's throat, and when Danette leaned over and looked to where the blanket had been drawn back, she saw what had caused the reaction from Foolish Heart. Lying there, purple in color, Longbow made a peaceful corpse. . . .

Flailing her arms about, Foolish Heart rose her face to the sky and mournfully cried out her son's name. Then she was led inside the tipi by the two Sioux, leaving Danette standing there, alone with Longbow's body, staring blankly down at the blue tinge of his lips. Shivering in the cold, she knew that she should be glad that Longbow was dead. But her feelings went farther than that. They were for the mourning mother, who still chanted, and whose cries echoed throughout the forest and across the river, over and over again, creating quite a stir in the village as everyone moved toward her tipi, as though they were being pulled by strings.

Attired only in her thin buckskin dress and leggings, Danette was quickly feeling the wrath of winter on her flesh. She began to step back inside Foolish Heart's tipi but stopped when the two Sioux braves rushed out and lifted Longbow's body from the sledge and carried it past her, inside to Longbow's waiting mother.

"Now what can I do?" Danette worried, hugging herself, shivering even harder as the wind whipped around her, turning her cheeks to scarlet. She didn't wish to enter the tipi where the dreaded Longbow lay. Even in death, he seemed still to be a threat to her.

Yet where else could she go? No one in the Sioux camp had befriended her. Then Danette's heart began to thump wildly. If Longbow was dead . . . didn't that have to mean that Gray Wolf and Chief Yellow Feather were near? They surely were responsible for Longbow's death.

Having no other recourse but to go back inside the tipi that had housed her for the past two days, Danette stepped gingerly through the doorspace and stood silently watching, as the blanket was released from about Longbow's body. Gasping, Danette looked toward his chest, seeing how his buckskin shirt was bathed in blood. She had to know how . . .

Tiptoeing to Foolish Heart's side, Danette gently placed a hand to her arm. "I'm sorry," she whispered. "Please let me help you in any way I can." She couldn't come right out and ask how he had died! It would be heartless!

Yet her insides were trembling with the need to know! If Gray Wolf was near . . . so was her rescue.

Foolish Heart stood mournfully over Longbow, nodding a thanks to the two Sioux braves as they moved, backwards, to the doorspace. And after they were gone, Foolish Heart knelt down over her son.

"Gee-mah-mah will prepare son for Dance of Ghosts," Foolish Heart murmured. "You will be dressed in finest clothes and your hair will be freshly braided."

Danette stood by, silent, feeling helpless. She paled as Foolish Heart began disrobing Longbow, until he lay crudely nude, exposing his lean, blemished body and the raw wound in his abdomen.

"My son fell on own knife," Foolish Heart suddenly blurted, giving Danette a quick glance.

"He killed . . . himself . . . ?" Danette gasped. "Gray Wolf . . . Chief Yellow Feather . . . ?"

"Gah-ween. Your husband did not kill my son. *I* did."

"You?" Danette said, settling down next to Foolish Heart, though hating having to be near the corpse of the man she had so hated. Even in death he looked evil. . . .

"Ay-uh," Foolish Heart said. "Don't you remember? I sent him away. I said that he was not my son. And I shamed

354

him in front of you and all Sioux by not letting him enter his own tipi. It was the same as clipping his braids. *Ay-uh,* it is Foolish Heart who will forever be guilty for son's death.''

''I understand how you must be feeling, but you musn't blame yourself,'' Danette argued softly. ''His death was imminent. Once he was found by Gray Wolf, Longbow would have died a slow, torturous death. This is probably why Longbow killed himself. He wanted to die quickly. In private. He saved face by killing himself instead of being killed.''

''No matter,'' Foolish Heart sighed. ''He is dead. Now I must prepare his body for burial rites.''

Danette's eyes moved away from Longbow as she rose to her feet and began a slow pacing. If Gray Wolf hadn't killed Longbow, that had to mean that Gray Wolf probably wasn't even near. Hopes for rescue dwindled. Now that Longbow was dead, what would happen to Foolish Heart and herself?

Danette stepped aside as Sioux squaws began filing into the tipi, carrying an assortment of paraphernalia that Danette surmised must be for the preparing of Longbow's burial. She watched as Longbow's body was washed by several women and cleansed of all blood. His cheeks were painted and his hair rebraided, shining with a fresh application of bear grease.

Another squaw entered, carrying a white, beautifully beaded doeskin outfit. They all worked over Longbow, meticulously changing him from an evil, vile-appearing person to one almost angelic in appearance. But all of this was suddenly and quickly covered up when the women began wrapping his body in a thick bark.

Foolish Heart, tears rolling down her cheeks, began gathering together Longbow's personal possessions and placing them at his side. ''Longbow must be buried same day he died,'' Foolish Heart said, glancing toward Danette. ''His spirit is lingering, waiting to be set free, to go on to the camping ground of eternal bliss.''

Danette was beginning to feel quite uncomfortable, though Foolish Heart hadn't forgotten her in her grief. It was the other women and the way they kept looking at her, as though she had committed some sort of sin. She stepped farther back, into the shadows, feeling the threat around her growing more and more intense. She seemed to have even become the subject of gossip between the squaws, as they talked with their heads together, giving her even more hateful looks.

Then their faces took on a different sort of expression after Foolish Heart spoke quietly and at length with them.

Danette watched, wide-eyed, as the gaping squaws inched past her and on outside the tipi, just as quickly re-entering it with several Sioux braves. Once more Danette had to watch as Foolish Heart spoke at length with them.

The Sioux braves then turned and eyed Danette carefully for a moment before rushing out of the tipi, along with the gathering of the squaws, leaving Danette once more alone with Foolish Heart and the corpse of Longbow.

Danette went to Foolish Heart. ''What is happening?'' she whispered. ''Why do I feel as though I have been the main topic of conversation these past several minutes?''

Foolish Heart fell to her knees beside Longbow's wrapped body and touched the bark wrap with her twisted, thin fingers. ''It was believed that you were my son's wife,'' she said.

Danette paled. ''What . . . ?'' she gasped.

''At first, the women thought it so strange that you were not mourning the loss of husband,'' Foolish Heart said. ''The widow of dead Indian husband should wail loudly to show outward grieving.''

''Good Lord . . .'' Danette said, now realizing why the squaws had been looking at her with faces filled with so much displeasure. She had shown anything but remorse for

356

the Chippewa Indian whom she had grown to hate with a passion.

"But Foolish Heart tell them truth. That you not son's woman, but son's captive," she said. "They bring Sioux braves here, and I even tell them."

"And . . . what . . . is my fate now?" Danette asked, her voice shallow with fear.

"When they found out that you . . . you had been brought here as a hostage by my son, fear began to swell in their hearts."

"Fear . . . ?" Danette softly murmured.

"Fear for their village of Sioux," Foolish Heart said. "They now know to expect Gray Wolf and Chief Yellow Feather to arrive, to rescue you. And they fear much bloodshed if they can't find Yellow Feather and Gray Wolf to talk to them before this happens. There has been peace between our two tribes for too short a time. The Sioux do not want war to start all over again. They have discovered peaceful ways . . . and they like them."

"So what are they going to do?" Danette asked, yet fearing the answer.

"They at first thought they might take you to Chief Yellow Feather's village, but then they had to think that to see you with them would be the immediate cause for bloody battle."

"Then what are they going to do?"

"Some braves and the Sioux chief, Chief Dark Cloud, are leaving the village to search for Gray Wolf and Yellow Feather and have a peaceful powwow with them, while others are staying behind to prepare the village for an attack, should that happen."

"Attack?" Danette whispered, growing cold inside. It wasn't enough that she had been taken captive by an evil Indian but now to be the cause of a confrontation between two tribes of Indians! Oh, how long ago had it been that she had spent innocent, peaceful days and nights in Duluth, awakening in the mornings, knowing that she was safe, and

357

wanted . . . needed . . . for nothing? Now her life was filled with one traumatic experience after another!

It would be easy to think she had been better off under the protective wing of her uncle, but she knew that hadn't been so. All these struggles were so that she could be with the man she loved.

"And what about you, Foolish Heart?" she asked. "Since Longbow is the heart of the trouble brewing between the Chippewa and Sioux, are the Sioux going to blame you, his mother, since Longbow isn't alive to accept the blame?"

"They see I'm a crippled, aging woman," Foolish Heart said softly. "They hold nothing against old woman."

"At least we have that to be thankful for," Danette sighed. She went to the deerskin entrance flap and held it open only slightly and peered from it. Things seemed no different. There was no excitement, as she would have expected. Then she saw several Sioux braves leaving a larger tipi and guessed they had just been with the chief, receiving instructions.

Not wanting to be seen gawking, Danette dropped the flap closed and stood there, breathless, wondering how long she would have to wait to see if she was to be rescued by peaceful or warring means.

Chapter Twenty-Three

Love is a passion which kindles
Honor into noble acts. . . .
—Dryden

The sudden heavy snowfall had sent the Chippewa braves on a retreat, back to their village, empty-handed and discouraged. Dismounting before Yellow Feather's council house, Gray Wolf looked back toward his wigwam, and then toward his mother's log cabin. His eyebrows forked, quickly noticing that smoke spiraled from his mother's chimney, yet there was none from his wife's wigwam!

"Longbow hide himself well," Yellow Feather grumbled, securing his horse's reins. He brushed snow from his horse's thick, handsome mane. "But we will leave again. Soon. On sledges we will find him."

Gray Wolf placed a hand on his father's shoulder. "Father, something is wrong," he said. "No smoke rises from smoke hole of my wigwam. Sweet Butterfly knows to not let fire die. The walls of wigwam too thin. She would soon freeze."

"*Mah-szhon,*" Yellow Feather said. "Go and see what is the matter. I will begin getting sledges and dogs ready to leave again in search of Longbow."

With his moccasined feet sinking deep into the snow, having not thought to need snowshoes so soon, Gray Wolf trudged onward until he reached his wigwam. With a rapid pulse rate, he stepped inside into darkness. Fear laced his heart as he began feeling his way into the room, smelling dead ashes in the firespace. He reached and touched empty blankets, then fell across Danette's easel, knocking her canvas from it.

Grumbling, Gray Wolf reached for the canvas, getting a glimpse of what had been painted onto it from the small trace of light shining down from the smoke hole above his head. "What is this?" he whispered. "Something is written across the front."

Taking the canvas with him, Gray Wolf stepped outside, into the light, and grew numb inside as he made out the words "Longbow" and "Sioux." Hatred burned into his heart as he realized what had happened. Somehow Longbow had managed to slip into the village and had taken Sweet Butterfly.

"No!" he cried, slinging the canvas away from him.

Yellow Feather rushed to Gray Wolf's side and placed his hands to his son's shoulders. "What is it?" he asked, seeing the canvas lying in the snow. "What did you find?"

Gray Wolf's face was drawn and his eyes narrow with hate. "Longbow has stolen my woman," he said. He nodded toward the canvas. "Sweet Butterfly left me a message on the picture."

Yellow Feather picked up the canvas, brushed flakes of snow from it, then read in silence. *"Ay-uh,"* he then said. "We made a big mistake by thinking Longbow was far from our village. He was probably waiting, watching for us to leave."

Gray Wolf gestured with his hands, looking desperately about him. "Why didn't anyone see?" he shouted. "Do our braves have blind spots before their eyes?"

Yellow Feather took a step into the wigwam and placed the canvas against the wall, then went back outside, to Gray Wolf. "This is not the time to ask why," he grumbled. "This is the time to go rescue Sweet Butterfly. Each added moment she is with Longbow . . ."

Gray Wolf clenched his teeth and frantically kneaded his brow. "Do not speak the word you have in your mind," he growled. "Should Longbow touch her in such a way, he will die many deaths."

Yellow Feather looked toward his own dwelling, worrying. Hadn't Red Blossom known about Sweet Butterfly's disappearance? Surely she would have alerted the braves, had she known! If Red Blossom hadn't been aware of what had happened, it had to indicate that Red Blossom still mourned too deeply for her sister.

Ay-uh, such a mourning was understandable. She hadn't only lost a sister, but would find it impossible to return with White Blossom's body to St. Paul for the white man's kind of burial. With an infant to care for now, and with the weather so questionable, Yellow Feather had urged Red Blossom to stay behind when the brave had left with Amanda's body.

Everyone's silent fear had been for Rettie Toliver. How would she take her niece's death . . . ?

"We must leave soon," Gray Wolf said, stiffening his back, straightening his coat of rabbit fur. "We must get our snowshoes and leave immediately."

"Dogs are being harnessed to many sledges," Yellow Feather said. "After I check on Red Blossom and get my heavier coat and snowshoes, we will leave, my son."

"Ay-uh . . ." Gray Wolf said. He went back inside his wigwam, hating the empty quiet of it. He left the blanket at the doorspace thrown back, enabling him to see without building a fire, then looked wistfully around at all the things that reminded him of his wife.

His wigwam had been magically transformed, now even more hers than his, with her painting paraphernalia, her lacy underthings stacked neatly inside an open valise, and the sweet fragrance of her perfume, coming from a bottle that sat next to the wooden basin where she bathed.

Thinking of her with Longbow and what he might force

her to do caused a low, anguished cry to come from the depths of his soul. A hate so profound ate away at his gut that in his mind he had already killed Longbow, over and over again. . . .

Picking up the portrait she had once again painted of him, Gray Wolf studied the strokes she had taken with her brush. He could see his likeness exactly in the painting, and then he hated Longbow even more when he let his gaze settle on the two words that had been smeared there. He shook himself, knowing that lingering, becoming lost in thought, was the last thing that he should be doing. He had to act!

"If I'm just not too late," he said, now busying himself by stepping into his racket-shaped showshoes. Their frames had been made from an ash tree and were crisscrossed with moosehide thongs.

He then hurried to the council house ground, where his father was already waiting, with at least four dozen other well-armed braves. No time was taken to smoke the stone pipes or to plan war strategy. Their destination was the Sioux camp that was the closest, and they wouldn't even send a scout on ahead to check the position of the Sioux lookouts. Blood was to be shed, and much of it.

All of the Chippewa braves were ready for the fight, fully realizing that some of them might not return. They were ready to face death, all in the name of their St. Croix band of the Chippewa, realizing that the man being hunted had at one time been one of them, but one who had made a wrong turn somewhere along the way.

Chief Yellow Feather raised his hand, silencing his waiting braves. "Let us now go," he shouted. "And many scalps must be taken. We must show the snakelike Sioux that it is not wise to harbor outcast Chippewa in their camp."

Gray Wolf stood proudly beside his father. "Gray Wolf's wife is being held captive in the Sioux camp," he shouted.

362

"She must be safely rescued. She must be at my side tonight, my brothers!"

"And death to Longbow!" Chief Yellow Feather yelled, circling his upthrust hand into a threatening doubled fist.

Shouts and confusion followed as the fur-wrapped braves grew increasingly excited with the thought of a fight ahead. Taking a Sioux scalp on the warpath enhanced the stature of a Chippewa male in the eyes of the village maidens and the ruling council. The Chippewa villagers would lavish the greatest praise on the leader of a successful war party, and on those who distinguished themselves in battle. The war party's return would be celebrated with a scalp dance, and the scalps would be treasured and displayed for everyone to see on five-foot-high scalp poles.

Harnessed in tandem with collars and side straps, the many wolflike dogs howled and snarled as the Indian braves readied themselves for the new hunt.

Stepping onto the long runners that reached out at the back of the sledge, Gray Wolf cracked his long whip and shouted to his dogs as they dashed off down the trail. His sledge followed Chief Yellow Feather's, and the others followed his. The chief and his son had rarely battled together, and all were eager to be able to participate in such an event.

Overhead, the sky was gray and threatening. The clouds appeared heavy with more snow. The wind whistled and moaned past Gray Wolf's face, where rabbit fur whipped against his cheeks from the hood of his coat.

With the lowering temperatures, Gray Wolf could feel the mucus in his nostrils freezing and his eyes burning from the cold air blasting against them.

But nothing would stop him in this hunt. Ah, what satisfaction he would receive in taking Longbow's scalp while Longbow writhed, screamed and watched before he died. It would be a different sort of pleasure than that of making love, yet it gave Gray Wolf a similar sort of thrill to think of this man he hated as finally dead. . . .

"The Mide priest refuses my son necessary funeral ceremony to ensure Longbow's journey to Happy Hunting Ground," Foolish Heart said solemnly. "Since Longbow bring trouble to the Sioux they refuse him even a place of burial. In death, my son is still shamed, as his mother also continues to be."

Danette's heart ached for this mother, yet, hating Longbow, it was hard to offer her any sort of help, since she didn't care if the evil Indian's spirit didn't find peace. In life he had brought much suffering to others. In death it seemed only right that he would have a share in this suffering.

Yet, Danette did have feelings for Foolish Heart, and she thought it only right to try to ease the elderly Indian's burden of the heart. "What can I do to help?" she asked, averting her eyes away from the bark-encased body.

"Dogs and sledge wait outside. They were at least kind enough to offer it for carrying Longbow's body from the village," Foolish Heart said, rising, securing a heavy blanket around her shoulders. "The Sioux only do this, though, to rid the village of the evil spirit of Longbow."

"Where can you take him?" Danette asked, drawing a blanket around her own shoulders, knowing that she had to at least help Foolish Heart carry Longbow's body to the sledge.

"To the forest, away from the circle of tipis," Foolish Heart said. "I will find a white birch tree and place him in the snow beneath it. It is the sacred tree of the Chippewa. Longbow will be safe there. The Chippewa have offered many sacrifices to the tree for bark taken. The spirits of the birch tree will remember and watch over my son who will not have proper burial in ground."

"I will help you to take him ... to ... the sledge," Danette murmured, shuddering at the thought of touching the body, though it was securely wrapped.

Feeling her back muscles straining, she lifted the end that held Longbow's feet while Foolish Heart groaned as she struggled with the other end. Together they crept from the tipi and placed Longbow's body on the sledge. Then Danette watched as Foolish Heart led the dogs away, toward the forest.

As a few desultory snowflakes began to settle onto Danette's face, she peered up into the sky, fearing an added snowstorm might delay Gray Wolf's arrival at the Sioux camp. The wind was already whipping the earlier fallen snow into high drifts against the tipis and trees. More snowfall could even bring danger to Gray Wolf and his father and the many braves with them.

Shivering, Danette looked slowly around her, seeing Indians peeping around the corners of partially drawn-back entrance flaps. In their eyes, Danette could read mixed feelings, a combination of fear, hate, and dread. She was beginning to wonder how safe she was. She was the only white woman in the camp. . . .

Hoping that getting out of sight might remove her from their minds, Danette rushed back inside Foolish Heart's tipi. Kneeling before the fire, she placed pieces of wood on the flames. She cringed when in the distance she heard mournful wails and knew that it was Foolish Heart spending her last moments with her departed son.

The wailing finally stopped. Danette sighed heavily and relaxed her shoulders, now hoping for a semblance of peace, with Longbow finally removed from her life. With the warmth of the fire seeping into her flesh, making her finally comfortable enough to remove the blanket from around her, she let it drop from her shoulders, onto the bulrush mats.

While waiting for Foolish Heart's return, Danette busied herself, making two hot cups of spruce tree tea, something that had only recently been introduced to her by Foolish Heart. It was a bitter concoction, but one that warmed one's stomach.

With the two cups ready, steaming and inviting, Danette looked toward the entrance flap, wondering what was keeping Foolish Heart. The sledge dogs should have delivered her back to her tipi by now.

A ripping sort of noise drew Danette quickly to her feet. She tiptoed to the side of the tipi where the noise was the loudest. She leaned her ear closer to the wall of the tipi, unable to make out what she was hearing as it continued incessantly.

"There's only one way to find out," Danette whispered. Throwing the blanket around her, she once more stepped out into the snow. She tried to step lightly, not wanting to sink any more than she had to into the snow, but feeling her feet growing quickly wet, she hurried on her way and put at least that worry from her mind.

Circling the tipi, Danette reached the back side. What she discovered caused her heart to skip a beat and her mouth to drop wide open.

"Foolish Heart, what . . . are . . . you doing . . . ?" she said, barely audible.

"*Gee-mah-mah* must not stay in place where son has dwelled and died," Foolish Heart mumbled, continuing to peel the birchbark from the frames of the tipi. "Foolish Heart must dismantle lodge."

"But . . . why . . . ?" Danette gasped.

"Longbow's spirit soar about inside his dwelling," Foolish Heart said. "It must be released. Longbow's earthly dwelling must be destroyed, to let his spirit travel to his new dwelling at the Happy Hunting Ground."

Danette's teeth chattered in the cold. She rushed to Foolish Heart and grabbed her by the arm. "You cannot do this," she cried. "Without a place of shelter, we will freeze. We will die. You know that the Sioux won't do anything to help us. Should you destroy our shelter, you will be destroying all our means of survival here.''

Danette discovered quite quickly the strength of this old Indian woman, who was mostly bone with skin stretched tightly over it. Foolish Heart jerked herself free of Danette and continued dismantling the tipi while Danette stood by watching, until the remains of the tipi stood fleshless, leaving only what appeared as skeletal bones rising, leaning from the ground.

Looking solemnly into the wall-less tipi, Danette felt like laughing and crying at the same time. Beside the embers of the fire in the firespace, two cups of spruce tree tea sat, untouched, and everything else that had comprised Longbow's and Foolish Heart's personal belongings was quickly being covered by snow, as the threat of a new snowstorm became instant reality.

Danette looked toward Foolish Heart, seeing her total grief as Foolish Heart's shoulders slouched heavily beneath her blanket and she lowered her eyes, softly crying. Trying to understand the strange custom that had led Foolish Heart to destroy the tipi, Danette went to her and placed an arm about her waist.

''Come,'' Danette murmured. ''We must go to the communal fire. Perhaps we can huddle there together and stay warm for at least a while longer.''

''You are kind,'' Foolish Heart said, patting Danette's hand.

Trudging through the snow, absorbing the cold wetness into the flesh of her feet and ankles, and fighting off the snow that was blowing harshly against her face, Danette tried to hold back tears of fear, praying that Gray Wolf would somehow sense her plight. . . .

Over the white, pathless snowfields, and beneath snow-encumbered branches, Gray Wolf hurried his dogs onward.

He cracked his whip across the dog's backs unmercifully, watching the snow falling harder, settling in layer after layer of white as far as the eye could see.

Heavy-hearted, Gray Wolf sensed that Sweet Butterfly was in even more danger than before. Somehow, Gray Wolf had to place the blame on the fierceness of the snowstorm. He felt that if he didn't reach the Sioux camp soon, it might be too late. . . .

Gray Wolf's thoughts were quickly drawn to the present as Yellow Feather raised a rifle into the air and shouted, *"No-gee-shkan! Nadoues-Sioux!"*

Hearing his father's warning to stop, that he had spied the snakelike enemy in the distance, Gray Wolf reached for his own rifle from his sledge. Stopping his dogs, he peered through the haze of snow and was able to make out the approaching figures of many Sioux, also on dog-drawn sledges.

Yellow Feather moved from his sledge and went back to Gray Wolf. "They come to us to stop our approach to the village," he growled. "So we fight them here and spill their blood to look like red poppies blooming from the snow."

"Father, what about Sweet Butterfly?"

"We will fight our way to village. We will rescue her. Do not doubt the guidance of Wenebojo."

"Ay-uh . . ." Gray Wolf said, lowering his eyes, sometimes feeling less than wise standing in the shadow of his father, the great leader of the St. Croix.

Gray Wolf followed alongside Yellow Feather, instructing all of the Chippewa braves to draw their dogs and sledges into a circle. Readying them for the fight, the sledges were tipped to stand on their sides, to serve as protection. And then, with rifles poised, ready, the braves stretched out on their stomachs in the snow and waited.

The barking, snarling, and howling of the Sioux's dogs came closer and closer. Gray Wolf watched over his sledge, hoping to get the first shot at Longbow, traitor and murderer that he was. His intention was not to kill him, but to wound him, then to continue with Longbow, torturing him. A scalp pole would hold his prize most proudly high for all to see what happens to a Chippewa Indian who betrays his people!

Gray Wolf's shoulder muscles corded tightly when he saw the Sioux stopping. But what was this? They weren't preparing for a fight as was expected! Instead, one Sioux, recognized to be Chief Dark Cloud, walking proudly as a chief would, had left his sledge and all the others behind, and was moving toward the waiting Chippewa. Without a weapon in either hand, he raised them above his head and kept walking straight ahead, alone.

Gray Wolf looked over at Yellow Feather. "What does it mean, *gee-dah-dah?*" he whispered. "Do they not hunger for a fight? Is Longbow not with them?"

"Chief Dark Cloud wants to talk? Chief Yellow Feather talk," Yellow Feather said flatly, handing his rifle toward Gray Wolf.

"Father, what if it's a trick?" Gray Wolf protested. "How can you trust our enemy?"

"Then, my son, it will be up to you to avenge my death," Yellow Feather said, placing his hand heavily on Gray Wolf's shoulder. "Take my gun. Keep it for me until my return."

"But father . . ."

"Gray Wolf, as long as I have been chief, I have never shot a man, not even a Sioux, if he shows sincerity in wanting to talk. Talk better than fight, if that can possibly settle a disagreement between Indians. Remember that, my son. Always remember that. Never kill in haste. Wars begin in such a way."

Gray Wolf accepted Yellow Feather's rifle and stood it before him, against his sledge. "My rifle will be aimed on Chief Dark Cloud's heart," Gray Wolf growled. "One false move and he is dead."

"Never in haste, my son," Yellow Feather said. He rose

to his feet and moved out into the open. Tall and proud, he moved across the straight stretch of snow-covered meadow.

Gray Wolf's heart thundered inside him, so fearing for his father's life. He aimed at the Sioux's heart with his rifle, and waited, breathless, as his father began a lengthy debate with the enemy. And it was when Yellow Feather placed his back to the Sioux and began walking back toward his own Indians that Gray Wolf became the most concerned. If Chief Dark Cloud hadn't agreed with whatever Chief Yellow Feather had said to him, it would be so easy to give the command to kill!

Gray Wolf inched over and let his eyes scan the waiting Sioux, watching for any sudden movement or the quick flash of a rifle barrel, indicating worsening danger. It seemed an eternity before Yellow Feather finally reached the safe circle of his Indians, and when he did he began shouting commands to ready their dogs and sledges, so they could retreat, back to the Chippewa village.

Gray Wolf rose quickly to his feet, lowering the barrel of his rifle. He studied his father's face for hidden answers. Then he spoke his worries aloud. "Father, are we giving up? Why are we returning to our village?"

"You and I will not return with the others," Yellow Feather said, straightening the twisted dog's harnesses.

"What does it all mean?" Gray Wolf insisted. "Why are we going separately?"

"The strength of many rifles is not required this time, my son. We will enter the Sioux camp in peace."

"Sweet Butterfly?"

"She is alive and well."

Gray Wolf sighed heavily, as though a weight had been lifted from his heart. Then he frowned. "Longbow?" he asked.

"He is *nee-boo*."

"Dead?" Gray Wolf gasped, his dreams of vengeance fading. "The Sioux? They kill him?"

Yellow Feather patted Gray Wolf's back fondly. "Longbow died as the coward he was," he said. "He fell on his own knife."

"Longbow . . . did . . . that . . . ?"

"*Ay-uh.* And Sweet Butterfly waits for us to come to her."

"The Sioux. Why are they being so understanding about all of this? Why are they behaving as friends instead of enemies, as they always have been?"

"They have only recently learned the rewards of a peaceful way of existence. They meet us before we get to their camp to stop bloodshed. This is good. We return home victorious, without firing even one rifle."

"I still don't understand many things," Gray Wolf growled. "If the Sioux want peace, why did they let Longbow stay in their camp?"

"They didn't know he was bad," Yellow Feather said. "They accepted him into the camp in good faith. They thought it would make the Chippewa chief happy to see the Sioux become friends with one of our people."

"Friends! Ha!" Gray Wolf exclaimed. "Do they deny helping Longbow in all his bad deeds?"

"*Ay-uh.* They knew nothing of any of his evil deeds."

"Time will tell who does and does not tell truth," Gray Wolf grumbled. He straightened his sledge and climbed aboard, waiting for his father to lead the way. Though his face was chaffed and raw from the icy breath of winter, his heart was warm with the knowledge that Sweet Butterfly was alive and even now waiting for his arrival into the Sioux camp, to take her safely home again with him.

But a part of him was still angry and filled with disappointment that he had been denied the opportunity to kill Longbow in the way in which he had seen fit. Longbow had surely expected to die a slow, painful death. By falling on his own knife, he had died a much less violent death than had been due him!

Keeping his eyes on the band of Sioux in the distance, Gray Wolf began concentrating only on Sweet Butterfly. He had been going through hell, not knowing what had happened to her.

Then his recurring nightmare struck him again. What if Longbow had raped her . . . ?

The first signs of the Sioux camp came into view, nestled into the restful scenery of white-cloaked cedars and pines, with the wider expanse of the trees of the forest as its backdrop.

Gray Wolf struck his whip across his dogs' backs and anxiously raced them on, ahead of Yellow Feather's team of dogs. But when they had reached the outskirts of the camp and the Sioux dogs were already being unharnessed, Gray Wolf became more cautious.

Slowing his sledge, stepping from it, Gray Wolf was met by Chief Dark Cloud. After exchanging brief words, Gray Wolf abruptly asked to be taken to Sweet Butterfly. A nod sent his way by the chief and the gesture of a hand, and Gray Wolf walked behind the chief, feeling many eyes on him as Indians stepped quietly from their tipis.

Gray Wolf looked slowly about him and when his gaze stopped where the communal fire hissed and spit flames back at the falling snow, he stopped in midstep, disbelieving what he was seeing. He closed his eyes and shook his head, thinking it was surely an apparition, because of his anxiety to see Sweet Butterfly. . . .

But when he opened his eyes and looked once more toward the two women huddled there on the ground beside the fire, so close together they looked like only one person, a loud cry tore from deep inside him as he recognized one of them to be Sweet Butterfly.

His feet wouldn't carry him quickly enough. He stumbled over his snowshoes, his breath tearing from his throat, and when he finally reached the clinging women, he fell to his knees and began frantically brushing snow from Danette.

"Sweet Butterfly!" he cried. "Why? How?"

He clawed at her, fearing he was too late. Her face and lips were a soft purplish color, her eyelids closed, her lashes heavy with snow. The blanket that had been the only deterrent against the cold was stiff with the snow and ice covering it.

Gray Wolf drew Danette quickly up into his arms and half dragged her closer to the fire. "Sweet Butterfly, you're going to be all right," he said, half choking on emotion. "You've *got* to be all right."

"Gray Wolf, what has happened?" Yellow Feather asked, hurrying to Gray Wolf's side, stunned.

"Your Sioux chief told only half truth," Gray Wolf cried. "Sweet Butterfly is not all right. She was left outside, to freeze." He looked across his shoulder, at Foolish Heart. "Foolish Heart also. She even looks dead, *gee-dah-dah.*"

Yellow Feather went to Foolish Heart and drew her up from the ground, seeing nothing in her that he could remember her having been in her youth. A deep sadness tortured his insides, as he remembered so much about her. At one time he had admired her fiery spirit, but she had learned how to misuse it, and that hadn't worked in her favor, being a wife of the next-chief-in-line. He could remember the day she had left the village ... beautiful, angry, and *ay-uh,* deeply hurt. ...

"Foolish Heart, you're too full of spirit still to let cold kill you," he whispered harshly. "Come. Let Yellow Feather help you to get warm again. Then ... then you will return with me to your rightful place ... to the village of the St. Croix band of the Chippewa." He swallowed hard. "You see, the Sioux explained how you protected Sweet Butterfly from Longbow. You are to be rewarded. Never again will you be cold or hungry."

Foolish Heart's eyes slowly opened. A slow smile broke through the snow on her face and a tear droplet sparkled in the corner of one of her eyes. ...

373

Danette could hear voices. One of them sounded like Gray Wolf's. But the hurting, the aching of her entire body was causing everything else to be fuzzy.

Gray Wolf rubbed his hands over her face. The friction was causing a warmth to rise to her flesh. She could feel it. She could hear him now. He sounded far away, yet he was there beside her. Yes! She could feel him!

Slowly, she opened her eyes. She tried to speak, only able to emit scratchy sounds. But that was enough. Gray Wolf had heard. He picked her up into his arms, laughing and crying at the same time.

"You are going to be all right," he shouted. He began running with her. And when he came to his sledge he placed her on it and began tucking great bearskins all around her.

Danette reached her hand to his face. "My . . . love . . ." she managed to whisper. "Once more . . . you . . . rescue me . . . ?"

Chief Dark Cloud was suddenly there beside Gray Wolf. Gray Wolf turned on his heel, fists doubled at his side. Then his mood softened when he saw what the chief was offering. It was two heated stones, one to place on Danette's lap to keep her hands warm, and one to place at her feet.

Gray Wolf didn't thank the Sioux, thinking the Sioux chief owed that much to Sweet Butterfly for letting her almost freeze to death in his camp. He placed the heated stones in place, then watched, silently, as Foolish Heart was taken to Yellow Feather's sledge and treated just as respectfully. He puzzled over this.

Danette slowly turned her head and managed a smile, seeing how warm Foolish Heart now looked under her many bearskins, on Yellow Feather's sledge. "She has . . . to . . . live," she murmured, glancing up at Gray Wolf. "If not . . . for . . . her . . . I would be dead, Gray Wolf."

She then tore into a fit of coughs, gasping for breath. Gray Wolf knelt down over her and framed her face between his hands. "Do not talk," he said. "Save your energy for later."

He gave Foolish Heart a quizzical look, then once more focused his attention on Sweet Butterfly, giving her a warm, sweet kiss on her lips. "We'll be home soon," he said hoarsely. "Life will only be good to you from this day forth."

Danette looked adoringly up into Gray Wolf's eyes, breathing hard, yet content. *"Ay-uh,"* she whispered. *"Ah-pah-nay."*

Happiness swelled inside Gray Wolf, proud to have his wife with him again, and proud to hear her speak in Chippewa so fluently. He boarded his sledge behind Danette and cracked the whip across his dog's backs, smiling confidently at his father as Yellow Feather's sledge came alongside his. It had been good . . . being a part of the hunt with his father.

"Ay-uh," he said to himself. "Everything in life is suddenly good again. . . ."

Chapter Twenty-Four

When she comes home again!
A thousand ways I fashion,
to myself, the tenderness
of my glad welcome.
—Riley

"First you heal my wounds from a fire, then from near frostbite," Danette said, amazed at how quickly her numbed fingers and toes had sprung back to life. She sighed rapturously as Gray Wolf continued with his warm, tender kisses along each finger, feeling the flames of desire inside her igniting, like a torch, kindling her heart.

Gray Wolf's lips now playfully traveled up to her inner arm, to her soft, sensitive spot there, and then just as quickly moved to her breast. Cupping the breast with his hand, he led its pliable nipple into his mouth and darted his tongue around it.

Half reclining, nude, on a bulrush mat beside a roaring fire in the firespace in her and Gray Wolf's wigwam, Danette leaned her head back and closed her eyes. She feasted on Gray Wolf's nearness and his art at making her mind leave her. All thoughts of where she had just been were erased from her brain, and now the present was all that was important to her.

"Your body temperature is still rising?" he teased, giving her a passion-filled glance.

"Very high," she sighed. "Love me, Gray Wolf. Just love me."

His hands began trailing over her, first at the soft, silken curves of her thighs, then upward where her hips spread only slightly, and on to her thin, tapering waist, where he placed his hands firmly and lifted her body to his lips. His tongue circled her navel, then worked its way on up to once more discover the hardened peak of her breast.

Danette's insides were now becoming like molten lava. She reached her hands to Gray Wolf and began her own exploring. She watched the glimmer in his emerald eyes as she played with both his nipples, letting her forefingers and thumbs work magic on him as they squeezed and toyed with the brown mountain of what felt like rubber to her.

Leaning up closer to him, she placed her mouth to one of his nipples and sensuously sucked, letting her teeth sink into it only enough to torment him. When she heard him sigh, she relished the pleasure she was arousing inside him. His pleasure meant her pleasure. Her pleasure was his.

Danette now sent feathery kisses across the copper flesh of his chest, up to his neck, then flicked her tongue in and out of his left ear. This seemed to intensify his need of her even more, for he let out a sort of growl and gathered her fiercely against him.

His hard maleness lay in full bloom against her lower abdomen. She could feel its heat and velvet softness, pulsating slightly, and when she looked down at it, she could see a pearly sparkle of wetness on its tip.

Quivering, she placed her hand to him and led him on inside her, thrilling at the way he so magnificently filled her. She closed her eyes, lifted her hips and twined her arms about his neck. She worked with him. She met his eager thrusts with abandonment.

His lips came down upon hers with softness and kissed her long and sweet. His tongue sensuously entered her mouth and found hers waiting and anxious. Theirs was a union that carried them to the heavens, where their minds led them to a peaceful bliss of togetherness. Their hearts and souls blended into one, soaring . . . clinging . . . floating. . . .

Danette let her hands creep down the strong structure of Gray Wolf's back. Splaying her fingers against the round hardness of his buttocks, she sank her fingernails into his flesh there and spread her legs even more, as his movements inside her became as driven as her own need to feel the rapture of release.

Breathless, perspiration-covered, Gray Wolf drew his mouth away from hers. He burrowed his nose into the jasmine of her neck and inhaled her flower scent. Placing his hands beneath her hips, he lifted her to meet his feverish strokes, becoming dizzy with the building passion. And as he felt the blinding moment of release engulf him, he shuddered violently against her, releasing his love seed inside her, his ever present proof of undying love for her.

Danette felt his warmth inside her, and this triggered her own response of release. Beautiful visions blossomed inside her brain as she was swept up into the powerful inner glow that her union with Gray Wolf always so magically offered her.

Then she felt the descent from heaven and was once more a normally breathing human being, aware of the coolness of the wigwam and the howling of the wind outside, where a fresh snowstorm was endangering the village of the Chippewa.

"I feel so wicked," Danette said, easing out of Gray Wolf's embrace.

"Why do you?" Gray Wolf asked, reaching out his hand in a futile effort to stop her from rising.

Danette pulled a blanket around her shoulders and scooted up closer to the flames of the fire. "Because I'm so happy," she murmured.

Gray Wolf pulled on his fringe-trimmed leggings and then his buckskin shirt. Kneeling, he began placing more wood on the fire. "It's about time, don't you think?" he growled. "No thanks to Longbow."

Danette's heart palpitated. She didn't want to remember. For a while there, she had thought she was dying sitting in the blizzard with Foolish Heart. Even in death, Longbow had almost succeeded in his plan of vengeance.

Gray Wolf's eyes narrowed and his jaw set hard as he looked toward Danette with a mask of hatred. "The time with Longbow . . ." he said thickly. "Did . . . he . . . ?"

Danette's face suddenly flamed. Her eyes felt hot. Her throat was dry. But shouldn't she have expected such a question from Gray Wolf . . . ? It would appear that Longbow would have raped her if he could have.

"He didn't," she quickly reassured.

"All the time you were with him . . . he . . . didn't . . . ?" Gray Wolf persisted, appearing to doubt her.

Anger flamed Danette's face even more. "Gray Wolf, if I tell you something, it is always told you in truth," she said flatly. "When have I ever given you reason to doubt my word?"

"Gah-ween-wee-kah," he said. He went to her and drew her up into his arms, causing her blanket to flutter down, away from her, to rest against her ankles. "Never, my love. Gray Wolf never question you about Longbow again. He is dead. So shall all our thoughts of him be dead."

Searching with his lips, he showered kisses on her closed eyelashes. He cupped her breasts with his hands, then lowered his mouth over one, sucking on the nipple until it rose to a stiff peak between his teeth.

Danette moaned, feeling the fluttering of her heart as renewed desire began to run rampant inside her. "Good Lord, Gray Wolf," she whispered. "I'm melting inside . . . literally melting."

"That is good," he chuckled. "Gray Wolf is seeing to it that wife never grows cold again."

"How could I ever be cold in your arms?" she murmured.

380

She slipped her hands beneath his shirt and ran them over his chest, stopping her hand where she felt his heart pounding so erratically.

She opened his shirt and pulled it aside and kissed the spot where her hand had discovered his heartbeat. "Your heart is going wild," she then said, looking up into his eyes, seeing them filled with need of her.

A sensuous shudder enveloped her and she was guided by her own wants and needs to place her hands at the waistband of his leggings. Brazenly, she began to lower them down over his hips, lower, to expose his swollen maleness risen to great heights . . . and lower then, to his ankles.

Breathless, her heart pounding, Danette knelt down before him and began tracing his muscled legs with her hands. Where her hands traveled, then so did her lips. She looked up at Gray Wolf, seeing his neck arched backward and his eyes closed. His body stiffened, then trembled, as she continued her gentle assault of his senses.

Danette's fingers and lips traveled upward, past his thighs, to where his shaft of desire shone from his patch of curly hair. Smiling warmly, she moved from her knees and leaned herself against his maleness and began a slow, seductive movement, until his gasps for breath warned her that the time for teasing had to be drawn to a halt.

"Gray Wolf, please let's not waste any more time," she sighed. "Take me again, my love. Take me now."

Gray Wolf placed his hands at her waist and began to lower her to the floor, but she didn't comply. He questioned her with his eyes.

"Not that way," she whispered.

"How then . . . ?"

"Lift me up, into your arms," she encouraged. "I shall place my legs about you. Then let's make love."

Gray Wolf chuckled. "You teach me ways of loving?" he said.

"Only in my fantasies have I known different ways of being with you," she said.

He lifted her and fit her in place against him as she locked her legs and arms around him. Holding her there with his hands beneath her round, smooth buttocks, he at first began slow movements inside her. His lips trembled against hers. His eyes closed in his drunken stupor of growing rapture.

Danette clung. She rocked with him. She tasted him. She smelled him. Her senses were reeling, filled with only him. As his thrusts increased, so did her heartbeat. She felt as though there were no tomorrow, no yesterdays.

When his lips moved from her, she placed her enflamed cheeks against his shoulder and cried out as together they once again found that time in life when, for a brief moment, there was a perfect joy.

"I wish that it could last forever," Danette whispered, lacing her fingers through his unbraided hair. She lifted her lips to his brow, separating his bangs to kiss him passionately there.

"We have forever," Gray Wolf said, lowering her to the floor, to stand before him. His eyes spoke of his devotion to her.

"Ay-uh," she said. *"Ah-pah-nay.* Forever."

Gray Wolf laughed throatily, pleased. "You know Indian words well," he said.

"I will know all Indian words soon," she said, running her forefinger down his chest, to his waistline. Knowing that surely he couldn't become aroused again so soon, she thought better of letting her finger wander lower.

Instead, she spun away from him, fulfilled and even smug, and settled down by the glow of the fire. The orange blaze once more reminded her of dancing elves as the flames flickered up and around the logs.

Gray Wolf knelt down beside Danette and placed the Indian blanket back around her shoulders. "You will know more than words," he said. "You will know all customs of the Chippewa."

"*Ay-uh,* I will," Danette said, smiling softly up at him. She watched him step into his leggings, laughing to herself about how he had not stayed dressed long the last time he had placed his leggings and shirt on his beautiful, masculine body.

"Gray Wolf guarantee this," he said. He rose to his feet and slipped his snowshoes and fur-lined rabbit coat on.

Danette's smile wavered. "Where are you going?" she asked, having planned to snuggle into his arms and stay there the rest of the afternoon, had he agreed to let her.

"I have chosen one of our brightest squaws to be your companion," he said, giving her a stern, forceful look. "I go to get her. Now."

"What . . . ?" Danette gasped. She rose quickly to her feet, holding on to the blanket, which persisted at wanting to loosen itself from her. "What do you mean . . . companion . . . ?"

"During the day while I am hunting in the snow of the forest and fishing through the ice of the river, she will see to all your needs and teach you the women's way of the Chippewa," he said. "At night she will leave, giving you to me for lovemaking."

Danette felt anger rising inside her. She took a step toward Gray Wolf and held her chin proudly high. "Gray Wolf, I need no one with me during the day," she said dryly. "What I learn of the Chippewa ways I will learn from you, and what I don't learn from you I will learn from observing all your Indian men and women. I will not be saddled all day to any woman, be she Indian or white. Even my personal maid, Amy, knew that I required privacy and never interfered in my day's activities unless I asked her to."

Gray Wolf's eyes darkened into many shades of green. "Gray Wolf says squaw teach, so squaw teach," he growled.

383

"Gray Wolf, I absolutely forbid it," Danette said, doubling her fists at her side.

Gray Wolf clasped his hands to her shoulders. "You are now wife, and a wife obeys," he said, emotionless.

"Gray Wolf, how dare you," Danette gasped, wide-eyed. She jerked away from him, now more hurt than angry. She turned her back to him and bit her lower lip in frustration.

"Do you forget that you lost one child?" he asked, gently forcing her around to face him.

"What does that have to do with this?"

"If you become with child again, you will need to be pampered, to make sure you are well," he said. "This is why it is necessary to have squaw here to do the household chores and duties."

"A wife usually does these things," Danette softly argued.

Gray Wolf's brow furrowed. "You are no ordinary wife," he said. "You are Chippewa wife of the next-chief-in-line."

"Oh, yes," she said sourly. "Did you really believe I could forget? How many times and ways must I be reminded?"

A look of hurt flashed across Gray Wolf's face. His mouth went slack and his eyes softened. "You sound less than pleased that you are the wife of the next-chief-in-line," he mumbled. "Are you now sorry that you are here with me? Does my love not sustain you, Sweet Butterfly?"

His pain was her pain. His sadness was her sadness. Feeling guilty for her harsh words, she threw herself into his arms and hugged him tightly to her, in the process hurling the blanket from about her again. "I'm sorry," she whispered. "I didn't mean what I said. I love you so, Gray Wolf."

His strong arms wrapped around her, his eyes feasting on her naked beauty, never getting enough of her. Her breasts were ripe and full, once more an invitation to his lips. He kissed the swell of one, then smiled warmly down at her.

"Hurtful words from you are rare," he said. "Gray Wolf forget you said them."

"I am sorry," she said, then pleaded with her eyes. "But, Gray Wolf, I still don't want anyone but you sharing this wigwam with me."

"It has to be," he said. "Now I must go. I sent word earlier for her to prepare herself for task ahead. Her family proud that she is chosen from the many maidens of our village."

"Even in this blizzard you plan to carry through with this . . . this plan? You will get her now?"

"Orders were given before snowstorm," he said flatly. "Snow stops nothing. If it did, the Chippewa would die."

Danette eased away from him, sulking. "What's this squaw's name?" she asked, resigning herself to what had to be, to please her husband.

"Laughing Rain," he said, then rushed from the wigwam, leaving Danette standing there, already missing him and dreading meeting this squaw who might interfere too much in her life.

After a while, she stamped her foot. "Laughing Rain?" she said. "Will she be as pretty as her name?"

A keen jealousy tore at her heart, knowing that not only would she be around this . . . this Laughing Rain too much . . . but Gray Wolf would, as well. Danette realized the dangers of this and already disliked the squaw, without even having met her.

Remembering her nudity and not knowing just how quickly Gray Wolf would return with Laughing Rain, Danette busied herself by dressing. She slipped the softness of a buckskin dress over her head, tied it securely in place about her waist with a belt trimmed with tiny, colorful beads, then stepped into moccasins.

Grabbing a mirror, steadying it in place on a makeshift shelf on the wall, she began taking long strokes with a brush through her hair. With each added stroke, she grew angrier.

The thought of another woman meaning something special to Gray Wolf, no matter how slight, was cause for her not only to dislike this woman, but to resent her.

With her hair finally glistening and hanging in its full, natural curls down her back, she focused her eyes on a canvas that was hidden partially from view, behind several others. To try to forget her frustrations over Laughing Rain, she went and drew the one canvas out away from the others and slowly turned it to face her.

Shuddering, she read the words "Longbow" and "Sioux" painted awkwardly across what had at one time been the proud portrait of Gray Wolf. It came back to her in a flash . . . the moment when she had been painting those words with Longbow standing there before her, a threat to her life. . . .

Shaking her head to clear her thoughts of Longbow's blemished face and cold eyes, she was reminded of the good things in life that were all rolled up into one person . . . namely Gray Wolf. If not for him, Danette would not be alive.

"How many times has he rescued me . . . ?" she whispered. "I must always remember and not only give him my love . . . but also my loyalty."

Danette began running her fingers across the portrait, wondering if she could somehow remove the two words that totally ruined it. She cocked her head to one side, still pondering over this, then jumped, startled, when she saw movement out of the corner of her eye.

Turning abruptly, her heart took on a dull, aching pain when she got her first look at the companion Gray Wolf had chosen. Partly hidden beneath a hooded fur cape, her face was still visible. Dots of snow sparkled like sequins on the Indian squaw's tiny-featured face, seeming to enhance her delicate beauty. Her cheeks were rosy from the cold, her dark eyes luminous, and the soft curve of her lips surely

386

hauntingly inviting to all Indian braves who chanced a look at her.

Danette slowly placed the canvas back among the others, wordless, glancing from Gray Wolf to Laughing Rain. Gray Wolf stood next to Laughing Rain, smiling almost boyishly . . . and Laughing Rain stood, clinging to his arm, smiling coyly back at Danette.

"So this is Laughing Rain?" Danette said icily, fitting her hands together behind her back, digging her nails into each palm.

Laughing Rain laughed softly. *"Ay-uh,"* she said. "Laughing Rain comes to assist Gray Wolf's wife."

"So you not only know everything there is to know about Indian customs but you speak the English language as well?" Danette asked, much too sharply, hating herself instantly after letting her venom show.

"Yes. Gray Wolf taught me as a child," Laughing Rain said, casting him an admiring glance.

Danette's eyes sent sparks of anger toward Gray Wolf. "Oh, I see," she said. "Gray Wolf didn't tell me that. What else have you neglected to tell me, my husband?" She could see growing irritation mask his face.

Gray Wolf went to Danette and leaned close to her ear. "You behave like a child bride in your jealousy," he growled.

"How else should I act?" she whispered back. "Gray Wolf, she is beautiful. She's one to be jealous of, especially with a handsome husband like you to worry about. And don't you see how she looks at you? Are you blind?"

Danette tensed as Laughing Rain loosened the cape from around her and placed it across her arms. What Danette then saw caused waves of relief to splash through her. Because of the bulkiness of the fur cape, she had not seen Laughing Rain's pregnancy.

Gray Wolf glanced toward Laughing Rain, then back at Danette. "Laughing Rain looks at me with pride in her eyes because of my status with our people," he said. "Her eyes . . . her heart . . . have been for only one man. Can't you see that she is swollen with child?"

Danette felt a rush of shame course through her, for doubting Gray Wolf, and for her petty jealousy. Her face flamed with embarrassment. *"Ay-uh,"* she murmured. "I see."

"Time will pass more quickly for Laughing Rain if she is busy," Gray Wolf said. "This and her intelligence are the reasons for choosing her."

"We shall get along just fine," Danette whispered. "I promise you that, Gray Wolf."

"Then I will leave you two alone to get better acquainted."

"Must you leave? The snow. The storm."

"I will only go as far as council house. It has been a while since I have had time to smoke leisurely pipe with father and Chippewa braves."

"How long will you . . . ?"

"When night creeps over village, I will return," he said, then walked out of the wigwam, leaving an awkward silence between two women behind him.

Danette was the first to speak. "Let me have your wrap," she said, taking a step toward Laughing Rain.

Laughing Rain took a step backwards. "I am here to help you, not you me," she said, taking it upon herself to place her cape beside the doorspace. She wiped some sparkles of snow from her coarse black bangs and straightened her two braids to hang down her back. Bending, she slipped her snowshoes off, then strolled to the fire and warmed her hands over it.

"In your condition, how is it that you can take over my household duties?" Danette said, glancing toward Laughing Rain's stomach. Another sort of jealousy was suddenly invading her senses, like pinpricks in her heart. A child. Yes, the importance of a child. . . .

"Though with child, I am strong," Laughing Rain said. Her eyes took on a daring, assuming look. "Gray Wolf understands my strength. He has always admired this in me. As a child, when Gray Wolf scaled a bluff, Laughing Rain scaled a bluff. When Gray Wolf swam in icy rivers of winter, Laughing Rain swam beside him. A boy-girl is what he always called me. I laugh even now when I remember him calling me this."

"Yes. That's quite humorous," Danette murmured, not at all amused. She was remembering how Gray Wolf had become so sensual when swimming with her. Had he been that way with Laughing Rain? Surely in the summer when the sun was sweltering, he and Laughing Rain had shared such swims as well. . . .

Laughing Rain looked toward the canvases. She went to them and began pulling them out, one at a time, admiring Danette's paintings. "You use your hands well," she said. "Will you teach me how to make colorful designs on cloth?"

"Do you mean to say that you do not know how to paint?" Danette said wryly. "I'm surprised. You seem to know so much about everything else."

Laughing Rain gave Danette a slow smile. "You do not like me very much, do you?" she asked, placing the canvas back with the others. "Why is that? Am I a threat to beautiful white woman?" She patted her swollen abdomen. "Me? A woman with child a threat?"

Danette tossed her head, flipping her hair back from her shoulders. "I'm surprised you are even wondering such a thing," she said. "You have a husband. Why would you think for one moment that I would consider you a threat?"

Laughing Rain pulled the tip of one of her braids around and brushed its loose ends against her chin. "Didn't Gray Wolf tell you?" she said, half smiling.

"Tell me what?"

"That my husband is no longer alive . . . ?"

Chapter Twenty-Five

> *Do you ask what the birds say?*
> *The sparrow, the dove and thrush say,*
> *"I love and I love!"*
> —Coleridge

Nine months had passed.

It was mid-September, called the month of the "Turning of Leaves Moon" by the Chippewa. The wild rice had once more been gathered and stored for the winter and corn was piled in golden heaps against the outside walls of Danette and Gray Wolf's wigwam. The harvest had been good for the Chippewa and as fruitful, singly, for Gray Wolf.

Rising slowly from her bed of blankets, Danette placed her hands to the small of her back, groaning. The weight of the child inside her womb had become almost unbearable this past week. Each day it was more of an effort to arise, to face another long day ahead of her.

"Sweet Butterfly have another sleepless night?" Gray Wolf spoke from behind her as he roused himself from his deep, restful sleep.

Danette ran a hand over the swell of her stomach. "Our child kicked all night," she sighed. Attired in a silk nightgown she had brought from Duluth, she bent down over Gray Wolf. She reached for one of his hands and placed it where their child still kicked unmercifully.

"Do you feel it, Gray Wolf?" she asked, laughing softly.

Gray Wolf's eyes lit up. *"Ay-uh,"* he said. His hand traveled over the full contour of her stomach. "A son. Only a son could be so active!"

Danette couldn't find the courage to ask if it really would matter so much to him that it just might not be a son he talked and boasted of continuously. She moved away from him and went to the doorspace and drew back the Indian blanket. She looked out, onto the patchwork effect of the trees in their crimsons and golds. She inhaled the fragrance of early morning, so fresh and clean in this northwoods country!

Then her eyes focused on the log cabin that housed Lorinda and Chief Yellow Feather. Two rooms had been added to make space for Rettie Toliver, who had been brought to live with Lorinda after Amanda's death, and for North Star, the soon-to-be toddler who was now the ruler of the house, able to twist even Chief Yellow Feather around her tiny finger.

Though the log cabin was rustic, it was beautiful to Danette, and she envied anyone who lived in anything other than a small, confining wigwam!

So far Gray Wolf hadn't taken it upon himself to be so generous to his wife. Now that she was his, he seemed to take her for granted. It was only at night, in bed, that Danette was able to forget her unhappiness at being away from her old life style. When she lay next to Gray Wolf, everything else was quickly placed in the back of her mind.

Strong arms slipped around her waist. Danette's heart pounded when she felt the hardness of Gray Wolf's risen desire for her probing her from behind. It had been a full month now since they had been able to share in lovemaking, and this added to Danette's mental anguish. She knew that his needs were just as great and wondered if he was getting these needs fulfilled elsewhere! Laughing Rain had had a healthy son and was now small and exquisitely beautiful again. . . .

"What is wrong with my wife this morning?" Gray Wolf whispered into her ear, his breath hot on her cheek. "Another moody day ahead for you?"

Danette placed her hands over Gray Wolf's, which lay possessively on her stomach. "The last couple of days it's been worse," she sighed. "I guess I'm just tired from being pregnant for so long. My activities have been restricted so much."

"Laughing Rain takes burden from your days," he said, kissing her cheek.

"I don't need her," Danette said coolly. "She has her child to care for. She doesn't need me to fill her days any longer!"

"It is for you that I insist Laughing Rain stay, to attend to you, not for Laughing Rain," Gray Wolf growled, drawing jerkily away from Danette.

Danette swung around, hating her spiteful words, but she was in such a state she couldn't help her sour flow of words.

"I'm sorry, Gray Wolf," she murmured.

He didn't respond. He instead began dressing. And after he even had his hair in fresh braids and shining with deer tallow, he gathered up his bow and quiver of arrows and brushed past her.

A sudden, sharp pain in her abdomen caused Danette to let out a loud gasp. She reached for Gray Wolf just before he stepped from the wigwam.

"Gray Wolf . . ." she whispered, eyes wide as another pain tore through her.

"What is it?" he asked, dropping his bow and arrows to the floor. He placed his hands to her shoulders, seeing how perspiration was suddenly beading her brow.

Danette flinched as another pain grabbed at her insides. "Can it happen . . . so . . . quickly . . . ?" she asked, leaning her arm heavily against Gray Wolf as he studied her, as though seeing her for the first time.

Danette laughed softly, seeing how this was affecting him.

"Darling, it's our child," she said. "I do believe ... it's ... time."

She closed her eyes and panted, trying to block out the painful, bearing-down sensation at her lower abdomen. But then her eyes shot wide open as a watery substance gushed from inside her, wetting her nightgown and the bulrush mats at her bare feet.

This seemed to awaken Gray Wolf from his daze of wonder. *"Ay-uh,* it *is* time," he said, swooping her up into his arms.

"Gray Wolf, what are you doing? Where are you taking me?"

"You are going to *gee-mah-mah*'s cabin, where you will be more comfortable to give birth to child," he said, rushing from the wigwam.

Realizing her scanty attire and how it was now clinging even more because of its wetness, Danette began to struggle in his arms. "No, Gray Wolf," she softly argued. "You can't take me looking like this. Anyone who looks my way can see clear through my nightgown!"

"They only see wife of Gray Wolf who is ready to give birth to son," he argued back.

The word "son" burned an imprint into Danette's brain. She became oblivious of eyes on her as Gray Wolf rushed her past the outdoor firespace where many women gathered, preparing venison on a spit. She was swept up in too much pain to now think of anything else ... except ... for that word ... "son."

Gray Wolf took Lorinda by surprise as he carried Danette unannounced into her cabin.

"My word, Gray Wolf," Lorinda gasped, wiping her hands on an apron. "Is it time? Is she in labor?"

"Ay-uh ..."

Lorinda spied the wetness of Danette's gown. "And her water has already broken?" she whispered.

Gray Wolf's eyebrows forked. "Water?" he murmured.

394

Lorinda laughed softly. "Never mind," she said. She guided Gray Wolf into a smaller room off the main, outer room, where a baby crib and a larger bed filled almost the whole space. "Place her on the bed beside the crib."

North Star, tiny, blond, and beautiful with her round, copper-colored face was standing in the crib. She was dressed in a deerskin dress and moccasins and her hair was freshly braided and hung, unusually long for a baby her age, almost to her waist. She was clutching onto a rag doll dressed like an Indian.

"And take North Star to Laughing Rain," Lorinda quickly added. "Tell Laughing Rain that I'll come to get North Star as soon as Danette has had the child and both are out of danger."

"Out . . . of . . . danger . . . ?" Gray Wolf said, his eyes wavering, placing Danette gently on the bed. He flinched as her face took on a grotesqueness as she grabbed at her stomach and softly moaned.

Lorinda lifted North Star from her crib and placed her in Gray Wolf's arms. "Gray Wolf, take North Star, then come back and help me," she said.

"*Ay-uh . . .*" Gray Wolf mumbled. He held tightly on to North Star and hurried from the room.

Danette reached a hand to Lorinda's arm. "This can happen so quickly?" she whispered.

"Some are slow, some are fast," Lorinda said, tying her long auburn hair back from her face. "Your little one appears to be one of the most impatient ones and should be born quite soon."

As a fresh pain spiraled through her insides, Danette grabbed onto the sides of the bed and bore down. Her teeth ground together, her hair was wet with perspiration.

"Just give in to it," Lorinda said, lifting Danette's gown. "Just let it happen." She pressed her fingers easily along Danette's stomach, then smiled. "It seems to be turned the right way. There shouldn't be any danger to you or the child.''

"Thank . . . God," Danette sighed, then gasped for breath as she gave in to another sharp contraction.

Gray Wolf came back into the room, breathing hard. Lorinda began to hand out instructions right and left, and soon many bowls of hot water were sitting beside the bed, ready for use.

Danette lay limply, spent of energy, waiting for the moment. Gray Wolf held on to one of her hands, while Lorinda held on to the other.

"It won't be long now," Lorinda reassured.

Danette smiled weakly from Lorinda to Gray Wolf, and then her attention was drawn to a scraping and a thud-thud sound on the hardwood floor of the cabin. She looked toward the door, watching as Rettie Toliver came wobbling into the room, dragging her left foot and leaning heavily on a cane.

Rettie was at least one hundred pounds lighter than she had been when Danette had first met her, and she was now only a wisp of an elderly lady. Yet the loss of weight had worked in Rettie's favor. She was now at least able to get around on her own volition at times, though she was still partially paralyzed on the left side.

Losing Amanda hadn't lessened Rettie's will to live, it had only strengthened it . . . to prove to the world that Rettie Toliver could stand up against all odds . . . that she could possibly live forever!

"What have we here?" Rettie said in a low rasp of a voice. "Another young'un comin' into the world?"

Rettie made her way to Gray Wolf and patted him fondly on the back. "So my nephew is about to become a father?" she said. "A little playmate for our North Star?"

"*Ay-uh* . . ." Gray Wolf said proudly. "My son will be younger than North Star, but he will be her protector against all harm as they grow up together."

Danette turned her eyes away, so fearful of disappointing him.

Rettie teetered a bit. Her wrinkled face paled as her eyes took on a glassiness. Lorinda saw this and hurried to her side. She placed an arm about her waist. "Rettie, why do you insist on leaving your rocker unassisted?" she scolded. "You know how lightheaded and disoriented you become at times."

"Precious, will you quit scoldin' me as though I was a child?" Rettie fussed. "And I want to help with the deliverin' of the baby. I helped Gray Wolf enter the world, or do you forget that?"

"I remember," Lorinda said. "But this time is different. You were much stronger then, Aunt Rettie." She began guiding Rettie from the room. "You should be in your rocker beside the fire. Come on now. Take it easy. Only a few steps and we will be there."

Danette's eyes widened and her heart thundered inside her as she felt a contraction, much worse than the others. She began to breathe heavily, tossing her head fitfully from side to side.

The pain was so severe, it seemed to block everything else from Danette's mind. Gray Wolf and Lorinda's voices blended together, sounding as though they came from the depths of a deep well.

There was an instant sensation of relief, and then Danette was hearing another sound from inside the well. She blinked her eyes, licked her parched lips, then looked slowly toward Lorinda, who was holding a tiny thing in her arms.

Wiping her eyes, Danette was now able to focus them, and she now saw her child and knew this new sound that she had heard had been its first cries of life.

"She's perfect," Lorinda cried. "Every tiny feature is perfect. And, Danette, look. She is an exact replica of you. Her skin is so fair." She gently placed the baby beside Danette, freshly cleansed but not yet wrapped.

"A . . . daughter . . . ?" Danette whispered. She looked at the fragile, wriggling child that had been born from love and she was torn with feelings. Oh, how she loved her daughter, yet she so feared Gray Wolf's reaction. She was too afraid even to look his way. Instead, she touched her baby's cheek, oh, so soft, oh, such a miracle, with ten tiny toes and fingers and a nose that barely turned up at its tip. The baby's dark eyes squinted toward Danette . . . mother and daughter . . . in communication for the first time ever.

"We must wrap her now," Lorinda said, lifting the baby, securing a tiny blanket of rabbit fur about her. She walked to Gray Wolf. She held the baby out to him, seeing how his disappointment was placing a wall not only between him and his wife, but also between him and his daughter.

"My son, your daughter is beautiful," Lorinda said. "She waits to be held by her father."

Danette's heart had never ached so much as it did at this moment . . . a time in her life that should mean serene happiness! But Gray Wolf's denial of his daughter . . . and his neglect of Danette too at this moment were just cause for her heart to be slowly breaking, possibly never to mend again.

When the baby began crying, Danette reached her arms out to her. "My child is hungry," she murmured. "I shall feed her now."

Holding tears back, not wanting to transfer her feelings to her child, Danette turned to her side and welcomed her daughter into her arms. Though hurt by Gray Wolf, she felt a strange euphoria when her daughter's tiny lips were placed at her nipple and began sucking nourishment from it.

A joyous peace settled over Danette. At this moment, there were only herself and her daughter.

Her spell was suddenly broken, but delightfully so, when Gray Wolf came and knelt beside the bed, looking at her with what she hoped was pride in his eyes.

Danette swallowed hard, not wanting to cry, when Gray

Wolf reached a hand to the breast from which their child was feeding. As he touched it, a soft tremor of ecstasy traveled through Danette, thinking now that surely there was hope . . . that everything was going to be all right. She smiled softly toward Lorinda as Lorinda inched out of the room.

"Gray Wolf shares breast now with daughter?" he said hoarsely.

"Ay-uh . . ." Danette murmured. "You do."

His hand traveled lower and touched the baby's cheek. "She is beautiful daughter," he murmured. "She has your . . . your pale skin. She doesn't look Indian at all."

"Yes, she is beautiful," Danette murmured. "And, no, her skin is not like yours. Does that matter, Gray Wolf? Have I now disappointed you twice in one day?"

Gray Wolf jerked his hand away as though he had been shot and his eyes narrowed. "What do you mean . . . disappoint . . . ?" he said softly.

"I bore you no son. A daughter is our first born. Are . . . you . . . disappointed?"

Gray Wolf turned his head away then turned it slowly back toward her. He took her free hand in his and gently squeezed it. "Happiness shines in your eyes. Your cheeks are pink with pride," he murmured. "This makes Gray Wolf happy."

"That is not what I asked you," Danette said, already knowing the answer without prodding him further.

"A son will come later," he said.

"I can measure your feelings by your voice," Danette said. "And I sense much that you don't confess to, Gray Wolf."

"A son will come later," he repeated icily, releasing her hand and rising to his feet. "I must go now. I will leave you to your child. You both need rest."

My child? Danette thought to herself. *Our* child, she wanted to scream. She turned her eyes from him as she heard him leave the room.

"What am I to do?" she whispered. "He doesn't seem the same now. What am I to do?"

She turned her attention to her child. "And he doesn't share in naming you?" she sighed. "So I shall do it alone!"

She paused for a moment, then said, "Hope. I shall name you Hope."

Chapter Twenty-Six

It hammers at my heart the long night through—
This want of you.
—Wright

The autumn leaves fell to the ground, making a colorful carpet too soon covered by *sisibakwatagon,* a snow fluffy as eiderdown. And then, the world was no longer muffled in the breathless silence of snow but was awakening to the new life that came only with springtime.

Danette lay clinging to Gray Wolf, in their passionate foreplay of love. This hadn't changed between them during these past seven months, yet, at other times, when they were away from their bed, Danette could feel the strain between them, and she had finally decided that a trip to Duluth was needed. Perhaps apart they both could work out this thing gnawing at their insides. . . .

"Gray Wolf will miss you," he said huskily, trailing his fingers across her abdomen, then upward, to cup her breast. He let his forefinger explore the hard peak, hearing how this caused Danette's breath to escape her in a slow, quivering sigh.

"But I must go," Danette whispered, lifting a leg lazily around him, flowering herself open to his fingers as they now gently probed between her thighs. "It's time for me to check on my lumber business. You know that I haven't since we've married."

It was a good excuse . . . one she was thankful for having. She would never confess to Gray Wolf that this was really a test . . . a test of the strengths of their love for each other. If it proved a failure, she wouldn't return to the Indian village of the Chippewa.

"You should leave white man's world alone," he growled. "Your life is here. With me."

And our child? Danette worried to herself. Always, when referring to family, Gray Wolf managed to omit Hope. Yet he did show love for Hope when he held her. It confused Danette. Was a daughter so worthless to an Indian? Then she had only to recall the time he spent with Laughing Rain's son, Running Deer, and how Gray Wolf laughed and played with him to have just cause to hate Gray Wolf.

Such thoughts caused Danette to move away from Gray Wolf. She brushed his hands from her body and started to rise from their bed but was stopped as he grabbed her by her wrist and jerked her back down beside him.

"Why you do that?" he growled. He leaned down over her, framing her face between his hands.

"I must get ready to leave," she said, flinching when she saw the anger flashing in his eyes. She glanced away and toward the cradle where Hope lay peacefully asleep. "I need to pack Hope's things for the journey and I'd like to do it before she awakens."

"You put journey and daughter before Gray Wolf?" he accused.

"No," Danette denied. "It's just that . . ."

"We make love, then you prepare for journey your husband disapproves of," he said. "What of husband's needs while you're gone?"

Thoughts of Laughing Rain and her clinging to Gray Wolf every chance she got made jealousy swell in Danette's heart. But that was another part of the test. Danette wasn't ready to give up the fight for her man all that easily, but in a sense she felt that she had already lost him; and, leaving him alone, hopefully to miss her, seemed to be the only answer to her present dilemma. She had made things too easy for Gray Wolf. Now he would have to prove his love to keep her as his wife forever, and, hopefully, he wouldn't decide to take a second wife.

"You will have to practice restraint," she finally murmured. "There are times when this is needed, you know."

"Gray Wolf's needs are like the wild bear," he said huskily. "Fierce. Insatiable. A man is young only once. A wife is needed each and every night. How can you deny me this so easily, as though I am just a toy to be played with?"

"I also have needs," Danette said softly, now wishing she hadn't said it. She had never complained to Gray Wolf about her worries. She felt that it was up to him to discover the weaknesses in their marriage in his own way, or the marriage was not worth saving. She had even refrained from continuing to bring Laughing Rain's name into the conversation . . . never pointing out to Gray Wolf how obvious it was that Laughing Rain was trying to win him away from her. The other times that Danette had shown jealousy of Laughing Rain, Gray Wolf had only shamed her for her lack of faith in him . . . the man. . . .

"Gray Wolf fulfill those needs now," he growled. He drew her lips to his and kissed her savagely, while his body worked against her until his hardness found entrance inside her.

Danette didn't want to give in to the mounting passion welling inside her, but his lips . . . his body . . . were stealing her sanity from her and she was once more being swept away on wings of desire.

She twined her arms about his neck and weaved her fingers through his hair, wild now, lifting her hips to meet him in a mindless euphoria. His lips tore away from hers and rained kisses across her face and down to the hollow of her throat. His hands worked feverishly on her breasts.

"Gray Wolf . . ." Danette whispered in a soft sob, lost

in her love for him. When the peak of her rapture was reached, she let the warm, melting sensation consume her and clung to Gray Wolf until the quivering inside her stopped.

She closed her eyes, breathing hard, and after his wild trembling ceased, only then did she let her thoughts return to now and what the day had in store for her. It was her first journey back to Duluth since the day she had left, after having lost her first child. . . .

Gray Wolf kissed her gently on the lips, then rose to his feet and began dressing. "The buggy that was used to bring Aunt Rettie to the village will be made ready for your journey to Duluth," he said. "My most dependable braves will accompany you and see to your safety."

Danette pushed herself up from the floor. "It is best that you don't go with me," she murmured. "This separation will . . . do . . . us both good. You'll see."

Fitting his headband around his head, he gave her a bitter look. "If I can't understand such a separation, my people will understand it even less," he grumbled.

"Why should they even question my going?"

"Have you done this before?"

"No . . ."

"There is your reason for my people not understanding. Why now, when not before?"

"The reasons are private," Danette murmured, lowering her eyes. "They are not for everyone to know. Your people shouldn't have to know everything in your life."

"Because I am chief's son, that is reason enough for questions about me and my wife. One day I will be their leader, and they have to learn to trust and revere me."

Danette went to Gray Wolf and placed her hand to his cheek. "Gray Wolf, do not be blinded by ambition and lose sight of other things in life of importance to you," she said. "In the end, you would, yes, have your village of people surrounding you, but would that be enough?"

He jerked away from her. "You can say that . . . knowing how I feel about you?" he growled. He turned back and glared down at her. "It is you who have lost sight of what is important in life. The proof of that is in your need to once more mingle with the white man."

He grabbed his rifle and stormed from the wigwam. Danette choked back a sob, reaching for him. She was filled with torn emotions, but the soft cries from the just awakened Hope helped her forget her conflict with Gray Wolf, at least for the moment.

Grabbing a robe and slipping quickly into it, Danette rushed to Hope's cradle and watched as her daughter pulled herself up to a wobbly sitting position, to smile good morning to Danette.

Danette lifted Hope up into her arms and hugged her tightly to her, smoothing her fingers beneath the tiny buckskin nightgown that she had made herself. This was another reason she wanted to go to Duluth. She wanted to purchase some frilly dresses for her daughter, though she knew she would get an argument from Gray Wolf over this.

"Morning, darling," Danette cooed. She let her cheek rest against the dark, soft fuzz of Hope's head. "We're taking a trip today. I know someone who is going to have a fit over you! Amy will adore you, Hope. Just adore you!"

It felt good to be decked out in a fine dress of silk with pleats and lace at the bodice and the skirt, fully gathered, with a layer of petticoat beneath it. And, with a matching bonnet tied with a satin bow beneath her chin, Danette rode into Duluth in the buggy, with Hope packed safely in a papoose case, secured to the seat beside her.

The Indian braves who had accompanied Danette through the forest had fallen back into the woods at the first sight of Duluth on the horizon.

Fresh sprouts of trees dotting the forest where the fire

405

had left its path of destruction welcomed Danette. New buildings and homes had been constructed along the streets of Duluth.

Danette's heart raced, anxious to see how her uncle's . . . no *her* house . . . had been restored. Had she been right to leave Charles Klein in charge of all the financial aspects of both her personal and business affairs? Had it been an imposition on Amy, asking her to live in the Thomas mansion and look after it?

"I shall soon have the answers to all these questions," Danette whispered to herself.

She snapped the reins, urging her horse to make a turn on the cobblestone street, to begin its climb up another steeper street, leaving the waterfront and business district behind her. The time to check and see how her lumber company was doing would come after she saw Amy and left Hope in her care. Then she would ask to see the ledgers that Charles Klein had been keeping for her.

Danette glanced back over her shoulder, seeing how her lumber company building rose above the other smaller businesses along the waterfront. A strange thrill of possession and power came over her, so strong that it frightened her. She didn't want the same things out of life that her uncle had wanted! She didn't! It had turned him into a cold, calculating person, living for only himself. Did she want such a life for her children?

"It depends on the individual," she thought further to herself. "If I instill love and compassion into my children, they can have a kind heart *and* wealth, if that's what they choose to have."

Shaking her head to clear her thoughts, she grew angry at herself for letting her mind wander so. This was not the time to speculate about a future that might never be. So far, only one daughter played a role in that future. She might never have a son who would have to choose between being a rich businessman and being an Indian chief.

But should she have one . . . which way of life *would* he choose?

"What am I doing?" she fussed to herself. "Gray Wolf may not even want me back now that I've left the village. Even for the short time I planned, to him it is an eternity. I may not even want to return myself . . . should he not prove his sincere love for me. . . ."

Danette guided her horse and buggy onto a side street. Her heart beat more rapidly as she traveled on past the familiar two- and three-story mansions that lined each side of the road. No signs of the fire were evident. All the houses had been refurbished and were even more breathtakingly beautiful than Danette could remember them being before the fire.

Then she scoffed at this. She surely only felt this way because she had been away from this way of life long enough to forget. A village of wigwams could not compare. . . .

Guilt tore at her heart. In her mind's eye she could see Gray Wolf's handsome face and the pride always in his eyes when he spoke of his people and village. To him, these were what was beautiful in life. . . .

And since I'm his wife, I should be as happy, Danette silently worried. All along I knew what he had to offer me. I had thought loving him would be enough . . .

Seeing her house only a few houses away, and, yes, so wonderfully restored, even to the replacement of the stained glass windows on the half that had been gutted by the fire, Danette was quickly swept up into her anxiety to enter the house to be surrounded by space and gorgeous furniture. How wonderful it would be to relax in a deeply upholstered velveteen chair, to eat at the wide expanse of the dining table, and to sleep in a bed with a mattress of fluffy feathers to cozy down into!

And Amy. Danette was so anxious to see Amy.

Looking over at Hope, whose dark eyes were wide, looking all around her, and who had been so good throughout the ordeals of the journey, though most of the time she had been confined entirely by the wrappings of the papoose case, she couldn't be any prouder of her daughter than at this moment.

"We're almost home," Danette whispered to Hope. "A real house, Hope. You will have soft carpets to crawl on and much floorspace to explore."

Guilt once more sprang forth in her, as she realized that she had called this place "home," when in truth "home" was the wigwam she shared with her husband!

She shrugged and giggled to herself. "Our second home, darling," she murmured. "There's no harm in that."

Clucking to her horse and snapping her reins, she traveled on past the neighboring mansions then turned into a drive that led up to her own. A mixture of feelings now encompassed her. There were many memories crowding in on her . . . some good . . . and some bad. She shook the bad from her mind and let herself be wrapped in the warm, delicious cocoon of only the good.

Drawing her horse up next to a hitching rail, she jumped from the buggy and secured the horse's reins. With a racing pulse, she unwrapped Hope from her papoose case, then secured her in her arms as she moved toward the house.

The lawn was a fresh, bright green with flowers of all colors and descriptions bordering the gravel walk Danette was now hurrying along. The two-story, Victorian house stood proud, displaying its wide porch along the front, its granite windowsills pale gray against the warm brick facade. Even the granite steps leading up to the porch were still the same in their magnificence.

Not stopping to knock, Danette opened and closed the heavy oak door and stepped into the wide entrance hall that opened into the three spacious parlors and the dining room.

To her right she could see into what had always been her favorite parlor. A comfortable fire was burning in the fireplace, its warm glow settling onto the upholstered chairs and matching divan and magnificent oak tables.

A gentle peacefulness settled around Danette's heart, drawing a sigh from inside her. But this peacefulness was short-lived, when she slowly turned and looked into the other room, and her memory of falling and landing on the floor there was suddenly upon her. She shivered.

She hugged Hope more closely to her. "I have you now, Hope," she whispered. "Thank God I have you."

Danette rarely thought of the child that she had so tragically lost as a result of that fall. She wouldn't torture herself with thoughts of "Had my child been born, would it have been a son?"

Her eyes were drawn to the walls that lined the long hallway. "What . . . ?" she murmured.

A slow smile touched her lips as she began walking down the hallway, absorbing the paintings one by one. Amy had removed the family portraits to instead display Danette's paintings . . . and . . . Danette approved! She had known that the Minnesota State Bank couldn't display them forever.

A swoosh of skirt, a rustling of feet, and a loud cry of her name caused Danette to turn quickly around to see Amy. "Amy," she sighed. "Oh, Amy, I'm home!"

Amy, dark eyes wide and in her usual calico dress and ruffled apron, ran toward Danette with her arms outspread and tears soaking her eyes. "Land sakes, Danette," she cried. "And Hope! You've brought Hope!"

Danette laughed softly as Amy embraced her and Hope at the same time, then gently took Hope from her arms.

"Isn't she just too beautiful, Amy?" Danette murmured, reaching a hand to Hope's chin, cupping it. Hope truly looked adorable in her tiny buckskin dress and moccasins, yet Danette couldn't wait to see her in ruffles and lace!

Hope's lower lip began to quiver as she reached for her mother.

"Now, now," Amy crooned, cradling Hope in her arms,

rocking her back and forth. "You in Amy's arms. And ain't you a pretty one? You a tiny replica of your mother." She looked toward Danette. "Her skin is fair like yours. Does Gray Wolf mind that she doesn't look at all Indian?"

"He's never spoken of it," Danette said, clearing her throat nervously. Then she blurted: "Amy, how are things?" She was relieved that Hope now appeared content enough as she eyed Amy and played with a button on the front of Amy's dress.

"Things are just fine," Amy said. "And are they as fine for you? What brings you here?" She looked toward the closed front door. "Did Gray Wolf make the journey with you?"

Danette untied the bow to her bonnet, then removed it, stepping into the parlor where the fire was so inviting. She heard the rustling of Amy's feet behind her. "No," she finally said, giving Amy a half glance across her shoulder. "He didn't." She placed her bonnet on a table and ran her fingers through her long black hair.

"You traveled alone through the forest?" Amy asked, settling down onto a chair to steady Hope on her lap.

"No," Danette said, going to the fireplace mantel. She chose a porcelain figurine and took it from the mantel and pretended to be studying it, hating to reveal all of her doubts of her marriage to her longtime maid and confidante.

"Then who?" Amy protested.

"Gray Wolf sent his most trusted braves along with me," Danette said, replacing the figurine on the mantel. "They are making camp in the forest right outside Duluth. They plan to stay there until my return to the village."

"How long are you going to stay, Danette?" Amy asked cautiously, seeing much in Danette that hadn't yet been spoken about.

"I'm not sure," Danette replied. "I tried to tell Gray Wolf's braves not to wait. I'm hoping for Gray Wolf to come to me, to take me back with him."

"You're hopin', Danette?" Amy said, lifting a heavy gray eyebrow. Her dark face lined with worry. "You ain't sure about your husband?"

Danette forced a smile and swung the skirt of her dress around. "Amy, why are we talking so seriously when I've just returned to my house after such a long absence?" she said, letting her eyes take in the expensive furniture, the wall decorations, and the plush carpeting at her feet. "Amy, I must rush through the house and see it. It looks like it was never gutted by fire! You and Charles Klein are absolute marvels at what you do. I first want to see my room. Though it's sinful to say, I have missed it."

Amy rose heavily to her feet, grunting as she began moving alongside Danette, out into the hallway and on up the staircase.

Danette noticed how much effort it seemed to be for Amy to take each step. She further noticed how much thinner and grayer Amy's hair had become and the added weight that seemed to encumber her movements. The loose flesh of her jowl hung over the stiff white collar of her dress, and her eyes had dark circles beneath them, contrasting against the brown of her skin.

She then glanced at Hope, suddenly worrying over her welfare. "Amy, is Hope too heavy?" she murmured. "I could carry her up the stairs."

Amy laughed. "If I'm strong enough to keep this large house on its toes, I'm certainly capable of carryin' this sweet bundle in my arms," she said. "Child, you do worry so."

"I'm no longer a child, Amy," Danette said, stepping up onto the second-floor landing.

"No. You ain't," Amy said, once more wishing to know more about what had prompted Danette's sudden unannounced visit to Duluth. Danette was most certainly unsettled about something, and it appeared to Amy that the source of this gloom that seemed to be hanging over her like a dark cloud, ready to burst, had something to do with her marriage.

411

"In fact, as soon as I'm rested from the trip, I plan to go and check on my lumber company," Danette said, stopping to wait for Amy to take her final step onto the landing. "And I had planned to leave Hope with you while I do that little chore. Would you mind, Amy?" She wanted to ask Amy if she was up to taking care of a toddler, but she thought better of it, for fear of further injuring Amy's feelings.

"Would I mind?" Amy laughed. "Land sakes, Danette, need you ask such a foolish question? I love your child, as I've always loved you."

"I'm sure you do," Danette said, leaning to kiss Amy softly on a cheek as Amy finally reached the landing. "And I'll always treasure your love, Amy, as my daughter also will."

"I'm just an old broken-down colored mammie," Amy sighed.

"No, You're not," Danette scolded. "You're something quite special, Amy."

Amy laughed throatily. "Let's get on to your room," she said. "If my skin weren't so dark and leathery you'd see me blushin'."

Danette joined in the soft laughter. She swung the skirt of her dress around, once more absorbing the surroundings, so immaculately clean and bright that it was hard to imagine that a fire had ever threatened the house.

The same hand-blown glass chandelier still hung from the ceiling, lighting Danette and Amy's way down the hallway as they headed for Danette's bedroom.

Reminded of the downstair's hallway, Danette said, "Amy, I saw how you've placed my paintings where the family portraits once hung."

"Do you mind?"

"No. Not at all."

"Havin' them there, for me to see every day, is almost the same as havin' you in the house with me."

"Oh, Amy," Danette giggled. "How sweet." She pushed

412

open the door that led to her bedroom. She stepped inside, flooded with memories of the past, when she had spent so much time there alone, in her own little corner of the world. Her first fantasies of Gray Wolf had sprung to life in her mind here, stretched out on her bed remembering his first embrace.

Danette looked about the room, admiring its decor anew, as though seeing it for the first time. Her Queen Anne pencil-post bed stood across the room, with its splay-leg nightstand next to it. The soft, thick comforter on the bed matched the yellow satin draperies at the windows and the soft yellow carpeting that was crushing splendidly beneath her feet as she took light steps across it.

Hope began to fuss in Amy's arms. Danette stopped and eased her gently from them, then placed her on the softness of the carpet. "Just watch her, Amy," she laughed. "She crawls already. It's so cute. And she'll love the carpet and the floor space she has for exploring."

Danette and Amy stood side by side, laughing over Hope as Hope scooted on her hands and knees over the carpet. The skirt of her dress occasionally tangled between her legs, causing her to bounce over on her side. But she would just as quickly recover and resume her crawling.

Danette tensed as Hope discovered the open door that led out into the hallway, which itself led to the dangers of the stairs. With a rush of heartbeats, she grabbed Hope up from the floor and into her arms. "No, no," she gently scolded. "You can't go out there. You might fall down the stairs."

Danette looked soberly toward Amy. "And, Amy, while I'm gone, please remember the stairs," she said. "It just occurs to me that Hope doesn't even know what stairs are. There aren't any in the Indian village. The stairs are a definite danger, where Hope is concerned."

Chapter Twenty-Seven

> A lovely Apparition, sent
> To be a moment's ornament. . . .
> —Wordsworth

Climbing the stairs that led to the sixth floor of Danette's lumber company, where her Uncle Dwight had made his private office, Danette felt a strong sense of the past closing in on her. This being her first time in this place since her uncle's death, it felt to her as though he wasn't even dead, and should be there, busying himself over his ledgers. She sniffed. The aroma of cigar smoke was even there, heavy in the air, as it always had been in the past, along the staircase.

A cold shiver ran across her flesh. Her uncle's presence was too real to be ignored. And the dark, gloominess of the steep staircase didn't lighten the mood any.

Lifting the skirt of her dress into her arms, Danette hurried on up the stairs, panting when she finally reached the sixth-floor landing. The sun shone in many colors of the rainbow through a stained-glass ceiling skylight window. It was at this moment that even more vivid recollections of her uncle seized her. How often had she stood beneath this very skylight as a child, with her uncle saying that the end of the rainbow was there, shining down upon her. He had said that she was that pot of gold that everyone searched for at the end of a rainbow, but was unattainable for everyone but him, because she was his. . . .

At the time, she had felt such a deep love for her uncle, believing that he had only her best interests at heart, and that his love for her was the clean, decent, and cherishing kind. Only before his death had she discovered his true plans for her, the designs of a twisted mind.

"Enough of this," Danette said. She straightened her bonnet, lifted her chin, and strolled on toward the door that led her inside the office that in every sense of the word was now hers.

Not stopping to knock, Danette turned the doorknob and entered a room that, surprising to her, lay heavily shrouded in cigar smoke. Through its haze she could see the familiar paneled walls, the dull finish of the hardwood floor, and the wide expanse of a great oak desk. The desk was cluttered with papers and books, and piles of stubs of half-smoked cigars lay in an ashtray.

Behind the desk, in the outline of the window across the room, Danette could make out the back of a high-backed leather chair. A lazy spiral of smoke rose from the front of the chair, giving Danette an eerie feeling. Her uncle had so often sat behind his desk, turned to face the window in such a way, lost deep in thought.

Should the chair swirl around, would her uncle . . . be there? Had he, somehow, survived the fire and no one had yet broken the news to her? Had Amy even been ordered by Dwight Thomas to keep her silence . . . for some morbid reason?

Trembling, caught up in fear and wonder, Danette took a step backwards. The cigar smoke slowly worked its way up her nose and down her throat, unmercifully tickling her in both delicate places. Covering her mouth, she tried to stifle a sneeze. But nothing could hold back the sneeze that erupted from deeply inside her, sounding like an explosion in the absolute silence of the room. Her eyes involuntarily shut with her sneeze. And as she opened them it was in time to see the chair turn abruptly around.

"Good Lord," Danette gasped, paling. "You. What are *you* doing here? How is it that you are here and sitting at my uncle's . . . no *my* desk, as though you belong?"

"Well, if it ain't the little Indian lover," Raoul said, rising from the chair. He rested his cigar on the edge of the ashtray on the desk and walked from around the desk, studying her closely, raking his eyes over her. He was clean-shaven, dressed expensively in a suit, yet still burly and unpleasant-looking, with his evil, colorless eyes, and a smirk curling the narrow line of his lips menacingly upward.

Danette stood her ground, stunned. "I asked you why and how you happen to be here?" she said icily. "This office is private. It belongs to me now. You have some gall! I even thought that when I last saw you, you said that you were leaving Duluth."

"I did leave," he said, now towering over her as he stood only inches away from her.

Danette was becoming aware of his massive chest, shoulders and hands. "Then why did you return? And why are you here?"

"Charles Klein paid me quite well to get me to leave St. Paul after I had made my residence there," Raoul bragged. He reached a hand to Danette's creamy white, bare shoulder and dared a touch. He laughed hoarsely when she visibly shuddered and took a step away from him.

"And why would Charles Klein do that?" she hissed, narrowing her eyes as she showed her intense hate for him through them.

"Because it was I, Raoul, the Frenchman, who earned a reputation of knowing the lumber business," he once more bragged, sitting down on the edge of the desk. "The rumor of this reached Charles Klein when he was searching for someone to manage the business at your request. And being that I worked *with* Dwight Thomas right before his untimely death, that was proof enough to Charles that I was the best man for the job!''

Danette placed a hand to her throat. ''You worked . . . with . . . Uncle Dwight?'' she gasped. ''Right before his death?''

''Exactly.''

''But he knew about you . . . about what you tried to do to me . . . !''

''Exactly.''

''And he still . . . ?''

''He wanted the best man for the job and I was the best. Nothing else mattered.''

Danette turned her head away. When a bitterness rose to her throat, she feared that she might retch, but feeling the importance of becoming quickly in charge of this situation, she forced herself to face him again, with strength showing in the forced set of her jaw.

''Well, Mr. Frenchman, now that *I* am the owner of this lumber company, your services are no longer needed,'' she said dryly. She pointed toward the door. ''Get out. This minute. And don't ever let me hear that you've come near here again. From this point on, I shall keep in better touch with Charles. It would have been better for me today if I had first consulted with Charles before coming here. At least I would have been saved the unpleasant task of having to look upon your face again.''

Raoul slipped from the desk and went to the door and closed it, then leaned against it, smiling crookedly.

''What do you think you're doing?'' Danette asked, suddenly realizing how vulnerable she was six floors above the activities of her employees and the throngs of people down below her on the street. If he dared anything with her, no one would even hear her screams!

''There ain't no Indian here to protect you this time,'' Raoul laughed. ''I even heard that you're livin' with the savage. Now ain't that a waste of a beautiful white woman like yourself?''

Danette began to move backwards, across the room, away from him. "How dare you talk to me in such a way," she hissed.

"Just because your uncle's death left you financially set for life don't mean you're a lady," he said. He began taking slow steps toward her. "No lady fornicates with a savage willingly. So that makes you what? A whore? A rich whore?" He closed his eyes and threw his head back into a fit of laughter.

Danette took full advantage of his moment of carelessness and rushed to the desk and began searching frantically through the strewn papers for the silver letter opener that she could remember her uncle using so often through the years. Her heart racing wildly inside her and her fingers violently trembling, she looked anxiously toward Raoul, watching him continuing to move toward her, now sober, his eyes filled with lust.

Danette's hand made contact with the cold, sharp tip of the letter opener at the exact moment Raoul reached across the desk to grab her by her other wrist.

"You can't get away from Raoul this time," he growled. He held tightly to her wrist and edged around the desk, closer to her.

Danette circled her fingers around the handle of the letter opener and slowly drew it across the desk, still hidden beneath the papers. "How do you think you'll get away with this?" she asked, grimacing as he squeezed her wrist even harder. "I shall see to it that you are hung. You have to know that there will be no out for you this time."

"Who'd believe a woman who chooses Indians over whites?" he snarled.

"My uncle was always respected in this city. *I* have always been respected as well," she hotly argued. "And you are wrong to think that the fact that I have chosen an

Indian to be my husband changes any of the feelings of the people of this community for me."

"Raoul will take this chance," he laughed. "Gettin' a taste of your flesh before was just enough to whet my appetite for all of your body."

"You're vile," she hissed.

"I've been haunted by your loveliness since the day I first saw you with that Indian in his wigwam," he said, licking his lips hungrily.

"In Gray Wolf's wigwam?" Danette gasped. "You spied . . . on us?"

"I wasn't smart," he growled. "The day I finally decided to have you for myself I didn't leave ahead of the Indian soon enough from where we were working together in the forest. If I had of, I'd of had you that day . . . all of you . . . not just a touch."

"You planned the rape?"

"For several days," he chuckled.

"Well, Frenchman, your plans were foiled once, so shall they be again," she cried, wriggling as he drew her roughly into his arms. When his lips bore down upon hers, she raised the letter opener and started to plunge it into his back, but she was stopped by the sound of the door opening and a loud voice erupting from across the room.

"Raoul! Danette! What's going on here?" Charles Klein shouted as he raced across the room and grabbed the letter opener from Danette. He dropped it to the floor, then placed a hand to Raoul's shoulder and swung him around, away from Danette. "What do you think you're doing?" he accused, facing Raoul with squinted, dark eyes. "You do know who this is whom you are treating so crudely, don't you? She isn't just any woman!"

"Unhand me," Raoul snarled, knocking Charles's hand aside.

Danette stepped back away from them both, limp with exhausted fear. Her bonnet had slipped from her head and swung awkwardly behind her, still tied beneath her chin. "Thank God you arrived when you did, Charles," she said, shuddering when she recalled how close she had come to murdering a man.

Yet one plunge of the sharp letter opener would have removed Raoul from her life forever, and now she wished that she hadn't been stopped!

Still breathing hard, she let her eyes run over her lawyer/ business partner. Though she hadn't had too many face-to-face dealings with him, she knew that she had been wise to continue his services, knowing that her uncle had chosen him carefully for his knowledge of the corporate world.

In his wool navy pin-striped business suit, stiff white collar and a wide, colorful bow tie, he looked every bit the businessman. His reputation said that he was the best in the city. His smoothed-down dark hair, brown eyes, and square, set jaw were attributes of an attractive man. He was said to be a womanizer, and was still unwed at the age of forty.

Charles went to Danette and lifted her chin with his forefinger. "I'm sorry about this," he said thickly. "It's apparent Raoul doesn't know who you are."

Danette shot Raoul an angry, daring glance. "Oh, yes, he knows quite well who I am," she murmured. "We have met before under such . . . uh . . . similar circumstances."

Charles's face shadowed as he swung around to face Raoul. "And what do you have to say for yourself?" he asked, his voice deep, tight, and threatening.

Raoul shrugged. "She lies," he said. "I do not know who she is. Raoul just sees a beautiful lady who comes and flaunts her body around, asking to have a man touch it."

Danette's face flamed with humiliation and growing anger. "You are not only a vile, disgusting person but also a liar," she said. She doubled her hands into tight fists at her side, giving Charles an authoritative look. "See to it that this man is taken from the payroll and that he is accom-

421

panied to the edge of town. Duluth has no need for such vermin walking its streets."

"You heard the lady," Charles said dryly, nodding toward Raoul. He went to the door and gestured with his hand toward it. "You'd best leave now, Raoul, while you have the chance. And I trust that you have the sense to leave Duluth on your own volition. It wouldn't be so pleasant for you if I had to have you escorted from town. You'd be left outside of town minus a few teeth and with a broken limb or two."

"You'll both be sorry for this," Raoul shouted, waving his fist in the air. He turned and hurried from the room.

Danette tensed, listening to the loud echo of his heavy footsteps on the wooden steps, seeming to last forever, having six full flights to thunder down. The slamming of the door that led out onto Front Street was evidence that he was finally, indeed, gone from the building, giving Danette reason to breathe easier and to crumple down into the chair behind the desk. Placing her face into her hands, she leaned heavily into them, sighing.

Charles came up beside her and bent to untie the bow beneath her chin and slowly drew the bonnet away from her. "I didn't know, Danette," he softly apologized. "I had been told by many that he was crude, yet he is knowledgeable of the lumber business. How was I to know that he would cause such problems as this for you?"

"That's all right, Charles," she said, raising her face from her hands. "There wasn't any way for you to have known." She raked her fingers through her hair and let her back rest against the soft leather of the chair.

Charles placed her bonnet on the desk. His eyes wavered as he looked her way, then he went to the wide expanse of windows and looked across the rippling waters of Lake Superior. He kneaded his chin nervously, then turned and placed his hands on the back of Danette's chair and slowly spun the chair around, so their eyes could meet.

Danette felt a chill race across her flesh, seeing something else in his eyes, much more than an apology for having hired the wrong man to run her business. "What is it?" she murmured. "Why are you looking at me like that?"

"It's my reason for having come here," he said. "It wasn't for business."

"Then why?"

"Amy sent word to my office," he said, looking away from her. He went and picked up the letter opener that he had earlier dropped to the floor. "She . . . Amy . . . said that you could probably be found here."

Danette slowly pushed herself up from the chair. The chill that she had earlier felt was quickly changing into a numbness. She inched toward Charles, eyes wide. "Why would Amy send word to you?" she said in a near whisper. "Why would it be necessary? I don't understand."

Charles toyed nervously with the letter opener, avoiding her eyes. "You are needed at home," he said. He placed the letter opener on the desk, then reached a hand toward her. "I'll take you in my carriage. We'd best leave now, Danette."

Danette ignored his proffered hand. Instead she clasped hers together behind her in an effort to steady them. "Tell me what has happened," she said flatly. "Now, Charles. What is it?"

"It's best that you wait until you get back to your house," he encouraged. He took her by an elbow and began guiding her from the room, but she stubbornly stopped, and boldly faced him.

"I will not move another inch until you tell me what has happened," she said, her voice breaking with nervous frustration.

Charles took both her hands in his. "In your absence from Duluth, we've never had the opportunity to become better acquainted," he said. "So I feel it is not my place to be the one with you when you are told." He nodded toward the staircase. "Let me take you home. Amy is waiting for you there."

"Charles . . ." she once more protested.

"Trust me . . . ?" he murmured. "It is best, Danette."

Worries about the ones she loved most in the world flooded her mind. She began sorting through faces, Hope's always being the strongest in her mind's eye. Amy wouldn't know of any of Gray Wolf's activities, so the news had to be about her beloved Hope.

Fear laced her heart. Had something happened to Hope in the short time that they had been separated—just an hour?

With weak knees and tears threatening to spring forth from her eyes, she followed silently alongside Charles. She let him help her into his carriage, then sat as bravely as possible beside him as the carriage carried them away from the waterfront, on up the steep street, and to her house. Another stately carriage was there, parked in front of her house, and Amy was standing on the porch, waiting, nervously twisting the tail of her apron around and around her fingers.

When Danette looked up into Amy's eyes, she saw grief and many swells of tears rushing from them.

"No . . ." Danette softly cried, now knowing that it had to be her daughter. As the carriage stopped, Danette jumped from it. She ran up the steps, on past Amy, and into the house.

"Hope!" she screamed. "Darling, it's Mommie. Where are you?"

She hurried from one parlor to the next, then stopped at the foot of the staircase and looked upward. She continued to stare upward, now taking the steps slowly, achingly, one at a time.

"Danette . . . honey," Amy cried from behind her. "No . . . honey . . ."

Danette placed her hands to her ears. Blinded by tears, she broke into a run. When she reached the second-floor, she continued to run, tears like rain now, being torn apart inside, fearing what she would find in her bedroom.

Throwing her bedroom door open, she rushed on into the room, then stopped. She let out an agonizing scream when she found herself staring down at the body of her daughter, stretched out, lifeless, on her bed. She fell onto the edge of the bed and drew Hope into her arms and began slowly rocking her back and forth. "It's all right, darling," she mumbled. "Mommie is here. Mommie is here."

Amy came into the room in a flurry, panting from her efforts. She gently took Hope from Danette's arms and once more arranged Hope peacefully on the yellow coverlet, then guided Danette over to a chair and down into it. "The stairs," she said, sobbing. "Hope just beat ol' Amy to the stairs. . . ."

Danette's heart floundered in her pain, and thoughts of Hope tumbling down the stairs became more than her mind could handle. Everything began to spin before her eyes. "Gray Wolf . . ." she sobbed. "Our daughter, Gray Wolf . . ."

She sank into a dark oblivion, thankful to be given at least this blessing in her life of continuing tragedies. . . .

Danette struggled in and out of consciousness for days, fighting to try and keep hold of her sanity. When the nightmares became less and less, she awakened to find herself in her bedroom, which was softly lighted by a lone kerosene lamp beside her bed. The strong aroma of flowers lay heavily in the air, overpowering, even stronger than any of the expensive French perfume that she had sampled in St. Paul's most elite shops.

Blinking her eyes, Danette let her eyes adjust to the semi-darkness of the room, then managed to make out bouquet after bouquet of spring flowers sitting around the room. There were the fresh blossoms of lilacs, forsythia, jonquils, tulips, and even twigs of apple blossoms arranged neatly in vases.

And then she saw dozens of roses, gardenias, and many other assortments of flowers. Who could have been so generous? And why? For some reason, she couldn't even remember why she would be the recipient of such abundant gifts of flowers!

With her tongue heavy and thick and her lips dry, she began scooting up on her bed, trying to clear her thoughts of a fuzziness that kept invading her senses. Looking down, she recognized the silk, lacy nightgown, but she couldn't remember having put it on.

She glanced toward the windows of the room. Though the drapes were closed, she could see daylight peering around their edges and was even more in wonder as to why she would be in bed when it was so obviously daylight outside! She had much to do! She had to go check out her lumber company . . . she had to go shopping, to find Hope some of the frilliest dresses she could to show her off in.

Something began to flash off and on inside her brain. A warning of sorts? Thinking of Hope had caused this sort of strange tugging at her heart and an emptiness at the pit of her stomach.

She sat abruptly up in the bed, eyes wide, and looked desperately about her, reaching frantically across the bed. Her heart began to pound so hard, she was finding it hard to breathe. Her pulse thundered wildly in the hollow of her throat, now remembering. . . .

A low sob rose into a harsh, painful scream as memory began to swallow her up, as though she was in a river . . . drowning. . . .

A rush of feet into the room and Danette gratefully accepted Gray Wolf's arms about her as he sat down on the bed beside her.

"*Mah-win* the pain away," he said, holding her face against his chest. "Cry it all out, Sweet Butterfly. Then you will be able to accept that nothing can be changed. She is gone. Our *gee-dah-niss* is now with all those others in the Happy Hunting Grounds."

"Gray Wolf," she cried. "I can't stand it. My heart cannot stand this torture of the loss of our child. What did we do to deserve this? Didn't we love her enough? Did God take her away because we failed to love deeply enough?"

"Gah-ween," he said. "You loved her enough. It was Gray Wolf who failed her. But your God . . . my Wenebojo does not work in such a way. They do not take child just because Gray Wolf was disappointed in her skin coloring."

Danette clung to him, shaking her head desperately back and forth. "No," she cried. "Do not say that you failed her. I don't want to think of it."

"But I did," Gray Wolf said, swallowing back a throaty sob. "Because she was born not looking Indian, I feared that I would look less a man in the eyes of my people. Birthing a child, daughter or son, who doesn't have any Indian features takes away from Indian male's virility. This is the only reason I paid so little attention to Hope. I didn't love her less, though. I did love her, Sweet Butterfly. I did."

He burrowed his face into the thickness of her hair and began a harsh sobbing. This sobered Danette, never having seen Gray Wolf let his emotions become so free and open before. And to cry? It wasn't at all like him. It had to mean that he was hurting as much as she was. His love for Hope had been as strong. It had been his Indian pride that had stood in his way of this love. . . .

"It's going to be all right," she crooned, caressing his back. "We will be strong for one another. We have to be. Please . . . please . . . stop crying. Hold me, Gray Wolf. Please . . . hold . . . me. . . ."

With a groan, Gray Wolf raised his face from her hair and drew her into his arms and hugged her tightly to him. Their tears mingled as their cheeks pressed together. *"Ay-uh,* we will be strong," he said. "We have faced sadness before. And before our life is over, so shall we again. Our love will sustain us through it all. . . .''

"Hope?" Danette said, paining inside even more, speaking her name aloud. "Where . . . is . . . Hope . . . ?''

"A white man's way of burial was already performed while you were in strange sort of sleep," he mumbled. "Amy saw to the . . . the . . . special arrangements.''

"No," Danette softly cried. "I didn't even get to attend my own daughter's funeral?''

"It is done. Do not torture yourself so.''

"Amy? How is Amy?''

"Guilt is strong in her heart," he grumbled. "She blames herself for Hope's death.''

Danette remembered the stairs . . . her warning to Amy about them . . . and she couldn't help but, yes, also hold Amy to blame. But she would never voice this aloud. Too much sadness already shrouded this mother-daughter relationship that had been between them for so long. And Danette knew that she wasn't even completely free of this thing called "blame" herself. Had she not come to Duluth for her own selfish reasons, wouldn't Hope still be alive?

"Gray Wolf, take me home," she quickly blurted. She shuddered as she looked slowly around the room. "Take me away . . . from this . . . place. There is something evil here. We have lost two . . . children . . . in this house . . .''

"*Ay-uh,*" Gray Wolf grumbled. "I feel it also. As though your uncle is still here.''

A coldness seeped into Danette's heart at the mention of her uncle. But, no! She wouldn't let herself be haunted by him any longer.

She eased from Gray Wolf's gentle embrace and hung her legs over the side of the bed. A lightheadedness swept over her, and she welcomed Gray Wolf's comforting hand at her elbow.

"When we return to our village, a new maiden will be chosen to look after you and our wigwam," Gray Wolf said.

428

Danette searched his face. "What did you say?" she murmured.

"Laughing Rain is gone," he said matter-of-factly. "I must choose another companion to see to your daily needs."

Danette's face grew hot with anxiety. "Where did Laughing Rain go?" she asked, wary of the answer.

"To next Chippewa village to make home with new husband."

A keen relief caused Danette to let out a long quivering sigh. "She is married?" she whispered.

"*Ay-uh.* She tell me she grow tired of waiting to become my second wife," Gray Wolf said. "In next village she will be the only wife of a very brave Chippewa warrior."

"All along she *had* wanted you as her husband," Danette said. "I had been right to worry."

"*Gah-ween,*" Gray Wolf growled. "You needn't have worried. It had never been my wish to have her as my second wife. I am sorry that you did not understand this."

Danette's eyes lowered remembering all of the torment that she had placed upon herself because of her jealousies. "I am also sorry," she sighed. "I was wrong to doubt you."

Once more she attempted to settle the spinning of her head as she moved her feet near the floor. "I'm so weak and dizzy," she murmured. "I guess because I've been in bed for so long."

"That not the only reason," Gray Wolf said, helping her to her feet.

"What else, Gray Wolf?" she said, placing a hand to her chest, feeling the nervous beating of her heart in her total weakness.

"While in bed, in your deep sleep caused mostly by medication given you by Dr. Ross, he examine," Gray Wolf said, holding her in his arms as she leaned against him, panting. "He said it best to examine you since you have troubles in past."

"And . . . what did he find?" she asked, gazing up into

his green, worried eyes. "Besides my grief over Hope, I am in perfect health. This is what he discovered, isn't it?"

Gray Wolf lowered a soft kiss to her lips. "No. That is not what he discover," he said hoarsely.

"What are you not saying, Gray Wolf?"

"Sweet Butterfly, we lose our daughter but will soon be blessed by another child to take her place. The doctor say you are again . . . pregnant."

Chapter Twenty-Eight

Too blest for a sinner
Is he who shall win her!
—Irving

Though the snow had thinned in the forest, Gray Wolf had urged Danette to wear snowshoes while she was out for exercise and air, fearing hidden patches of ice beneath the snow-soaked dead leaves of winter.

The smell of the snow in the air drifted out of the deeper woods, where some still lay under the ledges of rock never touched by the sun. And, as today, the sun's warmth set little runnels of melted snow trickling down the sides of the trails, and tiny streams glistened here and there beneath the shadow of leafless trees.

The snowshoes strapped onto Danette's feet were woven with intricate patterns of rawhide and added decorative touches of red, black, and brilliant green, so beautiful against the white of the snow, as she made her way further into the forest. Gray Wolf had wanted to accompany Danette on her outing, but she knew that he had his chores to do and felt very capable of taking care of herself, so she had encouraged him to stay behind. She had promised not to wander far, but she had hoped that the exercise just might help to bring on her labor pains.

This pregnancy wasn't behaving as her first had. When the time had come to deliver Hope the pains had started with a bang, and Hope had entered the world shortly afterward. But this time Danette was carrying her child heavy inside her for one month longer than she should have been.

"And I am so extremely large," she said, waddling along beneath the trees, winded.

Her stomach was twice as large as it had been in her pregnancy with Hope, and the baby seemed to be all feet and hands, endlessly wrestling inside her. All through the night she got no rest. Yet the child still refused to be born!

Sighing, Danette pulled her rabbit-lined fur coat more snugly beneath her chin. She laughed at how the coat no longer completely reached around her, with her large ball of stomach protruding from it in front, almost comically. She was a sight and was glad to be alone in the forest, to relax and waddle as freely as she desired.

Pushing a low-hanging tree limb aside, Danette kept up a steady pace. She could see stumps where Gray Wolf and his braves had cut trees for their personal cabin, which was finally under construction. She had wanted the cabin built and furnished by the time their child was born. But the Indians, only being skilled at building dwellings of sapling poles and birchbark, were finding it hard to build the five-room cabin ordered by Gray Wolf for his wife.

She laughed softly to herself. "I can't even believe he's doing it," she whispered. "But I certainly do approve!"

She had given orders to Charles Klein to sell the Thomas mansion but to keep certain furnishings and her paintings and equipment in storage until the completion of this house in the Chippewa Indian village. She had decided not to sell her lumber company, but instead to give Charles the full power of attorney over all legal aspects of it. She had told him to make wise investments from her profits, and she had promised a portion of all that her company made to him, to make him a wealthy man in his own right, for the rest of his life.

Danette had given Amy enough money to buy herself a

comfortable home and had told Charles to give her a sizable monthly allowance, up until the day Amy died.

"Yes, I feel good about my choices," Danette said aloud. "And it's good to know that Gray Wolf's love is sincere. I shall never doubt him again."

Deep down inside her, she was greatly relieved that Laughing Rain was no longer a threat, never missing Laughing Rain's openly shown infatuation for Gray Wolf.

And now she did understand Gray Wolf's antagonism toward Hope while she had been alive. It had been easy to see the awkwardness Hope's outward appearance had caused Gray Wolf in the eyes of his people. She was trying to refrain from worrying about this child that she was carrying. Danette plucked a twig from a tree and began breaking it into little pieces, refusing to be haunted by her daughter's death. Somehow, she had learned to live with the loss.

Winded and breathing hard, Danette leaned against a tree to rest. She looked slowly about her. Lost in her thoughts, she had traveled much farther than she had planned. There was now nothing familiar in her surroundings and she had lost sight of the village through the break in the trees.

She let her gaze move to the snow, relieved to see that her footprints were still there, to lead her back home. And, fearing they would melt away and blend back into the rest of the snow, she decided it was best to start back, though she was still short of breath.

Placing her hands to the small of her back, she leaned away from the tree and began to walk toward her path in the snow. Suddenly a narrow bright red band tied to a tree next to her grabbed her attention. "What on earth is that?" she said.

Glancing quickly around her, she could see the same type of red band secured to the trunk of other larger, healthier trees, most of which were oak.

Steadying her feet on the snow, Danette went to one of the trees and ran her finger across the smoothness of the red band, seeing how it was tacked into the bark of the tree so that no wind or rain could loosen it.

"I remember seeing such bands," she said aloud, going from tree to tree, inspecting them. "In the forests surrounding Duluth, where trees were marked for cutting!"

A coldness swept through her, surrounding her heart. She tensed, listening hard for any sounds other than those made by the birds calling out to one another in the trees. To her relief, everything else was dead silent. But the bands had to mean that someone besides the Indians had been in this part of the forest. It was quite evident that these trees had been chosen to be cut by some intruder on the Chippewa Indian property. How would anyone have ever known how to find this land? The land had been kept secret from intruders, to be used only by the St. Croix band of the Chippewa. Why now? What did it mean?

"I must get back to the village and warn Gray Wolf," she whispered, now hurrying along her path. "There has to be something done about this. Now. Before the lumberjacks come with their axes!"

Knowing how sacred this forest was to the Chippewa, Danette knew that such an intrusion from the lumberjacks could be cause for much bloodshed. The Indians wouldn't give up their land so easily . It had been theirs for too long now, and they had even succeeded in not having it taken away from them to be divided into reservations, like most other land taken from other Indian tribes all across the country. Gray Wolf had said that Wenebojo had kept them safe. But now? Had Wenebojo failed them all . . . ?

Huffing and puffing, finding it hard to lift her feet, Danette stopped to get her breath. She closed her eyes and clutched onto her stomach, feeling a slight twinge of pain circling around inside it.

When the pain disappeared, the activity of her child began again, and its wrestling match now seemed to have grown in strength. The corners of her stomach felt as if they were

434

being pinched. Her rib cage had grown sore long ago from the constant assault of the baby's feet and legs. If she didn't have this baby soon, her whole insides were going to be bruised, it seemed!

Rested, regaining her breath, Danette once more began her journey beneath the trees and across the pressed-down snow. She squinted her eyes, trying to see through the break in the trees for the first signs of the village. But nothing! How had she traveled so far? Why hadn't she noticed?

Irritated at herself for being so careless, she tried to move faster, knowing that Gray Wolf was surely missing her by now and wondering about her and their child's welfare. Though she had asked him to go on with his chores, she knew that his thoughts never left her, and he was like a hawk, watching her each and every movement.

"I can't be lost," she fussed to herself. "I know these are my footprints that I am following. Oh, if only I hadn't come so far."

Another pain in her abdomen, this time much sharper, drew a dry gasp from deep inside her. She clutched at her stomach and gritted her teeth, now realizing what was happening. She was in labor! Her child had finally decided to make its entrance into the world, and at the most inopportune time possible!

"I must get back to the village," she said, stumbling as she tried to make her way on through the forest. "I can't . . . have . . . my child way out here . . . all alone. . . ."

A snapping of a branch behind her caused her heart to leap. She stopped and slowly turned to see what had caused the noise, then smiled lazily when she saw a doe standing alone in a thicket of blackberry bushes, all freckled and dappled with shimmering rays of sunlight showing through the trees.

"So you are also alone in the woods, pretty thing?" Danette said, relieved.

Then her eyes grew wide with alarm when another sound

erupted from the other side of her. Never knowing what to expect in the wilds of the forest, she began to tremble and slowly looked in that direction. What she discovered there, large and burly and as threatening as always before, was the last thing that she would ever have expected to see!

"You!" she gasped. "Oh, no, not you again. Why . . . ?"

Raoul stepped into the clearing, carrying a rifle in the crook of his left arm. His features were hidden behind dark whiskers and he was dressed heavily in a red plaid wool jacket and knit hat pulled low, almost to his eyes.

"Why?" he chuckled. "Trees were Raoul's first reason for being here, but now I can say that I had always hoped that I would find you here, away from the savage Indians."

A horse whinnied in the distance, drawing Danette's attention. Perhaps . . . Gray Wolf . . . ?

Raoul moved quickly to her and grabbed her by the wrist. "Come. My horse ain't far. Frenchman will carry you away from this place and show you how he gets vengeance for wrongs done him."

"Release me this minute," Danette screamed. "Don't you see that I am . . . heavy . . . with child . . . ?"

Raoul laughed throatily. "That makes vengeance much sweeter," he said. "Come. My duties in the forest are done this day, anyway."

Danette cringed as he drew her against him, holding her there as he guided her away from her path. "Are you responsible . . . for . . . the marked trees?" she asked, once more breathless and trying to show bravery, though another contraction in her womb was beginning.

"There are riches to be made in this forest," Raoul said, nodding toward the thickest trees in the distance. "The Thomas Lumber Company will look small in comparison to what mine will be."

"How on earth do you expect to come in here, take the trees, without a fight from the Indians?"

"I have worked alone up to now, to draw less attention

to what I am doing from both the whites and the redskins," Raoul growled. "But when the snows are cleared, I will hire many men to bring in with me, and the Indians will have quite a fight on their hands if they try to stop us!"

"How did you know . . . of . . . this place when no other white man does?" Danette said, gulping, trying to keep her mind off the bearing-down pain that was engulfing her.

"It was easy," Raoul bragged. "Raoul followed you and the Indian when you left Duluth. All winter I waited for the time I could come and begin marking trees. They don't legally belong to the Indians, you know. I will lay claim to them, and they will be mine."

Raoul shoved Danette clumsily toward the waiting horse. "You will be a sight ridin' a horse with me," he laughed. "But that don't matter. What matters is gettin' you to my cabin. Even pregnant women can be fun."

"You're disgusting," Danette hissed. When he placed his hands to her waist, to try and lift her onto the horse, she turned and spat in his face. "That is what I think of the likes of you. And Gray Wolf will find you and do worse. He will *kill* you, Frenchman!"

Raoul's face shadowed darkly as he wiped her spittle from his tangle of mustache and facial whiskers with the back of his hand. "You . . . witch . . ." he snarled. "You will get just what you deserve. And to hell with the baby! Let me give you a taste of your own spit!"

He drew her roughly into his arms and crushed his mouth down upon hers. His hands found the swell of one of her breasts beneath her coat and he groaned lustily when he discovered the large size of it.

Danette struggled, pushing against his chest, but his other hand was behind her head, holding her mouth in place against his.

Raoul finally set her free, smiling wickedly down at her. "We hurry now," he said. "If not for the snow, Raoul would take you even before going to cabin."

"You ... can't ..." Danette said, weakening in her responses. "Surely you are more human than that."

"Get on the horse," he said, giving her a shove toward it. He stood back, laughing at her awkwardness as she placed her foot into the stirrup.

Danette strained. She pulled. But she couldn't get herself up onto the horse. She crumpled down onto the ground, sobbing. "I can't," she whispered. "I just can't." She grabbed at her stomach and doubled over in pain. "God, my child ..." she cried. "It can't be long now. ..."

A gurgling sound suddenly erupted from behind her, coming from Raoul, and then a loud thud, drawing Danette's head quickly around. She grew numb and gasped when she saw Raoul stretched out on the ground, clawing at the arrow that had pierced his back and had come through to his chest.

His eyes were wide ... blood was streaming from the corner of his mouth ... and his body was doing a strange sort of spasmic dance now along the snow, leaving a scattering of blotches of red behind him. Sometime in her past, Danette had seen a chicken beheaded and had watched it performing the same sort of dance ... after having lost its head. ...

Gray Wolf stepped into view, his eyes dark with hate and his chin held proudly high. He lowered his bow and tossed it to the ground and rushed to where Danette lay, now only half-conscious.

"Gray Wolf, darling," she managed to whisper. "Thank God, Gray Wolf. ..."

He lifted her gently into his arms as she drifted away into semiconsciousness. As heavy and burdensome as she was, she could feel the sensation of being carried as he began running through the forest, toward home.

The next thing that Danette was aware of were many voices above her. She recognized Gray Wolf's and Lorinda's, and cared not that she didn't know the others, because she knew that she was safe ... in Lorinda's cabin ... ready to become a mother again.

Still slowly drifting in and out of consciousness, she felt her body reacting to each added contraction. She bit her lower lip as pain wracked her body and then finally felt the relief that came with having successfully given birth.

When she heard her baby's weak cry, she opened her eyes and looked toward Lorinda, who was holding the tiny bundle in her arms. Danette started to hold her arms out to Lorinda, but then she was strangely engulfed by another strong contraction, and she was awake enough this time to know that she had given birth . . . again!

"My Lord, *twins!*" she heard Lorinda cry out in amazement.

Gray Wolf began loud chanting sounds over Danette, then knelt down beside her bed and grabbed her hands in his. "You have just given birth to *two* children," he said quietly.

"I . . . have . . . ?" Danette said, laughing softly. Then her smile faded. "Are they . . . all . . . right?" she added, not having heard a second cry.

"You will soon see," Gray Wolf said proudly, showering her face with kisses.

Lorinda placed first one child beside Danette, then a second. Danette's eyes grew wide and tears flowed down her cheeks. "Gray Wolf, why didn't you tell me?" she sighed. "They are both boys. I have just given birth to two sons at once."

She looked from one to the other. "And, Gray Wolf, they are . . . all . . . Indian in coloring and features. They are an exact replica of you."

"*Ay-uh,*" Gray Wolf said thickly. "Gray Wolf proud."

Danette's eyes widened. "But, Gray Wolf, which of our sons . . . will . . . be next chief-in-line, after you . . . ?"

Chapter Twenty-Nine

> We'll live our whole young lives away
> In the joys of a living love.
> —Wilcox

The newness ... the aroma of pine, cedar, and oak ... hadn't worn off, though the five-room log house had now stood at the edge of the forest, beside the St. Croix River, for three full years. It had gracefully withstood the cold, sharp winters, the mild, sweet springs, the hot, yet fulfilling days of summer, and the crisp, refreshing days of autumn.

Through the glass of the window the dipping sun in the west cast its fiery glow onto Danette as she stood, watching her two sons at play outside, chasing one another from tree to tree, where one would pounce out on the other.

Attired in their fringe-trimmed buckskin leggings, shirts, and moccasins, it was almost impossible to tell them apart. Their copper-colored faces with the distinct Indian features, dark eyes, and coarse black hair proved they were, indeed, their father's sons.

The only trait inherited from their mother had been given to the one son who had been named Mush-ka-wah-kayk, Indian for Strong Hawk, the firstborn of the two sons. It was the stubbornness of his hair. It had been gifted with some of Danette's natural curl, and the only way to keep others from noticing this was by applying layer after layer

441

of deer tallow to it, to encourage it to lie flat against his head.

Otherwise, Strong Hawk and his twin brother Mak-kood-wa-goosh, Silver Fox, were identical in appearance. But Danette had begun to be aware of their different interests in life. While Strong Hawk was becoming enamored of books, showing evidence of being as gifted as Danette had been at the age of three by already knowing how to read, Silver Fox was only happy outdoors, learning the skills of bows, arrows, and the art of hunting.

"Why are you so quiet, Sweet Butterfly?" Gray Wolf asked, suddenly at her side, placing his arm about her waist.

In a blue-flowered cotton dress, with her hair swept into a coil atop her head, she turned her eyes up to look adoringly into Gray Wolf's face. "I'm watching our sons at play," she murmured.

"Gee-mee-nwayn-dum?" he asked, lowering a soft kiss to the tip of her nose.

"Ay-uh. I'm very happy," she said. "How could I not be? You've given me everything. Your love—and we have two healthy sons whom we both adore."

She let her gaze move past him, taking in all her surroundings. "You've let me furnish our house with my own furniture, and you've even let me turn one of our rooms into a studio for my paintings."

In one sweep of the eye, she saw a room paneled with cedar, a stone fireplace along one end wall, and upholstered chairs, a divan, and oak tables placed comfortably around the room. Sheer curtains hung at the many windows, and a braided oval rug lay on the floor in the center of the room.

"There have been many heartaches for you to get over," he said. "And to help you, I have done all of this for you."

"Even though your people do not yet understand why I prefer my silk and cotton dresses to their buckskin? And that I prefer a house and furniture to a wigwam?"

"Don't you remember that my mother prefers the same

442

type of house and furnishings as you?" he laughed. "The St. Croix band of Chippewa understand more than they let on. They have had many years now, since Chief Yellow Feather brought first white woman to live with the Chippewa, to learn to accept the differences."

Danette sighed. "I'm glad they do accept it all," she said. "Because I am very happy here. I never want to live in the city again. My life is here with you and our sons. I could never be as content anywhere else."

The sun was now gone and the moon was slowly slipping into view through the branches of the trees. Danette stood on tiptoe, looking outside. "Look, Gray Wolf," she said anxiously. "The fireflies are rising from the grass. Winking their lights off and on as they do, they look like eyes of ghosts."

"Are the jars ready?" Gray Wolf asked, chuckling.

"Yes," she said, rushing from him, to take two jars from a table. "I've made many holes in the lids so the fireflies will not suffocate through the night. I've explained how important this is to Strong Hawk and Silver Fox. Will you come with me, to give the jars to our sons?"

"*Ay-uh,*" he said. He walked outside with her and watched proudly as she gave each son a fruit jar. There had been many struggles to reach this level of complete happiness, but the waiting had been worth it. And it thrilled his soul to see Danette so at peace with herself and life. Her peace was his peace. Her life was his. . . .

Danette giggled, a child again herself as she raced about the yard, catching fireflies in the palms of her hands and dropping them into each of her son's jars. Once filled, each jar set off quite a glow. Danette shooed her sons into the house, and eventually into bed.

Sitting on the edge of the bed, looking from Silver Fox to Strong Hawk, their faces scrubbed and shining clean against their pillows, Danette opened a book of poems. She scooted closer to the light from the kerosene lamp that sat on a table beside the bed.

"What are you going to read to us tonight, *gee-mah-mah?*" Strong Hawk asked, looking anxiously toward the bound book in his mother's hands.

"A very small portion from 'The Song of Hiawatha,' a poem just written by Henry Wadsworth Longfellow," she said, glancing from one son to the other. She didn't scold Silver Fox for his noninterest as he held possessively on to his jar of fireflies, knowing that he was more anxious for the lamp to be blown out than to be read to from some book. He had waited all day to capture them, and then to see how the fireflies would glow in the darkness of his and Strong Hawk's bedroom.

"Who is Henry Wadsworth Longfellow?" Strong Hawk asked in his inquisitive way.

"He is a poet of our time," she replied. "I will leave the book here, for you to read further, if you wish."

"No," Silver Fox argued. "If you leave the book, the lamp will burn all night because Strong Hawk will want to read. *I* want to see my fireflies glow in the dark."

Danette reached a hand to Silver Fox's brow. "The lamp will be blown out as soon as I leave," she promised. "Strong Hawk will promise to wait and read the book in the morning, won't you, Strong Hawk?"

"Ay-uh . . ." Strong Hawk said, sulking.

"We must be fair, mustn't we?" Danette said, now gently touching Strong Hawk on his cheek.

"Ay-uh . . ." Strong Hawk murmured, then his eyes lit up. "But, please read now, won't you?"

"This is a poem written about an Indian like you, my sons," Danette said. "It is a poem written about a Chippewa Indian brave named Hiawatha. . . ."

* * *

444

When Danette was finished, she closed the book, bent, and kissed first Strong Hawk and then Silver Fox, then blew out the light in the lamp. She smiled when she heard her sons' sighs as the glow from the fireflies showed through the darkness, as the fireflies blinked off and on, almost magically.

"Now hold the jars for only a little while," Danette said, placing the book on the table. "They should be on the table before you go to sleep. And early in the morning be sure to take the fireflies and release them back into the woods, or they will perish."

"*Ay-uh, gee-mah-mah,*" Silver Fox and Strong Hawk said in unison. "Good night, *gee-mah-mah.*"

"Good night, darlings," she said. "*Gee-mah-mah* loves you."

Full of a warm, delicious contentment, Danette glided from the room, then laughed softly as she ran into Gray Wolf as he stepped from the shadows. "You were there all along? Listening and watching?" she said.

"It is beautiful," he said huskily. "You with my sons is a beautiful experience, Sweet Butterfly."

Danette twisted her arms about his neck. "And is it also as beautiful when I am with you?" she teased.

Gray Wolf surprised her by suddenly sweeping her up into his arms. "Always," he said, carrying her into their bedroom. With his foot he closed the door and went to the bed and placed her down on the yellow comforter. A kerosene lamp reflected light about the room . . . a room with pale yellow curtains, yellow-flower-bedecked wallpaper, and splendid oak furniture.

"And, kind sir, what are your plans for me now that I've tucked our sons snugly into their beds?" she further teased, already lifting his headband from his head, tossing it aside.

"Words," he growled. "They are a useless thing when my heart is beating so wildly."

"Then, my darling husband, let me show you my skills

445

at doing . . . not saying," she said, busying herself at removing his shirt. She pulled him down onto the bed, then crept up on her knees, to have easier access to his body. She heard his breath catch as she began kissing him along the muscled lines of his chest, stopping to flick her tongue around one of his nipples.

Her hands went to his leggings, and she slipped them down over his hips and lower, until he was nude.

Gray Wolf reached a hand to her hair and freed it of its pins, then loosened it to hang long around her shoulders. Then his hands cupped her breasts through her dress. "Undress slowly for me," he said huskily. "Stand in the glow of the lamp. Let my eyes feast upon your beauty."

Breathless with desire for him, Danette rose from the bed and unbuttoned her dress from behind, then slowly slipped it from her shoulders and let it drop to the floor. And after she shook herself out of her petticoats and stepped out of her shoes, she felt Gray Wolf's hands begin a slow, tormenting exploration of her body.

Her breasts were soft to his touch. He cupped them each in his hands, letting his thumbs sensually circle her hard nipples, arousing such a heat inside her that she let out a rapturous moan.

She closed her eyes, arched her neck, and let his hands continue their search. She felt her skin quiver . . . felt the goosebumps rise along her body.

Feverish, she looked at Gray Wolf, seeing how glazed his eyes had become. "Darling . . . ?" she whispered.

Gray Wolf led her back to the bed and urged her down upon it, then knelt over her and placed his lips and tongue where his fingers had just been. Almost mindless from the exquisite sensation his tongue was now causing, she writhed and placed her hand to his face, urging him upward.

"I can bear it no longer," she sighed. "Love me as only you know how, my husband."

His lips covered hers gently as he worked his maleness

446

inside her. Their bodies began working together, practiced. Danette clung about his neck, her lips quivering against his in her intense ecstasy of their shared passion and love. His hands were hot in their touch to her breasts, his tongue like a burning flame inside her mouth. Only a few thrusts were required before their bodies shared the ultimate in pleasure, yet they continued to embrace, breathing heaven against each other's cheek.

"Darling, could anything make you happier than you already are?" Danette whispered, curling her fingers through his hair.

"Gah-ween-geh-goo," he said hoarsely. "No. Nothing."

"Then I guess you don't want to hear . . ."

"Hear what . . . ?"

"Gray Wolf, darling, I am with child again. . . ."

Gray Wolf drew away from her, his eyes reflecting his joy. "Sweet Butterfly, you were wise choice for this next chief-in-line," he chuckled.

Then they fell into each other's arms, laughing. *Ay-uh,* they had come a long way together, sharing the joys and sorrows of their . . . savage . . . innocence.

If you enjoyed SAVAGE INNOCENCE,
you won't want to miss

SAVAGE HEART

From the most beloved name in Indian Romance, with
over ten million copies of her books in print, Cassie
Edwards presents a tale of unbridled passion and high
drama on the wild frontier. . . .

Lured by fortune, Christa and her family leave the comforts
of Boston for the rugged hills of the Pacific Northwest.
But tragedy strikes when her parents are taken by cholera,
leaving Christa and her brother David with nothing but an
isolated cabin to their names. The only escape from poverty
lies in Christa's untouched beauty being sold to the highest
bidder—and David knows just the man to marry her . . .

But Christa rebels against reason—and riches. Her fiery
heart belongs to no man. Yet in the fateful instant her
eyes touch upon a perfect stranger, she proves herself
wrong. Lean, dark, and utterly forbidden, Tall Cloud is
the powerful chief of the Suquamish Indians—and
Christa's destiny. Now nothing can come between a
passion that knows no boundaries—neither an engaged
brother, nor a savage enemy from a rival tribe. . . .

A woman's heart loves no fear . . . SAVAGE HEART

Coming from Kensington/Zebra in January 2007.

"A sensitive storyteller who always touches
readers' hearts."—*Romantic Times*

"High adventure and surprise season this
Indian Romance."—*Affaire de Coeur*

www.Kensingtonbooks.com